PRAISE FOR ERIN HART'S FAST-PACED THRILLER

LAKE OF SORROWS

"Myriad twists and turns juice the plot and deepen the atmosphere in Hart's moody second offering."

—*Kirkus Reviews*

"Full of riches for readers who savor the multidimensionality of literary fiction."

—*Booklist*

"A beautifully told mystery, lush in its language, rich in history and characters, full of ancient rites and modern treacheries, this is a treasure of a tale."

—William Kent Krueger, Anthony Award–winning author of *Copper River*

PRAISE FOR THE CRITICALLY ACCLAIMED MURDER MYSTERY

HAUNTED GROUND

Winner of the Friends of American Writers Award, the *Romantic Times* Best First Mystery Award, Nominated for the Anthony Award and the Agatha Award for Best First Novel, and a Book Sense 76 Pick!

"Chilling . . . masterfully weav[es] Irish folklore and traditional music into an eerie plot. . . . Immensely enjoyable."

—*Minneapolis Star-Tribune*

"An utterly beguiling mix of village mystery, gothic suspense, and psychological thriller. . . . A debut to remember."

d review)

Also by Erin Hart

Haunted Ground

LAKE OF SORROWS

ERIN HART

[signature]

SCRIBNER

NEW YORK   LONDON   TORONTO   SYDNEY

SCRIBNER
A Division of Simon & Schuster, Inc.
1230 Avenue of the Americas
New York, NY 10020

First Scribner trade paperback edition August 2007

SCRIBNER and design are trademarks of
Macmillan Library Reference USA, Inc., used under license
by Simon & Schuster, the publisher of this work.

For information about special discounts for bulk purchases,
please contact Simon & Schuster Special Sales:
1-800-456-6798 or business@simonandschuster.com

Text set in Goudy Oldstyle

Manufactured in the United States of America

1   3   5   7   9   10   8   6   4   2

Library of Congress Cataloging-in-Publication Data
Hart, Erin, [date].
Lake of sorrows / Erin Hart.
p. cm.
PS3608.A785L35 2004
813'.6—dc22   2004052234

ISBN-13: 978-0-7432-4796-2
ISBN-10: 0-7432-4796-5
ISBN-13: 978-1-4165-4130-1 (Pbk)
ISBN-10: 1-4165-4130-6 (Pbk)

To my mother and father

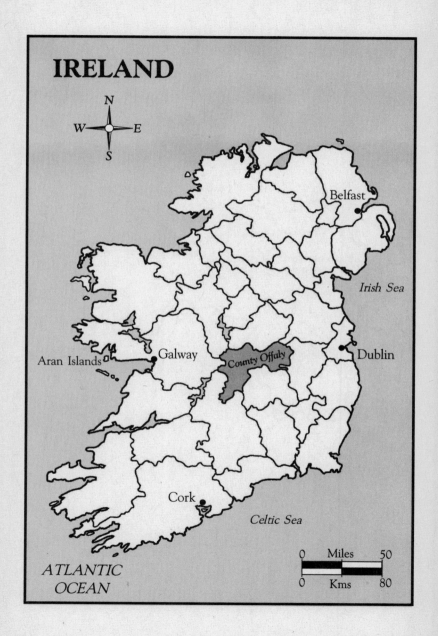

IRELAND

N
W E
S

Belfast

Irish Sea

Aran Islands

Galway

County Offaly

Dublin

Cork

Celtic Sea

Miles
0 50

Kms
0 80

ATLANTIC
OCEAN

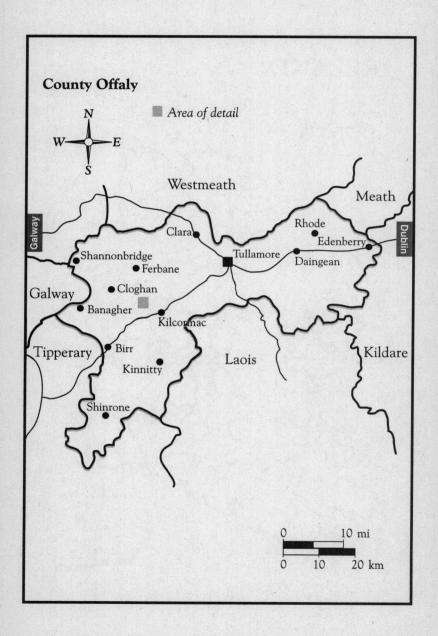

County Offaly

N
W · E
S

■ *Area of detail*

Westmeath

Meath

Galway

Dublin

Clara

Rhode

Edenberry

Tullamore

Shannonbridge

Daingean

Ferbane

Galway

Cloghan

Banagher

Kilcormac

Tipperary

Laois

Kildare

Birr

Kinnitty

Shinrone

0   10 mi

0   10   20 km

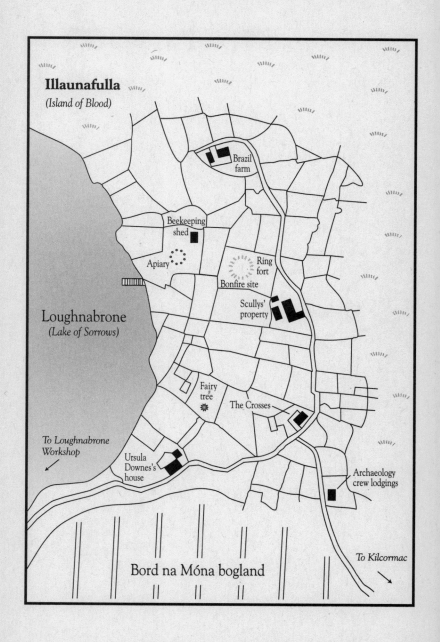

Illaunafulla
(Island of Blood)

Brazil farm

Beekeeping shed

Apiary

Ring fort

Bonfire site

Scullys' property

Loughnabrone
(Lake of Sorrows)

Fairy tree

The Crosses

To Loughnabrone Workshop

Ursula Downes's house

Archaeology crew lodgings

To Kilcormac

Bord na Móna bogland

I am the womb: of every holt,
I am the blaze: on every hill,
I am the queen: of every hive,
I am the shield: for every head,
I am the grave: of every hope.

—*from the* Song of Amheirgin,
an ancient Irish poem

CONTENTS

LAKE OF SORROWS

BOOK ONE

DEEP CRIMSON ON THEM

A Feidelm banfáid,
cia facci ar slúag.

Atchiu forderg forro,
atchiu ruad.

"O Fedelm, woman prophet,
What do you see on the host?"

"I see deep crimson on them,
I see red!"

—*from the Old Irish epic* Táin Bó Cuailnge

PROLOGUE

It was the cold that roused him. The moment he plunged into the frigid water at the bottom of the bog hole, his eyes fluttered open, and his mind grasped the fact that he would certainly die here. He knew it was the reason he had been brought to this place, the reason he had been born. His body, however, seemed to require further persuasion. He shook his head, groggy, as though awakened from sleep. Was all this real, or only a vision of what was to come? He remembered running, a glancing blow, and before that—

For a moment he remained very still; then he struggled to right himself in the bog hole's narrow fissure, pressing against the walls with his hands and elbows, treading slowly against the dark, pulpy liquid into which he'd already sunk to his hips. It was pulling him in, downward. Nothing would stop him now. He gasped for air, feeling the leather cord encircling his throat, all at once aware of a strange, spreading warmth upon his chest—blood, his own blood, sticky and metallic. But the primary sensation was cold, a deep, numbing chill combined with an utterly astonishing softness, whose deceitful purpose, he knew, was to draw him into its familiar, bosomy grasp and keep him here forever.

Above his head the midsummer evening remained fair and mild, and his eyes reflected the waning twilight still visible at the top of the bog hole, scarcely more than an arm's length above his head. His muscular shoulders were those of a man who had herded cattle milked at daybreak and evening, who each spring broke the virgin soil with his plow, who sowed corn and reaped it with sharpened blade—a man ruled by circular, circadian rhythms of light and darkness. The slight hollows in his clean-shaven countenance bespoke hard labor and scant harvests.

He knew this place, this bog. It was a mysterious, holy place, home to spirits and strange mists, a place of transformation and danger. He had crossed it countless times, treading carefully among glittering blue and green damselflies while tracking a hare or a slow-moving grouse. He'd seen the same evening light in its pools of standing water that recalled a hero's footprints or fragments of firmament fallen to earth. At their edges he had crouched, watching crimson masses of bloodworms as they transformed almost before his eyes and rose from the water to join quivering clouds of midges that hovered, faintly droning, above. He would never see them again, for he had entered a place from which there was no return.

Trapped by the weight of his own body, he could feel himself sinking with every passing second, could feel his hands moving uselessly against the seeping walls of the bog hole. Letting go an involuntary howl, he began to twist and claw furiously, reverting to the instinctive behavior of a trapped animal, baring his teeth and straining with every fiber, unable to reason or comprehend. But his feet were firmly mired in the slurrylike peat and would not come away. He was getting light-headed. His legs were numb, and as the frigid water seeped steadily higher, he began to tremble violently. Even as he felt the dread chill envelop him, he knew that his heart's blood would soon begin to slow. He ceased struggling and kept still, feeling each breath flow in and out, each one shallower than the last. A memory brushed like spider silk across his consciousness—a luminous face, a woman's voice soft against his ear. He had sunk to his shoulders; soon he would be swallowed up, devoured by the insatiable earth, the origin and end of life.

In the last few moments, it was only instinct that kept his chin above the surface, as each involuntary shudder drew him further downward. The water stung as it touched his wounds, and began to trickle into his ears, slowly shutting out all sound but his own beating heart. Soon only his face and hands lingered above the surface, but his eyes remained open, staring upward, so that the last image imprinted there was the dim, familiar outline of a head and shoulders, framed in the jagged opening above him by the dying light of evening. His savior, or his executioner? An instant later, living moss and damp peat showered down upon him from above, closing his eyes and filling his nostrils with the scent of sweet grass and heather as he abandoned all resistance and finally yielded to the bog's chill embrace.

1

Seventy miles straight west of Dublin, at the northern perimeter of Loughnabrone Bog in the far western reaches of County Offaly, Nora Gavin had already formed a distinct image of the man she was supposed to rescue today. It was not a complete figure she imagined, for the man she was going to see had been cut in half—jaggedly severed by the sharp blade of an earth-moving machine. The image lodged in the back of her mind was of frayed and slightly shrunken sinews, ragged patches of skin tanned brown from centuries spent steeping in the bog's cold, anaerobic tea. She knew she should feel grateful that even a portion of the body was intact; a few more seasons of turf cutting and he might have been completely scattered to the winds. It made her suddenly angry to think that an entire human being had been preserved for so long by the peat, only to be destroyed in the blink of an eye by the thoughtless actions of men and their machines. But the bleak reality was that she might never get the chance to examine an intact bog body, so she had to make the most of each fragmentary opportunity.

It was Monday, the seventeenth of June. The excavation season had begun only a week earlier, and the bog man had turned up the previous Friday. The business Nora would be engaged in today was just a recovery operation, to salvage the torso dug up by a Bord na Móna excavator. It remained to be seen whether the body's lower half was still embedded in the bank beside the drain. That mystery would probably have to wait for the full excavation—something that would take several weeks to coordinate, since it involved a whole crew of wetlands archaeologists, forensic entomologists, environmental scientists who analyzed pollen and coleoptera and ash content, and experts on metal detection and film documentation. But since the bog man's upper half had been removed from his peaty grave, the recovery was urgent. Without the proper conservation procedures, ordinary bacteria and mold would start their destructive march in a matter of hours.

Nora glanced down at the large-scale map she'd laid out on the passenger seat of the car. Driving into the West from Dublin, you couldn't be blamed for missing County Offaly. The two major motorways managed to skirt it almost entirely. The county had a reputation as a backwater, perhaps befitting a place that was one-third bogland. The Loughnabrone workshop, her destination, showed as a cluster of industrial buildings on a dryland peninsula, a scrap of solid earth jutting out into the bog. Bord na Móna, also known as the Turf Board, was Ireland's official peat-production industry, and had dozens of operations like this all over the midlands. The bog itself appeared on the map as a set of irregular blank areas between the River Brosna and the few hectares of arable land.

She was surrounded on all sides by bogland, and had evidently missed the turn for the workshop. It seemed too arduous to backtrack; the easiest way to navigate now might be to steer toward the looming pair of bell-shaped cooling towers at the nearby power station. That should put her within a quarter-mile of the workshop. The power station looked like the old nuclear plants at home, but chances were the electricity produced here had always been generated by burning peat. No smoke poured from the stacks now, but the towers remained still and silent landmarks in this strange landscape.

Scale was definitely the overpowering element here, where each furrow was fourteen meters across, and human beings were reduced to miniature among the gargantuan machines and the mile-long mountains of milled peat. Deep drains cut through the bog at right angles to the road. Ahead, Nora saw an enormous tractor with fat tires that kept it from sinking in the spongy peat. The extensions suspended from its cab on long cables looked like vast wings. Bearing down on her, with two front windows glinting in the sunlight, it took on the aspect of a monstrous mechanical dragonfly. Far in the distance, several similar strange contraptions in a staggered formation churned up huge clouds of brown peat dust. She drove on, toward the very center of the vast brown-black desert.

The sun was still low, but strong. Racing before her on the road she could see the car silhouetted in the golden morning light, a shape that contained her own weirdly elongated shadow. There was no one else on the road for miles. She opened the window and thrust her hand out into the wind, the way she sometimes had as a child, and felt her whole arm swimming, salmonlike, against the strong current of the cool morning air. She glanced over at the passenger seat and imagined her sister Tríona as a child, red hair trailing down her back, her arm out the window as well. She grasped Tríona's hand, as she had done years before, and they flew along together for a few moments, reveling in their sisterly conspiracy of wickedness and giddy with the sensation of being at least partially airborne. Suddenly her mother's voice echoed in her head: *Ah, Nora, please don't. You know she insists on copying everything you do.* Tríona's bright face vanished, and Nora pulled her arm back into the car. There was little comfort in such memories. Tríona was gone, and these fleeting images had become a precious, finite commodity.

Eventually, the road's surface became so uneven that Nora had to slow to a crawl to keep her head from banging against the roof of the car. Bog roads provided only the illusion of solidity; they were merely thin ribbons of asphalt, light and flexible enough to float above the shifting, soggy earth beneath. At this level, right down on the surface of the bog, you could see an unnatural barrenness where the earth had been stripped, year after year, to prevent the spread of living vegetation. It was only in comparing this landscape to what she knew of ordinary boglands that she could understand what was missing here—the teeming proliferation that existed in a natural bog—and could grasp the fact that the dark drains stretching to the horizon and beyond were actually bleeding away the life-giving water.

She imagined what the bog must have seemed to ancient people—a strange liminal region, half water and half earth. To them it had been the center of the world, a holy place, a burial ground, a safe for stowing treasure, a region of the spirits. She tried to conjure up an image of what this spot might have been like thousands of years before, when giant oaks still towered overhead. She had seen their sodden, twisted stumps resurrected from peaty lakes, the trunks used up for ritual structures, or plank roads to traverse the most dangerous marshy places.

It was astonishing to her that bogs, despite their role as collective memory, were still being relinquished to feed the ever-growing hunger for electric power. Up until a hundred years ago, the bogs had been considered useless, mere wasteland. Then the men of science had gone to work on them, devising ever more efficient ways to harvest peat—only to find out, too late, that this was a misguided effort, and perhaps the wrong choice all along. Twenty years from now, the outdated power plants would be gone. This bog would be stripped right down to the marl subsoil, and would have to begin anew the slow reversion to its natural state, layer by layer, over the next five, or eight, or ten thousand years. Without even realizing it, the men of science and progress had given up a book of the past, whose pages contained an incredible record—of weather patterns, and human and animal and plant life over several millennia—all for jobs in a backwater wasteland, for a few paltry years' worth of electricity.

Since prehistoric times bogs had served as sacrificial sites; it was strange to think that the bogs themselves had become the sacrifice. She thought back to the archaeology books she'd been reading steadily all winter. She had found a kind of fascination in the description of hoards recovered from watery places, including many of the artifacts she'd seen on display in the National Museum. Most had been discovered completely by accident. She had been stunned by the beauty and complexity of the ancient designs. Some of the objects were distinctly military: ornately patterned bronze swords and daggers, spearheads, serpentine trumpets like something from a fairy story. Others suggested domestic or ritual purposes: gold bracelets and collars, fantastic brooches and fibulae that mimicked bird or animal forms, mirrors with a multiplicity of abstract faces hidden in their graved decoration. The reason these objects had been deposited in lakes and bogs remained shrouded in mystery, the enduring secret of a people without written language.

And of course it was not only artifacts that had been found in bogs; nearly a hundred sets of human remains had turned up as well. Judging from the bare facts in the gazetteer of bog bodies she'd been updating, some people had simply gone astray and fallen into the deadly morass; the careful inhumations might have been ordinary burials, or suicides, or childbed deaths refused burial in hallowed ground. But there was still vigorous debate surrounding the assertion that some older bog bodies had been victims of human sacrifice. And this was not the only point of argument. The latest studies showed the difficulty of pinpointing radiocarbon dates, and experts debated whether bog men had colored themselves blue with copper or had absorbed the element from the surrounding peat, even whether they had been murdered, or had been the subjects of ill-fated rescues. Nothing was absolutely certain. When it came down to hard facts, all they really had were dots on a map, the points at which objects had been found.

Driving across the border into Offaly, she had been acutely aware that she was approaching the ancient region known as the Mide, the center.

It was a place that had been ascribed all sorts of magical attributes, the powerful locus represented by the central axes of the crosses on Bronze Age sun discs, from a time when the world had been divided up into four quadrants, North, South, East, and West, and a shadowy central place, which, because it was not There, had to be Here. Where was her own Mide, her center, that point where all the pieces of her life met and intersected at one infinitesimal but infinitely powerful place?

She had tried very hard to avoid thinking about Cormac on the trip down here, but she felt her resolve weakening. It was just over a year since she'd made almost the same journey westward, to the place where their lives had been bound together by the untimely death of a beautiful red-haired girl whose head they'd recovered from the bog. She hadn't meant to find someone like Cormac Maguire. She hadn't meant to find anyone; she'd come to this place as an escape, a retreat from too much feeling. It hadn't happened suddenly, but gradually, like a slow envelopment. There was no question that she had soaked up the warmth he offered like a person nearly perished from cold, but were those moments of intense happiness real, or only an illusion? It seemed as if the entire year had passed like a dream. With the coming of spring, she'd known that the dream couldn't last; that certain knowledge was like a goad in her side, sharp and getting sharper with each passing day. She couldn't wait to see him, but her eager anticipation was tempered by mounting anxiety.

She had no business fashioning a life for herself here. Her stay in Ireland was supposed to be temporary, a period of respite after her long struggle to find some semblance of justice for Tríona's terrible death. Sometimes she dreamt of her sister's battered face, and woke up weeping and distracted. The dream would linger, encroaching on her waking mind, a heaviness remembered in body and spirit that sometimes took days to dissipate. Worse still were the dreams where Tríona came back, whole and restored, as if she'd never been away. Though Nora knew these visions to be false even as her subconscious conjured them, upon waking from such a dream she still experienced new shock and sorrow.

She had picked up the phone two days ago, and heard the tremor in her mother's voice: "He's getting married again." There had been no need to ask; Nora knew that she meant Peter Hallett—Tríona's husband, and her killer.

Remembering the conversation, Nora suddenly felt her stomach heave. Afraid she was about to be sick, she brought the car to a screeching halt and climbed out, leaving the car door open and the engine running. She walked back along the road the way she'd just come. If she forced herself to breathe slowly, she might be able to keep from hyperventilating. She sat down abruptly on the roadside and dropped her head between her knees, feeling the pulse pounding in her temples.

After a moment the steady noise of the wind began to calm her, and she felt the nausea subside. Suddenly buffeted by a strong gust from behind, she raised her head. The breeze encircled her, then picked up a scant handful of peat dust. The tiny whirlwind danced over the surface of the bog, spinning eastward into the low morning sun, and then dissipated, nothing more than a breath of air, briefly embodied and made visible.

She sat for a moment longer, listening to the strange music of the wind as it whistled through the furze bushes along the road, watching the bog cotton's tiny white flags spell out a cryptic message in semaphore. Bits of organic debris danced overhead, caught in the updraft, and the strangely dry air contained something new, a mineral taste she could not readily name. When she stood up to return to the car, Nora understood instantly what had given the air its metallic flavor: an immense, rapidly moving wall of brown peat dust bore down on her from only about thirty yards away. She froze, momentarily stunned by the spectacle of the storm's overwhelming magnitude, then made a headlong dash for the car, but it was already too late. The dust cloud engulfed her, along with the road and the vast expanse of bog on either side, closing her eyes, filling her nostrils and throat with stinging peat. Suddenly unable to gauge any distance, she ran blindly until her right knee banged hard into the car's rear bumper. The glancing pain took her breath away. She didn't dare open her lips to cry out, but limped around to the driver's side and climbed in, closing the door against the dust that tried to follow her. After desperately trying to hold her breath out in the storm, she gasped for air and promptly burst into a coughing fit. Once the car door was closed, the dust could not penetrate the sealed windows, but a fair amount of peat had blown in through the open door, and now the tiny airborne particles began to settle, covering the seats and dashboard with fine dark-brown organic material. The outside world had disappeared, and Nora gripped the steering wheel, feeling like a cocooned caterpillar at the mercy of the wild elements. It was far too dangerous to try driving across a bog when visibility was so poor. There was little she could do except wait, and listen to the wind whistling under the car and around the radio antenna, furiously pummeling away at any object, animate or inanimate, that had the audacity to remain upright in its path. She rubbed her throbbing knee; she would have a lovely bruise tomorrow.

All at once, she made out a figure standing just ahead of the car. Although its general shape was human, the face was strange and horrible: huge exophthalmic eyes stood out above a flat black snout. She and the insectlike thing stared at each other for a surreal moment, then another heavy gust blew up, and it was gone. A second later, a solid thump sounded on the window just beside her ear, and she felt a rush of fear, until at last it began to dawn on her that the mutant creature was actually nothing more dreadful than a Bord na Móna worker in an old-fashioned gas mask. She could see that the man was trying to communicate, but his voice was hopelessly muffled by the mask and the wind. He pointed a gloved finger to her, then to himself, and then forward. He wanted her to follow him. The wind was beginning to diminish, and she could just make out the back end of a tractor about ten yards in front of the car. She realized in horror that she might have crushed her rescuer if she'd simply put the car in gear and started driving. She watched through gusty clouds of peat as he climbed up into the cab and turned the tractor around. When he drove forward, she followed.

It was impossible to tell how far they traveled; time and distance were distorted in the strange dark fog. Gradually the peat cloud began to thin away, the world began to reappear, and they were once again in the clear air. Nora watched the brown wall recede eastward, all the while keeping a close tail on the lumbering tractor until they reached the Bord na Móna sign at the entrance to Loughnabrone. Inside the grounds, the driver pulled up to a row of hangarlike metal sheds and climbed down from the cab; Nora caught up to him just as he was entering the large open door of a workshop, where several other men in grease-spotted blue boilersuits toiled over a huge earth-moving blade with acetylene torches.

"Excuse me," she said, reaching out to touch the man's arm in case he hadn't heard her. The other workers looked up, their torches still blazing. The tractor driver turned to face her, and it was only then that the gas mask came off, revealing a youthful face with strong features and intensely blue eyes.

"Excuse me—I just wanted to say thanks." She offered her hand. "Nora Gavin."

He looked at her for a split second, then dropped his gaze, and Nora wondered whether it was her red eyes, her dirty face, or her obvious American accent—or a combination of all those things—that had this young man so mortified. He took her hand very briefly. "Charlie Brazil," he finally said, pronouncing his surname the Irish way, with the emphasis on the first syllable. He colored deeply and glanced at the other men, who had stopped working when she approached.

"Well—thanks, Charlie. I'm grateful for your help." She could feel the workmen's eyes upon them, and understood that all poor Charlie Brazil wanted was to be shut of her as quickly as possible. "I'm afraid I have to ask another favor. Could you point me toward the manager's office?"

"Over there," he said, indicating a single-story pebble-dashed building about fifty yards away.

"Right," she said. "Thanks again." Heading toward the manager's office, she heard a leering voice behind her inquire: "What'd you do for the lady, Charlie?" There was an unsettling chorus of sniggers, and Charlie Brazil's deep voice muttered darkly: "Ah, feck off and leave me alone, why don't you?"

2

There was no one at reception inside the manager's office. Nora considered ringing Cormac to let him know she'd arrived safely, but decided against it. She wanted to put off talking to him as long as she could. Her emotions were too much in turmoil. A small sign on the nearest wall bore a single word, "Toilet," and an arrow pointing to her left down a short hallway, so she ducked in to have a look in the mirror. It was a shock: her eyes were horribly bloodshot, and her insides felt rubbed raw. Bits of peat dust clung to her hair and eyebrows, and to the tear tracks that lined her cheeks. No wonder Charlie Brazil had looked at her so strangely. What a fine state for meeting the brass here. She brushed as much of the peat from her hair as she could, and splashed her eyes with cold water, which stung as much as the dust had. As she dried her face on the cloth towel, the door swung open, and Nora stood face-to-face with a vigorous, casually dressed man of about forty, whose expression betrayed astonishment and a certain amount of suspicion. Perhaps she hadn't paid close attention to the sign and had accidentally wandered into the gents' by mistake.

"Sorry if I'm somewhere I shouldn't be," she said. "I got caught in a windstorm out on the bog, and I was just trying to get a bit of the dust off before I found the manager."

"You've found him," the man said.

"You're Owen Cadogan?"

"I am," he replied. "And you are . . ."

"Nora Gavin. I'm here for the bog body excavation." Surely he'd known she was coming down from Dublin. "I think you spoke with Niall Dawson at the National Museum—he said he'd explained all the arrangements." A subtle change came over Cadogan's demeanor; she thought it safe to surmise that the Dr. Gavin he'd expected was neither female nor American.

"Ah, right, Dr. Gavin. You're early." He ushered her down the hall toward his office. "We're not expecting the museum crowd until later in the day.

Anyway, sorry you were caught out there in the dust. Been dry as a desert here for two weeks, and that's one of the rare hazards of fine weather."

"I've never seen anything quite like it. But one of the workmen was kind enough to make sure I got here in one piece—Charlie Brazil?"

"Ah, yes," Cadogan said, with a grimace that suggested she ought to consider giving Mr. Brazil a wide berth in future.

"I have to admit the gas mask had me rather taken aback at first."

"Ah, he's all right," Cadogan said. "Bit of a quare hawk, Charlie is— an oddball." He led her back through reception and into his tiny office, where he gestured for her to have a seat. The place reminded Nora of her auto mechanic's office at home with its practical, no-frills atmosphere, its metal desk and uncomfortable vinyl chairs. "Afraid I'm fending for myself here at the moment," Cadogan said. "The girl's out sick today. Can I get you a cup of tea—or coffee, is it?"

Cadogan gave the impression that he was a very busy man: the quick gestures, the eyes that never settled in one place for too long. Whether consciously or not, he gave Nora the distinct impression that she was keeping him from duties much more important and necessary than her comfort. But breakfast had been three hours ago, and she realized that she was actually quite hungry. "Tea would be great."

"Won't be a minute." He ducked out of the room, and Nora tried to put a finger on what she sensed about him. Brisk, businesslike, still stirred by ambition—but on the cusp of forty, when a lot of men began to feel themselves softening into middle age, and to wonder why it was that the responsible job and the family and the new house weren't enough to keep them from feeling somehow anesthetized inside. A dangerous age.

She stood up to take a look at two large black-and-white charts hanging on the walls of the office. The first showed average rainfall at Loughnabrone over the past four decades, sometimes as much as a thousand millimeters a year. How was it even possible for the earth to soak up that much water? Alongside the rainfall chart was a bar graph showing annual peat production by the kiloton. She noted the inverse symmetry between the numbers, and the downward slope of the peat production stats for the past few years. Another poster on the wall had photographs of the various artifacts bog workers might encounter, and a series of exhortations:

Under Your Feet in This Very Bog
There could be hidden objects up to 10,000 years old.
Because of waterlogged conditions, the bog has preserved objects,
such as wood, leather, textiles, and even human bodies!
Once unearthed, these ancient finds begin to decay instantly and
if not cared for they will be lost forever.
Help us record our history by preserving these buried objects.

No doubt ignorance was the greatest enemy; if workers didn't know what they should stop the machines for, they might just keep cutting. But theft had to be a major concern as well. It must be tempting, if you did find something of value, to keep it to yourself. That was human nature. Nora wondered idly how much the average bog worker made these days. Probably the same as most other factory workers—not a fortune, certainly, just enough to keep a man with a family from cutting the tether.

Her attention was drawn to a framed and yellowed newspaper cutting. It was dated August 1977, and showed two lean-faced, unsmiling men in boilersuits looking up from a drain. One of the workmen held up what looked like a corroded sword blade. The caption read:

Illaunafulla men Dominic and Danny Brazil with the large Iron Age hoard they discovered while working at Loughnabrone Bog last week. The men uncovered numerous axe-heads, several amber bead necklaces, a scabbard and sword hilt, and twelve bronze trumpets. After excavation is complete, the artefacts will be transported to the National Museum of Ireland in Dublin.

Brazil, like her rescuer. She wondered whether it was one of those unusual surnames, like Spain, that had something to do with where your ancestors had traveled. Or maybe it was simply an old Irish name, misspelled by the English. She'd have to ask Cormac. At the picture's edge, almost entirely cut off, a third man leaned in above the Brazils, down on one knee at the edge of the drain. He was dressed, quite inappropriately for the bog, in a tweed jacket, collar, and tie. Three-quarters of his head had been cropped out of the frame.

"That was quite a find," said Cadogan from behind her. "Colossal. Nothing like it before or since. There was even a rumor that they'd turned up some gold pieces as well, but that turned out to be a load of—nonsense."

"Would these Brazils be any relation to Charlie?" Nora asked, accepting the mug of gray, watery-looking tea he proffered, and wishing she'd been prudent enough to refuse.

"His father and uncle," Cadogan said, taking a seat behind the desk. "We've got Brazils galore here. A lot of the lads come from families who go back four or even five generations on the bog. All the turf used to be hand-cut, of course, but even when they brought the big machines in we'd have whole families footing the turf for the summer."

"What happens to the peat you produce here?" Nora asked.

"Some of it goes to the briquette factory at Raheny, but most of what comes out of Loughnabrone is only suitable for use in the power plant."

"That place with the two towers down the road?"

"Used to go there, until a few years ago. It's closed down now. Obsolete. They're going to demolish it in a few weeks' time. No, all our production gets shipped up to the new station at Shannonbridge." Cadogan looked at her as if he didn't consider this a suitable topic of conversation for visitors, and abruptly changed the subject: "I was meaning to ask how you happened to be out in the storm. You weren't traveling on foot, surely?"

"Oh, no," Nora said, suddenly acutely aware that she wasn't prepared to give an exact account of how she had happened to be out on the road. "I stopped the car and got out to watch a—I don't even quite know what to call it, a small whirlwind. I'd never seen anything quite like it—"

Cadogan nodded, as if he understood. "The fairy wind."

"Excuse me?" Nora thought she'd misheard.

"That small whirlwind you saw. The lads around here call it the fairy wind. They also say nothing good comes after—ah, it's a load of auld rubbish, that kind of talk, but what can you do?"

"Well, in my case it was true. When I turned around, there was a huge dust cloud bearing down on me. I barely made it back to my car. Thank goodness Charlie Brazil came along when he did."

Again Cadogan studied her with a skeptical eye, as if he didn't quite believe the tale. Why did she keep feeling as though she was missing the joke here?

"If you'll excuse me just a moment, I'll get you fixed up here straightaway." He reached for his mobile and dialed a number from memory, then turned away slightly, with a small smile and a glance back in Nora's direction. He wanted to be rid of her, and soon. She was getting to be a nuisance.

"Ursula? It's Owen. Dr. Gavin's arrived in the office. Did you want to come round and fetch her—?" Cut off in midsentence, Cadogan listened for a moment, then colored and turned abruptly, as if the person on the other end of the connection had asked an embarrassing question. One hand flew up to the side of his face, an unconscious gesture of protection. "Look, I really can't . . . Yes, she's here with me now," he said, glancing up. Nora went back to perusing the office walls again, and did her best to pretend she wasn't listening. She stared at the newspaper cutting once more, at the nearly headless man in suit and wellingtons, noticing the interesting pin that anchored his tie—a sort of three-legged spiral. She'd arrived too early, and they didn't know what to do with her. Well, if that was the case, she could find her own way to the site. It beat standing around here like an idiot while they argued. She tried to catch Cadogan's eye. "I don't think that'll be necessary," he said, "but if you—" Ursula evidently cut him off again. "All right then . . . Yes, right away." Nora wondered idly whether it was a command or an acquiescence.

"That was Ursula Downes, the archaeologist heading up the bog road excavation on the site. She was first on the scene when the body was found." Cadogan looked vaguely preoccupied, shuffling through some papers on his desk, perhaps only to avoid having to make eye contact. "Since you're here, Ursula said she'd escort you out to the findspot, but she's rather tied up at the moment—so she's asked me to run you over there." He tried to offer a smile, but could only manage a worried grimace.

"Do I really need an escort? I'm sure I could find my way there if you gave me directions—"

"The trouble is that we're liable for your safety, and it's really much better if either Ursula or I or someone from Bord na Móna is with you out on the bog. It can be a much more treacherous place than it may appear. If you'd like to bring your own car, I'm happy to lead you out to the site—that is, whenever you're ready."

Nora glanced down at the brown film of limescale floating atop her now-cold tea. "I'm ready now."

As she followed Cadogan in her own car, watching him cut corners and shift gears a bit more forcefully than was warranted, Nora wondered what had passed between him and Ursula Downes. After speeding down the winding, tree-lined drive from the office, Cadogan turned onto the long, straight bog road. A set of narrow-gauge train tracks ran parallel to the road just below the ditch, and three rusting railcars sat idle upon them, with no engine in sight. Where the rails curved away from the road and out into the center of the bog, she could also see a jumble of extra track and several large bales of black plastic beside a high bank of turf someone had cut away by hand. A dirty wing chair faced the bank, as if someone had been sitting watching the cutter at work. It reminded her that in addition to its ancient use as a ritual depository, the bog had more recently taken on the role of communal rubbish heap. There was a pervasive air of abandonment here that surely didn't sit well with someone like Owen Cadogan, who still saw himself as young and vigorous. There wasn't much time to take in details; Cadogan's gray Nissan fairly flew along ahead of her, and she struggled to keep up on the bumpy road.

As they came near the site, she could see figures working at cuttings along the drain faces. In the distance, a brilliant white marquee tent out on the bog billowed slightly in the wind, looking oddly medieval in this dark, barren place. That's where the body was; it had to be. Cadogan finally braked abruptly when he came alongside a television news van and a couple of small rectangular trailers that seemed to have been dropped haphazardly by the side of the road. Between the sheds, a fair-haired woman was pacing and smoking a cigarette as she spoke on a mobile phone. She looked to be in her midthirties, and was dressed in standard work clothes for the bog: heavy-duty waterproof gear and industrial-strength rubber boots.

As they pulled onto the patch of gravel beside the first trailer, the woman closed her phone and approached Nora's car. Ursula's spiky fair hair and full lips were certainly arresting, but it was her large, luminous green eyes—set off by the delicate gold ring that pierced her left eyebrow—that added a not-so-subtle air of sensuality to her appearance. Whatever had passed between her and Owen Cadogan on the telephone had created a tension Nora could feel from several feet away, as Cadogan got out of his car and strode toward them, arms crossed over his chest in a posture that demanded acknowledgment. He opened his mouth to speak, but Ursula deliberately ignored him.

"You must be Dr. Gavin," she said, and Nora was surprised to hear a voice that immediately betrayed working-class Dublin origins. "Ursula Downes. I've heard so much about you, I feel as if we've already met." *Heard so much from whom?* Nora wanted to ask. As they shook hands, she felt the woman's eyes sweep her up and down, and had the unmistakable impression that she was being judged. It wasn't that Nora hadn't experienced this sort of scrutiny before—she was a Yank, after all, and had grown accustomed to being inspected—but the sincerity in Ursula's gaze had only to increase by the slightest margin before it crossed over into something much closer to condescension.

Ursula let go of Nora's hand and finally turned to acknowledge Cadogan. "Owen." The remarkable sea green eyes flickered across his face. "Mr. Cadogan usually pretends not to give a toss about what I'm up to out here, but he's actually terribly, terribly interested." Though these words were presumably addressed to Nora, Ursula's eyes remained on Cadogan. "Thanks for escorting Dr. Gavin," she said, glancing toward the television news vans. "I've been up to me oxters out here, trying to keep all the feckin' reporters from tripping into the cuttings."

Owen Cadogan's simmering annoyance was visible in his eyes, and in the grim set of his lips. "Could I have a word, Ursula?" he asked. "If you'd excuse us just one minute, Dr. Gavin . . ."

"I'll get my things," Nora said. She went around to her trunk to collect the gear she'd need for the day, and to climb into her waterproofs. She tried not to listen as she stepped into the baggy rubberized trousers, but couldn't help overhearing snatches of whispered conversation above the sound of the wind. ". . . *treat me like your fucking errand boy*," Cadogan was saying to Ursula, his right hand in a close grip on her elbow. She shrugged him off.

After Cadogan climbed into his car and roared away, Ursula Downes approached again, showing no apparent concern about the taut conversation.

"I'm sorry if I caused any trouble," Nora said. "I couldn't get exact directions—"

"Not to worry," Ursula said. "Owen's just in a poxy mood today. He got some bad news recently." She didn't elaborate, but somehow Nora got the impression that the source of Cadogan's dire bulletin had been none other than Ursula herself. "That was Niall Dawson on the mobile when you were arriving; he said they're about halfway here and should be arriving in the next hour."

Once again, Nora felt like a fifth wheel. "I'd love to have a look at what you're doing until the others get here."

"I suppose. Come along, then." Ursula led the way across a low-lying area beside the ditch, walking along in the impression left by a giant tractor tire. "It's still a bit soft in the low spots. Just put your feet down where I do."

Nora followed, carefully treading the same path Ursula took, her legs unsteady in the soft peat. To their right stood a rectangular pool—no doubt the end of a drain—reflecting the deep blue sky and billowy clouds. Beside it sat a twisted stump of bog oak, whose striated, ash gray surface had the segmented, half-burned look of charcoal. No fire had burned it, Nora realized. The effect came from the foreign touch of parched air after centuries of immersion.

"The wind is brutal today, isn't it?" she said, trying to make conversation.

Ursula turned back slightly, but kept walking. "I'll warn you—after a whole day out here, it feels as if you've been scrubbed raw. The peat gets everywhere: in your eyes, in your hair, even in your pores. It's almost impossible to get clean, and usually not worth the trouble." Nora glanced down at Ursula's hands, and saw black peat beneath the sculpted nails.

As they climbed the gentle rise of a slightly rounded field between two drains, Nora felt the familiar, not-quite-solid sensation underfoot. It was like walking on dry sponge. The first half-inch of peat had curled and cracked into irregular puzzle pieces, like the mud of a dry lakebed. It was clear that the peat in this area hadn't been cut in several years. Green plants sprouted at random; she recognized grass and sedge plants, sheep's sorrel and butterwort, and behind the clumps of rushes lay whitish pellets left by the hares who had used the rushes for cover.

"Your man's away down here," Ursula said. She pointed to the white tent, another hundred yards past the excavation site. A lone uniformed Garda officer sat on watch outside, his temporary seat an upturned white plastic bucket. The wind was still strong, and the blue-and-white crime-scene tape marking out the findspot trembled vigorously.

It was hard to imagine what this place must have been like thousands of years before. It must have taken a similar communal effort to make the roads that Ursula and the crew were digging up today, to cut down hundreds of trees, to fashion spikes, to weave hurdles from saplings. Whole villages must have turned out. If bogs had been sacred, then this area must have been a very holy place indeed. There were only sporadic patches of dry land, scattered like islands across the marshy center. What had it been then? A place of offering. Larder. Death trap. Quagmire. Healer of wounds. Nora tried to

imagine the time when all this had been wild bogland, crisscrossed by floating roads, a fearsome place roaming with wild beasts and bandits. She played
the picture in her head, of the last hundred centuries, from glaciers to forests
and solitary meadows, lakes gradually filling in, building up until the peat
was ten and fifteen meters deep, dead but undecayed, immune to corrup-
tion. Home to strange and primitive carnivorous plants, delicate orchids,
clouds of midges.

When she looked up, Ursula was yards ahead of her, easily jumping the
drain to the next bank. Nora's palms began to sweat as she approached
the drain, unsure if she could make it across. She saw Ursula turn to
watch her, a subtle challenge in her expression. What had she done to
earn this woman's scorn? They'd barely met, and already Ursula seemed
to dislike her. She gathered her courage and cleared the drain in one hop-
ping step. Safe.

"Who actually found the body?" she asked.

"I did," Ursula said. "We were clearing out this drain yesterday, getting ready to start another cutting here. I was directing Charlie Goggles,
one of the Bord na Móna lads, who was driving the Hymac, trying to
make sure he didn't put the spoil where the cutting was supposed to be.
After he dropped the first bucket, I saw something sticking up out of the
peat. Thought it was an animal bone at first, but it wasn't—it was the
bog man's thumb. Still attached to his hand, which was still attached to
his arm, which was still attached to his torso. Poor Charlie Goggles.
Nearly pissed himself when he saw it."

"Charlie Goggles? You don't mean Charlie Brazil?"

"Ah, you've met him. None other."

When they reached the tent, Ursula ignored the Garda officer's cautious gesture of greeting and ducked through the flap. Nora followed.
The space inside was an oasis of diffuse light and sublime calm after their
windy trek across the bog. Stepping inside felt like entering another
realm, another dimension. As she looked around, Nora felt Ursula
studying her once more, making sure that her anticipation reached full
fruition before lifting a corner of the black plastic sheeting that had been
staked to the ground over a mound of loose wet peat. Nora's eyes
searched the sodden heap until she saw a glistening, dark brown patch
that she knew immediately was human skin. Like the previous bog
remains she'd seen, it had an iridescent, slightly metallic cast.

"Do you think it would be all right if I—"

Ursula cut her off: "Do what you like. I'm not in charge of him; Niall Dawson has made that perfectly bloody clear."

Nora was aware for the first time that she had blundered into a potentially hazardous competition. Archaeologists had their turf wars, the same as everyone else, and maybe it was just the fact that she was part of the museum team that had put Ursula in bad humor. Whatever the politics here, she had to remain neutral. The problems of the living were the least of her business.

She knelt down and realized that she was holding her breath. The peat was wet and crumbly, like very damp, fibrous cake. She removed several handfuls of the stuff and saw how the excavator's gargantuan teeth had bisected the man at an angle just below his diaphragm, exposing muscle tissue and shrunken internal organs. The thought of such violence done to a fragile human being, even one centuries dead, suddenly made her feel queasy.

No one had mentioned how extraordinarily well-preserved this man was. His head, shoulders, and upper chest were almost miraculously intact. And if the Hymac had cut the body in half, there was a good chance that the rest of it was still under the bank below their feet. The man's skin was a rich dark brown, the typical tanned-leather appearance of a bog body. Tufts of hair about half an inch long stood out from his head, dark, but with the unmistakable reddish tinge of bog water. In the lab, they'd be able to tell how recently it had been cut, and with what kind of blade. Nora's eyes traveled the contours of his face again. She didn't want to forget anything about this moment, about the picture before her. In the next two days, he would be photographed from every angle, and finally removed from this place where he had slept so long undisturbed. There was no evidence of clothing, but a braided leather armlet circled his left biceps, and a thin piece of twisted leather lay coiled behind his head. Nora reached into her jacket pocket for a magnifying glass. Through the thick lens, she traced the cord to a triple knot just below the right ear, and saw how the leather cut into the wasted flesh. She crawled around to get a better look at the throat and noticed one end of a deep gash just below the ligature. From the position of the cut, inside the body's protected curve, she knew it could not have been made by an errant machine blade. By all appearances, someone had strangled this man and savagely cut his throat.

She raised her head and heard a hollow noise in her ears. That sound might have been the last thing he'd heard out on the bog as well: the gusting wind, or a faint whistle as it dragged through the sharp points of furze and heather. Or perhaps what he had heard were the few words whispered by his executioner just before the fatal blow. She wondered whether the armlet signified anything. Had he been a member of the society that killed him, a high-born leader, perhaps—or a prisoner, a hostage, an outcast? Had he gone willingly to his end, or been carried here bound and under protest? She imagined his killing carried out in darkness, some secret ritual witnessed only by the moon and stars, but maybe it hadn't happened that way at all. Maybe the bloodletting had been part of some public display.

She was suddenly aware of Ursula Downes standing beside her. "Looks like someone wanted to make sure he was dead," Ursula said. "Did you see the stakes? Look at his arms."

Nora saw several thin wooden stakes about an inch in diameter that had been driven through the flesh of the man's upper arms.

"I don't suppose you ought to do anything more until Niall Dawson gets here," Ursula said. She looked down at the bog man again and probed at his curled fist with the toe of her boot, a gesture that made Nora cringe. She wanted to shove Ursula away from the fragile body, out of the tent. But instead she slowly replaced the wet peat over the corpse and they stepped outside, back into the harsh sun and wind.

"Might take a couple of days to get him crated up," Ursula said. "I assume you've got accommodation sorted." The extraordinary green eyes shot her a stealthy look, and Nora suddenly felt foolish. Of course—everything was falling into place now; Ursula's having heard so much about her, the sideways glances that said she was under close scrutiny. It should have come as no surprise at all that Ursula and Cormac were acquainted—Dawson too. They were probably all old friends, and she was the mug. She should have remembered that here in Ireland, the world of archaeology was a tiny sphere, and Cormac knew everyone in it. Clearly Ursula had been toying with her since the moment they'd met, but there was no reason to let on that she knew it. Nora struggled to put on her blankest expression. "Yes, I'm staying with a friend nearby."

Ursula gave a mysterious smile, then looked across the bog toward her crew and sighed. "What the bloody hell are they up to now?" She checked her watch. "They're not due a tea break for another hour."

Nora followed Ursula's gaze. The crew were all standing about one of the cuttings. With the wind, it was impossible to hear what anyone was saying, but their postures communicated a disagreement of some sort. One young woman broke away from the group and started running toward them. "Ursula!" she shouted, voice faint against the wind, and her hail was followed by a gesture, a single sweep of the arm that said "Come." Nora followed as Ursula began to run.

When they reached the crew, Nora could see expressions of shock and dismay around the circle of fresh, windburned faces. A dark-haired girl crouched on the bank above the drain, her wellingtons covered in fresh muck to the midcalf.

"Jesus Christ, Rachel, why didn't you say anything?" demanded one young man.

"What's going on?" Ursula demanded. "And you—" she said to the television cameraman who had wandered over to see what was happening "—get the hell off this bank before I run you." He raised his free hand in a gesture of submission and beat a hasty retreat back to his van. Ursula turned to the crew. "Now, somebody tell me quick what's going on here."

Several of them responded at once: "Rachel fell into the drain—"

"We had to pull her out—"

"I was concentrating on what I was doing," the girl said. "I accidentally stepped off the end of the plank. I didn't ask anyone to rescue me."

Ursula's tone was incredulous. "I can't believe you're all in such a state about having to pull someone out of a drain. For Christ's sake—"

"It's not that," said the young woman who'd called them over. She stepped aside and pointed to the corner of the cutting. "We nearly stepped on him trying to get Rachel out."

Looking toward the spot the girl had indicated, Nora could just discern the outline of a distorted face. She dropped to her knees beside the cutaway for a closer look, and it took a moment for the totality of the terrible image to sink in. The skin was dark brown and the features slightly flattened, the nose smashed to one side, but the eye sockets, skull vault, and jawline clearly marked it as human. One skeletal, clawlike hand was curled into a fist and raised above the head, as though he'd been submerged and was trying to come up for a breath of air.

Ursula heaved an exasperated sigh. "You must be coddin' me. Two bloody Iron Age bog men in the space of a week."

"I wouldn't jump to any conclusions," Nora said, looking up into the circle of anxious faces peering down at her. "This man seems to be wearing a wristwatch."

3

Detective Liam Ward had just set the phone in its cradle when he noticed the fresh drops of blood staining his shirt front. The plaster he'd applied to the shaving cut on his throat had evidently come loose. He didn't really have time for this; the phone call had been from the duty officer, ringing with news that another body, the second in as many weeks, had just turned up at Loughnabrone Bog. The first had been officially declared at least five hundred years old, but this one looked as though it might be modern. Whatever the circumstances, it wouldn't do to have the detective in charge show up looking as if he'd just been in a brawl. He stripped off his shirt and went into the bathroom to clean the cut and apply another plaster. When he returned to his bedroom, the bloodstained garment lay crumpled on the bed. Like evidence from a crime scene, he thought, more mindful this time of the plaster as he buttoned his collar.

Lugh seemed restless. Perhaps it was something to do with the smell of blood. As Ward put the knot in his tie, he glimpsed the dog pacing down the hall and into the kitchen, setter's plumelike tail on alert, nails beating an anxious tattoo on the tile floor. For some reason the sound reminded Ward of his mother. He remembered the noise of her high-heeled shoes on the same floor, as she tried in vain to convince him to leave this house on the day after his wife's funeral. Of course he hadn't left, but had stayed on, anchored by memories, by the stones in the garden. He knew his mother thought he'd been relieved of a great burden when Eithne died. Could it already be eleven years this summer since his wife had walked down the riverbank, her pockets laden with dozens of small stones from their own garden, never intending to come up for air? He could see the stones: black, gray, white, pink, their smooth and rounded shapes. He'd put them out only a week earlier, to help keep the weeds down around the roses. He pictured Eithne at the edge of the grass, down on her knees but long past any hope of prayer, selecting the stones one by one and slowly filling the pockets of her dark green raincoat. He could imagine her performing that simple act, but he could go no further. Her final moments were obscure and inaccessible to him. They'd returned the stones with her personal effects after the inquest. He couldn't bring himself to put them back in the garden. It seemed wrong somehow, or perhaps just bad luck, so he'd flung them back into the river where they belonged.

He'd met Eithne at a spring wedding. One of his younger colleagues had taken the plunge. He remembered how the young sergeant and his friends had all slagged him as a perennial bachelor. Up to that point, he had never found anyone who had moved him enough—until the moment he'd glimpsed a wondrous creature playing a harp in the corner at the wedding dinner. He'd been struck at once by her sorrowful eyes, but above all by the dignity in her bearing, the graceful way she moved. She had seemed so regal, so self-contained, and he was a man who noticed such things.

He had been puzzled by the fact that he'd never seen this girl before, that he'd known nothing of her existence. He made a few discreet inquiries at the wedding party, and found she lived with her father and younger sister near Loughnabrone. She was considerably younger than he was—fourteen years—and astonished, embarrassed by his interest, her manner always somewhat diffident. He had not taken love easy, as the song implored, but uncharacteristically pursued her, wooed her, and eventually won her heart, although he sometimes wondered now whether she had finally consented to marriage more out of misplaced compassion than from genuine affection. At the time, it hadn't mattered. He had never experienced anything like it, the hunger that seemed to occupy every cell of his body, a chemical fire that would not be calmed or cooled. His all-consuming need to be with her, to possess her, had seemed sufficient to carry them both. But of course it had not been sufficient.

He'd told no one that Eithne had been carrying their child when she'd walked into the river. It didn't seem right to share a secret that had been revealed to him only through her death. She must have known about the child, and she had been so far sunk into confusion and despair that the prospect of a new life had not lifted that dark veil, but only made things worse. She had packed a bag before she'd walked down to the river that day, a single lucid gesture that had been calculated, he supposed, to save him the trouble of sorting through her things after she'd gone. He had opened the case and spilled the neatly folded skirts and blouses onto their bed, buried his face and wept into the silky underthings still suffused with her scent.

Lugh came through the bedroom door and stopped in front of him. The dog lifted his graying muzzle and sniffed the air, and Ward tried to reassure him with a friendly scratch. "It's all right, auld son. Relax." He felt great tenderness for his aging companion, who had arrived in this house as a tiny pup, a gift from his colleagues just after the first anniversary of Eithne's death. They had been together a long time, he and Lugh, and he knew the dog wouldn't last the year, if that. Lugh had come to the point in his existence where major systems had begun to break down, as they would for all creatures, Ward supposed, should they live so long. We are all vulnerable in that way, he thought—soft and imperfect, riddled with frailty. Long ago he'd forced himself to admit that he'd been drawn to Eithne Scully's dangerous streak, as if she could make up for that part of him that was afraid to live intensely in the present. He'd been fascinated by the dark, chaotic side of her nature, capable of great passion and creativity, but also subject to fits of paranoia and an inconsolable desolation. He'd once thought that if he could only surround her with peace and constancy, she might be able to hold some fragment of it within her, but once again he had been wrong. A capacity for contentment was something they had never shared. Eithne was always restless, chafing at any and all expectations. When he'd first brought her to this house after they were married, she'd followed him around as if on a tour, then gone home to her father's house for another fortnight before he'd convinced her to come back and live with him here.

In hindsight, of course, he felt he ought to have seen the signs earlier. At first, the changes had been gradual, imperceptible, mere hairline cracks. He'd taken to sorting through their lives, remembering gestures and looks, wondering about that certain blank expression that had said she didn't know who he was or what she was doing here with him. Eventually she hadn't been able to play the harp anymore; her hands would no longer do what she told them. He had arrived home one evening and found her sitting at her harp, with the instrument all unstrung, a web of golden wires across her lap. *It wasn't right, Liam,* she'd said. *I know I could play if only it were strung properly.* The harp sat, still unstrung, in the corner of the sitting room.

One day she had told him she'd taken up walking. At first he'd been encouraged, hoping that a daily dose of physical activity might help lift her mood. But even that had taken a bad turn as time went on. Coming home, he'd sometimes overtake her on the roadside, walking with her head down, lips moving in some silent litany, weighed down with the burden of words and numbers that had begun to crowd her mind. Eventually she was counting exactly how many steps it took to get to every one of her regular stops around the town: the post office, the newsagent, the chemist. He found her pockets jammed with small items she'd taken: scarves, gloves, lipsticks—all things she didn't use—which he would return discreetly. No one ever had the heart to confront her directly. Then she'd begun venturing farther afield. He remembered the terrible phone call from the Garda station in Ballingar, six miles away, where she'd turned up in the midst of a downpour, asleep at the foot of the Virgin in the grotto. She'd been completely disoriented when he came to fetch her, like a lost child. He still recalled her blank look when he'd tried asking what she had been doing wandering alone in the rain. She'd not ventured out for a few weeks after that episode, and he had thought she might be taking a turn for the better, not perceiving the nature of the disease that gripped her.

His colleagues had always treated her with deference and been discreet in their dealings with him, but it was a discretion born of pity rather than understanding. He knew what they said behind his back. "Poor auld Ward. You wouldn't wish that mad wife of his on anyone." She was slipping gradually into oblivion, and nothing he did could make things better. He lived each day in limbo, in dreadful anticipation. She shouldn't have been left alone, and yet he knew she would have found some means to get away. There was no such thing as enough vigilance. And if he had allowed himself to admit it, a part of him wanted to let her go, to let her have what she so ardently wanted.

The final phone call had brought him to the river's edge. Her body lay submerged in the clear water, and her long dark hair streamed away from her face, rippling in the current like the pale green weeds that trailed along beside her. The dress she wore under the raincoat billowed in the water. She had been so peaceful, so beautiful in death, suspended in her otherworldly, watery realm, that never-empty channel pouring itself endlessly into the sea. All at once he felt what she must have felt as the cold water closed over her—a relief that was almost like communion. But in his case, the feeling was brief and transitory. He remembered standing on the bridge as the ambulance men splashed into the shallow water to lift her out onto a stretcher, pale, cold, and heavy, once more subject to the earth's dreadful gravity. Had he contributed to that gravity, become part of what she could no longer bear? He tried to tell himself that nothing he'd done or failed to do had made the final difference to her, but in the end, that was the saddest testament of all. He thought of her every day, was still tied to her, as he would be always, those river weeds firmly twined around his heart.

Ward looked into the bathroom mirror, settling the knot on his tie and checking the plaster on his throat one last time before leaving the house. He was curious about this new body at Loughnabrone. He'd been out there a few days earlier, along with Catherine Friel, the new assistant state pathologist, who had been making a determination on another set of remains. He was glad that she would again be attending. He'd worked with Malachy Drummond many times, and they got on well, but he had only met Dr. Friel the previous week. He'd felt an immediate lift at the warmth and the acute intelligence in her eyes, and the slight frown of concentration that had furrowed her forehead as she worked. He hadn't felt anything similar in years—didn't even know how to describe it, except as a sort of forward momentum of the spirit. He hesitated for a moment at the bedroom door, then crossed back to the chest of drawers, where he removed his plain gold wedding band. He held it in his fingers, feeling the warmth and the weight of it, and finally set it in the shallow tray on top of the bureau.

4

Cormac heard the wind, and looked up from his work to see the leaves on the chestnut trees outside tremble in the stiff breeze. He hoped Nora was getting on all right out at the bog; he remembered what a strong wind could do to all that loose peat. He had urged her to come out with him, the night before she was to begin work on the excavation, but she'd insisted on getting up early and making the trip alone this morning. She needed time to think, she'd said. He had detected a slight pulling away in her recently, a greater detachment in the way she looked at him, a new tinge of sadness in her eyes. There was definitely something going on, something he was not privy to, and the thought disturbed him.

They'd never gone away for a proper holiday, and this hardly qualified. When he'd discovered that Nora was coming down for the excavation on the latest bog find, he'd arranged for them to stay at the McCrossans' cottage, which was only a short distance from the site. He was on deadline to finish an article, and the solitude afforded by this place would be ideal. But he had an ulterior motive as well, to try to clarify where he and Nora stood. He understood her reluctance to be drawn into anything serious. He'd tried not to read too much into her reticence. Maybe she had just had a lot of things to attend to before leaving Dublin. There was always work to do for classes, or her own academic work to catch up on at weekends. He sensed something terribly temporary about every aspect of Nora's life—the job, the flat, even her studies—and from the way she'd been behaving lately, he'd almost begun to feel as if he might be one of those temporary arrangements. Everything might carry on just as it had been, on and on. The trouble was that he didn't know whether that was quite enough.

He looked around the little house, where his old teacher and mentor Gabriel McCrossan had come every summer. Twenty years ago, Gabriel had started spending so much time out here, working on bog road excavations and living in somewhat shabby rented accommodations, that he and Evelyn must have thought it practical just to buy a house, so at least

they could have more time together. The cottage was small and compact, and despite having been completely fitted out and modernized, still
carried the atmosphere of age in its low ceilings, gray flag floor, and deep-
set windows. The place was not distinguished in location. There was no
breathtaking view, only wild bog and small hills, no doubt the remnants
of ancient monuments long since plowed under. A bland place, most
people might think, and yet some of Ireland's greatest treasures still lay
beneath these bogs. Gabriel had been the first to bring them to the
nation's attention. These treasures were not precious metal, but planks
of rough, hand-hewn wood, the wordless annals of the Iron Age, and
with them a fuller portrait of a whole society had begun to emerge.

Evelyn rarely used the house now, since Gabriel's death. A month
ago, she'd asked Cormac to dinner, and announced that she'd made a
will leaving the house to him, and that he ought to consider it his own.
She'd handed him a key, the same one he'd used to let himself in last
night. He'd been so touched by her gesture that he hadn't quite known
what to say.

"Just say you'll make good use of it," she had advised. "I'd hate to see
it empty and lonesome. Take Nora down for a few days."

When this opportunity to stay in the cottage had presented itself so
serendipitously, he'd quickly phoned Michael Scully, the old friend and
neighbor who had always looked after the house for the McCrossans
when they were in Dublin. Evelyn had warned him that Michael's
health was declining, though she hadn't been specific. But he'd seemed
happy to have them coming down for a few days, and had sent his
daughter to remove the dustcovers, wash the windows, and sweep out
the cobwebs and the cold ashes. She had still been in the house when
Cormac arrived. When he'd stepped into the kitchen, Brona Scully—a
slender, doe-eyed girl of about twenty—had retreated to the corner
beside the dresser and stood frozen, like a hare convinced that immobil-
ity would render it invisible to predators. He'd tried speaking to her, but
got no response; and when he came back from inspecting the rest of the
house, the girl had vanished without making a sound. Cormac didn't
know her background well, only the story—perhaps just a rumor or local
legend—that as a child she had witnessed her sister's suicide. Whether
or not the story was true, it was a fact that she had not spoken a word
since that day.

Cormac could feel his friends' presence strongly here: Evelyn in the colorful tapestry cushions and all the other things that made the house comfortable, Gabriel in the worn leather armchair by the fire, and both of them in the hundreds of books that lined the walls. He had been the anchor around which her energy swirled. To Cormac their union had always seemed a near-perfect balance: strong individuals married together to make a separate entity greater than either of them alone, a mystery unfathomable even to themselves. The deference they'd invariably shown each other used to calm him when he felt anxious. He remembered the way Gabriel sometimes used to catch Evelyn's hand when she passed by. He had always felt embarrassed but also fascinated by the tenderness between them.

He sometimes imagined that he could feel the same way about Nora as Gabriel had about his wife. Evelyn had come here, to a place not known for its amenities, and made a home for herself and Gabriel, amid the bogs that were his life and his passion. Cormac knew he wasn't Gabriel, that he could never be half the intellect, half the scholar, half the man Gabriel had been. He couldn't ask Nora to come with him to this remote place. She had her own work as well, with a different center, a life that was not his life.

It wasn't just that his work was here. He'd spent the past year trying to create a bridge with his long-absent father, now an old man retired from the world, living at his home place up in Donegal. It was not an inconsiderable thing for a man to know from whence he came. It was Nora who'd convinced him to keep trying, though the going had been rough at times.

It suddenly struck him that it was in this house that he had first heard her name. He'd been down for the weekend with the McCrossans, and Evelyn was already asleep. He and Gabriel had stayed up late, waxing philosophical over a few large whiskeys, and Gabriel was becoming more than usually sincere. Others might become uncoordinated, or belligerent from strong drink, but with Gabriel, utter sincerity was always the best indicator that he'd achieved a slight state of inebriation. He heard the old man's voice: *There's someone I'd like you to meet. Nora Gavin is her name. I think you might get on.* Cormac remembered protesting, as he usually did when any of his friends tried a hand at matchmaking. But Gabriel had persisted: *She's lovely, very intelligent, and she has a fierce good heart. And you need someone, Cormac, someone to get your arms around at night. Believe me, it makes all the difference.*

And of course Gabriel had been dead on, as usual. Nora was all the things the old man had said, and more. The idea of sharing his life completely with anyone had never before circled the edges of Cormac's consciousness. Now it hovered, light and capricious as a butterfly. In many ways, his daily life had not appreciably altered since they'd been together. He still rose each day at seven, and cycled to the university for morning classes three days a week. Tuesdays, Thursdays, and Saturdays, he'd go down to the boat club and take his scull out for an early morning row down the Liffey. When the water was calm, it was the nearest thing to flying he'd ever experienced. He loved the dank smell of the riverbank, the dripping green moss and algae on the bridge pilings, and the image that always filled his mind as he rowed, of the river water merging with the seawater, brown and green. These things were all part of the life he'd made, layer by layer, over many years. And Nora was the mercurial salmon, that bright flash of silver he glimpsed only occasionally, swimming against the current in that steady stream. What would happen if he caught her?

He thought back to the last time they'd made love. She'd begun to weep, quietly but uncontrollably, and when he'd asked whether it was something he'd said or done that had upset her, she had only shaken her head. Her wordless sorrow had moved him to the point of tears as well, though he hadn't shed them in years—not since his mother died, in fact. He hadn't even been able to cry for the loss of Gabriel, his truest father in any real sense of that word. But he had felt so helpless, so completely defenseless against Nora's tears. He'd wanted to gather her up like a small child, to tell her everything was all right, or would be all right, but he couldn't do it. Because it wasn't all right, and never would be, with that cleft in the world where Tríona used to be, where Nora's own life used to be. How often had she replayed that last conversation with her murdered sister, each time changing what she had said, so that circumstances would alter, the future would shift, and horror would recede into the realm of nightmare?

He wondered what she'd done to help build the case against her brother-in-law. He'd once found her poring over a file when he arrived at her flat, but she'd tucked it under a pile of papers, without letting him see what it was. Later, shifting the papers from the table, he'd scanned the heading: *HALLETT, Catríona. Autopsy report.* He sometimes tried to imagine how a family could be transformed by such a tragedy. He had often heard Nora on the telephone with one or both of her parents; it was easy to perceive her affection for them, and yet he detected a distance, a strain in the relationship—something in the tone of her voice, the duration of the pauses in the conversation. He imagined growing up in a close family, something that was as foreign to him as the place she was from. But when a thing is so horrifically broken, never to be put back together again, there must be all sorts of jagged edges.

Giving up on writing for the moment, Cormac put together his flute, hoping the distraction of playing a tune would get him thinking more about his article than about Nora. He felt the cool ebony against the underside of his lower lip, this once-living thing from the tropics now resident in a nearly treeless rainforest a world away. He felt the music pass through him, from somewhere unknown, out between his pursed lips and into his fingers, through the flute and into the air, the atmosphere he breathed and took into his lungs to make more music. So much of existence was like that: endlessly, thoughtlessly self-perpetuating cycles. His courtship of Nora—and he did think of it in that formal way—was part of another cycle of human life. He wondered where it would end, whether they would ever find enough common ground, but he remained hopeful. He had no choice.

He took another breath and began to play "The Dear Irish Boy," the tune that had become, for him, the theme of the *cailín rua*, the red-haired girl who had brought them together last summer. The *cailín rua* had suffered a needless and cruel death, but her son had survived, and three hundred and fifty years later, through another tragedy, her descendants had learned her story. He played through the tune's B part, feeling the cascade of high, keening notes pull like brambles at his soul. Slowly the theme resolved itself and flowed once more like a stream, with rippling, dark currents only occasionally audible under its surface.

He set down the flute and tried to go back to writing. The article he was wrestling with was a new look at Bronze Age and Iron Age gold from possible ritual deposits—and ritual deposits were always only possible because, as much as one wanted to believe in it, ritual intent was almost impossible to prove through archaeology alone. That whole period was fraught with riddles and mysteries to which they had only fragmentary answers. Why was it that the heaviest deposits of native gold were found in the rivers of Wicklow and Tyrone, and yet the most spectacular of the Bronze Age gold objects had been found all the way across the island in Clare? Why was there no direct evidence of beekeeping in the Iron Age, despite evidence that beeswax had most certainly been used for *cire perdue* metal casting? Why were gold objects so uncommon among grave goods—were they melted down, or passed on to the next wearer as a mark of office?

He studied the map showing the distribution of Bronze and Iron Age gold objects across Ireland. How many dots were missing because some-one had stumbled on the gold and kept it, buried it again, or melted it down and sold it, and lived on the proceeds in comfort for the rest of his natural life? There were also hundreds of unknown and never-to-be-told stories of gold-fueled strife—thefts and confiscations and no doubt murders as well—all over bright yellow metal. He wondered how the ancients had perceived it, who worked in rusting iron and green corrod-ing bronze. To cultures steeped in the ever-corrupting natural world, it must have seemed the only substance that did not decay, the sacred metal of the sun, of immortality.

A noise startled him—only a bird nesting in the eaves, but he realized how anxious he was, waiting for Nora's arrival. He didn't want a repeat of what had happened last night. Shortly after he'd arrived, he'd heard a rap on the door. He had answered it automatically, thinking the caller might be Brona Scully come back to see if he'd had any trouble with the boiler. He'd been caught off guard to find Ursula Downes on the doorstep. He thought back to the picture she'd presented. Ursula was slight and fair, and the hair cut tight around her ears gave her a rather self-consciously gamine look. The gold eyebrow ring was an addition since he'd last seen her, but somehow it was hardly surprising. It had been some time.

"I was just driving past, and saw the car," she said. "Thought it might be Evelyn, but I'm happy to find that it's you. Back on Loughnabrone Bog again. You'll never believe it—I'm over at the old digs. The house has been fixed up, but once in a while I'll open the door and expect to see you or one of the others standing in the queue for the toilet."

"It was all about making the most of a rare opportunity, as I recall."

They'd both spent several summers working out here with Gabriel nearly twenty years earlier, and seeing Ursula again brought it all back: the primitive student lodging, the aroma of wet wool jumpers drying by the fire, strong tea, cold rooms, warm beds. The very air in those days had seemed fraught with all kinds of physical hunger. From her expres-sion, he had no doubt that Ursula remembered it too.

"Listen, Cormac, I was very sorry to hear about Gabriel," she'd said, lowering her voice. "It must have been a complete shock. I'm sure we all thought he'd go on forever. I meant to phone you or Evelyn, but I'm no good at that sort of thing." She had seemed alone at that moment, wary and vulnerable somehow, still standing outside on the doorstep.

"Would you like to come in for a drink or something?" he'd heard himself ask. Even as he extended the invitation, he hoped it wouldn't be something that he would later regret.

"Maybe just a quick one. Thanks." She stepped across the threshold and glanced around. "This place hasn't changed much, has it?"

"What can I get you?" he asked, when she'd pulled up a chair at the kitchen table.

"Red wine?" She looked over at the half-dozen bottles waiting to be stowed in the kitchen cabinet. "Unless you're saving it. Trying to impress someone."

"Just experimenting."

As Cormac opened a bottle and poured them each a glass, Ursula continued, "I find I'm not at all particular about wine. Cheap plonk is just as effective as the posh stuff, if you're in the right mood. And I'm generally in the right mood." She turned to face him and took the glass from his hand, her luminous green eyes as mischievous as ever. The lamp on the table beside her cast a warm gold glow that caught her skin tone and highlighted the angular shape of her face, the slight hollows in her cheeks. Only a few lines at the corners of her eyes marked the passage of time. "So what are you doing down here?"

"Working on an article for the *Journal*. Some new findings about Bronze and Iron Age gold work."

"Really?" She started to peruse the books he'd strewn across the table in an attempt to get his materials organized. "You know, people always say there was gold in the Loughnabrone hoard, but the two brothers who uncovered it swore up and down they never found any." She pulled a book from a stack on the table. "Any chance I could borrow this one? I promise to return it promptly whenever you need it back." Checking the spine, Cormac saw it was one of the more obscure and detailed references on Iron Age metalwork.

He made a gesture of offering. "Be my guest."

"Oh, I would in a minute," she said, "but I believe you already have one."

Still quick as ever, Ursula. He didn't see any point in being coy. "I expect you'll meet her tomorrow—Nora Gavin. She's coming down to help with your bog man." He tried changing the subject. "How's your own work going these days?"

"Oh, you know. It's a living. We're finding bits of things, but it's a bit of a mess at the moment, a real hodgepodge of odd stuff: platforms and short stretches of plank trackway, a couple of nice willow hurdles. We've come across some really interesting peat samples—you might be interested in taking a look. But the regional manager is a desperate whinger, giving me a lot of pointless grief about hurrying it up so he can get this area back on his precious production schedule. The bog man turning up hasn't exactly made his day, although it's improved my mood considerably."

She looked at the open wine bottle, but apparently decided not to ask for another glass, for which he felt grateful. She leaned back in her chair and looked at him thoughtfully. "One of these years I'm going to give up fieldwork. Get myself one of those desk jobs. I'm sick to death of being out in all weather, of peat dust in my hair, and ten solid weeks of this—" She held up her hand, the fingers and nails black with ground-in peat. "Next year I'm going in for one of the consulting jobs, even if I have to switch firms. Those lucky sods barely get their feet wet once a year. It's either that or pack it in altogether." As she spoke, Cormac thought he perceived a change in Ursula. It had been a long time since they had met, and she no longer seemed to have that razor edge he had once so carefully tried to avoid.

She drained the last swallow of wine from her glass and stood up. "Time to push off home; I've an early start again tomorrow. Could I just run up to the loo before I go? I remember the way."

Cormac switched on the light at the stairs for her. He'd always had an uneasy feeling about Ursula. From the time they'd first met, he had sensed danger in her presence, a moodiness and manic energy that was draining to be around. There was, he had to admit, an unabashed and frank carnality about her, something he'd once been close enough to know about firsthand. But it wasn't that quality itself that he found worrisome; his reservations were about how she used it, as a weapon. Ursula had always possessed a very sophisticated—one could almost say scientific—understanding of sexual attraction in all its varying forms. He was still unsure whether "predatory" was the right word to describe exactly the way Ursula was, but she clearly got some sort of thrill from her ability to get another person's pulse racing. Years ago he'd watched her in action, toying with fellow students, then colleagues at otherwise deadly dull faculty functions. She loved causing a stir, and seemed to draw energy directly from the amount of social discomfort she could engender during the space of a single evening, with a glance, or with fingertips that lingered just a fraction of a second too long. She excelled at pulling every eye after her, making them see she didn't give a tinker's curse what they thought of her. He always imagined tense arguments erupting in cars as everyone headed home. Ursula had not made these people unhappy, but she was a catalyst who could concentrate unhappiness and set it loose.

He had once tried to convince Ursula that it was only herself she was damaging with those antics, but she didn't seem to care. He'd always sensed an edge of mistrust in her as well, of hurt or betrayal. Being in a room with her now filled him with unaccountable and overwhelming sadness. In all these years, had she ever found someone who was willing to risk everything, to get past all the defenses to reach her wounded soul?

She returned to the kitchen and breezed past him toward the door; he followed to open it for her. "Great to see you, Cormac," she said, and leaned forward, apparently to offer a quick embrace. But when he moved to reciprocate, she reached up with both hands, turned his face down to hers, and kissed him full on the mouth. He felt her tongue dart between his lips for an instant, and he pulled back reflexively.

His startled reaction seemed to amuse her. "Ah, come on, now. Don't pretend you wouldn't." Then she'd been out the door and into her car before he could say a word. He'd stood looking after the receding tail-lights, and when he'd reached up to wipe his mouth, his fingers had come away touched with plum-colored lipstick. He had rubbed his hands together, then scrubbed them against his trouser legs.

Feeling perplexed by the surge of emotion his memory of the scene had unleashed, Cormac climbed the stairs and looked at his clothes hung neatly in the wardrobe, his toothbrush and shaving things on the ledge above the sink in the adjacent bathroom. He sat at the edge of the armchair across from the bed, seized by a sudden gust of melancholy, similar to the feeling that had driven him from his own house to Nora's flat almost precisely fourteen months ago. The prospect then had been a different sort of life from his ordinary, orderly existence, and the decision he'd made at that time had certainly lifted him to a new level. Had he reached a point where another decision was required, where what he and Nora had was no longer enough for him? He thought of her tears again and felt far away from her, closed off from all those interior passages in her soul that he had once imagined. What impulse was it that pressed for access there? And was he really willing to reciprocate? Was he prepared to make an offer—to lay himself bare, metaphorically speaking, and hand Nora a knife?

5

Death set all sorts of wheels in motion, especially when a body turned up where it ought not to have been. Within a few minutes, a quartet of brisk young Guards in two police cars had arrived on the scene and set to work. They herded everyone away from the cutting and marked out the crime scene—if crime scene it should turn out to be—with their familiar blue-and-white tape. The archaeology crew had been banished for the moment to their roadside hut, but on discovering that Nora was a physician, the policemen had asked her to stay behind, to certify for the record that the man in the cutting was in fact deceased, and did not require medical attention. It was a routine procedure, but seemed the ultimate redundancy in this case. The coroner's crew had arrived a short while later; the uneven ground prevented them from erecting yet another tent over the cutting, but they did their best, rigging up some plastic sheeting to shield the body from prying eyes and cameras.

Nora was just about to inquire if they were finished with her when another vehicle stopped at the side of the road, and two people emerged. One was a tall man, well-dressed and serious—perhaps in his early fifties, she guessed, from the dark curly hair just going to salt-and-pepper gray. The dress shoes and immaculate raincoat looked out of place on the bog, but it was clear from the junior Guards' attitude that this man was in charge. The woman with him was evidently his partner. At the site, he nodded briefly to his fellow officers, then addressed Nora. "Dr. Gavin? Detective Liam Ward, and this is Detective Maureen Brennan. Are you connected with this excavation?"

"Not exactly. I'm actually here to help recover the bog body that was found the other day. I just arrived early." Nora glimpsed a plaster peeping out over the top of Ward's shirt collar, marked with a dark drop of blood.

"There's a whole van-load of people on their way from the National Museum as well. They should be arriving shortly."

"There's no way we could contact them, request that they delay the trip?"

"We could ring them, but they're nearly here, and I'm afraid it wouldn't be prudent to delay. The body they're coming to recover is in a very fragile state, and getting it to the lab as quickly as possible is critical."

Ward turned to Brennan. "Looks as if we'll need a few extra uniforms on crowd control." He motioned for Nora to accompany him to the cutting. "Is there anything you can tell me? Who was it found this body?"

"One of the archaeologists working here at the site. They called her Rachel, but I'm sorry, I don't know her surname. I only arrived a short while ago myself."

Ward consulted a list he'd been handed by one of the uniformed officers. "Briscoe, it says here. Rachel Briscoe."

They'd reached the edge of the cutaway. The policeman seemed unfazed by the sight of the corded brown arm that stuck up out of the peat. "Ursula Downes and I were having a look at the other findspot when they called us over," she said. "I think at first we both assumed this was another set of old remains, until we saw the watch."

Ward's eyebrows spiked. "A wristwatch?"

"Yes—I can show you, if I could just climb down into the drain for a second." Ward nodded. Nora dug out a foothold in the drain face and stepped down onto the board that rested on the mucky floor. She had to hang on to the edge of the cutting and tread carefully to keep the plank from tipping. If she fell off, she'd be mired to her knees in a second.

Through her magnifying glass, she examined the dead man's flexed hand, his long fingers with their well-formed oval fingernails, and noted the fibrous black peat embedded beneath the nails, which were slightly ragged, as though bitten off rather than clipped. The delicate flesh on the back of the hand was shrunken and slightly decayed from being near the exposed surface of the bog, but the palm appeared wonderfully intact, the fingertips wrinkled as if he had just lingered too long in the bath. With gloved fingers, Nora scraped the wet peat from around the watch, its wide metal strap buckled around a once-solid wrist now reduced to moldering flesh and exposed bone.

Ward crouched on the bank above the cutting for a closer look. "What else can you tell me?"

Nora peered through the glass at the disfigured face. The man was clean-shaven; his eyes were closed, but not sunken in the sockets. Reddish lashes rimmed the lids. It was impossible to tell his age; immersion in astringent bog water tended to make even youthful skin appear shrunken and wizened, and this man had already begun to take on a tanned-leather appearance. Though he couldn't have been buried here more than a few decades, this body was not quite as well preserved as the older corpse. There was nothing odd in that; bog preservation happened by accident, depending on fortuitous water levels and chemicals mixed by capricious nature. Sometimes the acidic bog water preserved skin and internal organs but had the opposite effect on bone; Nora remembered reading about a bog man in Denmark whose entire skeleton had been completely decalcified, leaving behind only a flattened, human-shaped sack of leathery skin. What could she tell Ward? The dead man's nostrils and open mouth were filled with peat. Perhaps it was only an impression, but to her he seemed to have been captured in the posture of dying, at the very moment when life's frenetic energy ceased: dividing cells stopped in their tracks, coursing blood slowed to a halt, the brain's constant storm of electrical impulses suddenly ceased.

Ward showed no adverse reaction to the gruesome sight before them, but a young uniformed Garda who came up beside him only looked at the body for a moment before turning away abruptly, and being violently sick all over his shiny black shoes. Nora saw the detective's hand rest briefly on the younger man's shoulder. It made her think that perhaps Ward had experienced similar distress when faced with his first corpse in the line of duty. Without a word, he signaled another uniformed officer to come look after their ailing colleague. Nora couldn't help feeling a surge of compassion for the ashen-faced Guard as well. She had never been affected by the sight of death; it was physical insult to living creatures that provoked in her an extreme visceral reaction. The embarrassing truth was that she'd barely made it through her surgical rotation in med school.

"Here's Dr. Friel," Ward said, ducking under the blue-and-white police barrier, and Nora looked up to see a silver Mercedes pull up along the road. She'd heard the state pathologist, Malachy Drummond, speak of his new colleague, but had never yet had the opportunity to meet Catherine Friel, despite the fact that their offices were only a short distance apart at Trinity. The slim, silver-haired woman who emerged from the car carried herself with a fresh, energetic demeanor. To look at her, one would never have imagined that Dr. Friel traversed the country several times a week on the trail of deadly violence. It was a regrettable sign of the times that Malachy could no longer keep up with the caseload all on his own.

Nora studied Ward's formal, deferential posture as he greeted Dr. Friel and escorted her to the excavation site. With his calm, soft-spoken manner, he seemed more like a family doctor than a cop. What had prompted him to join the Guards? What did he enjoy about a job that many viewed as nothing more than dredging up the unsavory details of other people's lives? She'd often tried to fathom what it took to be a detective, a person obliged to look behind hedges and ditches and through the walls of houses, stripping away the veils of propriety and convention to find a world of strange and untidy reality.

When Ward introduced them, Catherine Friel said, "Nora Gavin. That name seems so familiar . . ." Her face brightened. "I remember what it was. Malachy showed me an article you wrote recently for one of the anatomy journals, about bog chemistry and soft-tissue preservation?" Nora nodded. "Fascinating stuff. I'm certainly glad now that I read it with such interest." She turned to Ward. "It might be wise, as long as we have Dr. Gavin here, to make use of her expertise—if she's willing, and you have no objection."

"No objection at all from my end," Ward replied. "Carry on."

Nora felt her stomach begin to grumble; she hadn't eaten since six that morning and it was getting on toward one o'clock. But this was not the time to be worrying about hunger pangs; they would pass.

Moments later, outfitted in a white paper suit, Nora was down in the cutting again, this time beside Dr. Friel, who asked for her observations so far. At this point, she didn't have much to offer. "The position of the body, the presence of peat in the mouth and nose and under the fingernails—all of that could point to the possibility that this man just fell into a bog hole. But there's one thing that seems really strange." Nora reached for a handful of the black peat and rubbed it between her fingers. "Look at the texture of this stuff right around the body, how it breaks up into small clumps. It's definitely backfill. So even if he did just stumble into a hole, it looks as if somebody might have gone to a lot of trouble to cover him up."

"I knew there was a very good reason to keep you here," said Dr. Friel. "Let's see what else we can find."

They very carefully removed the remaining peat from around the dead man's neck and upper chest. "Odd that he's not wearing a shirt," said Dr. Friel. "How many people venture out onto the bog half-dressed, even in fine weather like this? And look here." Nora leaned closer and saw a thin leather cord. Dr. Friel traced its length to just below the man's left ear. "Could be a ligature," she said.

"Yes, but wouldn't it be tighter if it had been used as a garrote?"

"You're probably right." The pathologist's fingers probed gently at the leathery flesh beneath the dead man's chin. She lifted a small fold of skin, and Nora spied one end of a gash just under the jawline. "Doesn't look terribly deep," Dr. Friel said, "but it might have bled quite a lot—unless he was strangled first, and the throat wound was inflicted postmortem."

Nora realized she wasn't really listening; she was concentrating on the disjointed images that tumbled about in her consciousness: another length of cord, another knife wound, another dead man only a few hundred yards away. But this man was wearing a wristwatch. The two deaths couldn't possibly be related; they were separated by a few centuries at least. She said: "The body that was discovered here a few days ago—"

"Yes, what about it?"

"Well, it appears that he was garroted, and his throat was slashed as well."

"You think there's some connection?"

"I don't think it's possible. It just seems a strange coincidence that two men would be killed the same way, in the same place, hundreds of years apart."

Dr. Friel looked up at her. "What are you doing tomorrow morning, Dr. Gavin? I'm wondering if you'd like to attend the postmortem. Nine o'clock?" Before Nora could answer, the pathologist had turned her attention to the young Garda who stood above them. "Would you find Detective Ward for me? I want to let him know I'm listing the death as a homicide. And we can let the scene-of-crime officers begin their work, if they're ready."

Nora spied Ward up at the road, where the van carrying the National Museum delegation had just pulled up alongside the police cars. The detective was leaning in the window, no doubt explaining the situation.

She turned back to find Charlie Brazil standing behind her at the drain edge. He must have come walking across the bog, but the fact that no one had heard his approach was hardly surprising; four meters of peat soaked up sound like the ultimate underfelt. He was crouched beside the cutting, staring down at the dead man, his expression a complex blend of fascination and revulsion.

"Another one," he said. "What happened to him?"

"We don't know yet." She saw Charlie notice the leather cord, and the watch. He knew this body wasn't as old as the one he'd found. She could see the details pull him in, begin to work on him. He looked startled when she spoke. "Ursula said you were the one who uncovered the body the other day." He nodded. "I'd like to hear your version of what happened."

Charlie Brazil's eyes shifted, and he looked at the group that was headed toward the cutting. "I've got to be going now," he said. "I'm not supposed to be here." Then he turned on his heel and trudged off.

Now that the museum contingent had arrived, it was time to leave the realm of police work and return to the inquiry on the first Loughnabrone bog man. Nora went to greet Niall Dawson, who was getting his people set up at the far cutting. They wouldn't miss her for a few minutes; she excused herself and headed up to the hut for a long-delayed lavatory break and a bite to eat. She fetched her packed lunch from the car, and entered the Portakabin to find that the archaeologists had been sent home for the day. The place was deserted, and the floor was an inch deep in peat clods, as if a stampede of water buffaloes had just been through. As she bit into her green apple, Nora caught a flash of light on metal from a parked car outside and looked up to see Ursula Downes and Owen Cadogan engaged in conversation. The wind's steady whine swallowed up their voices, so they moved like figures in a dumb show. Ursula slouched against her car, looking up only occasionally; Cadogan paced the ground in front of her, arguing a point perhaps, but without much apparent success. All at once he stopped and raised one hand to Ursula's throat. It was impossible to discern at first whether the gesture was a caress or a threat, but when Ursula tried to move, he pinned her to the car with one quick motion. Nora felt a surge of adrenaline as she started from her seat. The only thing she could think to do was to slam her fist against the window. Cadogan lifted his head at the sound, and when he saw someone standing inside the hut, he dropped his hand and slowly backed away. Nora could hear the complaint of grinding gears as he drove off.

She left the hut and approached Ursula, who stood beside her car, one hand rubbing the place where Cadogan's fingers had rested on her throat.

"Are you all right? I realize it's none of my business—"

Ursula stopped her with a chilly glance. "You're right; it's absolutely none of your business." Nora felt as though she'd been slapped. She could only watch as Ursula turned her back and walked away.

6

The cottage wasn't difficult to find, with the directions Cormac had provided. The gate was open. As she pulled into the drive, Nora caught a whiff of turf smoke and saw a pale gray smudge rising from the chimney. Evelyn hadn't used the place in months, and yet it looked well cared for. Someone was making sure that the flues were cleaned and that damp and mold had no chance to set in. The rough exterior walls were painted a dull yellow ochre, the trim rusty blood-red. She could see the tail end of Cormac's jeep parked behind the house. It had been easy enough to put off thinking about their situation as the events of the day unfolded. Now she had no excuse—apart from being famished and thirsty, windburned and exhausted from all the fresh air out on the bog. What she really needed was a quiet evening without emotional upheaval. Nora gathered up all the resolve she could muster and opened the car door. As she lifted her case from the trunk, she checked the second-story window above; no movement, no indication that anyone was about. As she turned the corner, her bag brushed against the flowers in the window box, releasing a raft of dark crimson petals. She knocked three times.

The door swung open, and Cormac stood before her. He studied her for a moment, as if trying to decipher the day's events from her appearance. She tried to imagine the sight that greeted him. She'd taken off her waterproofs, but her work clothes were still a muddy mess.

"Nora—what happened? Your eyes—"

"Oh—I got caught in a dust storm first thing this morning. I'd almost forgotten about that. It's been an incredibly strange day. Another body turned up at the site, only it's not as old as the other one. The police were there, and the state pathologist. They think it's a murder."

Cormac's face clouded. "Jesus. And you were there when they found it?"

"Yes. I'm supposed to go along to the postmortem tomorrow morning too."

Cormac's eyes fixed her with a questioning look. He stepped forward to slide the bag from her shoulder, then reached out and brushed her face

with the backs of his fingers, the way he had first touched her, outside
the bar in Stoneybatter. The inner turmoil she had managed to keep at
bay all afternoon seemed to rise to the surface in response to this simple,
compassionate gesture. But her arms hung inert at her sides; she sank
forward, exhausted, to rest her forehead against his chest.

"You must be knackered," he said. "Why don't you come upstairs
straightaway and have a bath? Then you can tell me what happened."
He took her by the hand and led her up the narrow stairs, into a comfortable room with a low, sloping ceiling and a deep window that looked
out into the treetops in the orchard. He set her bag on the broad double
bed. Knowing what she had to do before she left this house, she felt
something false in the prospect of sharing this bed with him tonight. It
raised a pain in her stomach that wasn't remotely related to a lack of
food.

"Bathroom's through that door," he said. "There are clean towels in
the press, and there might be some drops in the cabinet to help your eyes.
I'm very glad you're here, Nora." He leaned down to kiss her, but for
some reason she couldn't respond; her whole body felt wooden. He could
feel it too, and he began to back away.

She wanted to reach out for him, but instead she said, "I'll be in a better mood to tell you everything after a nice long soak, I promise."

"Take as much time as you like. I'll fix us something to eat—is an
omelette all right?" She nodded. He turned from the doorway, and Nora
heard his quiet footsteps receding down the carpeted stairs. She started
the water running in the bath. Maybe a little warmth would help melt
away the stiffness in her limbs. She opened the nearest container from
the row of bath salts on a shelf above the tub and threw a handful of
powder under the tap, watching it bloom into a froth of soap bubbles.
Returning to the bedroom, she stowed her case on the floor by the night
table. She decided not to unpack; she wasn't going to be here long, and
there was certainly no point in hanging her work clothes in a wardrobe.

Nora quickly stripped off, leaving her dirty clothes in a heap on the
bathroom floor for the moment, and eased herself into the steaming
water. It was almost hotter than she could stand, but she slid down to
immerse herself completely for a couple of seconds, closing her eyes and
holding her breath. The heat was too much; she burst through the suds,
gasping for air, her chest heaving with the first tightness of a sob. There
was no relief, no respite from the grinding dissonance of her two impossi-

ble realities. She lay back in the tub and let the tears flow down her wet face onto her throat.

She remembered the first faltering steps that she and Cormac had made toward each other. Even as it happened, she hadn't been at all sure it was a wise or prudent thing. She'd denied the voice in her head, the one that kept warning her not to go there. Sometimes she felt like the selkie, the seal woman who comes ashore in human form, knowing that she cannot stay, that she must eventually return to the sea. She'd been on such tenuous ground, and he'd been so solid, so substantial. And now she was going to deliberately tear herself from his side, where she had felt so safe. She didn't know if she could take another keening, another period of mourning. Was there anything she could have done about the way things had unfolded between them? She was sure that Cormac had been as surprised as she by the rediscovery of desire, something she could only ever describe as a kind of wild, secret sweetness, like the fleeting taste of nectar on the tongue. It was far too late for any regrets. But every minute that went by sealed them together, and would make it that much more difficult when they had to part.

Two days earlier, when she had first received news about the Loughnabrone bog man, she'd dug around the high shelves in the bedroom closet for her waterproofs, unused since the previous summer. One of the shelf supports must have been weak; a box full of dog-eared files had upended, knocking her backward and sending a flurry of loose papers to the floor. She'd sat for a moment, dazed by the fall, looking around at the scattered documents. It was her own case file on Tríona's murder. She had read and reread every one of the papers in the file, scouring their neat typescript and scrawled ciphers for any pattern, any particle of information that might help the police prove who was responsible for her sister's death. She had felt a stab of remorse, remembering that when she first arrived in Dublin, this box had held a place at the center of her kitchen table. It was the constant reminder of what she'd left behind, unfinished. It had eventually shifted to the floor to make room for Cormac at the table. A few months later, she'd moved this box to the bedroom, but she had no memory of putting it up on the shelf in the closet. Was that how far she'd pushed Tríona out of her life?

Among the jumbled police reports, the autopsy findings and witness statements, she'd seen the corner of a color snapshot, and pulled it out. It was Tríona in profile, caught in a rare moment of contemplation, looking out the window into a grove of trees. Nora had taken the picture on a trip to the North Shore of Lake Superior. She had studied the lovely, lost features for a long, long time, then set the picture aside and begun sorting through the drifts of paper.

It had taken her nearly four hours to get the files organized again. How many times had she read all these notes and police reports? But this time one statement seemed to leap from the page: "Because the body was moved, the location of the primary crime scene remains unknown." *The primary crime scene.* The place that had witnessed an act of savagery. Places did not forget such things. But where was it? The police had searched the garage and basement of Peter and Tríona's house and found nothing; they'd searched Peter's office and come up empty there as well. And all this had happened nearly five years ago; what chance was there that any trace evidence would be left after such a length of time? The phrase kept echoing in Nora's consciousness: *the primary crime scene remains unknown.*

That night she'd awakened with Cormac sleeping beside her, knowing that she would have to leave him as soon as her work on the bog was over. She lay beside him, studying the outline of his face in the shadows, seized by desperate, overwhelming desire, but afraid to touch him. At last his eyes had slid open, and without a word he'd understood and answered. She knew that her fierce ardor that night had startled him; it had surprised her as well. But after they'd made love, she hadn't been able to keep from weeping. He thought it was something he'd done, and she couldn't find any words to explain.

The bathwater was beginning to cool. She lathered up one of the poufs that hung from the tap and began scrubbing at her face and forearms. Ursula had been right about the peat getting in your pores. Nora reached for a nailbrush to go after the black stuff under her fingernails, and remembered the peat under the dead man's bitten-off nails. What did that tell them? That he had worked in a bog? Or that despite his wounds, he had still been alive when he went into it? Tomorrow they might be able to find the answer—along with any other secrets he'd been keeping under the peat. She tried to imagine falling into a bog hole—the cold, the wet, the damp-earth smell, what it must be like to feel completely enveloped, paralyzed. She had read about air hunger; in cases of suffocation, the instinctive reaction to being deprived of oxygen was usually fierce struggle. That might explain the peat under the nails as well.

Out of the bath, she began to feel more human again. She dressed and ruffled her hair in front of the mirror, then clipped her fingernails as short as possible. Looking for a place to deposit the clippings, she opened the cabinet below the sink. Resting at the bottom of the empty bin was a single tissue, stamped with a perfect parenthesis of dark mauve lipstick. It was an absolutely precise impression, down to the tiny grooves bearing a slightly heavier stain of pigment. It was fresh, and not a shade she'd ever seen Evelyn McCrossan wear. Nora set the wastebasket back, shutting out a chorus of half-whispered questions as she quickly closed the cabinet doors.

7

No one was in the kitchen when Charlie Brazil arrived home from work, but the radio droned faintly into the empty room. They always ate their dinner without him; it was better that way. He removed his jacket and shirt and went to the sink to rinse away the peat dust that clung to his face and the back of his neck. He still had the uneasy feeling that something else was going to happen before the sun set. He was no more superstitious than the next man, but everyone knew that strange occurrences came in threes. First there had been the peat storm—a rare event; they'd not had more than two days in a row of fine weather in the six years he'd worked at Loughnabrone, and the wind had to be just right. He couldn't remember ever seeing such a storm, a wall of dust so vast it had blotted out earth and sky, even the light of the sun. He'd come across that woman and her car in the midst of it. He might have killed her, but he had stopped the tractor just in time. Surely that was a sign of something—but what?

Those gombeens in the workshop hadn't let up on him all afternoon, slagging him about the way the Yank had looked at him, asking was it true that American women were all mad for it? He detested that kind of talk, and he had felt as though his head would split. It was the same every day; they always found some way, large or small, of having a go at him. He'd almost grown used to it. He certainly knew that they talked about him, and even what they said, that he wasn't quite the full shilling. What they didn't understand was that all of his quirks were defenses, conscious choices he'd made to keep them at a distance.

A short time after he'd returned to the workshop, someone else had arrived with news that the archaeologists doing the bog road excavation had found another body, and this one was beginning to look suspicious, judging by all the police cars and vans. It was hard to keep anyone from knowing the score when police cars were swarming the place, visible from miles away on the empty bog roads. Word had spread until the air felt thick with shocked whispers, everyone trying to imagine who the victim might be—that young one from the next parish, some said, or another ancient corpse. There were murmurs, mutterings, and he could feel them all looking at him, asking the questions with their eyes.

Charlie slipped into the fresh shirt his mother had left for him on the chair near the hallway. He removed his dinner from the oven, using a towel to protect his fingers from the hot plate, and set it in the place laid for him at the table. He knew his father's illness would not let him live much longer. For a time they'd all tried to pretend that it wasn't so, but what was the point of denying it now, with the tubes and oxygen tanks, the death rattle at the bottom of his watery cough? In the meantime, someone had to keep the place from falling asunder. It wasn't a large farm, but there was still a load of work to do each day when he got home from the bog: feeding the calves, getting the hay in, not to mention keeping the house in good repair and the tractor running. He fell into bed exhausted every night and was up again at six in the morning for his shift on the bog. There was no end to it, ever. He deeply resented the position he was in, and still felt guilty for not doing more. He wolfed his food, eager to fill the gnawing void in his belly and be off. One boiled potato remained on his plate when his mother emerged from the sitting room, bearing a tray with his father's half-eaten dinner; each day he ate a bit less than the day before. The treacly music coming from the radio suddenly cut out, replaced by a heavy drumbeat signaling the seriousness of what was to follow:

"And here's the latest news from Radio Midlands. Gardaí have launched an investigation into the death of a man whose well-preserved body was found in Loughnabrone Bog this afternoon. The body was found by archaeologists working at the site, and has not yet been identified. A postmortem examination will be carried out in the morning, and Gardaí are looking into missing-persons cases from the area."

The newsreader's reassuring murmur continued, talking about shrinking dole queues and rural road construction grants, but Charlie's attention was concentrated on his mother's expression as she unloaded the tray full of dishes into the sink. She was someplace far away from him, away from his father, away from this place. He had studied her so often, tracing their similarities and differences: they had the same skin, pale and lightly freckled; the same cheekbones, nose, and hairline. There were times when she seemed to be illuminated from the inside, but there were also times like this, when she was unreachable, like something seen through a dark window that showed only his own reflection when he approached. Perhaps, like him, she had no idea how to gather up all those shape-shifting, unformed thoughts and begin to translate them into words. All at once he was back out on the bog, staring down at dark, wet peat cradling the dead man's misshapen head.

"I saw it," he said.

She turned to him as if she'd just awakened from a dream. "What?"

"That body in the bog. All black, it was—"

"For God's sake, Charlie! I don't want to hear that."

"It'll be on the television and in all the papers tomorrow. But they didn't even mention the strangest bit. I was there. I saw it. He had a leather cord around his neck with three knots in it—and he was wearing a watch." His mother's hands stopped suddenly, and she stood staring down at them, immobile in the soapy water. She spoke only after a long pause.

"What sort of watch?"

"I don't know—just an ordinary sort of wristwatch with a metal band. I couldn't see very well and it was all corroded."

Why had he told her about it? He'd developed a habit of telling his mother lies just to provoke a reaction. The story he'd just told her sounded like one of his more outrageous tales—except that it was all true. He hadn't told her what had unsettled him most—that the leather circlet around the dead man's neck was almost identical to the good luck charm he'd fashioned for himself from a length of cord.

Charlie stood and carried his plate to the sink. He knew his mother was watching him from the kitchen window as he left the house and walked toward the fencerow at the back of the haggard. He couldn't help it; he had to get out of the house, to take the fresh summer air deep into his lungs. Sometimes he began to feel suffocated in those rooms, weighted down with the silence. He wanted to cast it all off, all the expectations they had of him, and especially the desperate, killing worry about what people might think. He crossed the field behind the house in long strides, making his way toward the whitethorn tree in the corner, where he'd slip through the fence and follow the path up across the next small hill to his apiary.

There was a lot of work to be done this evening, and it was already getting on for six o'clock. It wasn't that he resented the work, exactly; he enjoyed the time he spent with the bees. But the farm work, though there was much less since they'd let most of the fields to neighbors when his father became ill, was still too much for one person alone. The constant grind was beginning to wear on him. If things stayed as they were, he'd end up just like his father, old before his time, and he wasn't going to let that happen. He remembered how hard his father had labored when he was a child, and look what those years of work had brought the old man: decrepitude and early death, from breathing in all that black peat. Charlie could feel the same thing for himself, in the constant wind out on the bog. That was why he wore the mask. He knew they all laughed at him, but he didn't care. They'd stop laughing when it hurt just to breathe.

He wondered what his mother had been thinking when he told her about the body. He knew she was intelligent; he caught the glimmer of it in her eyes, in the way she turned and looked at him when he asked her a question. But then the doors would shut again. She must once have had a desire for more than she had—endless days of labor beside a sullen ditcher driver of a husband who came home in the evening and had to put in another shift working the farm. She must have had dreams and ideas when she was young. What had happened? Charlie thought he knew the answer: his father, Dominic Brazil. Her family had never questioned the match. To them he was a good few acres, not bad to look at. What more could a girl in her position expect? He'd heard it often enough in their voices—what was life but a grim penance to be borne?

How his parents had come together in the first place had always been an unfathomable mystery to him. The only photograph he had of them was a blurry snapshot he'd found and now kept in the box under his bed: it showed his father looking defiant, even a little dangerous, as he leaned back against a wall, cigarette in his mouth, conscious of the camera. Teresa was leaning toward him, but half turned away, the side of her face a blur. Charlie thought he understood why she had turned away, even then. The one thing he'd always known was that Dominic Brazil loved his packet of fags and his pint of Guinness far more than he had ever loved any other human being. And yet she still washed his socks and made his bed, cooked his food, waited on him. And now hooked up a new oxygen tank when he needed it.

Charlie had spent a good deal of his childhood wondering what he'd done to earn his father's animosity. It was never an anger that expressed itself in physical violence, but the looks he received had done as much damage as blows. He'd sometimes watched other fathers with their sons, and he knew that his face had been a portrait of naked envy when he saw a bout of mock sparring, or when the sight of a man's hand on a son's shoulder would squeeze his heart into a cinder. Such things didn't hurt him the same way anymore, not really, but he wondered about them still.

He'd overheard his mother talking to her sister once, about his own difficult birth. From what he could understand, his entry into this world had very nearly killed his mother. "The doctor said I wasn't to consider having any more children," she'd said. He remembered wondering what that meant, whether it was anything to do with the fact that his parents kept separate rooms. From that point onward, the suspicion that he bore the dreadful responsibility for the rift between them had lurked in the nether regions of his consciousness. If he ever had a wife, he told himself, they would sleep and wake together. But what hope had he of ever finding someone? He'd always regarded girls as otherworldly creatures, as unapproachable as they were unattainable, on another plane of reality entirely from him, whose ears and face turned seven shades of crimson at the mere possibility of eye contact. He never thought of any specific woman when he gave in to temptation and touched himself, late at night, feeling the aching pleasure, the joy and shame at the moment of release. What hope, indeed?

He tried to remember how he'd come to the conclusion that his mother was at least as odd as he in some ways. Some of it had come from watching her work with the sheep. She always had soft hands, from the lanolin in the wool. He'd seen her work around the clock at lambing time, her shirt and trousers sticky with blood and afterbirth, and he knew she felt much more than she ever gave away. Once he'd watched her chasing a carrion crow away from a lamb, the firstborn of a pair of twins. As the ewe struggled giving birth to the second lamb, the bird had settled beside the firstborn and plucked out one of its eyes. He remembered his mother running at the crow with a strange, strangled cry in her throat, flapping her arms like a madwoman, and taking the wounded lamb into her arms. They hadn't been able to save it.

When he was fourteen, he had found out by accident that his mother wasn't at home some days. He'd mitched from school one day and sneaked back to the house, only to find that there wasn't any need for stealth; his mother wasn't even in the house. She'd returned about two hours later with no parcels, no evidence of where she'd been all morning. The following week he'd mitched again and followed her, ducking behind hedges, using all the skills he'd acquired playing spies. It had been a warm October day, and she'd taken the same path he was taking now, up through the pasture behind the house and along the lane that led to an old orchard. He'd gone there occasionally as a child, but eventually the bees had kept him away. He hadn't set foot in the place for years. He'd watched his mother wade through the tall weeds toward a small stone house with grass sprouting from its rotting thatched roof. No one else was about. He crouched by the roadside and watched, breathless with secret knowledge, as she pushed open the old door. There was no one else inside. Through the windows he could see her moving slowly around the small room, occasionally reaching out to touch an object on the windowsill or hanging from the wall. After a few minutes, she sat down on the cot against the wall opposite the door. She drew her legs up to her chest and sat like that in the ruined house for a solitary hour, in silence.

He'd had to keep shifting his weight so that his legs wouldn't go to sleep, and he breathed silently, conscious of every sound and movement that might draw her attention. As he crouched there, he heard a sound, a faraway droning; he didn't quite realize what it was until a single honeybee dropped onto the sleeve of his jacket. He held perfectly still as the bee clumsily traversed his coat's brown canvas hills and valleys. After about a minute it had given up and flown away, and he'd looked up to see his mother's face in profile through the door of the ruined cottage. Suddenly he remembered the feeling that had spread across his chest at that moment, the slow realization that every creature on earth had a secret interior life. The idea had filled him, traveled like electricity out to the ends of his fingertips. It felt enormous. And far from feeling betrayed, he remembered thinking it quite fantastic that his mother could be alone with her thoughts, away from him and away from his father, totally separate from them. He'd sunk down in the weeds and sat watching. He didn't know what this place was to her, and he decided at that moment that he didn't want to know.

After another thirty minutes, she'd risen from the cot and left the orchard, retracing the same path she'd taken earlier. This time he'd followed her only as far as the back fence. When he came into the house twenty minutes later, he searched for any sign that she'd seen him. But she was calmly laying the table for their dinner as usual, without a word, with no outward sign that she'd been out of the house all afternoon. His guilt about spying on her was assuaged somewhat by his gladness that she had another life.

He'd decided not to follow her again, but a few days later he had trod the narrow path up to the orchard, to explore the place. What he'd discovered was an apiary, a circle of nine rotting wooden hives half hidden beneath the nettles and *buachaláns* that had nearly taken over the grove. The first hive he'd uncovered was tipped over and encrusted with granulated honey. There was an enormous hole in the side of the box where bees were coming and going. The keeper had obviously abandoned them, but the bees had carried on, unmindful of human indifference. He'd tried to lean in and see into the hole, but when he lost his balance and tried to steady himself on the hive, a stream of angry bees started pouring out of the opening. He'd had to make a run for it, ducking under whitethorn branches until he was safely out of their path.

After that encounter, the notion of the bees had kept at him. He was plagued with curiosity about what went on inside the hive, and he wondered how people ever managed to extract honey if the bees were such ferocious defenders. On his third visit, he'd found a musty old book about beekeeping in the ruined house; he brought it home to read, making sure it was well hidden beneath his stash of maps and school papers. The book, with its descriptions of queens, workers, drones, nurse bees, and undertakers, of their orderly existence and mysterious chemical communications, only whetted his appetite for more. He haunted the libraries in Birr and Tullamore, returning from each visit with another beekeeping book secreted under his jacket, hands clammy with excitement over the new knowledge it might impart.

Once he had read every book he could lay his hands on, he'd sent away for a white beekeeping suit and veil. When he'd finally assembled the equipment he needed to set about putting the apiary to rights, his work had started in earnest. It could have occurred to him that his presence might be ruining his mother's place of solitude, but he was too caught up, and reasoned that she could simply go there when he was at school. He'd begun very gradually, using a scythe to clear away the tall weeds, setting up the tumbledown hives and repairing the holes in their sides. In doing so, he'd found one or two boards bearing the unmistakable impression of a sledgehammer. In the dozen years he'd been working at it, he'd turned the apiary into a haven. He hoped his mother still went there. If she did, she never acknowledged this thing they shared, not even when he brought her the first jar of honey from the hives.

He'd used the ruined house as his supply shed, just as the previous beekeeper had done. One day last autumn he'd found a small leather-bound book just inside the shed door, as though it had been left there for him. It was a beekeeper's journal, unsigned, anonymous. There was nothing about the keeper's own life; he wrote only about the bees. The pages contained a dutiful record of his daily work, the season's cascade of flowering plants, the weather, and the honey that was the distillation of it all. Tucked inside the book he'd found a whole handful of sketches by someone trained in technical drawing, as he himself had been. They were precise, detailed drawings of swords and daggers, mostly, but there were also strange Y-shaped objects, like old-fashioned hardware. Look-ing at them pleased him, and he had tacked them up in neat rows on the walls of his beekeeping shed. It was still a mystery where they had come from, and not one he was likely to solve.

This place was his sanctuary, away from the demands of the farm and the job, a place where he didn't have to measure time. He was nearing the apiary, wading through tall grass and wildflowers, aware of their scent and of the faint buzz in the air. Bees had moods, the same as peo-ple; the temperature and the weather and the light all affected them in different ways. He had spent time studying the ways they moved, from a swarm's quivering mass to the delicate, individual dances that spelled out the location of a clover patch somewhere close by. He'd studied the bees' tiny bodies, marveling at the detail, the perfection of their trans-parent wings and striped raiment.

The feeling came over him again, the anticipation of a third strange event yet to happen today. There was something unfinished about two of anything. He wouldn't feel right until it was settled. He could hear the bees' steady, collective hum as he approached, the reassuring, almost lazy vibration of more than a hundred thousand insects, their legs laden with the gold dust of pollen to be transformed into their precious hoard of sweetness. Bees were not good fliers; sometimes, especially in cold weather, he could sense the effort it took for them to become airborne.

Charlie pushed through the tangle of thistles and blackberry brambles and tall grass that was beginning to invade his small apiary meadow from the edges. He trailed his hands over the fragrant bearded grasses and sweet globes of clover. The bees would be getting their fill. He loved this protected place above the lake, nestled below the hill's crest, cut off from strong wind and heavy weather. He'd set his hives exactly where the old ones had stood, in an arc around the center of a small depression ringed by whitethorn bushes and apple trees. When the light was right, a person could mistake it for a stone circle, a holy place.

At times he was seized with a feeling that he really ought to keep this area in better trim, but the feeling vanished when he was here, amid all this profusion. The grass did not live in order to be cut down, but in spite of cutting. Its nature was to grow and go to seed and grow again. He felt the rebellion in his own soul swell sympathetically whenever he stood on this small patch of earth. The world was meant to be wild, unbridled. The place where he worked, Loughnabrone, was humankind's attempt to put its own shape on nature, but humankind never really won that fight. Drains filled in, grasses and bog plants encroached; they would soon take over again, once the humans were all gone.

He looked down to find a single worker bee attached to his wrist, apparently attracted to a small smear of honey on his shirt cuff. He watched the insect circle the spot, intoxicated by the scent of it. He watched her tongue looping outward onto the cloth, feeling as small as she was, the air around him buzzing, vibrating with life, the very atmosphere thick with the smell of nectar and flowers, the sheer overwhelming abundance of the universe. This sudden awareness passed quickly, and he was once more in his own apiary, studying the single bee as she worked to get the nectar from his sleeve. When she was satisfied she lifted off, flying unsteadily, he thought, drunk on the taste of her own honey.

There was someone in the apiary. Charlie stopped to peer through the dense and crooked whitethorn branches, half expecting to see his mother. Instead he saw a pale, slight figure in the center of his hive circle, a young woman about his own age. She wore a kind of shift—he knew no other word for the garment—a simple dress in some sheer material that caught the sun, which made her seem illuminated around the edges. A makeshift crown woven of twigs, clover, poppies, and other common roadside weeds adorned her dark head. He stood transfixed, watching as she lifted her arms and stretched luxuriously, like an animal. A single bee alighted on her outstretched hand, and she brought it down to have a closer look. It didn't sting her, as he had thought it might; she studied its trail across the back of her hand. Far from being frightened, she seemed curious.

She raised her thin arms level with her shoulders and turned slowly, raising her face to the sky. She seemed unaware of his presence; her eyes were closed, and he saw a cloud of bees gathering around her head, perhaps attracted to the flowers. He suppressed the urge to cry out, afraid he would startle the bees into doing her injury. But it was as if she anticipated, even invited the insects' attention. He remained still as a statue, barely breathing as they landed on her in dozens. Her neck and shoulders were awash in a vibrating mass of busy, winged bee bodies. He imagined their strange strawlike tongues against her skin, perhaps tasting her for the queen substance, the chemical reassurance they needed to carry on. This was swarming behavior, he realized, the main thing all his efforts as a beekeeper went toward preventing, and yet he could not disturb such a wondrous apparition. She was some deity, a force of nature incarnate, and who was he to disturb her communion with her subjects? For it was as if she commanded them, and they sought her out, the irreplaceable touch and taste of her. And she, for her part, seemed transported, rapturous.

He had no idea how long they stood there. It might have been two minutes, it might have been ten; his sense of time was distorted by this unexpected vision. It was almost as if their beating wings were about to lift her from the ground. He felt his center go with them, the girl and the bees, borne upward on a wish. He could have sworn there was a space beneath her feet, a miraculous millimeter, thinner than a bee's gossamer wing.

When the bees had taken their fill of her, it seemed, they departed as gradually as they'd come. She stood for a moment longer with her eyes shut, as if to retain the feeling of microscopic feet by the thousands upon her flesh. She shivered, clasped herself tightly, and heaved a sigh, the kind of wordless exhalation he imagined might escape from a woman whose lover has just left her. Then she dropped her arms to her sides and opened her eyes. Charlie was taken aback when he recognized the face, returned to earth from wherever she had been. It belonged to Brona Scully, the daughter of their nearest neighbor. Someone had cut off her long hair—that might have been the reason he hadn't recognized her earlier. Brona was perhaps the only person in the locality who enjoyed more pity than he did. People said she wasn't right in the head—but they said the same thing about him, he knew. Charlie wanted to be near her, to understand what she had just experienced. And with a kind of gentle, settling sadness, he knew he never would. He knew it in the same way he knew that this was the third strange occurrence, the thing he'd been waiting for all along.

8

The red wine swirled in her glass, and Ursula Downes studied the sediment as the eddying liquid slowed and came to rest. The bathwater was getting cold, and she was reaching the bottom of the bottle. She reached down and poured another splash; only a couple of inches remained. Her unsteady movement made the wine slosh in the glass, and several drops escaped and fell into the water. She watched as the inky red sank in ever-decreasing rings until it disappeared altogether. Her head felt heavy from the wine. She leaned back, letting the glass rest between her soapy breasts.

She remembered the look in Owen Cadogan's eyes this afternoon. She probably shouldn't have laughed, but he was so pathetic. He couldn't fathom why she wouldn't just pick up where they'd left off last summer, and resume those desperate bouts of coupling he'd no doubt begun to think of as their "affair." She had to admit that she had enjoyed watching his expression whenever she'd proposed anything slightly more adventurous than he was used to. But what right had he to assume that she would just take up with him again? Their relationship—if you could even call it that—had been based on physical need, nothing more. It wasn't as if they even really enjoyed each other's company. In fact, after what she'd seen today, she'd have sworn he actually despised her, so what was he on about? Owen didn't know what had changed for her. She had other prospects now, not just another permanently married man who liked having it off once in a while with someone younger and more imaginative than his wife.

And Owen wasn't her only problem. Plenty of strange things had happened today, almost as strange as a second body with a leather cord around his neck. The crew were not settling into their work. Maybe it was just her imagination, but the pool of qualified archaeologists seemed to include a larger percentage of head cases every year. Rachel Briscoe was getting moodier and more unpredictable with each passing day. And what exactly had Charlie Brazil been up to, scrabbling through her site maps in the office this afternoon? She'd walked in and caught him out, and though he'd pretended to be curious about the excavation, there was more to it than that. He'd always been far too interested in their business. She'd seen him often enough, climbing the small hill behind her house, or out on the smaller bogs around Illaunafulla. Did he sleep out there, or was it some other attraction? Everyone around here thought him soft in the head, and Charlie Brazil was anything but. She'd find out what he was looking for.

Actually, meeting Nora Gavin had been quite interesting. Ursula had to admit that she'd experienced the tiniest buzz shaking the woman's hand, remembering her brief encounter with Cormac Maguire the night before. She'd always found it impossible to resist needling people like Cormac. She wondered if he was ever sorry about the way he'd left things between them. She'd long ago given up being sorry for anything. There was no future in regret.

She set her wineglass on the floor, and began scrubbing at her nails with a brush, but gave up after a few seconds. It was no use; her nails would remain black until she left this place. She sometimes felt as though the peat was entering her very pores, filtering in through the microscopic cracks in her skin, filling her up with darkness. She was sick to death of bogs, weary of the people and the bleak rented house. Who would have believed it: two consecutive summers back in the same dreary squat from all those years ago? Somehow she thought her life would add up to something more by now. At least she'd insisted upon her own place—and why not, if Bord na Móna was paying? The crew's communal way of life, the shared kitchen and toilet, depressed her unutterably, perhaps because she'd lived that way every summer for long enough. Maybe this time next year she'd be someplace where it didn't rain ten months of the year. She relented for once and let herself imagine sun and heat, white sand, azure water. She knew she ought not to think about it too much. Bad luck.

She wetted her sponge and applied a few drops of body wash, working it into a frothy lather, then slid the rough sponge around the back of her neck and over her chest and shoulders. The image of that second dead body in the bog came back to her, the stillness of it, the spark long extinguished. And with the picture came the knowledge that staying here much longer meant extinguishing her own spark, letting it gutter out in perpetual rain. She wanted to see it burn brightly for as long as possible.

She felt nothing but pity and contempt for those who would stifle their own vital energy, from fear of what might happen—or even worse, from some false sense of morality. She knew she was an amoral person, by any definition of the word. The idea of morality held very little meaning for her. If the universe itself was amoral, why should the creatures governed by the rules of that universe be any different? There was no morality in gravity, for instance; it just was. Nor was there any sense or judgment in the way atoms formed into elements. Who was to say that one collection of particles had any more intrinsic value than another mass of particles with one electron more or less? The very coldness of it excited her, the hard, physical substance of the world. The rest was sentimentality masquerading as morality.

She lathered the sponge again, and went back to washing, feeling suddenly aroused by its roughness on her soapy skin. Then the sponge passed over the top of a scar that stretched the length of her back. Various lovers had asked about it, a question that usually meant they felt entitled to intimate knowledge of her. Whenever that happened, she made sure not to see the person again. It was her only rule. She couldn't bear inquisitiveness in a sexual partner; it seemed a singularly undesirable trait. Only one living person besides herself knew why she avoided dry cleaning shops and couldn't abide the smell of perchloroethylene.

Long ago, when she was still a child, she'd sought out confession, trying to get rid of that dirty feeling she couldn't seem to scrub away. The priest had instructed her to tell him everything. She had complied, choking when she had to describe what her stepfather had done. She had remained kneeling, innocently hoping for absolution, even as she heard the breathing on the other side of the curtain grow more labored. It had only dawned on her very gradually that the old priest was getting stirred up listening to her, imagining what was forbidden, taking twisted pleasure in her fear and shame. "My child," he'd called her. The bastard. The sick fucking wanker. She'd walked out in the middle of her confession. She didn't believe in goodness or morality anymore. It simply didn't exist, and people who did believe in it were deluded. She wiped away the single tear that slid down her face, and with it wiped the scene from her memory.

Ursula took another swallow of wine and watched, fascinated at how the liquid clung to the side of the glass. It was true what she'd told Cormac—that she didn't really give a damn about what vintage she was drinking, but maybe that would change. Desmond Quill said he would teach her about wine, and maybe she'd let him. She had to admit that Quill wasn't at all her usual type. For one thing, he'd pursued her. When they had first met at that museum reception in the spring, she'd been struck by the hard glint in his eyes, the strength of his handshake. He'd kept staring at her through the crowd, and when they bumped into each other at the bar, he'd slipped one hand around her waist and steered her right out the door and into a waiting taxi. She hadn't even asked where he was taking her, and when the taxi pulled up in front of a Georgian house, she had followed him inside and straight up the staircase to his bedroom. They had not spoken a word. The memory of that first encounter still excited her. She and Quill were very much two of a kind. He was probably at least thirty years older than she was, and he never seemed to have the desperate, guilty quality of the partners she usually chose. She felt transparent to him, in a way that she'd never felt with any other human being—as if he could see right through her, into her bones, into the darkest thoughts that occupied her existence. He had never asked about her scar, but he'd often traced the outline of the damaged skin as though it were the map of her soul.

Ursula's reverie was suddenly punctured by a loud crash, then another, and another. Jagged fear sang through her veins. It sounded like someone breaking down the door. She leapt from the bath, leaving the water lapping and sloshing in her wake. Her fingers felt clumsy as she quickly turned the key in the lock. Then she covered her ears and sank down to the floor, trying to imagine what she would do if someone started to batter down the bathroom door. But no one came. The house had gone dead quiet.

Ursula had no idea how long she waited—ten minutes, perhaps fifteen. She heard no movement, no sounds of life from the other side of the door. She knew it might be a ploy to draw her out, but she couldn't stay in there forever, and her mobile phone was out in the kitchen. She found a small pair of scissors to use as a weapon, then pulled on her bathrobe and silently turned the key. No figure loomed out of the shadows at her, no hand reached out to grasp her by the hair. The house was still. She almost thought she had imagined it all, until she turned the corner into the kitchen and saw the word scrawled on the glass in red paint: SLAG. Ursula looked down at the small scissors in her hand and felt as though she was going to be sick.

Returning to the bathroom, she saw that the nearly empty wine bottle had toppled over and was spilling onto the white tile floor. The dark pool shimmered in the electric light, its surface disturbed by drops that seemed to fall in slow motion from the bottle's open mouth.

Book Two

Human Crime
and Bloodshed

What then, think you, is the honor, what the piety, of
those who even think that the immortal gods can best be
appeased by human crime and bloodshed?

—*the Roman writer Marcus Tullius Cicero, writing
about the Gauls in the first century* B.C.

1

The postmortem on the second murdered man from Loughnabrone took place the following morning. The mortuary at the regional hospital in Tullamore, twelve miles northeast of Loughnabrone, was a drab, anonymous room with institutional tiled walls, anemic fluorescent lights, and two stainless-steel tables. Dr. Friel had gone into the next room to take a phone call, leaving Nora alone with the corpse, which lay partially covered by a plain white sheet on one of the tables, ready for their initial external examination. There had been no clothing to itemize and remove; upon taking the body from the bog, they'd found the deceased completely naked but for his leather cord and wristwatch.

Nora lifted the sheet and looked at the band still encircling the man's wrist, its metal parts corroded green and black. She could just make out the word "Waterproof" on its peat-clogged face, a watchmaker's assertion now disproved. The hands pointed to 9:55; faded red characters, TUE 20, showed through the window at three o'clock. Around his neck was the thin leather cord with its three knots, regularly spaced, about an inch apart. The Gardaí would have trouble identifying the corpse, if this and the watch were all they had to go on. She considered his still outline, wondering who had waited in vain for him to arrive; who had held fear inside like a clenched fist, waiting for any news of him; who, perhaps, was waiting still.

The left arm that had stretched toward the top of the bog now extended above the man's head, the partially skeletonized hand still bagged to preserve any forensic evidence. Dr. Friel would take scrapings from beneath the fingernails, to check for traces of skin or hair from another person—possible evidence of a struggle, if he hadn't gone quietly to his death. But the acidic bog environment typically destroyed fragile nuclear DNA, so even if there was any tissue residue from a struggle, it probably wouldn't provide concrete clues to a killer's identity.

She circled the table to take a closer look at the man's right hand through another polythene bag. This hand was much better preserved than the other, the palm and fingertips marvelously intact. Her primary impulse, on seeing this modern body, was to wonder whether she might be allowed to take a few small samples to analyze and compare to older specimens. But that would require the consent of the family, if the man's identity was ever determined, and might require a delicate diplomatic approach. Maybe Dr. Friel would have some advice.

At the other end of the table, the sight of the dead man's right foot was particularly arresting: brown skin stretched, tentlike, over a fan of bone and sinew. The flexed foot was delicately pointed as if caught in a dance step, from the toes, like five small dark stones in a row, to the wrinkled arch and rounded heel leading to the shapely ankle. Strange, Nora thought, that the glimpse of a bare foot should strike such an oddly intimate chord. But the feeling was not unfamiliar; she had experienced similar, fleeting flashes whenever she worked on a cadaver. Death allowed all kinds of intimacies never imagined in life. She wanted so much from this man, whose skin and bones and sinews had already begun to form answers to her questions. For as long as she could remember, the human body had been her subject, her instrument, her fascination. Most people misunderstood the pathologist's motivation; it was not a preoccupation with death, but a profound curiosity about life. She had seen a Latin inscription in some mortuaries that captured the philosophy exactly: *Hic locus est ubi mors gaudet succurrere vitae.* "This is the place where death delights to help the living." There was a procedure to be followed, a routine that broke the experience of death away from emotion and grief, and pushed it instead into the realm of scientific observation. It relieved her mind, at least for a while, to believe the illusion that she was dealing only with flesh and bone, with the comforting clarity of science rather than the murky world of human relationships. But even scientific detachment didn't last. Eventually every person on the autopsy table had to be recognized as someone who had lately had a life.

Catherine Friel pushed through the door, wearing a rubber apron over her lab coat and pulling on a pair of latex gloves. "Sorry to keep you waiting. Let's get started now, will we?" She pressed the button on her tiny tape recorder and began to describe the deceased in a calm, measured voice: "The body is that of a normally developed white male of slender build. Difficult to ascertain age because of the condition of the body." She lifted first one arm, then the other, then each leg in turn. "There is no rigidity, and no visible lividity, but the body is quite dark brown in color from deposition in a bog. The left hand is desiccated and partially skeletonized. The exposed bone is somewhat decalcified, and adipocere seems firmly established throughout. The exposed skin is darkened from contact with peat, but remains remarkably elastic. Deceased is wearing a wristwatch with a metal band on the left forearm." She gingerly removed the corroded watch and bagged it. "The deceased is clean-shaven and the hair on the scalp appears black and wavy. There's a slightly reddish tint to all the body hair, which I think we can assume is from immersion in the bog." She looked up at Nora, who nodded her concurrence. "There's no visible evidence of congestion in the face, and the skin discoloration prevents observation of any possible cyanosis." Dr. Friel set down the recorder and carefully lifted each closed eyelid, examining the surface of the eyes with a magnifying glass. "The irides appear blue, and the pupils are fixed and equal. There are no foreign bodies or contact lenses. There's noticeable focal petechial hemorrhaging in both eyes." The small blood spots were one of the typical signs of asphyxia or strangulation.

Dr. Friel concentrated on the man's head and neck, marking off his external wounds with her measuring scalpel. "There's an incised wound on the left lateral area of neck, four centimeters in length. We'll have to do a dissection to describe the wound path and see whether it's severed any major vessels. I don't know if you can see this . . ." She handed Nora her magnifying glass. "There's horizontal bruising just above the gash. A pretty definite ligature mark; see how it continues around the back of the neck? A rising peak in the back usually indicates a suspension point. That's one way we can tell the difference between an actual hanging and a rearward strangulation." She cut the leather cord from around the dead man's neck, bagged and labeled it, then gently opened his mouth and pointed a small torch inside to peer at the teeth and gums, which were only slightly discolored and clotted with peat. "There's some dental work. Gold crown on the first molar, lower right—and the first upper left bicuspid is missing. No visible injuries to the gums, cheeks, or lips. Looks like he got a mouthful of bog water at some point, though—we'll be able to tell more about that after we have a look at the lungs and the airways." She lifted and examined each arm in turn. "The hands and arms appear to have sustained a few defensive wounds. The right hand seems to be in fairly good shape; we might be able to get a decent set of prints."

Nora looked up to see Detective Ward standing at the door, and after a moment Dr. Friel noticed him as well. "It's all right, Liam, come in." He joined them at the table. "I'm afraid cause of death isn't going to be very straightforward," Dr. Friel continued. "There's a lot going on here, and it may take a bit of time to work it all out. I'm finished with his effects, if you wanted to take them. I was just about to ask Dr. Gavin if there was anything she could see, given her previous experience, that might give us a better idea about how long this man was in the bog."

Nora felt slightly discomfited by such deference; the "previous experience" to which Dr. Friel referred consisted of exactly one nonpreserved specimen. Ward ventured a question. "What exactly causes the discoloration?"

"The bog environment triggers what's known as a Maillard reaction." Ward looked blank, so Nora tried to explain: "In simple terms, it's a common protein-sugar reaction—the same chemical process that causes food to turn brown, actually. Some of the recent research using piglets has demonstrated pretty marked discoloration after a couple of years. So, in other words, I don't know if we can tell very much from coloration alone." She looked closely at the dead man's shoulder through the magnifying glass. "It'll be interesting when the larger incisions are made to see how deeply the color has penetrated the cutaneous and subcutaneous layers. The brown color doesn't seem quite as rich or well-established as in the older remains I've seen, but I've not seen that many bog bodies—to be honest, no one has, and they're all slightly different, depending on the particular environment."

Nora paused, realizing that what she was about to say might be all wrong, that she might have to backtrack somewhere down the road. She took a deep breath, hoping she wouldn't regret what she was about to say: "This man apparently went into the bog completely naked. He's probably been strangled with a leather cord, and his throat has been slashed. If he hadn't been wearing the wristwatch, we might quite naturally assume he was much older."

"And why is that?" Ward seemed intrigued.

"Well, he has similarities to the other body from Loughnabrone, and to remains found in England, Germany, and Denmark, and other places as well. The finds over the past fifty years or so have all been pretty well documented. Some of them had similar types of wounds: they were hanged or strangled, their throats were cut, and they were buried or staked down in watery places. Some people have taken those things as proof that many of the bodies were victims of ritual sacrifice."

Ward seemed troubled by this interpretation. "So what are you saying—you think this might have been some sort of ritual killing?"

"I don't think it can be ruled out. When we find the same evidence on an older body, it's always one of the possibilities. Any one of those wounds was probably enough to kill him, so why the excessive violence? If he were from the Iron Age, then the injuries would be consistent with what's been found before. But if he's clearly modern, then the mystery is why someone today would have used those three forms of violence in particular."

"Why, indeed? Shall we see what this fella can tell us?" Dr. Friel said, reaching for the garden shears that lay on the stainless-steel tray near the dead man's head. She didn't seem to notice that Detective Ward was already beating a hasty retreat out the mortuary door.

2

As he drove the twenty-three miles back to his station in Birr, Ward was thinking about Dr. Gavin's words. Ritual killings, or murders that looked like ritual killings, were rare, although probably not as rare as people might imagine. Some were committed by self-styled occultists, but murders carried out for other reasons were sometimes covered up by staging the scenes to look like ritual killings. He'd seen a few examples where the ritual aspect had turned out to be misleading.

The first challenge here would be to find out who the victim was. He pulled out his mobile and punched in a number. "Maureen, it's Liam. Do me a favor, will you, and pull all the missing-person files? How many are there from the last twenty years, do you reckon? . . . Maybe we should go even further back. . . . Yes, sort those out if you would. I'm on my way. I'll have a look at them when I get there. And I'll tell you more about the PM when I get in."

They'd be lucky if it was a local disappearance. If the victim happened to be from somewhere else, they'd have to search missing-person files from the whole country. It could take a long time just to establish identity, not even talking about evidence for a murder case. There was that date on the watch, but it only told the day of the week and the date. No indication of the year or month, unless . . . The watch had to know what month it was, in order to tell the date accurately. Maybe it had to be set by hand; but perhaps there was a mechanism inside the watch that calculated how many days were in each month. At the very least, they might be able to get a manufacture date for the watch and eliminate the years before it was made.

How strange was it that the victim was naked? He'd seen the body out in the bog; there was no suggestion that this had been a careful burial— just the opposite, in fact. So how had the victim come to be naked, and why—especially out on that broad expanse of milled peat? There was no evidence from the postmortem that he'd been bound—or was there? Victims of ritual killings were not usually cooperative, unless they were incapacitated in some way. Dr. Friel hadn't mentioned any blows to the head, and they'd have to wait for toxicology results to see if there had been any drugs involved. But the peat under the nails might suggest he hadn't been unconscious going into the bog. Ward was crossing a similar stretch now, along a straight bog road, the surface rutted and patched, crumbling away at the sides. He suddenly realized that he relished this moment in a case, when the whole thing lay before him, complicated as a Chinese box, waiting to be opened, to confound and mystify.

He parked outside the station and walked around to the front entrance, a tiny room with a window for the duty officer and a row of hideous molded-plastic chairs opposite. No one was at the window, but a woman sat in one of the chairs, waiting. She cast a brief, anxious look in Ward's direction, then turned back to the empty window and sat a little straighter in her chair, arms crossed across her chest. Her handbag hung over one shoulder and two bulging carrier bags rested at her feet. She'd come in after doing her shopping for the day, after trying to decide whether to speak to the police. She wouldn't stay long if no one came to her aid.

Crossing the waiting area to the inner door, Ward formed an impression instantly. The woman was perhaps his own age, he decided, fifty-ish, though she looked younger. He would have described her as handsome rather than delicately beautiful. She had dressed with care, and the clothing, though not in the latest fashion, was of good quality: a tailored trouser suit, a crisp white blouse, and just a touch of makeup. A farmer's wife, Ward decided. Respectable. Her face showed concern, perhaps that she would be seen sitting in the reception area of the Garda station, but there was something deeper as well. In his years in the Guards, Ward had learned to read many different layers and grades of concern. There was the annoyance of parents come to fetch unruly offspring who had committed some relatively minor offense such as public drinking or joyriding; complainants about noisy neighbors often brought with them a nauseating air of moral sanctity. This woman's face had none of that. The idea struck him that she was here to make a confession, but perhaps it was better not to jump to any conclusions. He turned to her. "Excuse me, have you been helped?"

She looked up, startled by his sudden attention. "No. No one's been here. But I haven't been waiting very long."

Just then the duty officer returned from the inner room, pulling the door shut against the sound of laughter and the murmur of male voices. Upon seeing Ward in the outer room, he straightened and put on a serious face.

"I can help the lady now, sir," he said. Ward noted a few crumbs of seedcake on the young man's shirt front.

"That's all right; I'll look after her myself," Ward said. He returned to the security door to press in his code, then ushered the woman down the hall and upstairs to the plain beige office he shared with Maureen Brennan. The space was spare and impersonal, but at least they had a view, overlooking the street in front of the station.

"May I get you a cup of tea?" he asked.

She seemed surprised at the offer. "No, thank you. What I need—" She looked down at her knees and couldn't seem to find the words to continue. Perhaps she was unused to stating her needs so baldly, and to a stranger.

"Let me get you some tea," he said. "I won't be a moment." He stepped into the corridor and closed the door, watching her through the glass as he crossed the hall to the galley kitchen to fetch the tea. He poured the steaming water over the bag in the large mug, not watching the tea as it steeped, but instead studying the woman in his office. She continued to look straight ahead, not even glancing around the room. This woman was completely focused on whatever it was she'd come to say. Again he thought of a confession, but pushed the idea aside.

Ward squeezed the darkness from the teabag, added milk and sugar, and headed back to his office. As he handed the woman the steaming mug, he noticed her hands. Where he had expected to see skin rough and reddened from farm work, he saw long, delicately tapered fingers, fresh and pink as a young girl's. She began speaking before he could take out a report form, so he leaned back against his desk and listened.

She introduced herself as Teresa Brazil, then said, "I've come because I think the body they found at Loughnabrone yesterday might be someone I know—someone I knew, that is—my husband's brother. Danny Brazil." It came in a rush, as if she was afraid she'd stop before getting it all out. And having said what she had come to say, she fell silent and looked up at him, unsure what would happen next.

Ward considered for a moment; there'd been no details released, besides the fact that the deceased was a man. Why would she presume that it was someone she knew? He remembered the leathery corpse he'd just left in the mortuary and wondered whether this woman was just another case of wishful thinking. Whenever a body turned up, the relatives of missing persons came forward and prepared themselves for the worst, just in case. Somewhere way in the back of his head, the name Brazil seemed familiar; he'd met Teresa Brazil before, he was sure. The why of it might be a little longer in coming to him.

"We haven't even put out an appeal for information yet. We were just preparing to look through all these old cases—" he indicated the stack of missing-person files Maureen had left on his desk "—to see whether we could come up with anyone matching his description."

"You won't find Danny Brazil there," she said.

"And why's that?"

"We all thought he'd gone away, emigrated to Australia. He talked about it often enough. That's why they never reported him missing. He'd just gone, no long good-byes, just slipped away as he said he would."

"When was the last time you saw him yourself?"

Her voice was barely audible: "Midsummer's eve, twenty-six years ago." Very precise date, Ward thought. Teresa Brazil seemed uncomfortable sitting in the chair before him, but she evidently felt compelled to be there, to tell what she knew.

"So you're saying he never wrote, never came home, and no one thought that strange? No one from the family tried to find him?"

"What would have been the point, if he didn't want to be found?" she murmured.

"I'm still not quite clear why you think the man we found is your brother-in-law."

She looked up at him, suddenly back from wherever her distant thoughts had taken her. "There were some things found with him. My son was there; he told me. A knotted leather cord, a wristwatch with a metal band. I could describe the watch, if you like. It was a gift for his birthday that year."

Ward reached into his jacket for the two evidence bags and set them without fanfare on the desk in front of her. The corroded watch had left dust against the clear polythene, and he watched as the object worked its magic of recognition in Teresa Brazil's eyes. He followed her gaze to the narrow leather ligature, still stretched from being twisted tight around the young man's throat.

"That cord—" she said.

"What about it?"

"He always wore it," she said. "May I have a closer look?"

"I'm afraid not. It's evidence in a murder investigation."

"Murder?" She barely whispered the word, and the color drained from her face.

"I'm afraid so. That's all I can tell you right now."

"It is Danny," she said. There was no doubt in her voice. "I don't know anyone else who wore such a thing. It was for protection, he said. For luck." She turned away, and Ward watched her try to gain control. When she turned back to him, her face was calm.

"Mrs. Brazil, please understand that I'm not questioning your word on the identification, but it might be best to have some sort of corroborating physical evidence. Did your brother-in-law have any identifying marks that might help us—any noticeable scars or birthmarks?"

"He had a scar just above his left eyebrow, from hurling. I don't know about birthmarks."

"And did he ever see a dentist, here in the town or elsewhere?"

"They used to see Dr. Morrison, just here beside the station. The old doctor died a few years ago, but his son is in it now."

"If we're able to establish a positive identification, we'd of course have some additional questions for you and your husband, and any other family members as well." Teresa Brazil nodded and stood, and he escorted her to the top of the stairs. "Thank you for coming in. We'll certainly be in touch, whatever happens. And here's my card, in case you think of anything else." She took the card without comment and tucked it into her handbag.

As she started down the staircase, Ward spoke again: "One more thing, Mrs. Brazil. I was wondering why your husband wouldn't have come along himself."

Her expression said she'd anticipated his question all along. "My husband has been in poor health. He rarely leaves the house."

That ambiguous answer would have to suffice for now. Ward returned to his office window to observe Teresa Brazil as she left the station. What was it about her that was so familiar? He watched as she merged with a crowd of adolescent boys and girls, all limbs in their blue school uniforms. They didn't move as she passed them by, just another housewife weighed down with her messages, hurrying home to cook the family dinner.

When she disappeared around the corner, Ward turned away and sat down at his desk, where he picked up the phone and started dialing Dr. Friel's mobile number. While he waited for the connection, he spoke across the desk to his partner as she came in. "Maureen, do you know Morrison, the fella who has the dental surgery just beside us here? Looks like we'll have to request records belonging to a former patient of his father's. The name is Brazil. Danny Brazil."

3

As Nora made her way back to the excavation site, the dead man in the mortuary kept pulling at the fringes of her consciousness. She had an uneasy feeling that she was getting caught up again, as she had with the mysterious red-haired girl whose head she and Cormac had unearthed last summer. But she couldn't help imagining the murdered man as he had been in life, electricity humming through his nervous system, blood soaking oxygen from his lungs, all the thoughtless, automatic, repetitive cycles of physical existence brought to an abrupt and violent end. Why? Who was he, and why should he have been dispatched in a manner usually reserved for Iron Age victims? Had his death been deliberately planned to look like an ancient ritual killing—and if it had, who would have known enough about those practices to approximate such a thing? Maybe he had been a real sacrifice for some reason—the victim of mob violence for something he'd done, perhaps? It was difficult to imagine the sort of crime that might warrant a treble punishment. She pictured the naked victim, kneeling at the edge of a bog hole as the garrote tightened around his neck and a blade was drawn. Perhaps the blade was dull, and didn't cut as deep as it should have. Maybe the victim struggled, or the swordsman's aim was not true. Had he been drugged? Toxicology results and stomach content analysis could take weeks, but they might reveal how far the killer had gone in pursuit of authenticity, if it had been some sort of sacrificial ritual.

She arrived at the excavation site to find the small parking area jammed with Garda vehicles. The Technical Bureau van stood out above the cars, and a couple of television vans with satellite dishes had pulled up along the road as well. The place was turning into a circus, crawling with people. She had to park on the road about fifty yards from the hut. It looked as if the Guards had cordoned off access to the bog and were only letting people in if they were on a list. No sign of Ward. She wanted to tell him that the whole triple-death scenario he'd been so interested in this morning was probably not quite as concrete as she'd made it seem.

As she rounded the back of her car and got out her heavy boots and waterproofs, Nora saw Rachel Briscoe, the girl who'd found the new body, sitting cross-legged just inside the open door of the supply hut, on a large rectangular box like a shipping container that rested on blocks beside the shed where the archaeologists took their tea. A large pad of paper rested on her knees; she was drawing the worked ends of timbers that had been uncovered in the cuttings. It was all part of the excavation work, documenting each stroke of the ax; each gouge or facet was a direct line to the work of ancient hands.

Owen Cadogan's Nissan pulled up behind Nora as she struggled into her waterproof trousers. Cadogan passed her by without speaking and strode purposefully toward the tea shed. When he was almost at the door, Ursula Downes emerged, evidently ready for a confrontation; as Cadogan moved to speak to her, she drew back and slapped him hard across the face. When he recoiled and began to protest, she pushed him away with both hands, turned on her heel, and left him standing with his arms hanging uselessly by his sides. A few yards beyond them, Rachel paused in her drawing and watched intently from the door of the hut, only turning her eyes back to her work when Cadogan stalked off, still rubbing his face. Maybe, Nora thought, she'd been wrong in her assumptions about Ursula and Cadogan. Maybe she'd completely misread what had happened yesterday. Cadogan obviously didn't have the upper hand today. Maybe Ursula could handle him, and she had been butting in where she wasn't wanted or needed.

As Cadogan returned to his car and sped off, the shed door opened again and Charlie Brazil emerged, checking to see if anyone was watching him. He began walking slowly toward the Garda checkpoint, skirting the crowd of reporters and sliding in at the front.

When she was suited up, Nora approached the barrier through a small but persistent crowd of journalists and showed her ID to the young policeman. "You should have me down on the list there—Gavin. Nora Gavin."

The officer scanned down his clipboard and made a tick by her name. "Yeah, you're all right, Dr. Gavin. Go ahead." He waved her through, then held up his hands against the reporters who were clamoring for access and pressing up against him. Nora saw Charlie Brazil following a few yards behind her; he was let through the barrier as well. The crowd's buzz receded as she walked deeper into the bog, conscious of Charlie

Brazil's presence only a few paces behind her. She could see Niall Dawson's shaggy head among the group at the site, and felt somehow comforted to see his crew from the National Museum carrying on in spite of all the tumult.

Beside Dawson another figure moved slightly, and for a fraction of a second she thought it might be Cormac. In another heartbeat she realized it wasn't him, but she wondered how she had known, so quickly and so absolutely. She also understood that the same thing would happen to her again and again, perhaps for the rest of her life, if she turned away from him now. In the years to come she'd see the back of a man's head, a shoulder turning toward her, and his image would come to her like a ghost. Was it possible for the living to haunt their fellow creatures? For something as intangible as the mere memory of a gesture to slip into the subconscious unbidden and remain there until some firing synapse, some chemical key set it free? She had studied Cormac with her anatomist's eye—how his bones were put together, how the layers of muscle and sinew lay upon those bones in a very particular way to create the face and form she loved. And she did love him. The knowledge filled her suddenly, like a great breath. She'd been fighting it, denying it out of guilt and fear, but now she felt overwhelmed by the certainty of the feeling. Strange how epiphanies arrived in between things, when they were least expected.

There was nothing to be done about it now. She hiked her bag up on her shoulder and tried to prepare herself to work.

The wind was cool today, and everyone wore jackets; great cloud towers billowing past periodically threw everything into high relief or heavy shadow. The white marquee still shielded the bog man; its sides puffed in and out with the strong wind—it was a wonder the thing hadn't lifted off and blown away. Niall Dawson, directing the crew that was building the transport crate for the body, looked up as Nora reached him. "Welcome back. How did your postmortem go?"

"Very interesting. A bizarre coincidence—well, bizarre anyway; I suppose we'll have to find out if it's really a coincidence. It looks as if he was killed almost exactly like our man here—strangled with a ligature, throat slashed—"

"Really? And how long do you reckon he'd been in the bog?"

"That's what's odd. From the style of the watch he was wearing, I'm guessing probably twenty or thirty years at the outside. Maybe less."

Nora saw Charlie Brazil turn toward them. He might have heard what she'd said about the cause of death, and she realized that she probably shouldn't have said anything—to Niall Dawson or to anyone. "You'll keep all this under your hat, won't you, Niall? It's officially a murder investigation, and I don't want to get anyone in trouble."

"You know me, Nora—the soul of discretion. We're just about to do the honors here, if you're ready." He held the tent flap as Nora ducked into the white marquee.

Inside, she paused for a moment to put on a pair of latex gloves. It was difficult to believe this was real. All the hours she'd spent digging through musty old files and museum records, trying to string together known facts into never-before-discovered patterns—all the hours she'd spent trying to imagine from quaint, antique descriptions the reality faced by earlier discoverers of ancient bog remains; and here was another whole trove of information, in the flesh.

The purpose of this partial excavation today was to photograph the bog man in situ before removing him to the National Museum conservation lab at Collins Barracks in Dublin. Because the body had already been removed from its original location, there was an extra urgency about getting the remains into the protected and controlled environment of the lab. Today they would expose the arrangement of the limbs, record the things that might change once the body was moved, just as police photograph a crime scene—as an aid to memory, capturing empirical evidence exactly as it lay. The crew had already taken the obligatory shots of the telltale body parts that emerged from the peat, with markers to show the scale. Now it was time to draw back the peaty blanket and to find the full, fascinating horror that lay beneath.

First Nora uncovered the crown of the bog man's head, bare except for a matted carpet of skin and hair. She remembered reading an account of bog workers finding and tossing around something they jokingly called a "dinosaur egg," only to find later that it was a badly decayed human head, a vessel that had once held memories, sensations, fears, the spark of an individual life. She uncovered a deeply furrowed brow, a left ear bent nearly in half, a left eye squeezed shut. She looked up at Dawson; he was uncovering the man's right forearm, which was flung out away from the body, chasing the sodden peat from between the finger bones so that they would be distinct when photographed.

Nora was astonished to see the raised outlines of blood vessels beneath the skin of the dead man's right temple, distinct though the pulse they had contained had been stilled centuries ago. His delicate, papery eyelids were likewise preserved, and there was a deep crease between his eyebrows, an expression of fierce concentration. He had a full lower lip, and a strong chin covered in fine stubble the color of fox fur.

It was difficult to make out many details when everything was the same shade of brown and the invading peat had filled every recess. They'd be able to see more once they had him in the lab. The cord that had been tied around his throat looked like leather, though Nora knew, from reading about previous bog discoveries, that it might be hard to determine definitively what sort of animal hide it was. The knots would have to be examined further by a forensic specialist, but they seemed fairly simple: a stopper knot at each end of the narrow cord, and a third knot linking the two ends. That was one difference between this victim and the newer bog body.

The withered skin on his throat had gathered in folds, but with the help of a pocket mirror she could see that the near edge of the cut was still sharp, and there was a distinct layer of adipocere at its lip. They'd have to examine the wound more carefully in the lab to determine whether it had been made by a piercing or slashing action; from that they might be able to discern whether the blow had been intended to kill the victim, or merely to spill his blood—an important distinction when studying possible ritual significance. It was tempting to imagine this excessive violence as part of a complex ritual, but it was also possible that the bog men who had been subjected to such apparent overkill were simply being punished multiply for multiple crimes.

When they'd finished exposing the front and sides of the body, the photographers came inside the tent to do their portion. Nora sat on the ground outside and closed her eyes, trying to imagine what this spot had looked like twenty centuries earlier. No doubt it had been covered in a thick blanket of bog, scattered with stands of birch trees and standing pools. What was it about wet places—rivers, lakes, and bogs—that prompted offerings? Perhaps ancient people saw in the water's surface another world, a reflection of this world turned upside down, or a place inhabited by shades and spirits. She'd often listened to Cormac talk about how the Celts saw life and animus in everything, eyes peering out from the leaves of the forest, grinning faces disguised as abstract spirals and curved lines. The Romans had certainly portrayed the people who lived here as bloodthirsty savages—but didn't every conquering culture paint that portrait of the people they tried to subdue?

Perhaps the whole community had gathered here to witness as the man inside the tent bled and died, or perhaps his death had been clandestine, a well-kept secret. Some bog bodies, from their undernourished state, were thought to be people of low status, while some were very well-fed. What had this man's status been—outcast, scapegoat, fatted calf? Had he ventured out here to the bog willingly, understanding that he was to die, knowing that his blood was the necessary price for his people's survival, or had they carried him, unconscious or drugged, against his will? The whole idea of sacrifice recurred in religion to this day, Nora thought; modern Christians still drank the blood and ate the flesh of their God, if only in symbolic form. And it wasn't just Christians; nearly every culture, every human endeavor from sport to politics to the cult of celebrity, had a way of selecting scapegoats to receive punishment that would otherwise have been borne by all.

As she felt the eternal wind on her face and watched the sun still riding high across the southwestern sky, Nora felt as if she'd just discovered the key to a locked doorway into the distant past. She wasn't sure whether it was disturbing or reassuring to open those doorways and find that human beings had not fundamentally changed at all in the intervening years. Perhaps they never would.

She checked her watch; nearly six o'clock. They'd soon be finished for the day and covering up the bog man in preparation for his journey to Dublin tomorrow. She climbed to her feet and started cleaning off her tools.

Niall Dawson came up behind her. "That's the bog man finished. We'll start searching the spoil tomorrow, if that'll suit." He meant the sopping heaps of loose peat that Charlie Brazil had been removing from the drain when he'd uncovered the body. They'd have to go through it all by hand, looking for any more clues to the Loughnabrone bog man's fate. "Good for you to get your hands dirty, Nora. It'll give your research much greater depth and credibility if you've participated in all these different aspects of an excavation. Who knows, you might even get a book out of it." He smiled at her. "A few of us are heading over to Gough's in Kilcormac later if you and Cormac would fancy coming along for a drink. They've a regular set dance night there on Tuesdays. I assume you know the Clare set, at least?"

"Are you joking? Of course I do." She lapsed into a broad West Clare accent: "Didn't I spend every summer at my granny's below in Inagh? What else was there to do on a Sunday night?"

Dawson laughed. "Very good."

Nora smiled back at him, and her own American voice returned. "Been a while, though; I'm probably very rusty. Thanks for the invitation, Niall. We might see you there."

At the parking area, she spotted Charlie Brazil unloading several welded metal grids into the supply shed. He hadn't had cause to employ his gas mask over the past couple of days, but it was still hanging around his neck, facing backward. In profile, he looked like a strange two-faced Janus. He set down the heavy grids, then gave one of the joints a proprietary check. "Did you make those?" Nora asked.

He seemed startled. "I did, yeah."

"What are they?"

"Drawing frames. The archaeologists use them as grids when they're drawing the cuttings." His ears went bright crimson. "I'm allowed to make what they need here, as long as all my other work gets done."

"I've been meaning to ask you about a newspaper cutting I saw in Owen Cadogan's office when I first arrived. It had a picture of two men who made a big discovery here years ago. Their name was Brazil too. Owen Cadogan said they were relations of yours?"

He answered quietly: "My father and his brother."

"How did they come across the hoard, do you know?" Charlie's expression told her he'd heard this question before. "Sorry. You must get sick of people asking about them."

"It's never been any other way. I only get tired of people asking me where the gold is buried."

"They don't. Really?" At first she couldn't tell if he was serious; another quick glance told her that it was true, but that he managed to keep a sense of humor about it. Charlie Brazil was a quare hawk, all right, just as Owen Cadogan had described him.

"Do your dad and uncle still work on the bog?" she asked.

Charlie's defenses came up again, and quickly. "Why do you want to know?"

"It's just that I might like to talk to them as part of my research."

He looked away, then down at the ground. "My father took the pension last winter. Had to—his lungs are gone." From the set of his jaw, she sensed some rift between father and son.

"I'm sorry."

"Not your fault, is it?"

"And what about your uncle?"

"Never met him. He emigrated before I was born." Charlie lifted two more drawing frames up into the high container door. "I'd like to have known him, though. I've been looking after his bees, and I have a few questions." He spoke as though he was just a temporary caretaker—typical, Nora realized, of all the beekeepers she'd ever known.

"My grandfather used to keep bees," she said, "down near the bog in Clare. He'd let me help him tend them sometimes. He never let me mark the queens, though; I always wanted to but he said it was too dangerous, too delicate." Charlie looked over at her with a new appreciation. Nora thought he was probably one of those keepers so enmeshed in the bees' world that he would be one of them, if only he could. She suddenly saw him veiled, hands sheathed in white gauntlets, sorting through the writhing insect mass, gently brushing aside the courtiers to capture the queen in her tiny cage, making the mark that set her apart as the necessary mother of replicants, a unique being in a universe of clones. Her grandfather had explained it to her: the queen was the anointed one, chosen at random—the first to hatch. Her first royal duty was to dispatch every one of her sisters, to the last. No sentiment, just a quick spike to the head.

"You must get heather honey, this close to the bog," she said. "You don't happen to have any left from last year's run?" She felt a sudden craving for the taste—dark, almost musky, and never liquid. It was like end-of-summer fruit, sweetness teetering on the edge of decay, the last breath of summer, intensely distilled. "I'd love to see the apiary. I could just stop by—"

"No!" His vehemence seemed to surprise even himself. "There's no need. I can bring you some."

Perhaps the place was remote and hard to find. And an apiary could be dangerous to someone with no experience of bees. But the alarm in Charlie Brazil's voice had seemed slightly out of proportion. Was there something at the apiary he didn't want her to see?

4

"A set dance night?" Cormac's eyebrows lifted as he repeated the phrase, and Nora understood it might not have been his first preference for something to do that evening. "You're aware that Gough's is reputed to be the dirtiest pub in all of Ireland?"

"Well, no, I wasn't. But now I've got to see it. Come on, Niall Dawson is going down with a bunch of his people. He said you could join the session if you were afraid to dance."

As they walked through the front door of Gough's, Nora understood the designation, but thought it a bit exaggerated. True, the floor was plain concrete and could do with a good sweeping. But the bar's reputation was probably due to its bohemian decor—no tidily upholstered tapestry benches and barstools here, but swaybacked antique settees in threadbare brocade, as if the owners made a habit of haunting country-house estate sales and snapping up the worn castoffs of a dwindling aristocracy. Above the bar, an antique pendulum clock advertised Golding's Manures. Behind the front room and up a few steps lay a modern addition, a large open room with a fireplace and limestone walls lined with benches and tables. The stout pine dance floor was already filled with eight-person sets.

While they waited for drinks at the bar, Nora looked up at the fluttering streamers of green, white, and gold that made a bright pinwheel above the punters' heads. The championship season was in full swing, and hopes were high this year for the Offaly hurlers. Hurling wasn't a sport in this part of Offaly, Cormac had explained; it was closer to the local religion. And of all the sports Nora had ever halfheartedly followed, it was one of the most beautiful. It was an ancient game, played since the days of legend—the hero Cúchulain was supposed to have been a great hurler, though in his time the losing team was usually put to death after the match. There was something still very primal in watching lean young men racing down the field, scooping up the small leather ball with flat hurley sticks, balancing it while running at full speed, then batting it over the bar for a point—from a hundred meters out. Set dancing and everything else would be forgotten on Sunday afternoon during the match.

Drinks finally in hand, they headed toward the back room and spotted Niall Dawson and his group at the far side of the dance floor. The crowd was an interesting mix of older and younger people; the musicians sat in one corner near an upright piano, leaning hard into a set of reels, and four couples stood in squares, the ladies lacing their way surefootedly around the gentlemen with a brisk battering step. Then the couples faced one another, and danced around the square, stopping in each place with two emphatic stamps. When they reached home to their original places, the figure was over, and the dancers returned, flushed and perspiring, to their tables, while the musicians started up another set of tunes.

"This will be a Plain set," shouted the organizer, an energetic white-haired man in shirtsleeves and a loose tie. "Who's for a Plain set?"

Nora set her drink down on the table in front of Dawson, then took Cormac's pint and flute case from him and pulled him out onto the floor. "Back in a minute, Niall."

"Oh, I don't know, Nora," Cormac said, hanging back. "It's been too many years."

"Don't fret," she said. "I'll pull you along."

She placed Cormac's right hand snug against her waist, lifted his left arm and let her hand rest lightly against it. The music began with two thumps on the piano, and they both fell naturally into the subtle toe-heel rhythm of the Clare set. They stepped in tandem, forward and back, then Cormac swung her into ballroom position and around the square. It was clear this wasn't his first time on a dance floor.

"You're a man of many surprises," she said.

Cormac smiled and spoke quietly in her ear. "I gave it up when I started playing music, but it's like riding a bicycle. You never forget."

When the dance ended, they headed back to Dawson, who was deep in conversation with the couple at the next table. He waved them over and introduced them to Joe and Margaret Scanlan, an elderly pair who'd been sitting out the set. Joe, silent and barrel-chested, was filling his pipe and barely nodded in greeting, but Margaret Scanlan leaned forward and shook hands, scanning their faces with bright eyes. Dawson said, "Would you ever enlighten these fine people with what you were just telling me, Mrs. Scanlan?"

"We got chatting," Margaret said, "and when I found Mr. Dawson was working on the excavation over at Loughnabrone, I asked if he'd heard the latest on the murder victim. Everyone around here thinks it's a fella from these parts, Danny Brazil."

Dawson broke in: "The strange thing is, Brazil's family—"

"Says he emigrated," Nora said.

"That's right. How did you know?"

"I was just talking to his nephew this afternoon." Joe and Margaret Scanlan exchanged a significant look. "I was asking about Danny and his father finding the Loughnabrone hoard, and Charlie said people still ask him where the gold is buried."

"Seems we've nothing to tell that you don't already know," Dawson said, feigning disappointment.

"No, it's news to me that people think the body belongs to Danny Brazil. Mrs. Scanlan, why do people think it's him?"

"Well, Joe's niece Helen works at Dr. Morrison's dental surgery right beside the Garda station in Birr. About half-ten yesterday morning she saw Teresa Brazil—that's Charlie's mother—going into the station and leaving again a few minutes later. And the Guards came 'round to the surgery that very same afternoon, asking for Danny Brazil's records."

Nora said, "I hate to seem skeptical, Mrs. Scanlan, but surely the man's own family would know whether he emigrated or not. How could he be missing for twenty-five years and his family know nothing about it? That doesn't make sense."

Dawson said, "It all depends on the family."

Margaret Scanlan leaned forward. "Indeed. And it makes great sense if you knew the Brazils. All a bit quare in the head, if you know what I mean—every last one of 'em."

Cormac asked, "Any theories about why he might have been killed?"

"I think everyone assumes it's something to do with the gold," Mrs. Scanlan said. "It's been a great source of speculation for years."

Dawson broke in: "Everyone thought—maybe just assumed—that there was more to the Loughnabrone hoard, that the Brazils hadn't turned quite everything over to the museum. I suppose it's what people always think, even when it isn't true. It's nicer to think of treasure still being buried somewhere, accessible."

Margaret Scanlan said, "But now Danny's turned up dead, everyone's looking for answers about the brother and the gold."

"But there's no actual evidence that the Brazils kept anything back from the hoard?" Nora asked.

"None that I'm aware of," Dawson said. "We'll probably never know for certain."

"But it's certainly not the first time that family have had their dealings with the police." Margaret Scanlan took a sip of sherry and settled herself in to tell the story, while her husband sat back, sucking on his pipe and nodding. "About ten or twelve years ago there was an awful scandal, over terrible things that were done to several sheep and a kid goat—too horrible to mention. I don't even like thinking about it. Everyone said it was Charlie Brazil that did it, but they couldn't prove anything against him, so he was never up in court. Dreadful, it was. Shocking. And you know what they say, the apple doesn't fall far from the tree."

5

By the time Nora reached the bog on Wednesday morning, the Lough-nabrone man was already packed into his crate, ready for his trip across the Bog of Allen to Dublin. She felt sorrow for some reason, seeing him leave this place where he had been cradled for so long. But she told herself she would see him again, get to know him through whatever intimate secrets his flesh and bone and marrow might divulge.

When the museum van drove out of sight, she turned to Dawson, who was remaining to oversee the next step in the excavation process. Over the next few weeks, a full-scale excavation of the site would look for any additional remains beneath the turf. But today they would begin the search, going through every scrap of spoil looking for bone fragments, skin, and any associated artifacts. They'd have to go through a ton and a half of wet peat with their bare hands, looking for objects as small as a single fingernail. The ridge of spoil had been marked out into sections, so that each person had a manageable amount, and any finds could be pinpointed on a drawing. Nora's section was just beside Niall Dawson's.

One of the bog man's fingernails turned up after three-quarters of an hour, but it was slow, painstaking labor. Nora finished going through her fourth bucket of wet peat, and had just shifted to another position to keep from going numb, when something jabbed her, hard, just below the knee. She gasped and rolled to one side to find whatever it was that had made such a sudden impression. Straightening her leg, she found a sharp point stuck right through her trouser leg and a good quarter-inch into the flesh of her shin. She pulled it out.

Dawson was up on his knees, peering over her shoulder. "What is it?"

"I don't know. Looks like part of a clasp." She rubbed the place where it had stabbed her and tried to remember when she'd last had a tetanus shot, then held the thing out to Dawson. He gave a low whistle, and she saw his eyes grow large. "What is it?"

"It's a fibula. I'm sure you've seen them in the museum collection—Iron Age safety pins."

Nora turned the thing over in her hand. Most of the ones she'd seen had been bronze, but the body of this pin—bright yellow metal, uncorrupted by damp—was unmistakably gold. It was exquisite: a stylized bird with furled claws, its eyes set on either side of a long beak that formed the arching bow. Even with Dawson looking right at her, the first impulse she felt was to fold this beautiful object into her palm and slip it into her pocket. It was almost like the urge she'd felt as a child, to hide when another person entered the room.

Watching Dawson mark the findspot and deposit the pin in a clear polythene bag marked with the excavation number, Nora felt a small part of herself resisting the very idea of collection, collation, enumeration. Her hand remembered the pin's lovely heft. How easy it would have been to slip it into her pocket, and say not a word to anyone. She remembered the poster in Owen Cadogan's office, requesting bog workers to report the things they found. An idea began to rattle around in her brain.

As they were going back to the shed at the tea break, Nora caught up with Dawson. "Niall, supposing I found something valuable out on the bog, and decided to keep it."

Dawson seemed a little reluctant to engage on the subject. "If you were caught you'd be looking at a hefty fine, and probably jail time if it was deliberate poaching and not done just out of ignorance. The National Monuments Act is very specific and very strict."

"What's to keep me from coming out here with my trusty metal detector and looking for treasure?"

"You mean apart from it being illegal and unethical? Even archaeologists have to have a license when they're using metal detectors on sites. The answer, unfortunately, is not much."

"Supposing I wasn't caught?"

Dawson threw her a look. "You'd be lucky. Illegal trade in antiquities is big business, but hard to keep secret for long. There was a pair of cousins prosecuted a few years ago. The Guards got a tip-off and nailed them with more than four hundred artifacts in their house—figured they'd probably made off with hundreds more before they got caught. Another woman down in Wexford went around wearing a thousand-year-old Viking brooch as a lapel pin for about three years before anyone realized it was a valuable artifact."

"So how do you get people to resist temptation?"

"Well, with ordinary law-abiding citizens, fear of prosecution is a great motivator."

"What about rewards and finders' fees?"

"Oh, there's that as well. Things found on private property are handled a bit differently from discoveries made on Bord na Móna lands. But according to the law, the finder's fee is at the discretion of the state—more specifically, the museum's director."

"So that pin I just found—how much would it have been worth if I'd just dug it up perfectly legally in my back garden?"

"Are you asking about its value, or what the museum would actually pay?"

"What's the difference?"

"The reward is usually just a percentage of the actual value. It can be a delicate negotiation, particularly if we know somebody's got something we want, and we're not sure who they are, what the object is, and whether they'll ever turn it over."

"Does that happen a lot?"

"More than we like to admit."

"So what's your estimate?"

"I couldn't really say, not without examining it further. I'm not just being coy, Nora; that's the way it is. Depends on the object's value, the archaeological and historical value, and the amount of rewards made for similar objects. And it all comes from the state treasury, so we're usually talking a maximum in the thousands rather than the millions. Just to give you an example, when the Derrynaflan hoard turned up in Tipperary in 1990, the finder and the landowner received about twenty-five thousand pounds each—and that was for a whole hoard that included a silver chalice inlaid with gold."

"But depending on what you found, it could be serious money."

"Oh, aye, surely—if it was found legally, and reported as required. Why this burning curiosity all of a sudden? Tell me you haven't been tainted by one touch of saint-seducing gold?"

"Not to worry, I've no plans to turn treasure hunter. Thanks, Niall."

Someone else farther back in the group called for Dawson's attention, and Ursula Downes maneuvered into his place beside Nora.

"How's your accommodation working out, then?" she asked.

Something in the innocent way she'd posed the question made Nora suddenly wary. "Just fine," she answered cautiously, curious about where Ursula might be heading.

"What do you think of the Crosses?"

"It's a wonderful place."

"You don't find it a bit . . . I don't know—cramped? When I used to stay there, I always found it a bit confining. Old houses are like that, I suppose. Some people like quaint. I always preferred something a bit more up-to-date, myself." They'd reached the shed, and Ursula cast a frankly lubricious glance over at Charlie Brazil, who was building a new staircase for the supply shed out of broad planks, his shirt loose and unbuttoned in the afternoon heat. He was about ten yards away and couldn't have heard Ursula's remark, yet Nora felt her face unaccountably burning for his sake, or perhaps her own. Was it true, what Margaret Scanlan had said about him last night? She hadn't even tried to imagine what "terrible things" had been done to those animals. What she really wondered was whether Charlie Brazil was a true misfit, or just one of those unfortunate people whose odd behavior naturally draws suspicion—a scapegoat.

The afternoon's work was slow and hot. Like footing turf, Nora thought; you're better off not looking up. At a quarter past three, she climbed to her feet and set out for the nearest lavatory, a portable toilet with no running water. It was swarming with bluebottles and the floor was caked with peat. She had just closed the door of the Port-a-loo when she heard noises outside under the vent to her left. The compartment suddenly rocked as a body was shoved up against it, and she heard a struggle, like two people wrestling. Male and female, from the silhouettes on the fiberglass walls. Was she a witness to violence or lovemaking? Even at this proximity, it was almost impossible to tell. Finally the tussling stopped, and Nora recognized the voice: Ursula Downes, out of breath. "Don't worry, you won't hurt me. That's what you're worried about, isn't it, Charlie? To tell the truth, I like it a bit rough. What about you?"

Charlie Brazil didn't respond, but Nora could hear his ragged breathing. Through the louvered vent, she could see them outside on the ground, Ursula astride Charlie with her knees pinning his arms. He couldn't move without shifting her off him by force.

Ursula leaned forward and extracted something from the front of Charlie's shirt. "What's this—some sort of good luck charm? It's very like the one your uncle Danny was wearing when we found him. Only it didn't turn out very lucky for him, did it now?"

"I don't know what you're talking about," Charlie said. "What do you want from me?"

"Why do you think I want something, Charlie? Maybe I have something to give you. Did you ever think of it that way?"

"Whatever it is, I don't want it."

"Is that any way to talk? You haven't even heard my offer. I've been up at your place, Charlie—the place where you have the bees. People have told me Danny used to keep bees there as well."

"What about it?"

"Randy little devils, aren't they, bees? I heard once that the drones put it to the queen while she's flying, ride her in the air. Is that really true?"

"I don't know. Let me go." He struggled again, but she held him fast.

"I think you do know, Charlie. I think you know all about that and much more. I've been watching you, Charlie. I know what you're hiding."

He writhed beneath her, but she leaned forward into his face and whispered, "It's not as if you'd get nothing in return. I wouldn't tell anyone, for a start. And I'm very inventive, Charlie. You've no idea. I can be very sweet when I want to be, and I know you appreciate sweetness, Charlie. I can feel it. There's just one thing I have to mention, and it's that little girlfriend of yours, Helen Keller—"

Out of Charlie's throat came a deep groan full of anguish, swelling into a roar as he heaved Ursula from his midsection and scrambled to his feet to make an escape. She couldn't resist one parting shot: "When you do come and see me, Charlie, wait until after dark. You know how people talk."

When he was gone, Ursula sat on the ground and began to laugh to herself, a dusky sound in which Nora thought she recognized a bright note of triumph. Eventually Ursula climbed to her feet, brushed off her clothing, and went back around the side of the shed. Nora kept still for a moment, trying to think. She felt somehow stained by having witnessed the scene. She couldn't shake the sound of Ursula's laughter from her head, and she felt it setting loose the darkness that sometimes welled up inside, washing through her. She felt as though it had the power to turn her blood a deeper shade of red, and it was something she could not just wish away.

A few minutes later, when she headed back to the parking area, Nora found a jar of dark golden heather honey sitting on the hood of her car. A solitary bee had found it as well, and was tracing a circle around the edge of the lid, trying to find a way in.

6

Owen Cadogan hated the train station—the cold tile floors, the huge ticking clock, all the lifeless gray cinders that lay beneath the tracks. Perhaps the aversion was left over from his childhood, when the whole family would go down to see his father off on his way back to work in England. All that false hope, the forced emotion, the tears . . . it was dreadful. The father had made it home every few months at first, then he'd come back only at Christmas, and eventually he'd stopped coming back altogether. He had to find work, he'd said, and England was where the work was, but they all wondered what else he had found over there. Owen knew he wasn't in any position to judge, considering what he'd done with his own life, but that didn't make his father any less guilty.

He stood in the ticket queue, looking back occasionally to where Pauline sat with the children on a wooden bench against the wall. They were going up to visit her mother in Mayo for a fortnight, something they did every summer without him. A holiday at the seaside did the children good, Pauline said. And she was probably right, because Pauline was always right. The worst thing wasn't the fact that she was always right, but that she knew it. The woman's awareness of her own superiority hung around her like a stifling cloud. He'd never understand women. First they laid traps for you with their soft voices, the way they smelled and felt under your hands, and once you were reeled in and caught it was too late; you were marched before the judge and informed of the way things were going to be. When she finally had the two children she'd always wanted, Pauline's interest in him had abruptly terminated. Then she was off-limits, the door closed in his face whenever he came near her. She didn't want to have to move to a separate bedroom, she'd said, for the sake of the children, but she would if he persisted.

So he played his role as provider—the wallet, the moneybox, the bank—he'd always played that part all right. It was just in every other area that he couldn't seem to measure up. No one really understood his position, at home or at the job. He thought of all the workers who'd be losing their jobs at the end of this season. They couldn't see into the future for themselves, didn't even fucking try; they just put their heads down and went to work every day, hoping desperately that no one would force them to think too hard about the choices they had made. In many ways they were like overgrown children, and they expected to be taken care of like children for the rest of their lives. He was the one who had to tell them that things didn't work that way anymore.

He glanced back again at his family. They were his family; why should he feel like such an outsider? He studied the dark hair falling down Deirdre's back and wondered what his daughter thought of him. Children were very sensitive about these things. Did she see him for the failure of a man that he was? Stephen raised his eyes at the same moment, and Cadogan felt himself shrink under their gaze. The roundness of Stephen's head and the set of his shoulders, that confidence of youth, suddenly made him feel like weeping. They knew all about him, it was clear. And they had always been their mother's children, never his. He looked at his daughter's hands clutching the small suitcase, her knuckles still dimpled with a babyish plumpness—touching, but already lost to him. If they never came back from Mayo they wouldn't miss him a bit. He wished the train would come and take him away, once and for all, so that he would never have to look at them or think about them ever again. But just then the woman in front of him stepped away from the ticket window, and the clerk addressed him: "Where to, sir?"

"Three return tickets to Westport, one adult and two children."

"The missus taking the little ones on holiday, is she?"

"Yes."

"They're a fine-looking family."

"Yes." Cadogan's hackles rose as he watched the man's eyes flit over toward his family once more; the gray eyes glittered, the pink tongue darted out to moisten cracked lips. But when the clerk handed over the three return tickets with nicotine-stained fingers, Cadogan saw the man for what he really was: a harmless old bastard stuck behind a ticket counter for forty years. What was wrong with him? He must be losing his mind, seeing the iniquities within himself manifest themselves in everyone around him. He felt queasy, and turned away without a word of thanks.

The children led the way out to the platform. The train wasn't due for another couple of minutes, and his son went immediately to the tracks and peered into the distance for it.

"Will you get away from there, Stephen?" Pauline scolded. It was the very same tone of voice, Cadogan realized, that she often used with him as well.

"Stop fussing me, will you?" Cadogan recognized his own voice in the boy's response. When Stephen was out of harm's way, his wife turned to him, but kept her distance. "You know when we'll be home. You'll have to fend for yourself until then." What did she think he was, a schoolboy? Why had it taken him so long to realize that this was the way she'd always treated him, like a stubborn child?

Finally, the train pulled into the station. No false hope, no forced emotion, no tears. Cadogan felt relief as he watched his family climb the steps into the carriage.

"I won't wait, if you don't mind. I'll just be off."

"Whatever you like," Pauline said. "I'll ring you from Mam's. Behave yourself." With that final admonishment, she turned to catch up with the children, who were already arguing over who would get to sit facing the front of the train.

Cadogan turned and threaded his way through the loose clumps of travelers disembarking and waiting to get on. Freedom stretched before him, fourteen days in which he would not follow his wife's advice. He felt enormous relief at getting out from under his family for a few days, and wondered briefly what it might feel like to be shut of them altogether. He dared not think about that—at least not until he'd seen his plan through, until he'd found out what his worst side was capable of at the bottom of it all.

Once out of the station, he passed a self-imposed threshold and allowed himself to think about Ursula Downes. When he'd arrived at the excavation site today, she'd accused him of trying to frighten her the night before. He hadn't responded, just listened to her fume and sputter on. He wasn't going to dignify her accusations with any reply. Who did she think she was, coming out here with airs and graces, rejecting him, after what they'd got up to almost every day last summer? Why should he tell her anything? Let her fucking wonder, the bitch.

7

Two days after the new body had turned up at Loughnabrone, Liam Ward sat at his desk finishing the paperwork on a couple of recent cases. They'd just closed the inquiry on a local farmer who was making and selling his own quack cures for cattle, and were now waiting for a determination on the charges to be filed by the Director of Public Prosecutions. And just last week they'd cracked a stolen car case purely by accident; on their way out to interview the suspect, they'd found him trying to bury the car in the bog with a backhoe. Far from being sporadic, the detective work—even in a rural district like this—was usually small-scale, but relentless. This was the first homicide he and Maureen had faced in several years, and it was possible that the unusual circumstances of the case would mean they'd have some interference from above.

Maureen came through the door with a brown envelope. "Preliminary autopsy on the Loughnabrone case. It's addressed to you."

Ward studied the envelope. The address was in Catherine Friel's regular, slightly feminine hand. Still no word on Danny Brazil's dental records; it might take a few more days. He opened the envelope and slid the autopsy report onto his desk. There was a note attached:

> Liam—
> I hope this preliminary report will be of some use. It could be a couple of weeks before the toxicology and serology results come through, but please ring me if you have any questions. The findings are fairly conclusive, but let me know if you need clarification on any point. I'd like to help the investigation in whatever way I can.
>
> —Catherine

Ward felt an unfamiliar catch just beneath his solar plexus as he set the card aside. He scanned the first few paragraphs, looking for the one phrase, the key that would help him unlock this puzzle.

Evidence of injuries:

1. *Sharp force injury to the left side of the neck. This is a complex injury, a combination stabbing and cutting wound. The initial wound is present on the left side of the neck, over the sternocleidomastoid muscle, 6 cm below the left auditory canal. It is diagonally oriented, and after approximation of the edges, measures 2 cm in length. Subsequent autopsy shows that the wound path travels through the skin and subcutaneous tissue, without penetration or injury of a major artery or vein. This is a nonfatal sharp force injury.*

2. *Lateral contusion measuring 3 mm in width around the neck superior of the hyoid and traversing C4 at a 10-degree angle ascending anterior to posterior. There is a ligature crossover pattern 3 cm from posterior midline at C4, suggestive of a slightly off-center rearward ligature strangulation. This is a nonfatal injury.*

3. *Oblique and slightly curved laceration of the left posterior head, located 12 cm from the top of the head and 6 cm from the posterior midline. The laceration extends through the scalp and is associated with subgaleal hemorrhage. No skull fracture is present. This is a nonfatal injury.*

4. *Multiple incised wounds to scalp, face, neck, chest, and left hand (defense wounds).*

5. *Multiple abrasions on the upper extremities and hands (defense wounds).*

6. *Peat particles present in trachea and in both lungs.*

7. *Multiple small contusions on the calves, ankles, and heels.*

From there, Dr. Friel embarked on a more detailed description of each wound. Ward read quickly through the details, then skipped over the internal examination to the final page, for the summary of the findings:

From the anatomic findings and pertinent history, primary cause of death is ascribed to drowning. However, from the character and number of lacerations, contusions, and defensive wounds, inflicted trauma is clearly the result of a homicidal assault.

Drowning. Strange that despite all the other injuries, he had ended up asphyxiating at the bottom of a bog hole. The defensive wounds said the man hadn't gone willingly to his death. Cuts on his hands and forearms were evidence that he'd been conscious while being attacked with a knife. There had been a fierce fight.

Ward tried to put himself in the dead man's place, to reconstruct the events in logical sequence. He opened the evidence box and removed the leather cord. Someone surprises the victim. He naturally tries to escape, so the attacker takes hold of this cord, twists and pulls him backward, to hold him, probably with the left hand. That's one reason the ligature mark on the neck would be slightly off center. The attacker tries to reach around and slash the victim's throat with the knife, but he's still struggling, and the attacker doesn't get a good strike; the wound is only superficial.

In the struggle, the victim twists around and falls. His head strikes something hard, giving him that curved laceration, and he's knocked unconscious. He might even appear to be dead. At this point the attacker drags him across the bog and throws him down the bog hole. But the victim isn't dead; he's only unconscious. He regains consciousness in the hole, and struggles even then, sinking in the sloughy darkness, trying to dig his way out, until finally he sinks and the attacker fills in the bog hole with spoil.

Ward felt exhausted, just thinking about the scenario. But what were the weaknesses? There were always weaknesses. It was all a bit too much to believe—the garrote, the knife, the drowning. Unnecessary overkill. But had it been planned that way, or had it just happened? Unwilling victims had a way of upsetting people's carefully drawn plans.

And there was still the puzzle of the missing clothing. If the victim had been fully dressed when he was attacked, why would the killer bother to strip the body? If you were simply trying to make identification difficult, why not take all the effects—the watch, the leather necklace? Dr. Gavin said that the bodies thought to be sacrificial victims were usually found naked. .

There was another problem as well. The scenario he had just imagined assumed only one attacker, and there might have been more. A conspiracy? Stranger things had happened. In the famous Missing Postman case, several upstanding citizens had been involved in covering up an accidental death, transporting the body and concealing it down a well.

Now that they knew how the man had died, they would have to wait and see if he turned out to be this Brazil fellow. Once again, thinking the name, Ward felt unsettled. Ever since Teresa Brazil had sat here in his office yesterday morning, he hadn't been able to shake the feeling that he should know that name, but he couldn't place it. Nothing recent—it was something old, unfinished.

He turned to the computer on the corner of his desk, typed "Brazil" into the system, and started scanning the dozen or so items that came up: joyriding, petty burglary, public drunkenness. No, none of those; the first names were wrong. Then he spotted it, and everything came back to him. The case had been one he'd handled himself, eight years earlier, with his old partner, Eugene Larkin. A postman making his rounds on the bog road between Kilcormac and Loughnabrone had discovered a lamb hanging by the neck from a scrub tree at the edge of the bog. Whoever had put the creature there had also cut its throat, and with the blood had drawn three circles in a sort of triangular formation on the ground below. It was just the sort of incident that fanned the flames of fear and intolerance in a small rural place. The killing had been discovered just after a full moon, and a sort of mass hysteria had taken hold of the community. The air was rife with rumors of clandestine rituals and blood cults. Perfectly innocent activities became suspect. When a second animal was found slaughtered after the next full moon, on the same stretch of road and in much the same condition, anonymous tips began pouring in. Ward had taken several of the calls himself, and could still hear the voices: *Better look to that Brazil lad, Charlie. He's a right quare one, he is—a desperate odd character. Not the full shilling, out walking on the bog at all hours. What's he get up to out there? No good, I'll promise you.*

After the second incident, they'd decided to interview the boy, if only to eliminate him from the inquiry. Why the community had all settled on this boy in particular was a mystery. All that set Charlie Brazil apart from his fellows, apparently, was that he kept to himself, displayed a pointed lack of interest in football and hurling and girls, hadn't been seen inside the church these last two years, and was seen walking in the bog at all hours of the day and night.

But after the official visit from the Guards, it seemed as though the suspicion and whispering only escalated. Emboldened by their neighbors, more voices began chiming in, a chorus of indictment. One person claimed her cousin's daughter had seen the boy in nothing but his pelt, dancing around a bonfire. But whenever they had pressed further—for proof, any physical evidence, eyewitness statements placing Charlie Brazil in or near that part of the bog on the nights in question—the anonymous accusers had vanished like mist. They'd all heard about Charlie and his midnight rituals from a neighbor or someone in the pub. For some of them it was proof enough that the animals involved belonged to the boy's mother; naturally she wouldn't be interested in pressing charges against her own son.

The last and most violent incident had involved a kid goat. The third time they'd questioned Charlie Brazil with no result, Larkin had tried flashing a few photos from the scene. But the boy hadn't looked at the pictures, nor at the men who were questioning him; he had maintained his composure, kept his eyes averted, and calmly continued answering their questions, with the photographs strewn on the table before him. Ward recalled that to Larkin, the boy's lack of reaction had been proof enough of guilt. He himself hadn't been so sure.

The Brazils were an odd family; that much was true. Ward had sensed a deep disconnect in the room with them—three individuals completely separate from one another, each consumed with maintaining that separation. He recalled the father's dark expression, the way he'd hung back beside the door while the boy was being questioned, as though he wanted to be able to bolt at any moment. A powerful man, Dominic Brazil was, with hands like two spades. Ward had interviewed dozens of fathers like him, inexplicably silent men whose own fathers had been rigid and unforgiving, fearful of any weakness in their offspring. At least the mother had been concerned about what was happening to her son. Teresa Brazil, the woman who'd been in his office this morning, had looked at every grim photo that day so long ago without flinching. He was surprised that he hadn't remembered her; she'd impressed him back then with her unwavering support for the boy. After looking through the pictures, she had turned and spoken slowly to him and Larkin, shaking her head. *My son could not have done this.* As though trying to convince herself, Ward had thought. As though willing it not to be so was enough. It was possible the boy had done it, of course. Anything was possible.

In the end, they hadn't been able to find a single scrap of physical evidence tying Charlie Brazil to the incidents and consequently had never charged him. After the third and most grisly occurrence, the mutilations had stopped, and the case had eventually been shelved for lack of evidence. Ward hadn't seen the lad since. He must be in his early twenties now, probably working for Bord na Móna as a ditcher driver like his father.

Ward remembered what he'd been going through himself at that time—it hadn't been long after Eithne's death—the night sweats, the fearful dreams of drowning, of watching her head slide beneath the water and being frozen with horror, unable to act. He'd probably been easier on the boy than he should have been. But there had been no compelling evidence. And inflicting needless suffering had never been one of the attractions of his job.

It was both curious and disturbing that the animal mutilations and the body from Loughnabrone seemed to involve similar ritualistic spilling of blood. But was that a connection or just a coincidence? What age was Charlie Brazil—about twenty-two, twenty-three? That meant he hadn't even been born when Danny Brazil left home.

The key to the Loughnabrone case was how long the body had been in the bog. At this point Ward only had Teresa Brazil's word for the date when Danny had disappeared from Loughnabrone. Maybe he'd never gone away. Or maybe he'd left for a while and come back, tried to get in contact with someone he shouldn't have. Ward looked down at the list of known associates he'd been working on, people they might have to interview in the next few days: the Brazil family, of course; Danny's coworkers at the workshop; his former mates on the hurling team, those erstwhile local heroes turned middle-aged butchers and electricians and publicans. He wondered whether Danny Brazil had been headed to Australia of his own free will, or whether he'd been banished there—and if so, by whom.

When he got back to the office, Liam Ward watched Maureen on the phone with her husband, cradling the receiver against her left ear, and wondered whether he'd ever again have the opportunity to hear a woman's voice soften like that over the telephone. He thought about picking up his own phone and ringing Dr. Friel. Perhaps she was still in the area, and wouldn't mind having dinner with him. That was all it would be: a meal and some conversation.

He flipped through the numbers in his diary, and was just about to dial her mobile when Dr. Friel herself appeared in front of his desk. She was wound up about something, but from all appearances, it looked like something good.

"Hello, Liam. I hope you don't mind me just popping over like this, but we've got a positive ID on the second body from the bog. It *is* Danny Brazil, no question about it. I made the preliminary comparison, and the odontologist just confirmed it; he says there are too many matches in the dental work for it to be anyone else. I have both sets of X rays here if you want to have a look."

Maureen overheard, and put down the phone to join them at the window. In the ghostly image against the pane, the dense teeth glowed white, the fillings and metal crowns a translucent gray.

"Can you see the missing bicuspid here on the left? And the gold crown is pretty unmistakable in both. A person's teeth have very distinctive features, very individual facets and root systems." Ward looked, and saw some of the similarities, and was glad there were experts whose obsession served the greater good.

"These are a bonus," Dr. Friel said, pulling out a pair of X rays and holding them up to the light. "Turns out Danny Brazil was treated for a blow to the face during a hurling match—they tell me he played midfield for Offaly. These X rays were taken at the time of the injury and were in his file at the dental surgery."

Ward looked more closely at the shadowy radiographs of Danny Brazil's skull. On one he could see the leather cord still hanging loose around the throat. The soft tissue—the eyes, ears, and the tongue— were gone, the sockets round and staring. It was probably best not to imagine all that was inside us, Ward decided. Not to dwell on it at least. And yet she thought about it all the time, Catherine Friel did. It was her life, the same way his life was thinking about what went on inside people, perhaps in a somewhat less literal, less visceral way. But there were those who preferred not to think about either. He was acutely aware of her close beside him, of the hand that held the X ray up to the window. No wedding band.

"It was great of you to bring these by," he said.

"I have to admit I had an ulterior motive."

Maureen cleared her throat and excused herself with a look that said Ward had better be listening carefully. Was his attraction to Catherine Friel that obvious? They both watched Maureen go, then Dr. Friel turned back to him. "I was wondering whether you might join me for dinner. I've another case over in Athlone tomorrow, so I'm here for another day at least. I'd love to talk over this case a bit more—if you're free."

It was as if she knew what he'd been thinking since the first day they'd met out on the bog. Of course, he'd have to go and speak to Danny Brazil's family before he did anything else. "I really should—"

"Perhaps another time."

Ward could see that she was reading his hesitation as reluctance, and he wanted to dispel that notion. "No, it's just that I should go and talk to the family right away this evening. What about tomorrow?" He felt sudden perspiration on his palms, but was relieved when she smiled.

"I'm staying at the Moors. It's out the Banagher road—do you know it? There's quite a nice restaurant in the hotel, if that would suit. Is eight o'clock too late?"

"I'll see you there tomorrow at eight."

As he drove out to the Brazils' farm, the fact that he had a grim visit to pay to a bereaved family kept Ward from thinking about dinner with Dr. Friel the following night—and that, he reflected briefly, was probably just as well. He passed by the Scully house and felt a tug of guilt. Ward hadn't been to see Michael for nearly a fortnight. He could stop by after talking to the Brazils—but something just beneath his breastbone told him he wouldn't do it, not tonight, in any case. There would be enough of bereavement tonight. Perhaps tomorrow.

He pulled into the yard at the Brazils' farm and wondered how significant it was that Teresa had come forward so early to identify the body. He decided to play it neutral and not mention that fact just yet. Better hold it in reserve to see if he needed it later.

One car stood in the yard. The place looked like a lot of the smaller farms in the area, barely able to justify the burden of work it took to maintain. Crowded into an old foundation beside the house, small green cabbages stood in three neat rows. Alongside them ran a dozen potato drills, a few rows of runner beans, and various other vegetables. Two sheds with horseshoe roofs stood at a right angle to the garden, one housing a load of turf, the other a small tractor; muddy hoof-prints, evidence of cattle, tracked across a corner of the yard. Washing flapped on the line, but Ward knew from experience that it was impossible to keep things clean out near the bog. Everything got covered in peat dust—the laundry, the tabletops, the people. Got inside them as well, muffled their speech, their thoughts.

The large single-pane window faced the back garden, and through it he could see Teresa Brazil expertly peeling potatoes with a small kitchen knife. He watched her sure, rapid motions as the long spiraling ribbon fell away and the glistening, naked potato slipped under the surface of the water in the saucepan. Then she looked up and saw him, and immediately understood the reason he'd come. She grasped the edge of the sink and bowed her head. She'd known it was Danny; that was why she'd come forward, after all, Ward told himself. But to have it confirmed, and so quickly, must still be a shock.

She came to the door, and waited until Ward had stepped several paces into the room before she turned to face him once more.

"It was Danny," she said. The words were not a question.

"Yes, I'm afraid so. We just got a positive identification from the dental records. I'm very sorry."

Teresa Brazil spoke in a low voice, glancing toward the door to the sitting room. "He doesn't know I came to you. He doesn't even know about the body. Couldn't you just tell him that—I don't know—that someone phoned anonymously?"

"If you wish," Ward said. He would go along with that for the moment at least, to see how that simple omission colored things. After all, her husband would be a primary suspect in this case. Always look closest to home when investigating a murder; that was one of the rules.

Teresa Brazil finished wiping her hands. "Let me speak to him first. I'll be right back." She disappeared down the hallway, her footsteps silent on the carpeting.

Ward turned to take in the space behind him, a sort of combination kitchen and sitting room. Blue delft stood on display in a dresser against the wall, and two places were laid at the table. In addition to the potatoes Mrs. Brazil had been peeling, the makings of a substantial dinner sat ready beside the cooker. The room spoke of order and cleanliness, the kind of existence where you knew exactly what you were going to get for your dinner seven nights a week. The radio, tuned to the Midlands station, droned in the background. In the corner farthest from the kitchen area stood a trio of tall sea green oxygen tanks, their shiny cautionary labels warning against use near an open flame.

"You can go in to him now," Mrs. Brazil said, and ushered Ward into the sitting room. Her husband sat stiffly in an overstuffed chair. One might almost have imagined that, apart from his barrel chest, the man was slowly disappearing into his clothes. A thin, clear tube snaked up to his face, which had the hollow eyes and bluish-gray complexion that accompanied afflicted lungs. Dominic Brazil was perhaps sixty, but looked older, blue veins standing out on the pale hands that emerged from his sleeves, his once-dark hair now a dull gray. Voices tinkled merrily from the television in the corner, but above its sound a faint hiss filled the room, like air escaping from a slow puncture, and Ward realized it came from the oxygen tank that stood beside Brazil's chair. What was this before him but a man slowly drowning, dying a little more each day?

Teresa Brazil hovered at the door, apparently unsure whether she should stay or return to the kitchen, until Ward said, "I'd prefer you to stay, if that's all right." She sat down in a straight chair near the door.

Ward moved to sit down opposite Brazil on the sofa, feeling like an awkward suitor in his collar and tie. Brazil's wheezy breath grew perceptibly faster, in through the nose, but out through pursed lips, and each exhalation seemed to take more effort than the last. "Mr. Brazil, my name is Liam Ward; I'm a detective."

Brazil nodded, evidently not wanting to waste his breath in responding when every ounce of oxygen was precious. Ward continued: "I'm here to tell you that workers at Loughnabrone Bog discovered a body two days ago. I'm sorry to inform you that it's been positively identified through dental records as the body of your brother, Danny."

Brazil said nothing, but closed his eyes and concentrated fiercely upon each breath. Just as he seemed about to speak, the man pitched forward in a violent coughing fit—a ragged, tearing sound from somewhere deep within. His wife was beside him in a second, pulling his shoulders back, and Ward noticed once again her smooth, youthful hands. Her husband gripped her forearm, hard enough that Ward thought it must be hurting her; he could see the pain in her face, but she said nothing. At last Brazil sat back in the chair, exhausted, bright tears streaming down his face, but whether they had been brought on by the news of his brother's death or by the coughing fit, Ward couldn't be entirely sure.

"I'm also sorry to have to tell you that your brother's death doesn't appear to have been accidental. I'll have to ask you a few questions. I can do that now, if you're up to it. If not, I can come back later."

"What do you want to know?" wheezed Dominic Brazil. "He left. Went off to Australia, we thought." His voice was like a child's wind-up toy running out of steam. His hand still rested on his wife's forearm, but she slowly withdrew it, and rubbed the spot where he'd held her fast. Had that grip been just a reflex, a spasm, or some sort of communication?

"When was the last time you saw your brother, Mr. Brazil?"

He thought for a moment. "It was Midsummer's eve, but the year— what was the year?"

His wife reminded him. "It's twenty-six years ago tomorrow."

"You say you thought he'd gone away. Did you ever hear from him after he left home?" Dominic Brazil shook his head fractionally.

"Did no one worry about him not staying in touch with the family?"

"He could be dreadful mulish."

"Why did he want to leave?"

"Nothing for him here. He hated the bog like poison."

"I understand he hurled for Offaly, but he was injured?"

Brazil nodded. "After that blow to the head, he couldn't play anymore. He suffered from fierce headaches. That's when he started talking about Australia."

"How did he have enough money to get to Australia?"

"He had the reward." Brazil's look suggested that everyone knew about the reward.

Teresa jumped in: "For the hoard they found on the bog. There was a finder's fee."

"Do you mind if I ask how much?"

"Twenty thousand—pounds, it would have been at that time."

Ward tried to imagine a couple of Bord na Móna lads with that kind of cash. "You split the money equally?"

"I bought him out, his share of this place. He had enough for Australia."

"And no one thought it strange that he never wrote? No one tried to find him?"

"What would have been the point, if he didn't want to be found?"

Ward was taken slightly aback; Teresa Brazil had said exactly the same thing in his office. "Who were his mates? Anybody from the workshop that you can recall?"

"Never paid much attention to any of them. He had a couple of mates on the hurling team, but when he quit playing, they fell out. All he really cared about here was those bees."

"Bees?"

"He kept hives above on the hill. Used to spend hours up there." Teresa Brazil rose abruptly and left the room.

"What about girls? Was Danny involved with anyone?" Brazil shook his head, saving breath.

"Had he had a dispute with anyone? Over something on the job, maybe? You said he had a falling out with some of the hurlers?"

Brazil shook his head again, but no words came. He launched into another violent coughing fit, and this time Teresa was not beside him to help until it passed. Ward felt helpless watching the man go through agony, and knew he'd gotten all he was going to get from Dominic Brazil today. He would come back when they'd had a chance to let the reality of the situation sink in. It was the same whenever you brought this dreadful news to a family—they could never imagine anyone with reason enough to kill. As if reason came into it at all. He waited as Brazil's cough gradually subsided, then rose and said, "I'll leave you now. I may have more questions in the next few days." Dominic Brazil nodded again, ashen-faced.

Ward found Mrs. Brazil in the kitchen, back at her cookery, scraping the skin from a carrot with furious intensity.

"Excuse me, Mrs. Brazil. You wouldn't by any chance have a photograph of Danny? It might help in our investigation."

She looked at him blankly, as if she'd never seen him before, then seemed to snap out of her slight trance. "Of course. I'll see if I can find one." She left him and went back down the hall. Through the cracked-open door, Ward could see that she went into a bedroom, and he heard her digging around, probably in the bottom of a wardrobe. She returned with a battered cardboard suitcase. "If there's anything at all, it would be in here." She flipped the latches and exposed a jumble of color snapshots and antique portraits, a collection of family history, corseted women and mustached men in well-worn Sunday suits, a dead child in its pram. He looked over her shoulder as she dug up ancestors, the jumbled details of their triumphs and tragedies long forgotten.

"My husband's family were never great for taking photos, and after Danny—" She stopped momentarily. "After Danny was gone, his mother threw the few pictures she had of him into the fire. No longer any son of hers, she said." Teresa Brazil turned her face away, apparently disturbed by the vivid memory. Ward's own mind formed the image of a vigorous young man in a fading color photo, suspended for a few seconds against the orange glow of a turf fire, then curling up and crumbling away into ashes.

She continued looking, and at the very bottom of the case she found a newspaper cutting. "This was in the *Tribune* when the lads found all that in the bog," she said.

Ward looked at the grainy image, softening into yellow and blurry gray with age and damp. Yet Danny Brazil's face was clearly visible, along with the sword he held in his hands, like an offering, while his brother looked up at the camera from behind. It was astonishing to think that one of the vital men in the photo was now the living cadaver who sat in the next room. And the other was the wizened brown flesh he'd last seen on the stainless-steel table in the mortuary. He tucked the cutting into his pocket, thanked Mrs. Brazil for her help, and took his leave.

Driving back to the station, Ward tried to put his finger on the feeling he'd got in the Brazil house. It was like walking the bog; you had to be very careful where you put a foot down, in case you'd sink in. Stick to the well-trodden paths, and you'd be all right, you'd survive the crossing. But how had Danny Brazil happened to stray from the path? How exactly had he put a foot wrong and ended up dead?

8

"We've got a standing invitation to have a drink over at Michael Scully's house," Cormac said, when they'd finished their evening meal. "We could go over tonight, if you're up for it. Michael keeps a bottle of Tyrconnell single malt for special occasions, and apparently we qualify. He's quite anxious to meet you."

Nora knew that Michael Scully had been one of Gabriel McCrossan's great friends; that was enough incentive. "I'm delighted to go along for a drink. But I can't understand why he'd be anxious to meet me."

"Gabriel told him about your research project. He probably wants to meet the mind behind it. Michael would be a good person for you to know. He's retired from the Heritage Service a good few years now, but his interest always ran much deeper than the job required. If you're interested in bogs, archaeology, antiquities, the history of this area, Michael Scully is your man. He's devoted years to going through all the annals and old manuscripts, especially the ones that mention this part of the county. I don't know if you've ever heard tell of hereditary historians, families whose job it was to remember the whole history of an area. He's a bit like that. An amazing character, for the most part self-educated, very grounded in the old culture. There are so many people around here who have nothing of it left in them at all. He's fluent in Irish, and reads Latin and Greek. An unappreciated treasure stuck out here in the middle of the bog."

When they arrived at the Scully house, the first thing Nora noticed was that the property seemed to be overrun with poultry, including strangely tufted guinea fowl, matronly buff-colored hens, and many black-and-white barred pullets, all bright-eyed and alert to movement, randomly scrabbling at the ground for things to eat. The sole rooster, a scrappy bantam, strutted among them, flicking his fall of beautiful black and brown and purple tailfeathers and eyeing the human visitors suspiciously as they approached up the gravel drive.

The house was plain and large like many farmhouses of a certain age, the yard beside it a small green patch edged with gravel. As they passed by one of the windows, Nora thought she saw a curtain flutter, but it must have been her imagination; when she looked back the drapery was still. Someone had made sure the grass was kept in trim, but the house didn't boast much in the way of plantings—or adornment of any kind, in fact, except for the heavy brass knocker on the door, which was painted a deep carnelian red. There was no movement visible inside.

Cormac rapped loudly with the knocker, then stood back. "Mind yourself," he said under his breath. Nora turned to see a black-and-white sheepdog creeping up toward them on its belly around the back end of the car parked outside the door. "That's a wicked dog," Cormac said. "He'll try to nip you. Stick close beside me." The dog moved closer, as if his rolling, innocent eyes and obsequious posture put him above suspicion.

A human figure appeared behind the rippled glass of the front door, and the dog slunk away silently, much to Nora's relief. The door swung open to reveal a man perhaps in his seventies, wiry and gray-haired, with brows that stuck out above his intense dark eyes like a pair of caterpillars. He was dressed rather formally, in wool flannel trousers, with a V-neck sweater over his shirt and tie, as if the routine of getting dressed each day provided a modicum of helpful structure. Scully moved with some difficulty, and his neatly pressed shirt collar seemed a few sizes too large for him, giving the impression that he was shrinking, slowly but steadily.

When Cormac introduced her, Michael Scully took Nora's hand in his own with an inquisitive, approving look. "Ah, Nora—delighted to meet you. Gabriel spoke of you very fondly. Since his passing the one thing this old house has most sorely lacked is good conversation." A look passed between Cormac and Scully that said there was something more in the remark, but she let it go.

They followed Scully into a large sitting room that could have been much the same in the nineteenth century. Heavy Victorian furniture claimed the floor, and framed family photos hung from a high picture rail on the flowery papered walls. A gramophone and a huge collection of 78s took up one entire wall. To the other side of the room stood a large table, completely drifted with books and papers, like the cluttered desk of many an academic Nora had known, a visual representation of the scholar's crowded mind. And yet the underlying impression was not one of squalor, but of order and cleanliness, as if the absent-minded chaos of one consciousness was underlaid by another that cared whether the floor was swept and the cobwebs dusted away. Someone—and clearly not the keeper of this disarranged archive—was at work to maintain cleanliness at least, if order was out of the question.

"I see you're still hard at work," Cormac said.

"Impossible to keep a rein on it," Scully said. "Some people collect stamps, some collect tunes; I collect what Fionn MacCumhaill once called 'the music of what happens.' And since I've retired, people insist on giving me these things. They tell themselves it's because I'm keen, but it's also partly because they don't want to deal with it themselves—all the boxes of old letters and newspaper cuttings in their granny's wardrobe. Some of the things I get are really beyond redemption. In a climate like this, paper can turn to mildew in a few weeks' time. It's impossible to keep up with the rate of decay. But I can't bear not to at least have a look through it all. You never know when something interesting may turn up."

"Cormac was telling me you know a lot about this area," Nora said.

"And not just paper history, either," Cormac said. "Michael has walked every tumulus and fairy fort for fifty miles around. He can tell you what's inscribed on every castle wall and standing stone, even take you to the spot where the ravens in legend sang over the grave of a king. A worthy heir to O'Donovan."

"Ah, pure flattery and you know it," Scully demurred. He turned to Nora. "It's invariably this way when he's craving my good whiskey. You'll have a drop as well, won't you?" He crossed to a carved cabinet beside the fireplace and, with much effort, searched for one particular bottle among a small collection. To Cormac he said, "I don't have to remind you that O'Donovan never had much affection for this part of the country. What's the verse he quoted from the *Dinnseanchas*? 'Plain and bog, bog and wood, / Wood and bog, bog and plain!'"

Nora looked blankly from one to the other, hoping one of them would take pity on her and explain. "*Dinnseanchas* means 'place-history,'" Cormac said. "It's actually a series of fragments of the old oral history that were set down in manuscript form during the twelfth century. Sometimes it's also called *Seanchas Cnoc*, the History of Hills."

"And who's O'Donovan?"

Michael Scully said, "John O'Donovan. One of the great Gaelic scholars of the nineteenth century. He and his brother-in-law, Eugene

O'Curry, were employed by the Ordnance Survey during the 1830s. O'Donovan worked in the field, traversing the country, documenting ancient sites and checking contemporary maps against old manuscripts. He sent letters back to the Ordnance Survey office in Dublin almost daily, with a sort of running commentary on all he was finding along the way, and he always sowed in snips of poems and songs and quotations— the letters make tremendous reading. And the depth of his scholarship is absolutely frightening. But he should have known better than to cover this part of the country in the dead of winter. It spilled rain almost every single day, and he often complained about the damp rooms where he had to spend the night. Survey work did him in eventually, poor fellow. Dead of rheumatic fever before he ever saw sixty years of age."

Scully finished pouring and handed them each a small tumbler of whiskey, which smelled sweet and smoky as a turf fire. Nora could imagine Michael and Gabriel and Cormac staying up too late over the last drop of this stuff. Scully lifted his glass. "As Gabriel always used to say, *Go mbeirimid beo ag an am seo arís!* May we all be alive this time next year." The defiance in his voice was tinged with sadness as he repeated his old friend's perennial toast. They drank to Gabriel in silence.

Scully finally roused himself from his brief reverie and moved to sit near the fireplace, gesturing to them to do the same. "I see you brought the flute," he said to Cormac.

"I've a new tune for you, Michael. Something of local interest, a set dance Petrie collected somewhere near Kilcormac."

"George Petrie, another of O'Donovan's contemporaries," Scully said in an aside to Nora. "He and O'Curry between them collected hundreds of tunes, and all kinds of information about the old music."

Cormac sat on a stiff chair beside the fireplace and began putting together the flute as he spoke, deftly lining up the finger holes, wetting his lips in anticipation of playing this tune for Scully, and Nora realized that to come bearing a new tune was like bringing flowers or a naggin of whiskey—it was an offering. Cormac had been storing this up for some time, she could tell, and now the notes seemed to fall from the flute in slow motion, suggesting a dignified, almost courtly dance. As he listened, Michael Scully filled his pipe with tobacco and lit it, the smoke curling around his head and shoulders. From time to time, his features took on a worn, gray pallor, as though he was suffering great pain but did not wish to acknowledge it. Eventually the pain seemed to subside, and a look of satisfaction stole once more across his face as the tune's main theme returned. The whiskey was good, and warming, and the windburn she'd gotten from a few days out on the bog made Nora's face feel warm and flushed.

Cormac set down the flute when he finished the tune and took up his glass. "Petrie called that 'The Hurling Boys.' Said it was a most popular tune in the King's County in the 1860s. It's probably an old set dance piece, but it's quite stately—almost like a walking march."

"Yes, isn't it? It would put you in mind of this one—" Scully broke off and began to lilt. He had to strain to reach the highest notes, but in the lower register his voice was rich and resonant. Nora had never learned how to lilt, and envied the ease with which some people made this sort of music. It was almost as if they heard it inside their heads all the time, like language. They were steeped in it, changed by it, down to the deepest recesses of their souls.

"I never played an instrument," Scully said, looking at Nora, "and I'm sorry for it now. But the music's here." He pointed to a spot just below his breastbone. "Cormac tells me you've got music in you as well."

"I don't know about that. I just can't help singing."

"Will you give us a song now, Nora?" She saw in Cormac's expression that her own presence was part of his gift to Michael Scully this evening. He sat apart from her, but it was as if she felt his hand at her back, pushing her forward like a child sent with flowers. She could not refuse. With a flutter in her stomach, she took a breath, and opened her mouth with no idea what song might emerge.

> 'S a Dhómhnaill Óig liom, má théir thar farraige
> Beir mé féin leat, is ná déan dhearmad;
> Beidh agat féirin lá aonaigh 'gus margaidh,
> 'Gus iníon rí Gréige mar chéile leapa 'gat.
>
> O are you going across the water?
> Take me with you, to be your partner;
> At fair or market you'll be well looked-after,
> And you can sleep with the Greek king's daughter.
>
> O Donal Óg, you'll not find me lazy,
> Not like some high-born expensive lady;

I'll do your milking, and I'll nurse your baby
And if you are set upon, I'll defend you bravely.

You took what's before me and what's behind me;
You took east and west when you wouldn't mind me.
Sun, moon, and stars from the sky you've taken,
And God as well, if I'm not mistaken.

The last verse contained such pure aching sadness, and Nora felt its familiar pain as she sang the words about a bruised and broken heart:

Tá mo chroí-se brúite briste
mar leac oighre ar uachtar uisce,
mar bheadh cnuasach cnó tar éis a mbriste
nó maighdean óg tar éis a cliste.

"Lovely, Nora." Michael Scully said. "Thank you."

She opened her eyes, feeling cool tear tracks on her face. "I'm not sure where that came from." It was true. She had known the song forever, but had never sung it particularly well. This evening something was different; maybe the good whiskey had helped. But underneath she knew it was more than that; she'd felt, while singing, almost as if she was being played like an instrument, as if she was a mere conduit for the unnamed young woman's despairing cry. And now that the song was gone, she felt uncomfortable and self-conscious.

It was Cormac who came to her rescue. He looked at her, not at Scully, when he spoke. "Michael, didn't you say you had something for Nora?"

"Ah, I do." Scully climbed slowly to his feet and went to his desk, carefully extracting a slim leather-bound volume from one of the piles so that he didn't set off an avalanche of papers. "I've been holding on to this for months, and it got buried underneath everything. But when Cormac phoned and said you were coming out, I did a little excavating.

"About a year ago, among one of the latest loads of old papers and photographs, I discovered a diary kept by a Miss Anne Bolton, companion to Mrs. William Haddington of Castlelyons. Miss Bolton began her record on the first of January, 1835." He handed Nora the small book and directed her to the place on the page with one thin finger. His eyes beamed his pleasure in this moment of discovery. "Read what she says about the second of May."

Nora read aloud:

> "The weather being exceptionally fine this morning, and Mrs. Haddington being in rare excellent form, we decided to traverse the countryside to take the view. We climbed the gravel ridge that lies just beside the Castlelyons gatehouse, and proceeded to walk along its back, across the moorland that lies along the southwest boundary of the castle demesne. If the weather is good, and one is properly attired, the bog can be a very pleasant place to take the air, especially for persons interested in botany (as I am), and it is a rare excursion that does not raise at least a few hares and pheasants. However, we had not ventured but a few minutes on our course when we heard the alarm raised among some workmen who were toiling in the bog. It is the practice of the country people here to venture out into the bogs to cut 'turf' as they call it, which, once dried, can be burned in place of wood in their hearths. When Mrs. Haddington stopped to ask the cause of their consternation, they shewed her what they had found, a man buried and quite marvelously preserved in the peat."

Nora's stomach tightened with excitement. Nowhere in her previous research had she seen any reference to this body or this location. She was looking at a new paper body—the name given to bog remains that survived only in written accounts. She tore through the succeeding paragraphs in which the extremely observant Miss Bolton described the man's glossy brown skin and the twisted withy made of sally rods around his throat, not to mention his shocking nakedness, from which the workmen had quite properly shielded her and Mrs. Haddingon. She also described in detail the leather armband around the dead man's upper arm, and the astonishing preservation of his face and feet. Of his disposition in the bog, Miss Bolton had written:

> Mrs. Haddington has sent for the vicar, so that this unfortunate soul may be re-interred at the paupers' cemetery outside the village. This discovery presents a most intriguing puzzle: how the peat and bog water could preserve both flesh and bone. Perhaps the cold may have some part in it, or perhaps there is some other reason. I have often heard the natives

of this place tell that the bog water of this locality, and indeed the peat itself, is an excellent treatment for wounds and afflictions of the skin, and wonder if there is not something in it that may contribute to this most astounding suspension of decay.

Nora raised her eyes from the book, feeling an electric shock of recognition and a surge of affection for Miss Bolton. Only then did she realize she'd been reading silently since the first paragraph, ignoring the two men who were waiting expectantly for some more visible reaction.

"I'm sorry, it's just—this is huge," she said. "I'm fairly sure it's a new paper body, one that nobody has in the records. To have this, and such a detailed description—what a gift."

"It gives me great pleasure to share it with the one person best able to appreciate its true significance."

"I wonder if I might borrow this book—just for a short while, I promise."

"You may have it. I've read Miss Bolton right through to the end, and there are several other passages you might find interesting as well. She struck me as extremely curious and well-read. What do you think of her theory about the bog water?"

"Amazingly accurate. You don't happen to have a map, so I could see the exact point she's talking about?"

"I do. Cormac, you know where the maps are—in the cabinet there." Scully was looking a bit drawn, and Nora knew they ought to go soon, but she felt an urgent need to find out how this new body fit in. Cormac brought out a flat map book, like his own, and opened it on the table before them.

"These are the maps O'Donovan was working on, originally drawn in 1838, and updated in 1914. Here's Castlelyons demesne," Scully said. "And here's the gravel ridge Miss Bolton mentioned. It was left behind by the last glaciers, and the ancients called it the Eiscir Riada, 'the Great Road.' People used it for centuries as the main east-west highway across Ireland. There are a few breaks, but for the most part it was a useful roadway. It stood above the rest of the landscape, you see—especially useful in this 'county of bogs and morasses,' as O'Donovan once called it. If the ladies were walking toward the bog from the house, they must have been right about here when they encountered the workmen."

Nora had seen the ruined shell of an eighteenth-century manor house near the crossroads she passed every day on the way to the excavation site. She tried to get her bearings from the map in front of her, looking for familiar names or features.

"Here's where we are right now," Cormac said, indicating a long, irregularly shaped land mass that seemed to be in the middle of a bog.

"So we're actually on an island?"

"Yes; there was a bridge built across the bog a hundred and fifty years ago," Scully said. "It looks like a peninsula now, but it was originally a dryland island. There were hundreds of islands like it, all across the bog. You often hear mention of such islands in the old place-names."

"Where's the excavation site?" Cormac pointed to an area only an inch away on the map, and the pieces began to fall into place. There was the place where the workshop was now, the tracts of bog that were all drained and measured on Nora's own map.

"The Dowris hoard was found just over here," Scully said. The Dowris treasure, one of the most famous Iron Age discoveries in Ireland, made up of hundreds of mysterious horns, crotals, and other votive objects, had been deposited in a bog about fifteen miles away.

"And where was the Loughnabrone hoard found?"

Scully's thin finger pointed to the spot only about a quarter-mile distant.

Nora said, "So we have a couple of major Iron Age hoards and two possible sacrifices that follow the pattern of the triple death—all this from the same small spot." She turned to Scully. "You haven't by any chance heard that another body was found on Loughnabrone Bog the other day? Not ancient remains—much more recent."

"No, but I miss a lot now that I can't get into town as often as I used to. Have they identified the body?"

"Not officially, but everyone thinks it's someone from around here—a guy named Danny Brazil, who supposedly emigrated twenty-five years ago and was never seen again. A strange name, isn't it—Brazil? Is it Irish?"

"Yes," Scully said, "from the Irish Ó Breasail. Historical sources say they were mainly found in Waterford, but there's long been a pocket of Brazils in Offaly as well."

"Did you happen to know Danny Brazil?" Nora asked.

"The family are our nearest neighbors. Danny used to keep bees the hill here behind the house. Was it an accidental death

"The police don't think so. They're calling it a murder.
say any more than that."

"Well, I'm stunned. Who would want to kill Danny Brazil? He was a hero, a champion in these parts, a splendid hurler. And his injury came at the worst possible time for the Offaly team. They were in with a chance that year, but when he dropped out—well, their chance dried up, vanished straightaway. An awful shame."

"You don't think his death had anything to do with that?" Nora asked.

"With dropping off the hurling team in the middle of the championship? Ah, no; he was very seriously hurt. I saw it happen myself, along with thousands of other people. No one thought he was feigning the injury—and why would he do a thing like that? He wanted them to win as desperately as we all did; they just couldn't pull it off without him."

Nora's brain began to simmer with unanswered questions. From what was known about the few triple deaths, it seemed as though the victims had been killed during periods of great social stress, especially when food supplies were scarce. What if there were other kinds of social stress— adversity or bad luck—that some people still believed could only be lifted through blood sacrifice? She cast the thought aside. There had to be another, more logical reason that Danny Brazil had been killed in such a mysterious, ritualistic way.

Cormac had been silent for some time. Now he asked, "Michael, do you happen to remember reading anything in O'Donovan's work, or in any of the older manuscripts, anything that mentions this area being known as a place of votive deposits or sacrifices?"

"Nothing that I can recall, not specifically. The medieval writers might not have known about such things, or might have chosen to suppress them if they did know. But it certainly fits with the ancient name of this place," Scully said. "According to O'Donovan, the patch of ground we're standing on is called Illaunafulla—'Island of Blood.' O'Donovan had no explanation for it; he just noted that that was the name he'd found in the annals."

Nora felt as though someone had run a cold finger down her spine. "And what about Loughnabrone?" she asked. "I meant to ask Cormac what it means. I know *lough* means 'lake,' but what's the rest of it?"

"It's quite a grand poetic name. Shares the same root as my daughter's name—*brón*," Michael Scully said. "*Loughnabrone* means 'Lake of Sorrows.'"

9

It was Midsummer's eve, the longest part of the year, and felt like it, Nora thought. Another eight hours on the bog today, and not even another fingernail. She looked with envy at Ursula's team, who were making great progress with their bog road, and sighed. They were finishing up for the day, gathering up their tools, tossing trowels and kneepads into their buckets, spades and rakes into the wheelbarrows for the trek back to the trailer. Some of the crew were spreading black plastic tarps over the cuttings.

Nora packed up her own tools, wished her fellow crew members a good evening, and started back to her car, passing Ursula's team on the way.

Rachel Briscoe seemed agitated as she searched through one of the buckets. "Where are they?" she demanded of the first person she saw, a young woman clearing away debris nearby.

"Where are who?" the other girl asked, irritated. "What are you on about?"

"My binoculars. I put them right on top of this bucket."

"Look, Rachel, how should I know? I never went near them."

Another of the archaeologists, a young man, approached Rachel from behind. "Here they are," he said. "I was just having a look at some wildlife—"

"Give them to me," Rachel said. She reached to take the field glasses from his hand, but he stepped aside and moved them just out of her reach, teasing. Rachel gave him a look of pure hatred and formed her words slowly: "I said, give them to me."

"Off to do a little bird-watching again tonight, are you?"

Neither of them noticed Ursula striding toward them. "Oh, for God's sake, grow up, will you?" Her voice cut through the air as she snatched the binoculars from the young man's grasp. She held them out to Rachel, who stared at her for a long moment before taking them and stalking off without a word. Nora was close enough to read Rachel's expression, and what she saw was a violent churning beneath the pale surface.

Nora had only been here a couple of days, but it was obvious to her that Rachel Briscoe stuck out among the archaeology crew. She thought it must be awkward for Rachel, effectively ostracized by her colleagues yet having to work and live and eat with them, day in and day out for weeks. No doubt this was like every other human endeavor; alliances and divisions were formed through no one person's conscious effort, under nobody's control. A group of people was something like a primitive organism, affected by mood and atmosphere and even weather, resistant to change, with each member playing a specific role. Leaders, followers, scourges, clowns—every group had them, and people slipped into their parts as easily as actors taking on familiar stock roles.

The boy had mocked Rachel for bird-watching, or was it for bird-watching at night? The bog was a great place for birders, Nora knew, but why should such an innocent interest provoke such an extreme reaction? Perhaps it wasn't innocent; perhaps there was some subtext, some implication she was missing. It wouldn't be the first time.

The Bord na Móna minivan pulled up beside the hut and the crew began to pile in for the ride home. Nora saw Rachel hang back, perhaps reluctant to face her tormentor. The minivan driver shouted, "Are you coming, then?" The girl shook her head, and the driver backed out of the gravel parking area and stepped on the gas. Rachel set out walking.

When she had packed up her things, Nora pulled the car alongside Rachel and let the window down.

"Can I give you a lift?"

The girl seemed annoyed that Nora was bothering her. She marched stoically onward. "I'll walk. It's only a couple of miles."

"You shouldn't really walk alone out here. Please, Rachel, I insist." At the use of her name, the girl hesitated momentarily, and Nora thought she might run. But there was nowhere to go, only black bog for acres and acres to the horizon. She finally climbed in, hefting her heavy rucksack onto her lap. She sat quite still, and her beetlelike posture spoke volumes about defensiveness and mistrust. Nora wondered what was inside the bag, besides her precious binoculars.

Nora said, "The friend I'm staying with is part of the archaeology department at UCD—you didn't happen to study there?"

"No," Rachel said curtly. She obviously hadn't accepted the lift because she was starved for conversation.

"You'll have to tell me where I'm going. I'm not sure." Rachel gave her the route, then was silent again. "Do you all share the same house?" A wordless nod. "What is there for people your age to do out here all summer? Sorry, I don't mean to interrogate you; I'm just curious. Ten weeks out here must seem like an eternity—"

"I don't know what the others do. I don't spend time with them when we're not working. They mostly go home at the weekends." Implying that she didn't. Rachel Briscoe seemed particularly young at that moment, vulnerable and alone. Nora didn't know what else to say.

They turned near the McCrossans' cottage, then navigated a few sharp turns on narrow little roads before arriving at an old two-story white farmhouse. The minivan was just leaving; Nora had to stop beside the gate to let it pass. When she pulled into the drive, Rachel opened the door and slid out quickly.

"Thanks for the lift, but I'll be all right on my own from now on." It was a final dismissal, as if Rachel had realized she shouldn't have let anyone get this close. Why not? She shut the door and marched stolidly toward the house. Nora could hear thumping music already coming from its open windows, and felt again what it was like to be somehow apart from all those around you. She had some firsthand experience of not fitting in, but she had early on taken refuge in books and music, in the elegant, abstract beauty of the biological world. She had spent many hours in school peering through a lens at microscopic bacterial colonies, oblivious of the corresponding macroscopic social activity around her. Perhaps it had been just as well. Solitary bird-watching might be Rachel Briscoe's escape. Making yourself an outcast was one way to avoid the pain of having it done to you.

It wasn't until she pulled into the driveway behind the McCrossans' cottage that she noticed a folded paper down beside the passenger seat. Unfolding it, she found a brief, polite form letter requesting the return of several books borrowed from the Pembroke Library in Ballsbridge, Dublin. It must have fallen from Rachel's pocket as she climbed out of the car. Scanning it again, Nora noticed that the letter was addressed not to Rachel Briscoe, but to someone named Rachel Power. Was the girl using a false name here? Unless Power was the false name. Kids knew enough to use fake identities on the Internet; maybe they did it elsewhere as well. She might have a very good reason for going by two different names. Nora left the letter folded on the passenger seat—she could return it in the morning.

She must have seen Cormac's yellow waterproof jacket and trousers hanging outside the back door before, but this evening something in the way the garments were draped over the peg made her do a double-take. With the wellingtons standing at attention below, they looked almost like a person pressed flat against the wall. Nora pushed at the yellow rubber and felt it collapse beneath her hand.

She heard music as she approached the door, so she opened it silently and stepped into the entryway to listen. It was not a recording, as she'd first thought, but Cormac playing the flute as she'd never heard him play—flat-out, ferociously, full of joy and pain and exultation, the attack of air, breathing the fullness of experience into the notes, so that life became music, and music became life, in all its frustrating, overwhelming glory. The movement from slow air to reel left percussive notes ringing in the air, and the reel's whirling pagan flow felt unstoppable. She closed her eyes, leaned back against the wall, and let the music lift her in its vortex. She didn't know the name of the tune, but she had heard him play it before, although never with this kind of intensity. There was something inspired in him today; he was on fire, stoked by the passion in the notes.

Finally the flow of music slowed, eddied, and died away. Nora pushed away from the wall and touched Cormac from behind, sliding her arms down his chest. He wasn't surprised; on the contrary, he seemed to be expecting her, and turned toward her to accept the hungry, searching kiss she offered. He set the flute down on the table and guided her onto his lap as they continued tasting each other, drowning in sensation, as if this were the first and not the thousandth time their lips had met. A fragment of a song came into Nora's mind, something about ivy twined around an oak. Which was need, and which was love? The question slipped away unanswered, replaced by a ferocious abandon, desire so strong she might have given up anything at that moment to see it fulfilled.

And then it shattered, dropping in shards and splinters around her feet. The change was so sudden and frightening that she jerked her head away and gasped, causing Cormac to catch her shoulders in alarm. She stood and staggered backward, marking the fear in his expression and knowing there was no way she could explain what had just happened.

She didn't know if she could bear the way he looked at her. She made a bolt for the stairs and shut herself in the bathroom, running the bathwater to cover the sound of her tears. A long soak would wash them away, the tears, the deceit, and make her feel whole again; at least she hoped it would. But the look on his face, the shock and hurt as she backed away—she knew that was only a fraction of what he would feel when she told him she was leaving, and the prospect made her shoulders shake more violently with each shuddering sob.

She'd been in the bath twenty minutes when she heard a soft rap at the door. "Nora, are you all right? Please talk to me."

"Come in." The door opened a crack and she could see his worried face. "You can come all the way in."

He crouched by the end of the tub where her head emerged from the bubbles. The house had been newly fitted out, but it still had an old claw-footed tub, wide and deep. She closed her eyes and felt his fingers brush against her cheek. He kissed her forehead, her burning eyes. She lay back and listened as he poured a drop of shampoo into his hands and began soaping her hair and scalp, massaging her pounding temples with slow, rhythmic strokes. She could feel her fear break up and wash away as he rinsed the soap from her hair. As she rose dripping from the water he wrapped her in a huge white towel, then carried her in his arms the short distance to the bedroom. And this time nothing shattered; there was only triumphal yielding, sweet blending.

10

Charlie Brazil waded through the tall grass at the edge of the apiary, his mouth dry and a twisting knot in his stomach. Strange things had been happening here the last few days. He felt eyes on him, heard whispers wherever he went, and rumors swirled through the air like ghosts. He'd come home this evening to find that detective, the same one from all those years ago, speaking to his parents. He'd listened, watching and waiting outside until the policeman got into his car and drove away. Apparently all the whispers had been true: the body from the bog was his father's only brother, Danny Brazil. But when he'd gone into the house a few minutes later, neither of his parents had spoken a word about it.

But Danny Brazil wasn't the reason for this clenched knot beneath his ribs—not exactly. How did Ursula know about what he'd got up here? She couldn't know anything; she couldn't. She was just having him on, playing him. But she must have been here—how else would she know about Brona? He felt the burning shame come over him once more, remembering how it had felt when Ursula sat straddling him, the edge in her voice when she'd talked about Brona. He'd wanted to throttle her, rip her for thinking that way; he couldn't bear it. Raising a hand to wipe the bitter taste of hatred from his lips, he heard something and stopped abruptly, midstride.

His beekeeping shed had no door, and he could hear a noise from inside, a faint tearing sound. It was her again. He crouched by the window, peering through the weeds up into the loft at Brona Scully, once again illuminated in a shaft of late-evening sun. She sat on her feet, deeply immersed in ripping some piece of cloth to ribbons. Surely she knew that he came here every day; surely she saw that the bees were looked after? But today he was earlier than usual. Watching her behave as though she were completely alone gave him a kind of guilty thrill, the same thing he'd experienced following his mother up here all those years ago. The sun shone through the edges of her shift, and her thin, pale arms looked gilded.

All at once a dog began to bark in the distance, and Brona got to her feet and bolted down the stairs before he had a chance to hide himself. It was the very first time their eyes had met, and Charlie felt electrified by her gaze. She, too, seemed shocked, momentarily paralyzed at seeing him not an arm's length away. As she came through the door, his arm shot out and snaked around her waist; for a brief, breathless moment he held her there, transfixed by the galvanizing jolt that passed through him as he felt her warmth through the thin cloth. The ground seemed to rise in a roiling wave beneath his feet when she let out a short gasp, the only sound he'd ever heard her make. Then she was gone, pushing past him before he could even react.

She was anxious, frightened—because of him? The idea upset him. He went back over the frozen moment in his mind: the terrified look in the girl's eyes; her face streaked with tears, he realized now, bright tracks down her pale, lightly freckled cheeks. It wasn't her eyes he'd stared at when they'd stood face to face, but her lips, moving noiselessly. He found himself wondering if she made any sound at all when she wept. He was seized with a fierce desire to hold her, help her in some way.

He hesitated, wondering whether he should follow her, not wanting to step from the place he'd first touched her, rooted to the spot as if under a spell, weakened by her gaze. Then the feeling passed; he turned slowly and sat on the steps up to the loft, turning over the scene in his mind, reliving the startling shock of touching her, going through in slow motion how he'd put out his hand, how his arm had circled her, briefly. He had only been trying to stop her so that he could see what was wrong, how he might help her—how could he communicate that? Most people said she was a deaf-mute, but others protested that she wasn't deaf, only refusing to speak, stubborn, touched. He knew the truth; she understood every word you said to her. And there was no mistaking the looks she got, a mixture of pity and contempt. Charlie knew those looks because he'd received them himself—cultivated them, in fact. It was easier than trying to fit in, which was hopeless in any case.

She must have known that they would sooner or later meet on this threshold. What had she imagined happening then? He'd tried to keep from thinking of it, alone in his narrow bed at night, filled with yearning for which there was no relief. He couldn't allow himself to think of touching her in that way, but sometimes he awakened drenched in sweat, the bedclothes sticky, and he felt ashamed of what his unconscious mind desired. He hung his head and tried to wipe that sensation from his memory, knowing it could never be erased—the feeling of her hipbone under his palm, the friction of the two fabrics rubbing together under the weight of his hand. It was automatic, he told himself, just a reflex. Anyone would have put out a hand to stop her.

Charlie climbed the ladder to the loft to see what she'd been at. He found a cardboard suitcase lying open, its contents jumbled about—a man's suitcase, by the look of it. Definitely a man's clothing. Where had she found it? Or perhaps she'd brought it with her. He'd been up here a few times and never found anything like that, but the loft was filled with boxes of nails gone to rust, old milk cans, spools of rotted baling twine. He knelt and lifted one of the shirts. Those were what Brona had been after. There were two completely torn up, the bodies and arms shredded to ribbons. What was she up to?

A pile of yellowed newspaper cuttings had been tossed aside; Charlie picked up the top one, gone soft with mildew and almost illegible. It was a smudgy photo of two hurlers struggling for control of a ball, one gripping the other's shirt, feet and ankles covered in mud, teeth gritted fiercely as they concentrated on the ball. He quickly pawed through the other cuttings; they were all about the Loughnabrone hurling club and the Offaly team. Beneath the cuttings was a polythene bag containing a few old snapshots. Most of the images were stuck to one another, the photographic emulsion turned sticky with age and damp. A single picture had been facing the polythene and was still intact except for slight discoloration at the edges. He edged nearer a hole in the thatching so that he could have a look at it in the light. A young woman stared at the camera thoughtfully, skirt pulled over her drawn-up knees. Charlie recognized the setting: it was the downstairs of this house, in better repair in those days. The photo was slightly out of focus, but not so blurred that he couldn't recognize the young woman as his mother.

A faint buzzing noise arose as he tried to make out the expression on the face in the photograph. Without warning, a large, sticky drop of golden honey fell from above, directly onto the photograph. He pulled it out of harm's way—too late—then looked up and watched another drop stretch from the ceiling and fall in the same place, onto a growing mound of crystallizing sweetness on the floor. The bees had gotten into the roof and recognized the dark, enclosed space between the beams as suitable for a hive. They'd have to be shifted, and a bucket put under the drip until he had time to do it. The bees, not knowing it was their own store escaping, would bring the honey back, one drop at a time, only to lose it again.

He looked back at the photograph, thinking how young his mother looked, and wondering if he could somehow rinse away the sticky residue without ruining it. Had this place been her retreat even then? But the suitcase was a man's, he was almost sure of it. Charlie felt something hovering in his consciousness, unnamed, unrealized, an idea that had yet to take shape. He tossed the picture aside. He'd have to think about it later. Right now he had to know if Ursula had been here. If she had—

He cursed himself again for his stupid mistake, letting Ursula catch him looking at her maps. He felt his palms go damp, remembering how she had circled around him and blocked the door, not letting him out until he was shaking and covered in sweat. And then yesterday afternoon she'd stopped him behind the supply trailer. At least he hadn't told her anything. She couldn't know.

He dropped to the place he used for hiding things, a hollowed-out space under one of the flagstones near the fire. He'd hidden a biscuit tin there, to make a safe place for the things he didn't want robbed. He used the poker to pry the flagstone up, and found the tin just where it should be. He'd looked in it only a few days ago, and everything seemed to be there. His eyes traveled over the familiar shapes: two fingerlike silver ingots; fourteen bronze rings—he counted to make sure they were all there; six coins; four bracelets, ends flared like trumpets; and a dagger, its greenish sheath graved with sinuous scrolls. Everything was exactly where he'd left it, he was sure. He glanced around, checking the windows and the door to see how anyone might be able to look into this protected space.

He couldn't leave the box here now; what if she'd found it and just decided not to take anything? But where could he hide it? She could be watching now, to see what he would do. He was caught again. He had no way to know for certain whether she had been there. Everything was in the box, but maybe she'd taken something else, left something for him.

He searched the walls and windows for any mark, anything out of place. Then he saw it: the blank space on the wall where he'd tacked up the other beekeeper's drawings. He started pulling down the remaining sketches, ripping them in his fury, heedless of the thumbtacks flying everywhere and rolling dangerously underfoot.

11

The long golden twilight was beginning to wane outside the bedroom window. Lying tangled in the sheets with Cormac, watching him sleep, was a rare luxury. But Nora felt her blissful, dreamy state dissipate as her stomach's emptiness made itself known. She'd have to get something to eat.

"Cormac, are you awake? I'm starving. Do you want anything?"

He opened his eyes and looked at her a long moment, and not as if he was thinking about food. Finally he said, "I'll come with you."

They were foraging in the kitchen when the bell sounded, and Nora turned to see Liam Ward's angular profile framed in the diamond window of the front door. "It's Ward, that detective I told you about."

When she answered the door, Ward's face wore a somewhat worried expression. "Sorry for intruding, Dr. Gavin. I was just at—I was passing by, and I had a few more questions for you about the postmortem, if you have a few minutes."

"Of course. Come in."

The policeman stepped into the tiny front hall and offered his hand to Cormac. "I don't believe we've met. Liam Ward."

"Cormac Maguire."

"Won't you sit down?" Nora asked, ushering him into the inner room. Ward eyed the two places set at the table and moved to one of the leather chairs near the fireplace. Nora sat down across from him, and Cormac perched on the arm of her chair.

"Any luck yet in identifying the body?" Nora asked. "Everyone's been talking about it."

"As a matter of fact, someone did come forward with information, and the positive ID came through yesterday. The victim was Danny Brazil. You probably heard some speculation about it. His family thought he'd emigrated to Australia twenty-five years ago. They say they didn't expect to hear from him, and they never did."

"How can I help you?"

"Well, you mentioned something yesterday at the postmortem, and it's been with me ever since—this notion of 'triple death.' Can you tell me any more about it?"

Nora felt embarrassed. "I'm not sure I'm the one you should be asking. Cormac probably knows much more about it than I do."

"There's not much to know," Cormac said, "but I can tell you what I've read. The whole idea of triple death stems from the fact that some bodies found in bogs seem to have sustained multiple mortal injuries. Up to this point, all the clearest examples have come from Britain and the Continent, but that could change as forensic methods improve. The man from Gallagh in Galway—he's on exhibit at the National Museum—is from the Iron Age, and it's quite possible that the twisted sally rods around his neck were some sort of noose or garrote. And from what Nora's told me, the older body from Loughnabrone was strangled with a narrow cord, then had his throat cut, and was deliberately sunk in the bog. At first glance that certainly seems like overkill, since any one of the three would have been enough to dispatch him. But taken together, they might add up to a classic triple death."

Ward pulled at his left ear. "So this triple death was a form of human sacrifice?"

"It's one possibility," Cormac said. "I'm not deliberately being difficult, but the Iron Age Celts operated in a completely oral culture; they never wrote anything down about their religious practices. Much of what we know about them was actually written by others, like the Romans, and a lot of that was based on hearsay rather than firsthand accounts. But something like the triple death probably did exist, according to the current scholarship."

"What was its purpose?" Ward asked.

Cormac said, "There are Roman sources that say each of the three major Celtic deities who required human sacrifice had a preferred method: the thunder god Taranis was appeased by fire or heavy blows like thunderbolts. Then there was Esus, who preferred his sacrifices hanged from a tree and cut until they bled to death. Sacrifices to the war god Teutates were usually dispatched by drowning. Personally, I don't think the Romans really had a firm grasp on barbarian religious practices. I think the reality was a bit more complicated than they imagined; after all, they considered other cultures inferior, barbaric. The Celts had numerous triple deities, one entity with three different aspects, sometimes three separate identities . . . when the early Christians were teaching about the trinity, the concept was already pretty old news in these parts. There's a strong streak of triplism that remains in us, even today."

Ward pulled at his lower lip and nodded slowly. "All those old pishrogues—making the sign of the cross three times."

"Exactly," Cormac said. "When it came to those ancient sacrifices, the three-in-one combination seemed to be all about augmenting power—both the power of the deity and of the person making the invocation. And a triple sacrifice, likewise, was intended to magnify and make an offering more powerful. To combine all three forms may have been a very powerful offering indeed, perhaps reserved for times of great crisis. And of course there were variations; sometimes the victim wasn't bashed over the head, or his throat wasn't cut. The hanging or strangling seemed to have been pretty consistent, as was disposition in the bog. Sometimes the victims were pinned down with wooden stakes."

"The older body from last week was clearly staked down," Nora said. "I didn't see any stakes around Danny Brazil's body, but it might be worth asking Rachel Briscoe if she remembers removing any sticks or branches from around the body—if someone is trying to make it look like a triple death, a small detail like that might be important."

"So who were the usual victims?" Ward asked. "How were they chosen?"

"Some of the bodies show no battle scars or evidence of hard labor, so one camp says that sacrificial victims were probably not warriors, and may have been fairly highborn individuals, possibly even priests. Of course, they may also have been criminals, or outcasts, or hostages taken in war. The Romans said that the Celts preferred sacrificing criminals, but if there were none, they would resort to using innocent people. But they also said the sacrifices were invariably performed in the presence of holy men or priests."

Nora said, "From what I've read, the victims were sometimes children, or people who were injured or malformed in some way—some had tubercular bones, some had extra fingers or toes. It's possible that they were chosen as scapegoats for those reasons."

"Or it may have been left to chance. Examination of some victims' stomach contents showed that they'd recently ingested blackened grain kernels. There's a theory that a burnt piece of bannock may have been used in a kind of deadly lottery. Several had apparently ingested grain contaminated with ergot, which can cause hallucinations and severe convulsions—so those victims might have been in some sort of altered state when they were killed. Archaeological evidence for any of these theories is very scant, especially here in Ireland, and what does exist is open to a number of different interpretations. In other words, no one really knows. Everything we've told you is built on a certain amount of speculation."

"Finding an ancient body that fits this pattern of multiple injuries isn't a complete shock," Nora said. "A number of victims have turned up, all across northern Europe, with similar wounds; most of them date from the Iron Age—about two thousand years ago."

Ward began to nod slowly. "But finding a modern victim with similar injuries only a hundred yards away . . ."

"Yes, that's what's really strange," Nora said. "It's a very odd coincidence, to say the least."

Ward's expression was thoughtful. "Or maybe it's not just a coincidence. Is it possible that someone might have discovered the older body at some point and not reported it?"

Nora said, "Yes, I suppose. But if you're asking whether anyone could tell whether something like that had happened, the answer is probably not. We can tell if an area is backfill, but not how many times it's been disturbed."

"But chances are the perpetrator in the more recent case would most likely be someone who's at least acquainted with this whole idea of triple death."

Cormac said, "If this Danny Brazil disappeared more than twenty-five years ago, remember that much less was known about bog remains in those days. A lot of the forensic information we have these days has only come to light since then."

Ward pursed his lips in displeasure. "Well, thank you both for the information." He rose and went slowly to the door; before opening it, he paused, pulled out a card, and handed it to Nora.

"I'd be obliged if you'd contact me if you think of anything else—just in case there are more similarities between your ancient man and our modern victim. Thank you again for your time."

12

All the way to the Moors, Ward kept seeing Danny Brazil, stripped of his clothes, a prisoner in the bog. Whose prisoner? Had there been one captor, or a whole group? They would have to look for connections to other cases, anything that might resemble a kind of sacrifice: animal mutilations, victims or crime scenes marked with any significant symbols or patterns, victims treated in any ritual way. If it had been a group of people, they must have had a trigger. Something must have precipitated the death. Perhaps it was tied to the calendar, or something less regular. What was it Maguire had said? *Times of great social stress.* That would include famine, obviously, or danger from an invading force. What about power plants shutting down, a way of life dependent upon peat going the way of all things? He knew it took less than people imagined to push things over the edge.

Working from the date Danny Brazil was last seen, Maureen Brennan had checked the date on Brazil's watch. Midsummer's eve, the twentieth of June, had fallen on a Tuesday in 1978. The date hadn't come around on a Tuesday again until 1989, then 1995, and then 2000; it was a very irregular pattern. That information, and the state of his teeth, told them that Danny Brazil had never left Offaly. He had gone into the bog at the same time he was last seen.

Ward knew he had to dig up yet another Danny Brazil—the one who had never really disappeared, who remained in memory, whose time on earth had left ripples when he sank into that bog hole. His job was to follow all those ripples and find out where they led.

Arriving at the hotel, he looked forward to seeing Catherine Friel's face. His wife's death had made him draw back into his tortoiseshell, closed off from the world of experience and risk. Catherine was pulling him out of that, ready to expose himself to hurt and danger. And it felt exhilarating, that primitive, mysterious chemical and biological phenomenon—an intense, unsettling feeling, rooted in the primeval senses of touch and smell. What was it that drew him to Eithne, to Catherine, to anyone?

As he walked across the gravel drive and glanced into the restaurant, lit only by candles and the setting sun, he imagined her sitting across from him at the table, glowing in the flickering candlelight, perceptive of his unspoken yearning and reflecting it back to him. How natural, then, that after they finished the meal and lingered deliberately over the last of the wine and coffee, they would climb the stairs together, she leading and he following, until they stood behind the closed door of her room. . . . The momentary dream was shattered as the flat-nosed grille of a gold Mercedes came to an abrupt stop only a few feet from his knees, and the driver let down the window to offer a few choice words of advice.

Ward didn't raise his eyes to the sputtering driver, but tramped slowly toward the door with measured steps. When he got inside, he was surprised by a bar stripped down to stone walls and wooden floor, with modern leather furniture in the seductive colors of exotic spices. He caught sight of Catherine Friel's silver hair; her back was to him, and as he approached, wondering whether he should touch her arm or call her name, she turned slightly and he saw that she was speaking on a mobile. He stopped his advance and stood a few yards away to afford her at least a small amount of privacy.

"I can't stay on the phone now, John, I've got to go. . . . Yes, I'm having dinner with a colleague. . . . No, no one you know, a detective. We're going to talk over the case. He's probably waiting for me now." She turned to check the room and saw Ward. "There he is. I should be home tomorrow evening. . . . Yes. . . . Good night now, love."

As he heard the last phrase, Ward felt foolish for entertaining notions about Catherine Friel. Her interest was in the case, that was all. It had been so long since he'd even allowed himself to imagine such a closeness, and now he shut the notion down, psychologically boarded it up, so quickly that by the time they entered the dining room he'd nearly forgotten the vision he'd had of himself and Catherine Friel there in the candlelight, and in the darkness upstairs, just beyond the locked door.

13

"I suppose the police are always reluctant to declare any death a ritual killing," Cormac said, digging into his second plate of pasta. "Given a choice, they'd probably prefer old-fashioned, understandable motives. And I'll bet a good portion of ritual killings turn out to be ordinary garden-variety murders dressed up after the fact to try and put detectives off the scent."

Nora chased the last couple of penne around her own nearly empty plate and took another sip of wine. "I wish there was more we could do to help. Think about it, Cormac—he was probably still alive when he went into the bog hole."

"But what else can we tell Ward? We don't know anything about the victim, the circumstances of the crime."

"We don't know anything about Danny Brazil, but we may know something about the circumstances."

"What do you mean?"

"We know something about the other people found with the same kinds of injuries. It would just be interesting to compare Danny Brazil to other possible triple-death victims—to take a really close look and see what the similarities and differences are. I should ask Rachel Briscoe, the girl who found him, if she removed any wood from around the body. The crime-scene people may not have been looking for stakes or branches, but if he was staked down, that would fit with earlier finds."

"How are we going to do all this research without the materials we'd need?"

She shot him a sheepish look. "All my research files are in the trunk of the car. I figured if you were getting some work done here, I might have a chance as well."

Cormac leaned back in his chair and laced his fingers together behind his head. "It's likely that the police will come up with something sooner than we would. I mean, it is pretty coincidental that the victim turns out to be one of the two people who'd found a cache of treasure only a short time earlier. This story is probably all about money or love gone wrong, and we might just be chasing wild geese."

"I know, but we still might find something useful. And anyway, it's interesting. I was thinking—if the injuries were deliberate, what sort of person would have known so much at that time about triple death? Danny Brazil went missing in the late seventies. Most of the research comparing causes of death has been done in the last ten years or so. But certain people would have had access to that kind of information before it was widely known—"

"Certain people like archaeologists, you mean."

"Maybe. Anyway, I can't help thinking about all this. It's a puzzle." And it wasn't the only one, either, she thought. There were the riddles of Owen-and-Ursula, Ursula-and-Charlie, and Rachel Briscoe/Rachel Power. Not to mention the difficult Cormac-and-Nora conundrum, which might not have any solution.

She got up to clear, trying to avoid Cormac's eyes. He caught her wrist as she was about to remove the plate in front of him, took the cutlery from her other hand, and set it on the table.

"Leave it, Nora. I can do all that later." He stood and slipped his hand into hers. "I know it's been a long day, but are you up for a short expedition? There's something I'd like to show you."

"What is it?"

"If I told you, it wouldn't be a surprise, now, would it?" He stopped. "You'll probably want to wear your wellingtons."

She eyed him skeptically. "Do I really want a surprise that involves wellingtons?"

He nodded. She retrieved her boots from the car and put them on while leaning against the back bumper, and Cormac did likewise. Then he led her up over the gap in the stone wall, into the pasture that rose to a small hill at the back of the house. The grass was cropped close to the ground, and the handful of cattle grazing the field watched their progress with that typical bovine mixture of curiosity and detachment.

"Where are we going?" she asked.

"You'll see." Cormac turned back to glance at her, but his close-lipped smile gave nothing away. The gentle slope had turned into a steep grade. "You can see Michael Scully's house from here, off to our right," Cormac said. "And the Brazils must be the next farm, way down at the other end of this ridge. The white house over there"—he indicated a plain but freshly painted bungalow just over the ridge—"is the Bord na Móna house where Ursula Downes is staying this summer." At the mention of the name, Nora felt a twinge of discomfort, remembering the conversation she'd overheard yesterday afternoon. She didn't ask Cormac how he happened to be in possession of that fact.

Breathing hard, they finally reached the top of the hill, a flat tabletop that afforded a view for miles around. It helped that the surrounding area was mostly bogland, stretching endlessly into the distance before them. About a quarter-mile to the northeast stood a pair of bottle-shaped cooling towers, the old Loughnabrone power plant due to be demolished soon. Far in the distance, Nora could see the red-and-white striped smokestack of the power station at Shannonbridge.

It was after ten o'clock, and the sun was setting under a bank of dark clouds, glowing golden and leaving the horizon bathed in oranges and pinks and purples. Despite its detrimental effect on the air quality, the peat dust in the atmosphere contributed to the beauty of the sunsets. There was always that tension in life, beauty walking hand in hand with danger.

"What do you suppose will happen here, when all the bogs are gone?" she asked Cormac.

"I don't know. I try to remember that it's in their nature to return. The moss can't help growing." That brainless proliferation, Nora thought; life asserting itself as it always did, and as it always would, please God.

"All right, you'll have to close your eyes from here," he said. "I promise I won't let you stumble."

Nora hesitated only a moment before closing her eyes and taking his hand. It was a strange sensation, walking through a field as though blindfolded. They were moving along the top of the hill, she thought, then down a gentle slope. She lurched dangerously a few times, but, as he'd promised, Cormac didn't let her fall. At last he stopped and stood behind her, setting her shoulders between his hands. "Here we are."

Nora opened her eyes. Directly before her stood a small whitethorn tree, covered in a colorful mishmash of ribbons and rags. Thick vines twisted up the trunk, and faded white blossoms peeped out from between the weathered scraps of fabric. Nora's mouth opened in wonder, and she moved to examine the strange man-made foliage, overwhelmed by the wild assortment of fetishlike objects that had been tied to the branches: neckties, old gloves and socks, numerous rosaries, a scapular, several handkerchiefs, a hair ribbon, a frilly wedding garter, three hairbands, a holy medal of the Virgin, a hairnet, a knitted bag, several plastic bags with bits of cloth inside, a tiny stuffed bear, a Sacred Heart bookmark. Around the trunk hung a black patent-leather purse, as though the tree had grown up through its handles. It was impossible to believe that this was the work of one consciousness, one pair of hands. Despite the fact that it had been created from a jumble of mad-looking, cast-off junk, the little tree presented an aura of holiness. It was like a prayer of some kind.

She stood still beneath the branches, absorbing its weird energy, until Cormac came up behind her and slid his arms around her waist. She shivered slightly and leaned back into him, feeling the roughness of his face on her neck.

"Astonishing, isn't it? I haven't seen anything like this in years. My grandmother's neighbor, Mrs. Meagher, used to save bits of things all year and tie them on the whitethorn bush outside her house on the first of May. I once made the mistake of asking why she did it, and she told me I'd no business being so bold. I don't think she even knew. I suppose she'd been doing it her whole life and didn't think it a good idea to stop. My grandmother said people used to do it as protection against the fairies. Anyway, I hope you like it—my offering to you."

"I love it, Cormac." She kissed him, and in the kiss was a fervent prayer that they might stay here, forever sheltered in this sacred place. She felt a breeze come up from the east, setting all the ribbons into an excited flutter, and had an unmistakable premonition that this deceptively calm evening held mischief or malice, or both. She shivered again, and Cormac held her more tightly.

"I saw Brona Scully up here the other day," he said.

"Tell me about Brona, Cormac. I think I saw her watching us from upstairs when we went over to the Scullys' house last night." The girl's sudden, erratic movement at the window came back to her. "Is she—is she all right?"

"Right in the head, you mean? Hard to say. As a child, she used to speak, but she suddenly went silent—about ten or twelve years ago, I think. I can't remember exactly."

Nora thought back to Ursula's conversation with Charlie Brazil, and her callous reference to Helen Keller. *That little girlfriend of yours*, Ursula had said. Who could she have meant but a girl who didn't speak? "Why would someone just stop speaking?"

"Most people seem to think it was brought on by some sort of trauma, but they're just guessing, and of course she can't—or won't—say."

"What sort of trauma?"

Cormac hesitated, then looked away. "Well, it was right around the time of her sister's death. Some people think Brona may have watched as the sister drowned herself."

"How awful."

"Nobody knows if it's true, Nora. It's only supposition."

She knew from experience how uncomfortable Cormac was in the realm of supposition, and she wasn't surprised when he changed the subject. "See that gravel ridge over there?" He pointed to a grassy knoll where the earth rose to a point and its rocky underbelly spilled out below. "Probably a bit of the Eiscir Riada that Michael Scully mentioned—the Great Road. What's left of it, anyway." Nora had begun to see the landscape differently since being with Cormac. She wanted to see what he saw, to know what he knew about these places, to see under the skin of the landscape down to the bones.

"I'm glad you liked the surprise," he said, when they were back home in bed. "I only wish I had such wonders for you every day."

Nora was silent for a while, listening to Cormac's steady heartbeat, mustering her courage. She would never be ready; she had to just open her mouth and speak.

"Cormac, I've been meaning to talk to you. I don't want to do it—I've been putting it off, but I can't any longer. It's not fair." She stopped to gather strength, preparing herself for his justifiable anger. "I can't stay here." She held her breath.

He was silent, unmoving against her. She hadn't wanted to blurt it out like that, with no warning, no preparation. What a coward she was, not able to look him in the eye.

But when he did respond, it was not in any of the myriad ways she had imagined. He only reached out and gathered her in closer until she could feel the warmth of his body all along the length of her own.

"I know," he said. "I've always known you'd have to go home. We've both been avoiding the subject. I just hoped it might be later rather than sooner."

She pulled away slightly and turned to look into his eyes, black pools in the encroaching darkness. "How did you know?"

"You're not a person who gives up, Nora." He ran one finger along the edge of her jaw and down her throat. "But neither am I."

She searched his face for proof that he would not give up, even when she was thousands of miles away, tangled up once more in the threads of a dark web that kept spinning and would never allow an end to grief. No matter how much Cormac might reassure her, and no matter how much she might wish for it, no such proof existed.

"Don't think about any of that right now," he said. "Rest yourself."

"But do you know why I have to go? I want you to understand. It's not that I want to leave you, Cormac. I don't. It's not just for Tríona's sake, but for my niece, for my parents—"

"I know," he said, pressing his lips close to her ear. "Shhh." She felt his arm close around her, locking them together at least for tonight, and she felt safe, surrounded, quiet inside. Eventually she drifted off, worn out by the long day, the wine, and a surfeit of emotion. She slept profoundly, heavily, like a person drugged.

14

At half past eleven, Liam Ward sat washed in the golden glow of his desk lamp, going through his coins. He wasn't a serious collector, not like the fanatical dealers with whom he'd corresponded from time to time. The coins in his collection were certainly old—mostly Roman-era English—but not all that rare; none of them could be considered extremely valuable. His was more an aesthetic appreciation; he enjoyed the artistry and symbolism of the form, liked feeling the weight of the coins in his hands, their surfaces worn smooth from touching the palms of generations before him. He liked to imagine their history, to envisage the multitude of debts each piece had paid.

They'd have to find out more about Danny Brazil's part in discovering the Loughnabrone hoard. Everyone had heard the rumors that there had been more to the hoard, that the Brazils hadn't turned everything over to the museum. Ward wondered whether Danny and his brother had shared everything equally. He had sensed some tension when Dominic Brazil spoke about the farm. It wouldn't be the first time that property had caused bitterness between family members, the kind of bitterness that sometimes led to murder. If Dominic had paid the brother for his share of the farm, where had all that money gone when Danny Brazil went into the bog? But if money was the motive, why go to such trouble—why not just bash him over the head, dump the body, and be done with it? No, the method suggested there was more to the story than simple money-grubbing. There were all the signs of sacrifice, and something in that smelled to Ward of revenge, of humiliation.

Another possible—though much less likely—theory was that Danny Brazil was a fallen hero, a champion cut down in his prime. Dr. Gavin's mention of damaged or deformed sacrificial victims had brought that into Ward's head. He thought about how seriously some of them took the hurling around here. You'd have thought it was their lives on the line with the outcome of a match. And what was sport, underneath, but a kind of sanitized, ritualized violence? Danny Brazil's injury had probably

cost his teammates the championship, the coveted McCarthy Cup. . . .
Ward had never been that much interested in sport himself, but he
thought of the faces he'd occasionally seen as a child—red faces con-
torted with pain and anger as a match slipped away. What was sport but
a thin veneer over the factional fighting it had replaced—ritualized violence, bloody entertainment?

Everywhere around them, in religion, in sport, in politics and entertainment, were daily reminders of how quickly one could go from being
carried on the shoulders of a jubilant crowd—greeted with palm fronds,
as it were—to being reviled, cast down, crucified and torn to pieces. The
pattern was too recognizable not to be seen. Blood lust he understood—
someone pushed too far over a tipping point. What he couldn't fathom
was the conspiracy that made it possible to carry out and cover up an
atrocity. But history was full of figures able to disconnect, to carry out
horrific acts and still pose as decent family men.

They'd have to get back to the Brazils, dig a little deeper. Ward had a
sense that Teresa Brazil and her husband knew more than they'd told
him, with the husband's illness providing an excuse when he didn't feel
like talking. And tomorrow he and Maureen could also start on Danny
Brazil's old hurling teammates, to see if they could shed some light on
the man. The farm, the family, the hurling, the workshop . . . where else
could Danny Brazil have got in over his head? Some of the seemingly
ritual murders carried out recently had turned out to be drug-related
executions. But illegal drugs—at least on the scale that usually accompanied killings—had been practically unknown in this area twenty-six
years ago.

There were plenty of leads to follow on this one—too many. And
many layers had settled over this murder in the years since the deed had
been done. Who knew what would come up when they started probing
around under the surface? Ward closed his coin album, placed it carefully back in the desk drawer, and turned the key in the lock.

15

Owen Cadogan drove to the abandoned storage shed at the edge of the Loughnabrone works and parked his car among the trees. He wasn't terribly worried about being seen. No one used the back road anymore since the pipe factory had closed down a few years ago. Thirty years earlier, when the bog was in full production, they'd built a factory adjacent to the workshop, to make cement drainpipes for siphoning the water off the peat. The factory had closed once all the drains were laid. Eventually it would all be gone, he thought, and himself with it.

He unlocked the storage shed with a key from the chain on which he kept his office and car keys. This was where he and Ursula had met last summer, hastily and on the sly. The taste of those illicit encounters lingered on the back of his tongue. She'd felt the same kind of excitement, he knew; now she claimed it was over, that she'd moved on, and didn't need him or want him anymore. After he'd spent the whole bloody winter dreaming of her, anticipating the next time.

He'd even started fantasizing about leaving Pauline, only to find out that what they'd done had meant nothing to Ursula. He had seen it in her eyes when she'd arrived this summer. He'd been a temporary diversion to her, nothing more. Anger and jealousy welled up in his throat, choking him. Nothing was over until he said it was over. He'd make sure she understood that.

No one else had a key to this building. He surveyed the small, crowded room, trying to keep alive the memory of how he'd felt there, looking at Ursula's glistening face, certain in the knowledge that he'd made her feel something. He'd enjoyed having her in this place, not at all like the comfortable marriage bed, but hard, rough, and dangerous. A person might get hurt here.

Moonlight filtered through the filthy glass of the window. He looked down and saw his own handprint on a bag of cement stacked in the corner of the shed, evidence of where, a few months earlier, he'd stood with his trousers around his ankles, gasping and straining against her. He'd never done with his wife the things he did with Ursula. The intensity of the release he felt with her actually frightened him, made him feel that he was somehow abnormal. But once tasted, it had spurred a hunger that nothing else would fill. And now she was demeaning him further by making him beg for it, by holding his need over him like a club.

He went over those first few moments again, as he had a thousand times before. He'd given Ursula a lift home after some official function over in Birr. The Carlton Arms Hotel. He remembered almost nothing about the journey now; it had been wiped out, obliterated by what had happened when they arrived at her place, what he'd come to think of as his final moments as an ordinary man. When he'd pulled the car up the drive of her rented house, she'd reached over without a word and unzipped his trousers. They'd both been half pissed, but not completely out of their heads, and he hadn't said no. How different everything would be now if he had.

After that night, they'd met almost daily in this old supply shed. There had been a few other places as well: in the woods bordering the canal, and once—only once, and most spectacularly—right out in the middle of the bog, on the sweet, yielding surface of a fresh peat stockpile under a full moon. That time had been so intense he'd thought he was having a heart attack, or a stroke at the very least.

Trying to re-create the intensity of that night, he'd emptied a dozen or more bags of peat moss onto the floor. Over the peat he'd draped woolen blankets. He now gathered them up and took them to the door and shook each one vigorously, until no more dust emanated with each snap of the rough fabric. When he had arranged the blankets once more, he stepped back and surveyed the scene. It was like a nest, an animal's lair. Perhaps that was why he'd never been able to recapture those few ecstatic moments out under the broad mantle of sky.

From behind a stack of cement bags, Cadogan coaxed a large metal toolbox. He flipped the latch to open the lid. No one had touched these things for a long time, the handcuffs, the velvet hood, the silk scarves. It was just games, he'd told himself, just elaborate playacting. Harmless, really. And it had all started innocently enough, when the necktie he'd taken off had become the rope in a playful tug-of-war. It was Ursula who'd suggested going further; he'd had to be talked into it. But the craving was within him now, had wormed its way into his mind like a sinister, corrupting force. He'd become an animal, a monster.

He took out the hood, felt the velvet fabric with his fingertips, and slipped it over his head, flushing with the memory of how Ursula had made use of it, teasing him to within an inch of his life. She might be finished with him, but he certainly wasn't finished with her. He pulled the hood off and put it back in the toolbox, then went to the door and flicked the light switch. The shed was well illuminated in the daytime, but he had to make sure he would have light at night. He counted the steps it took to get from the door to the makeshift bed. He threaded a strong cord through the leather cuffs. She wouldn't be able to wriggle free and evade him so easily here. He could talk to her all he liked. And he'd be gentle at first. But he'd make sure she felt his anger. She'd told him many times that she deserved to be hurt, and in this he was now more than willing to oblige.

Above the blankets was a shelf unit, through which was slung an assortment of hemp ropes and chains they'd rigged up to use with the cuffs. All very effective for his purposes. There was no danger the shelf would come down; he'd anchored it to the concrete wall himself, with six-inch bolts. He pulled one of the silk scarves from the toolbox, sliding it through his hands, pulling it taut. At first this had all been just a fantasy, but as he'd imagined it more and more, it had taken on a life of its own, and become a reality—or at least a possibility, and then a plan. She wouldn't suspect; it was nothing they hadn't tried before. He felt a frisson of excitement, thinking about the look that would come into her eyes when she realized that things were not going to go as they always had before, with her in charge.

Cadogan wound up the silk scarf and stuffed it into his pocket. Everything was ready. He walked slowly to the door, carefully going over all the details in his mind, then turned off the lights and locked the door behind him. No one would get into this place—or out of it—in a hurry.

The thought had crossed his mind a few times that perhaps she'd found someone else. If that was the case, he ought to warn the poor sod, before it was too late. It was too late for him, he knew—too late to go back to his former innocence. But what was done was done, and he'd never been one to wallow in misfortune. When something was finished, he forgot about it. He would forget about Ursula, too, as soon as he'd finished with her.

16

The fire was not difficult to start, given the recent dry weather. Charlie Brazil watched the flames leap higher as they consumed his broken frames, the bits of scutch he'd been saving for this night. The bullock he'd tied to the tree nearby lowed softly, alarmed by the fire's scent. Charlie leaned over to pick up a cup from the ground, and reached into his pocket for a penknife. He approached the frightened animal, moving slowly and speaking softly to allay its fears.

"You're all right, now. It'll all be over soon. Just keep still." The nervous bullock stamped its feet and eyed Charlie suspiciously as he inched nearer. He made a small but deep incision above the animal's left foreleg, and held the cup to the wound to collect the blood that flowed from it. When the cup was half-full, he pulled it away; the blood continued, coursing in a small stream down the bullock's leg. Charlie set his cup on the ground and reached into his pocket for a folded paper packet. He opened it and took out a flattened tangle of spider silk, and pressed it firmly against the wound. The bullock's dark brown eyes shone in the moonlight.

He returned to the fire, feeling its heat against his face and chest and thighs. He dipped his first three fingers into the blood and sprinkled the warm liquid into the fire, repeating the motion three times. The droplets sizzled as they came in contact with the flames. He murmured the old charm:

> "Three over me,
> Three below me,
> Three in the earth,
> Three in the air,
> Three in heaven,
> Three in the great pouring sea."

Then he poured the remaining liquid into the blaze and heard it hiss and sputter. He sat, knees drawn up to his chest, imagining that he saw fires on other hilltops in the distance, waiting for the flames to die down. By what he did tonight, he was making sure that Ursula Downes could not harm him, or anyone else, ever again.

17

The thudding music from the next room was giving Rachel Briscoe another grinding headache. She checked the clock; not time yet. Better to wait until after twelve, when it was really and truly dark. She closed her eyes and lay still, trying to quiet the thoughts, the colors and shapes that moved in her head.

The beat of the music coaxed her memory back to the spring. She'd been lying in bed at university, her windows open for the first time in the year. She'd emerged from sleep in darkness, to a noise coming from outside and above her bedroom window, a deep guttural sound. An animal, she'd thought at first. Then the cries had started to come faster and faster. When she'd realized what they really were—human noises, not animal—she'd felt embarrassed, repelled, fascinated. It had lasted only a few seconds, then all was quiet. People said it was a beautiful thing—but how could it ever be beautiful, she wondered, all that thrashing and howling like beasts? Her stomach knotted, remembering the disgust she'd felt. It remained one of the profound mysteries, what made men and women want to do those things to one another. But the worst thing was pretending that it was driven by love.

At eight minutes past twelve, Rachel got to her feet and looked around the room, surveying all it contained: a bed, a chair, a desk; herself and her rucksack. Nothing to tell anyone anything about her—no books, no music, no pictures. Only a few articles of clothing, a small clock, and some toiletries, all of which fit into her rucksack. She had to leave this room each night prepared never to return. And yet, so far, she always had returned, unable to let this part of her life go as eventually she must.

As she pulled on her jacket, she felt the pendulous weight of the binoculars in one pocket, her torch in the other—her two touchstones in this whole strange affair. She felt safer with them bumping against her legs. She checked to make sure no one was in the hallway, then left her room, shutting the door behind her. She would have locked it, if only she'd had the key. She passed the sitting room, seeing that Trish and Sarah were completely absorbed in some insipid pop-music program. They didn't give a toss what she did. It was the three lads who thought her strange, who couldn't resist slagging her, and who were probably puzzled by her total lack of interest in them. They had no way of knowing that she was here for reasons completely different from their own.

She quietly lifted her waterproofs from the hook and left the house by the kitchen door, careful to lock up after herself. Once outside, she struck out along the narrow lane, staying close to the verge so that she could avoid the headlights of any oncoming car, but sure there would be none. This road was dead quiet at night. A short distance down the lane, she climbed up and over a large metal gate, sinking into the soft ground churned up by the cattle that congregated there each morning and evening. She followed the field's bushy perimeter—a short, familiar walk over the hill, fifty yards this way, another thirty yards that way—until she came to the gap in the hedge. She ducked under, sure of her footing after treading the same path each night for the past couple of weeks.

Rachel began to feel the knot in her chest loosen as she approached her destination. She'd imagined it would be hard to live in secret. But she'd been shocked at how easy it was, how like second nature it had become for her to lie to people's faces. Perhaps it was more difficult when you were spurred by baser motivations. She felt herself to be above all that; it was love that was driving her, after all. This nightly trek was her own act of devotion, her own private pilgrimage. She always made sure no one saw her go out. And she had always made it back to the house before morning. But the late nights were beginning to take their toll, and she knew she wouldn't be able to maintain these sojourns forever. It had to come to an end, and soon. Perhaps tonight she'd have the courage to act. She tried to imagine what she would say, what Ursula would say, what they would both do, but she could not envision the scene. The future loomed empty ahead of her, beyond the point of confrontation, that precipice. She'd never pushed herself to a place like this before, and it was both frightening and exhilarating. She began to acknowledge that tiny flame inside her that relished the prospect that lay before her, the unknown, dangerous place she was about to tread.

Working with Ursula every day, watching her, studying her, was a chance she'd never even dared to imagine. She'd applied at the firm not even hoping for a spot on this dig, at least not right away. But it had fallen into place: first one of the archaeologists had got appendicitis just before work was to begin, and then her own application had been top of the heap when the position was to be filled. She couldn't have planned it better had she schemed and plotted for years. That had to mean something.

Rachel reached her place outside Ursula's house. She was sweating; her armpits and the small of her back felt clammy under her dark anorak. Taking the binoculars from her pocket, she let herself imagine briefly what her mother would say if only she could see her now. Rachel saw her mother's face, pale and luminous, beautiful as she herself had never been, never would be now. She cut off the thought, before any hint of disappointment was visible in her mother's face, before those lovely lips could utter her name.

The spot she'd come to was directly above and behind Ursula's house. She had a perfect view into the kitchen and the bedroom, the one where Ursula slept. The bathroom window was pressed glass, a translucent pattern through which Ursula's toweled head was sometimes visible after her nightly bath. Rachel knelt on the bed of leaves she'd arranged to make the spot more comfortable. She had been lucky in the weather. This summer had been incredibly dry so far; she'd only been rained on once—a minor miracle. She lifted the binoculars and focused on the kitchen table. An open bottle of red wine was there, as usual. No glass, though; she must have it with her. Rachel swung the binoculars from window to window, looking for Ursula's form or any sign of movement. She might be in the bath. But she usually brought the bottle if she was going to have a long soak. Rachel focused in on the bottle on the kitchen table. It was newly opened; probably Ursula had just gone into the bedroom and would return to the kitchen soon. She decided to settle in. She had waited so long for this opportunity, and everything was going so well, just as she had planned; what need was there to rush? She could certainly bide her time for another few minutes.

She opened her rucksack and felt around until her fingers found the flat bundle she sought, wedged up against one side. She drew it out, and slowly unwrapped a long-bladed knife, admiring the way the metal glowed dully in the moonlight. Sitting hidden in the hedge, feeling the blood pulsing through her temples and her breath slowly flowing in and out, Rachel suddenly realized that she had never felt more alive.

BOOK THREE

SPEAKING IN RIDDLES

They speak in riddles, hinting at things, leaving much to be understood.

—the Greek philosopher Poseidonius, writing about the Celts in the first century B.C.

1

When her alarm sounded at seven, Nora was first conscious of the fresh air coming in through the open window. She felt warm and comfortable in the bed, aware of Cormac's weight beside her. She resisted getting up right away; instead she turned to face him, luxuriating in this temporary illusion of domesticity. It was quite usual for her to fall asleep before he did, and that, added to the fact that they hadn't spent many nights together in the first place, meant she hadn't had many opportunities to study him as he slept. It was lovely seeing him so relaxed and oblivious, since that wasn't the usual picture she had of him. His hair was pushed into odd tufts where it rested against the pillow. She admired the natural embouchure of his lips that she found so pleasing, the slight concavity of the unshaven cheeks; her eyes lingered for a long while on the tiny whitened scar at the edge of his hairline. Her heart suddenly squeezed tight as a fist, thinking of all the stories she had not yet had a chance to know.

When she noticed a small smear of dried blood on the pillowcase, she suddenly remembered Detective Ward's plaster-patched shaving cut a few days earlier. Pushing the covers aside, she examined Cormac's neck and chest. No apparent wound. Then he stirred and turned over, and she saw three red lines on the side of his neck, fresh enough that they were still caked with a small amount of blood. She looked at her own fingernails, cut short. How could she have done that to him without knowing? But how else could he have acquired them? She tucked the duvet around him again. If she had hurt him, he had not complained.

Unwilling to wake him so early, she slid out of bed, slipped quickly into her jeans and work shirt, and carried her shoes downstairs. She moved around the kitchen, noting the dishes all washed and stacked neatly in the drainer. He'd been up again last night while she was asleep, tidying the kitchen, the books and papers on his work table. While she waited for the coffee to brew, she made some sandwiches to take out to the bog for lunch, and thought again about the night before: the fairy bush, her feeling that some mischief was afoot. Cormac hadn't seemed at all surprised when she'd finally told him she was leaving. He said he had always known—just as she had. But knowing didn't make it any easier.

When the coffee was ready, she poured it into her travel mug, added a drop of milk, and took it out to the car. Maybe it would be best to leave her files here today; that way Cormac could get started looking through them if he felt like it. She set the coffee in the car and went around to the trunk to unload her files. Lugging the heavy box into the house, she noticed that Cormac's waterproofs, which had been hanging on the hook outside the back door, were no longer there. It seemed curious. Why would he have moved them since last night? She didn't have time to puzzle over it at the moment. She was going to be late for her shift, sorting through drain spoil again today.

She knew her way to the bog by now, through the maze of crooked, unmarked lanes and hedge-choked byways. The distance was only a mile and a quarter, but the journey took at least fifteen minutes on these small roads. The power plant's strange, enormous towers were always a marker in the landscape. Cormac had been coming here for years, and must know every knoll and back road. Last night, from the hilltop, he'd given her a glimpse into the life of the place, into all the human activity—large and small—that had scratched the surface here.

She was approaching the house that Cormac had pointed out as Ursula's temporary home. Why did the woman make her so uneasy? Ursula's face rose up in Nora's memory, and for some reason she remembered the tissue in Cormac's bathroom bin, the soft, sensual impression of a woman's lips. She tried to banish the thought from her mind, but it clung like a cobweb to the edge of her consciousness.

It wasn't until she was past Ursula's house that Nora registered something odd about it. Checking to make sure that no one was behind her on the road, she slowly backed up to take a closer look. Her fleeting impression had been right; the front door was standing wide open, and what she presumed to be the sitting-room window was smashed.

Nora parked the car as far off the road as she could. She opened the trunk and reached for the tire iron, then slowly made her way up around the back of the house. The kitchen window was also broken, and the back door and shed door were wide open as well. Something was definitely not right here. Ursula should have been down on the bog already, and she wouldn't have left all the doors open. The house was still.

Nora approached, tire iron in hand, checking for broken glass on the ground. A few clumps of moss bloomed on the concrete foundation, and a painted clay drainpipe emerged from the wall under the bathroom window, probably from the tub or shower. She heard the *drip, drip, drip* of the pipe before tracing it all the way to the drain at the bottom, and looking down she felt a sharp electric jolt of fear. The small pool below the drain was dark crimson with blood. There was no mistaking the color.

She entered by the back door. A wine bottle and two glasses, one empty and one half-full, stood on the kitchen table. A few drops of blood spattered the floor in front of the sink and one of the chairs near the table. Nora moved quietly down the hall to the bathroom, barely breathing, and she looked in through the open door, unprepared for the full horror that awaited her there.

Ursula's wrists and ankles rested on the lip of the claw-footed tub, pale as porcelain. Her body was submerged beneath the water's surface, and mounds of peat had been heaped all around the base of the tub. The stillness, the strange and terrible intimacy of the scene before her, was so surreal that it took a moment to register. Then the natural flood of confusion and horror broke loose, and a thousand jumbled thoughts began rushing through Nora's head: she shouldn't be in here, she should phone the police immediately, she should get out, call Cormac, run away and hide. What if someone was still in the house?

Listening closely for any noise, she fought her fear and edged closer to the bathtub. Her conscious mind understood that it was too late, but she checked for a pulse inside Ursula's left ankle just to be sure, and found the pale skin cold to the touch. Nora withdrew her hand and cast her eyes around the bathroom. They would ask her to describe exactly what she had seen. Nothing was registering but the peat, the blood on the wall, and the pale, cold limbs emerging from the water. She forced herself to turn and look, to concentrate on the white tiles, the strange green walls, the purple bathrobe lying on the floor beside the tub, the single bare bulb that hung on a wire from the ceiling, the black peat under Ursula's fingernails. Several candles on the windowsill had burned down and guttered out. Nora backed out of the bathroom slowly with the tire iron still in one hand, trying to hold the scene in her mind. The faucet dripped slowly, and nothing else moved, only the bright clear water steadily dripping into crimson, counting the seconds.

She had worked with death almost daily for years, but there was nothing between her and this death, no buffer, no intention on the part of the deceased to become the object of scrutiny, and somehow that made all the difference. Her presence here felt like an affront to dignity. She reached into her jacket pocket, fumbling for her mobile phone, and dialed 999 for emergency services. While the forefront of her mind calmly answered the operator's questions, under the surface coursed a fearful, dark tumble of thoughts. Her memory replayed the angry gestures between Ursula and Owen Cadogan, his hand around her throat, her fists pushing him away. She remembered the confrontation, the threats Ursula had made to Charlie Brazil. But what was the pile of peat supposed to mean, unless—Nora's stomach churned when she thought of the strange way Danny Brazil had met his death. She leaned over the tub again to look at the still corpse beneath the water, and this time she saw the thin leather strand that encircled Ursula's throat, its dark line broken by three knots.

2

The house and yard were swarming with Guards. Soon they would be replaced by scene-of-crime officers going over the minutiae like white-clad ants, carrying bits of evidence away to their own anthill. Nora sat waiting to give her statement to Detective Ward, wishing that they would just let her go home. She wanted nothing more than to crawl back into bed, to go to sleep and wake up again, start the whole day over, and find this nightmare vanished.

"Thank you for staying, Dr. Gavin. We'll eventually need to get a detailed statement from you, but at this point it would be helpful if you could just tell me what happened this morning. What made you decide to stop and look in here?"

Nora's mind went back to the moment she'd seen the open door. What synapse made a person do or not do something? What if she hadn't seen the door standing open, or it had been open to a lesser angle? Would she have noticed, or flown past as she'd done all the previous days she'd been here? Had knowing this was Ursula's house made her more observant? "I don't know, really. I saw the door standing open, and I thought it was odd. I thought something might be wrong."

"Did you know who was stopping here?"

"Yes, I knew that Ursula Downes was staying here for the excavation season."

"How did you know?"

For some reason she felt a bit nonplussed. "Cormac Maguire told me last night."

"And how did he know that this was Ms. Downes's residence, if you don't mind my asking?"

Why did she mind the question so much? "I'm not sure how he knew. He never mentioned their acquaintance specifically, but I believe they knew each other from years back. Archaeology is a small field. Everyone knows everyone."

"I see," Ward said, and Nora knew he was making a note to put Cormac on his interview list. "Why don't you take me through what happened, from the time you saw the open door?" His brown eyes were not unkind, and she told herself that he had to be open to every possibility— even those that seemed extremely unlikely. Of course he had to look at Cormac. He'd probably have to interview everyone within a five-mile radius. She took a deep breath and plunged in, recounting all the details she could remember: the broken window, the drops of blood on the kitchen floor, the wine bottle on the table, her panicky journey down the corridor, and the jangling fear she had felt pushing the bathroom door open with the tire iron. She couldn't seem to go on.

"I'll let you go very soon," Ward said, "but I have to ask you, Dr. Gavin, where you were last night. Perhaps you'd oblige me, and go back to the time I left the house after talking with you and Dr. Maguire."

"We ate dinner after you left, then Cormac took me to the top of the hill behind the cottage. That was when he pointed out all the neighboring houses."

"And then?"

"We came home and went to bed. "

"What time would you say that was?"

"About ten forty-five, I suppose, maybe eleven."

"So you were together the whole evening, and all night?" When Nora looked up at him, he tried to reassure her: "Absolutely routine questions; I don't want to assume anything. I just need the facts."

"Yes." Nora thought of the clear evidence she'd seen this morning that Cormac had been awake and moving about the house.

"You didn't wake up in the night? Didn't go to the loo, or to get a glass of water?"

She wondered if Ward could see her hesitation. "No, I'd been working out on the bog all day, and I was exhausted. I didn't wake until the alarm went off this morning."

"How well did you know Ursula Downes, Dr. Gavin?"

"Not well at all. I only met her a couple of days ago, out on the bog. We hadn't really spoken very much."

"And what about Dr. Maguire? How well was he acquainted with Ursula Downes?"

"As I said, they may have worked together some time ago. I don't really know."

"I realize you've been here only a few days, but in that time, were you aware of anyone who may have wished her harm?"

Nora hesitated again. "I don't know about wishing harm; I can only tell you about things I witnessed."

"Go ahead," Ward said, interested.

"Ursula didn't seem to be on especially good terms with Owen Cadogan, the bog manager. I saw them talking on a couple of occasions, and neither was what you'd call a cordial conversation. At one point, Cadogan had his hand around Ursula's throat. I couldn't tell if he was threatening her or not, and when I asked whether everything was all right, she basically told me to back off and mind my own business. The next day, when Cadogan arrived at the site, Ursula tore into him. I don't know why; I couldn't hear what she was saying. And she hit him, a slap in the face. She seemed absolutely furious, but you'll have to ask Cadogan why."

"Anything else?"

Nora watched Ward noting all this in his book. If she was so willing to tell him everything she'd witnessed between Ursula and Owen Cadogan, why not mention the conversation she'd overheard between Ursula and Charlie Brazil?

"If that's all—"

"It isn't, actually." She might regret this but it was too late now. "I also overheard a conversation a couple of days ago between Ursula and one of the Bord na Móna men, Charlie Brazil. She had—" It was going to sound ridiculous enough, without mentioning how Ursula had wrestled him to the ground. "She said that she'd been watching him, that she knew what he was hiding. And it seemed as though she was threatening to expose whatever it was if he didn't do what she wanted."

"And what was that?"

"She wasn't really specific. She just said that he should come and see her, after dark."

Ward took all this in impassively, making a few notes in his book. "Anything else?" Nora shook her head, wondering why it was that she had left out Ursula's reference to Brona Scully. She told herself she couldn't be positive, and for some reason she felt a fierce protectiveness toward a girl she'd never even met. "You can go home now if you wish, Dr. Gavin. If you wouldn't mind coming down to the station this afternoon, we can finish taking a complete formal statement then. Thank you for your cooperation."

As Ward made his way back to the house, Nora saw one of the Guards at the gate turn to address someone approaching from the road. The lanky stranger had blunt, handsome features—a slightly flattened nose, down-turned lips, and a square jaw—and his short steel gray hair was combed straight back over the crown of his head. He wore a long gray raincoat that reached below his knees, and carried a black attaché case. Another detective? Not likely. He didn't seem like a reporter—too mature and too well-dressed for this sort of assignment—and it was a bit early for that, in any case. She heard the young Garda say, "I'm sorry, sir. I can't let you in without an okay from the boss."

"Where's Ursula?" the man in the raincoat asked. "Has something happened to her? Tell me what's going on here."

The officer looked at the attaché case. "You her brief, sir?"

The man looked at the young Garda as if he'd never encountered a greater class of imbecile. "No, I am not her 'brief.' Is there someone in charge of you here? I insist that you let me speak to the officer in charge."

Ward had evidently overhead and strode toward them. "Detective Liam Ward. I'm in charge of the scene. And you are—"

"Desmond Quill. I'm a friend of Ursula's, and I demand to know exactly what's going on here."

"If you'd step this way, Mr. Quill." Ward's calm demeanor withstood the waves of anger directed toward him. The two men stopped a short distance away, and Nora watched Ward speaking very quietly to Quill. There was a brief silence, then Quill's head tipped forward and the case he gripped in his left hand dropped abruptly to the ground. Ward reached out to steady him, but he pushed the policeman's arm away, rubbing his brow with one hand as the other, the one that had held the attaché case, slid up and down his side as if searching blindly for his raincoat pocket.

3

Nora drove in stunned silence back to the Crosses. She felt her right foot pushing too hard on the brake, as if she could stop time and back up to the previous evening when she had stood wrapped in the aura of that magical tree, when, for one brief shining instant, everything had seemed so right and possible.

When she pulled in beside the cottage, it seemed impossible that she should be reaching to open the car door, entering the house. All these mundane, thoughtless acts seemed somehow surreal after the bizarre and terrifying tableau she had just witnessed. And yet it was all real, all of it: Ursula's blood on the wall was as real as the birds in the trees outside the windows, as real as Cormac sitting at his desk inside the cottage. He stood up as she came through the door.

"Nora, what are you doing home? Is everything all right?"

"I never made it to the bog. I only got as far as Ursula's house. She's dead, Cormac."

Nora wasn't sure what sort of reaction she expected. What should a person say when presented with such news? He took a step backward, a deep crease furrowing his forehead, and looked into her eyes, searching for a sign that she was telling the truth. When she nodded, his head dropped forward and words finally escaped within a long, slow exhalation. "Ah, no. No."

"She's been murdered."

This brought Cormac fresh anguish. He lunged forward and seized her by the arms. "How do you know, Nora?"

As his fingers pressed into her arms, she found his reaction beginning to alarm her. She tried to wrest one arm out of his tightening grasp. "Because I found her body."

All his urgency dissolved in an instant. He folded his arms tight around her and whispered through her hair. "Ah, Nora. I'm sorry. I'm so sorry. Are you all right?" He pulled back to look into her face, to see for himself.

"I'll be all right. But what about you—are you all right, Cormac?"

He didn't answer for a moment; he looked away, the muscles in his jaw tensing. He finally looked back at her, and she could feel the anxiety that radiated from his eyes. "Nora, there's something you need to know right away. I was over at Ursula's last night. I'm responsible."

She received the force of that blunt statement as though she'd been struck in the face.

He realized his poor choice of words immediately. "No, no, I didn't— I wasn't even there very long. Maybe fifteen minutes, maybe twenty. She was fine when I left, Nora." He shook his head and raked his fingers through his hair. "But I am responsible, you see. She rang me up on the mobile after you'd gone to sleep, just after midnight. I was here in the kitchen, finishing the washing up. Ursula said she'd heard someone outside the house and asked me to come over. She wouldn't phone the police or the emergency services. I didn't know what else to do. She sounded a bit drunk, and she seemed genuinely frightened. I was just going to try to calm her down, get her to ring the Guards.

"I thought something was off as soon as I stepped inside the door. The kitchen window had been smashed. She was trying to clean it up, and she'd cut herself pretty badly in the process; it was a nasty gash, and I ended up with blood all over my clothes from helping her bind it up. When I came back from putting away the bandages, Ursula was calmly pouring two glasses of wine, as if nothing had happened. I asked her what the hell was going on, and she said something about how shockingly simple it was to mislead a decent man." He colored deeply. "I thought she'd made it up—the prowler. I thought she'd broken the window herself."

"So what happened?" Nora felt a hand tightening around her heart, the familiar signature of her old enemy, regret.

"When I told her that there was no way I was staying for a drink, I don't know what happened—she just went off." Cormac's anguish and humiliation were evident from the red flush that burned in his ears. "I turned to leave, and she came at me from behind. All I wanted was to get the hell away from there. I tried to shake her off, but she got in a good swipe at me, enough to draw blood." He put one hand to his injured throat. "All I know is that she was alive when I left, Nora. Halfway up the hill I looked back. I could see her standing there in the kitchen. She was holding up a wine glass and laughing at me."

He leaned back into the wall and sagged against it for support. On the left side of his neck Nora could see the three distinct scratches, still raw-looking. All at once she remembered the smear on his pillow.

"You'll have to go to the police right away."

"Yes. Of course."

An expectant silence hung in the air, and Nora could sense that she hadn't heard everything he had to tell. "There's something else. What is it, Cormac?"

He closed his eyes and drew another breath. "It's bound to come out when I talk to the Guards, and I don't want you to hear it from anyone else." He looked straight into her eyes. "I should have told you before now, Nora, and I apologize for that. Ursula and I were very briefly—involved, a long time ago. We were both graduate students, working out here with Gabriel. It only lasted for a few weeks one summer. I broke it off when I realized that Ursula was not . . ." He searched for the right words. ". . . not as honorable a person as I had imagined."

"And that was something you couldn't figure out before sleeping with her?" His eyes flashed, and she gazed into the wound her words had opened, quick as a blade. "I'm sorry, Cormac, I'm sorry. That was uncalled for."

"Not entirely. I don't know what made me go over there last night. When she stopped by on Sunday evening, I thought there was something different about her. She seemed calmer, more thoughtful. I thought per-haps she'd changed a little. Maybe she had, maybe she hadn't; maybe it was all an act."

She had been here. The lipstick-stained tissue in the bathroom bin—Ursula had left it there, deliberately planting seeds of doubt. Nora's mind crashed back through all the sly looks she'd received the past few days; Ursula had been probing, checking to see whether those seeds had taken root.

"I should have stayed last might. Maybe Ursula would still be alive if I'd just taken the time to talk to her and calm her down."

Cormac paused for a moment. "I wanted you to know what really hap-pened before things get crazy. Because they will get crazy; I think we can count on that. But I didn't hurt her, Nora. I would never—"

His dark eyes overflowed with remorse and supplication, and it seemed as though he was waiting for a response, for her to say something reassuring—*Of course, of course you wouldn't.* But she was thinking: *No one knows what he's capable of until it's done and he's face-to-face with it.*

People snap, they do stupid things, they don't think. Her throat felt thick; no words would come.

"Please say something, Nora."

She was suddenly aware that she was pressing her fingernails into tightly clenched fists. She uncurled her hands, and tried to unclench her stomach as well. He reached out and gripped her wrist. "I know. I know it's a crazy, stupid story. No one will believe me, and I don't blame them. But I can only tell you what truly happened."

She looked into the deep brown pools of his eyes, then down at the fingers encircling her forearm—the same fingers that had coaxed such wild, furious music from his flute, that had touched her and stroked her hair when she wept. "We'll get all this sorted," was all she said. But she could see the relief break over his face like a wave.

4

Ward stood for a moment in the light streaming through Ursula Downes's missing kitchen window. It had been a huge window of plate glass, unshaded. Must have seemed like a lighted stage to someone looking in at night. He looked out the window at the rise of the back garden, saw the sagging wires on the clothesline vibrate in the wind. He checked the locks on the back door, one of those that latch without a key, and a separate deadbolt. Both front and back doors had been left open. Neither one had been forced, which meant that Ursula Downes's killer either had a key or was someone known to her, someone she would have let into the house. Or the killer could have just entered through the smashed window. Most of the glass had been cleared away; there was a broom in the corner and the bin was full of broken plate glass. He drew out one shard with gloved fingers, and noticed tiny droplets of what appeared to be red spray paint on the glass. "Can we have a closer look at this?" he asked the first crime-scene technician who passed by. "Reconstruct the glass and see if it's graffiti or writing of some kind?"

The tech nodded and took the bin of broken glass. Ward turned his attention to the presses. Lots of tea and a few tins of beans and sardines, but the fridge was empty except for milk and several nearly empty take-away containers. Ursula Downes was not a cook, apparently.

In the sitting room, marks on the carpet looked as if someone had been moving the furniture recently—covering up a violent struggle, or looking for something? Ursula Downes had not left a large imprint on her temporary lodging; there weren't many personal items in the sitting room. He had a suspicion that her flat in Dublin wouldn't be that much homier than this. She didn't seem the type to go in for soft cushions.

A rucksack sat on the floor next to the table. He picked it up and unzipped the front pocket, and found a single lipstick, a mobile phone, a diary. The precious details that would help him unlock her life and death were here, waiting to be winnowed. He bagged the rucksack as evidence—he'd take it with him and have a closer look at the station.

Suddenly a white-garbed officer appeared at his elbow. "Dr. Friel's ready for you, sir."

Ward took several slow, deep breaths before walking into the bathroom where the body was. The scene-of-crime officers had removed and bagged the peat to allow Dr. Friel better access to the body. Ursula Downes's pale corpse was still partly submerged in the tub. The cloying smell of blood hung in the air. For him, the odor of death was usually worse than the sight of the body, but he wasn't prepared for this one. A thin black thong cut into the flesh of her neck just below the chin, and below it gaped a dreadful wound.

"Not a very deep ligature," said Dr. Friel, beside him. "Possibly not done to kill her, but to cut off airflow temporarily, or to control the bleeding. And there are three knots in the cord."

"Just like Danny Brazil." Ward mentally went through the list of people who would have known about the ligature on the previous victim. "What about the slashing?"

"Almost certainly a right-handed person, from the angle of the cut and the spatter."

"So you believe she was alive when her throat was cut?"

"Yes; look at the pattern on the wall. Very definitely arterial bleeding." Ward looked where Dr. Friel's eyes pointed, at the deep rust-red plumes on the wall. He counted: one, two, three, four, five. How long had her heart carried on beating before she died? Whoever had done this hadn't gotten away clean, he thought. He looked down at Ursula's wrists and ankles, still resting on the bathtub's gracefully rounded lip. "Any other visible injuries?"

"Just a gash inside the left hand here." She pointed to an incised wound between the thumb and forefinger. "It's a very recent cut, and the strange thing about it is that there are traces of cotton thread in the wound, as if it had been bound, but the bandage was removed. There may also be some skin and blood under the nails of her left hand. I won't be able to tell for certain until we get to the PM. She may have been unconscious, just this side of asphyxiation, when her throat was cut."

"And the knife found on the floor?"

"They'll have to test it, of course, but I'd bet it's not the murder weapon."

"Why's that?"

"The blade is serrated. According to everything I see, her throat was cut with an nonserrated blade."

Ward took this in. "Anything else, anything—I don't know—unusual?"

"Well, you're looking for a dull blade. Not new—maybe an antique; a kind of metal that doesn't hold a sharp edge for long." Ward raised his eyebrows in query. "Not that difficult to determine. Dull knives make for rough wounds."

"And how long has she been dead, would you say?"

"Based on general rigor and lividity in the limbs, I'd say roughly eight to twelve hours. But the fact that she's been mostly submerged in cold water gives us a larger margin of error. I should have the PM finished by early evening, if you want to check back with me then. You have my mobile number?"

As he left the scene behind, Ward reflected that sometimes the only witness they had to a horrific crime like this was the victim herself. It was fortunate for him, he thought, how well a body remembers. He removed his gloves before leaving the house and placed them carefully in his rain-coat pocket. Stepping out the back door, he heard a noise, like pouring water, and saw a crimson pool spreading out from the peat-clogged drain. He shouted to the officers standing beside the thing, but it was too late; their shoes had been surrounded.

"Detective Ward!" a voice rang out from a few yards away. "We've got something over here." The uniformed Garda hoisted the stick he'd been using to probe at the thick grass and held aloft a pair of green binoculars. Ward strode over to take a closer look, putting his gloves back on and pulling an evidence bag out of his pocket.

The binoculars were compact and waterproof, with a cloth strap—the sort you might imagine hunters would use, he thought. Had someone been watching Ursula Downes last night, waiting for his chance to strike? "Good work, Moran." Ward held up the polythene bag, and Moran let the binoculars slide into it. "Make sure you mark the spot and let the crime-scene boys document this area." He was nearly back at the house when another voice called from about fifty yards away. "Detective? I've something else here, sir." Ward turned on his heel and charged up the slope toward the sound of the officer's voice, through a gap in the hedge that defined the boundary of the pasture.

"I was just putting my stick down at the base of the hedge when I saw the yellow color, sir. There was this huge stone on top, so I shifted it and found this." Ward folded himself into a crouch to look at the spot where the Garda officer was pointing. Beside the large stone was a flattened waterproof jacket of heavy rubberized yellow canvas, like those worn by fishermen and by some of the archaeologists on the bog excavation. The jacket's right sleeve was spattered with blood. Ward pulled out a pen and flipped over the tag just inside the neck to see the owner's name written in block capitals: MAGUIRE.

He hadn't even had time to formulate any ideas about this strange turn of events when the mobile in his pocket began to ring. The duty officer reported that a Dr. Maguire had just rung, and would be coming in at three to give a statement on the Ursula Downes case. Not before time, Ward thought, looking down again at the blood-spattered jacket. He quickly returned to the house and finished up with the crime-scene team. As he climbed into his car, he found himself running through the questions they'd ask Maguire in the interview room. It was an elaborate form of negotiation—not unlike diplomacy or even courtship, he'd often thought—with each side trying to find out how much the other knew, how much had already been given away. His fingers thrummed a steady rhythm on the steering wheel as he drove the short distance to the excavation site. He hoped questioning the archaeology team wouldn't take too long. He couldn't wait to hear what Maguire had to say.

5

Ward arrived at the excavation site at a quarter past eleven, and was greeted by the uniformed officer who stood to one side of the sturdy wooden steps leading up to the door of the tea hut. Maureen was already there, taking the team's names and addresses down in her notebook. Five pairs of eyes followed Ward as he took a chair at the far end of the table, which was littered with boxes of teabags, biscuit packets, and several open milk containers. Someone had made a pot of tea, and several of them warmed their hands on mugs. Their faces were reddened from sun and wind. There was a reason they were all so young, Ward thought as he looked around the room at the apprehensive faces. The work was physically hard, temporary, grim, seasonal—a stepping-stone to other things, not an end in itself. Was he getting old, that they all looked so unformed to him, so unmarked by experience? The shed where they sat was a flimsy trailer; he could hear and feel the wind outside, trying to blow away the whole structure, this paltry affront to its power. Even if it didn't blow them away, the wind always succeeded, eventually, in wearing down the people who worked here. Soon enough they would all be gone, replaced by others, and the constant wind would still be blowing over the face of the earth.

Ward was acutely aware that he had to treat even such an inexperienced group as potential suspects, until they could safely be eliminated. "I don't know how much you've heard about what's happened," he began.

"Nothing," said a stocky lad with close-cropped sandy hair and large gray eyes. "We've heard nothing at all. We've been here working all morning, and all we know is that we were told to come in here and give our names." Ward looked down through the list Brennan had handed him, and she pointed to a name: Tony Gardner.

"Then I'm sorry to have to tell you. Ursula Downes was found dead this morning, and it appears that she's been murdered."

He could feel the collective jolt as his words registered around the room. He watched their faces for a reaction, that familiar first denial, parrying reality's brutal thrust, as if a simple "no" could reverse the facts. Such news was always too immense, too illogical, too impossible to accept. "I can't tell you any more at the moment, except to say that we've been in contact with your employers, and they're sending someone from the firm out here straightaway. I'm here to ask you a few questions about Ursula, and about your work here, to see if we can find a reason anyone might have had to wish her harm. What happened when she didn't show up at the site this morning?"

Gardner replied for the group: "Nothing. I mean, we didn't think anything of it, because she wasn't meant to be here this morning. She was taking the day off, she said—a long weekend. I'm not sure if she was going home to Dublin or somewhere else. She didn't tell us her plans."

"So the last time you saw Ursula was—"

"Yesterday evening when we were finishing up here." Maureen pointed to another name: Trish Walpole. She was an English girl in her early twenties, as Ward guessed most of them were. The natural color in her face had been heightened by the sun, and her fair hair was streaked and layered like straw from the constant wind. She played with a teaspoon as she spoke. "We all took the minibus back to the digs, and I presume Ursula went home as well. She had her own car."

Beside Trish was a quiet young woman with long dark hair and frightened eyes, who sat on her hands and never looked up. Ward looked down through his list again: Sarah Cummins. This must be terrifying for some of them, perhaps their first time away from home.

"How well did you all know Ursula Downes?"

"Not all that well," another of the young men replied. "Barry Sullivan," he added, looking at Ward's list. "Most of us were just hired on for the summer season. She had her own digs, didn't really hang around with us. We only saw her out here on the job."

"Given that limited interaction, were you aware of anyone who might have wished her harm?"

"Not really," Sullivan said. "I mean, she had a few rows with Owen Cadogan, but I guess I thought they just didn't get on. The managers have to put up with us, but most of them don't really give a toss about what we're doing here; I think they just see us holding up their bloody production schedules. The sooner they can get rid of us, the sooner they can get back to raping the landscape."

"There's no need to be melodramatic, Barry," said Trish Walpole. "They're really quite good to us here."

"But Ms. Downes's relationship with Cadogan was strictly professional, as far as you knew?"

"Yeah. As far as we knew," Sullivan said. None of the others disagreed.

"And what about her relationship with Charlie Brazil?" Several of the crew shifted in their seats, and Ward could see damp clods falling off their heavy boots onto the layer of brownish peat that already covered the floor.

"She was always trying to get him to come out here—making up odd jobs for him to do," said Trish Walpole. "She was very sweet to his face, but behind his back she called him Charlie Goggles. There was something strange going on between them. A couple of days ago I saw her come in here, and a few minutes later Charlie came out, looking like somebody had given him a right hiding."

"You said Ursula had separate digs from your own. But all the rest of you lodge at the same place?"

"Yes, we have a house about a half-mile around the bend past Ursula's place, on the Cloghan road," said the last young man, Tom Galligan.

"Five of you in the house?"

Gardner said, "Six, actually. One of our crew is missing today—Rachel Briscoe."

The girl who'd found Danny Brazil's body. Ward remembered talking with her. She had answered his questions that day, but had barely made eye contact.

"I knocked on her door this morning, but there was no answer, so I stuck my head in. She was still asleep. Had the duvet pulled up over her head."

"But you didn't go in, didn't speak to her?"

"By that time the minibus driver was already waiting, and we didn't have time to hang around. She just overslept. It's not the first time." His tone suggested that Rachel was a constant thorn in their collective side.

Sarah Cummins said quietly, "I went in. The bed was arranged to make it look as if somebody was in it, but Rachel wasn't there."

A cascade of guilty looks traveled through the group. Sullivan said, "Look, we all knew she went out nearly every night. Thought we didn't take any notice, I suppose. She was always back by morning."

"Any idea where she was going?" Ward asked. "To meet someone, perhaps?"

Sarah Cummins bristled defensively. "We don't know where she went. How could we?"

"I do," Gardner said. "I was coming back from the pub one night, and I saw her on the hill right behind Ursula's place."

"Anyone else ever see her there?" Ward asked. The uncomfortable looks and a couple of nodding heads told him that they had, but like Sarah Cummins, they didn't like to jump to conclusions. "Do you have any reason to believe she was somehow involved with Ursula?"

"More like obsessed," Gardner said. "I'm sure she thought we didn't notice, but you could see her staring at Ursula when she thought no one was around. Watching her like a cat when we were on tea break. It was weird." Ward looked around at the other crew members. No one jumped in to agree, but none of them protested either.

Ward reached into his coat pocket and brought out the bag containing the binoculars found at the crime scene. "Have any of you seen these before?"

Sarah Cummins said quietly, "They're Rachel's. She always had them with her. She'd go berserk if anyone borrowed them, even for a second."

When he'd finished questioning the archaeology crew, Ward excused them. He handed out his cards as they filed out of the office, and asked them to ring him personally if they remembered anything else, no matter how seemingly insignificant. Sarah Cummins lingered behind the others, and Ward waited until they were alone before he spoke. "Was there something else you wanted to tell me?"

"They're all seeing what they wanted to see. There's something bothering Rachel; she's acting strangely, and I don't think she's been thinking straight since she arrived here. I know the signs." Sarah pinched the ends of her coat sleeves as she spoke, balling her hands up in knots. "I walked in on her once in the bathroom at the house. I didn't know she was in there; the door wasn't locked. She was sitting on the edge of the tub, staring at a knife in the sink." The girl swallowed hard. "I know what she was thinking about, what she was going to do." She took a deep breath, and pushed up one of her sleeves, showing several whitened lines where the skin had once been cut. "It's not about killing yourself, or even about the blood; it's about the pain—about feeling something, anything. And about taking control again. I don't do it anymore."

"Do you think could Rachel have hurt anyone else?"

The girl's anxious eyes held him. "I don't know. I should have said something before now."

"You can't blame yourself for anything that's happened. I mean that. It's not your fault, Sarah. Have you got someone you can call—someone to talk to?"

The girl nodded and looked away. "My sister."

"And will you promise me you'll ring her today?" She looked back up at him and offered another wordless nod. How had this young woman come to bear the whole world upon her back? "I want to thank you for coming forward, Sarah. It took a lot of courage, and it might make the difference to this case. Will you ring me if you think of anything else— anything at all?" Sarah Cummins nodded again and left, tucking his card into her trouser pocket as she walked slowly back to her work. Unseen disturbances lurked everywhere, Ward thought. It was difficult enough to calm the situations that were out in the open. How could human beings hope to forestall the conflicts that raged within a soul turned on itself?

6

Owen Cadogan didn't look pleased to see two detectives approaching his office, but he was evidently expecting them. He got his secretary—a soft-looking woman, perhaps in her early thirties—to bring in a pot of tea and three mugs on a tray. She glanced at the detectives with that combination of fascination and dismay common in people who find themselves unexpectedly on the periphery of a dreadful crime. When she left, pulling the door closed behind her, Ward jumped right in. "Mr. Cadogan, tell us about your relationship with Ursula Downes."

Owen Cadogan fixed him with a stare, evidently annoyed at the assumption in the question. "There was no 'relationship.' She worked the bog last summer and came back again this year. She and her crew were under my charge here, so we were in fairly regular communication."

"About what?"

"About the progress they were making, if she needed any supplies, or anything from the workshop—that sort of thing." He went silent for a moment. "It's hard to believe she's—"

"You're sure that was the extent of it?"

"Extent of what?"

"Of your relationship?"

"I've told you there was no 'relationship'—"

"We have eyewitnesses who say that you had a couple of rather heated exchanges with Ursula a couple of days ago. What was that all about?"

Cadogan's eyes shifted away. "It was to do with a personnel matter."

Brennan took the ball. "And how confidential will it be when we have to go through all your employees' files to find out?" Cadogan looked up into her eyes, on the verge of challenging her authority, Ward thought.

"This is a murder inquiry," Brennan said curtly, and Cadogan backed down.

"Last summer Ursula got her hooks into one of the lads here in my workshop, and I saw how it turned out. It seemed that Ursula liked to try things sometimes, just to see if she could get away with them. I wasn't going to let her do it again."

"Or you'd do what? Seems to me taking her by the throat is a rather unprofessional way of making your point," Brennan said.

"I'd tried talking to her already, several times, and she wasn't getting the message."

Wasn't getting the message, Ward thought to himself. Here's a man who doesn't really like women. Doesn't trust them, sees them as alien creatures. He listened closely as Brennan continued her questions.

"Sure she didn't have her hooks into you?" Brennan asked.

"I'm married," Cadogan said. "Besides, a woman like that—"

"A woman like what? What did she make him do, this young man she seduced? Did you think about that a lot, Mr. Cadogan? Did it upset you—make you feel jealous, perhaps?"

"No! I'm just trying to do my job here."

"And who was this worker she was after, again?" Brennan asked. "This innocent lamb whose virtue you were defending? Presuming they're both of legal age, why should it be anything to do with you?"

Cadogan considered his answer. "It wasn't like that. I wasn't trying to interfere, but the way she carried on disrupted morale, that was all. We were stuck with her out here for ten weeks, and I was just trying to keep the peace."

Ward sat forward slowly, so as not to draw attention to himself, and watched Owen Cadogan's lips form the words of his answer—the truth this time, or a lie? They had no proof that Cadogan had been involved with Ursula Downes. But somehow his story seemed false. If only there were some foolproof clue to mendacity. The trouble was, most liars were clever enough to mix in some truth with their lies, so it wasn't whole cloth. You had to sort it out, check everything they said, not just the parts that seemed suspicious. There were many kinds of lies and many kinds of liars. There were embellishers, people who told things the way they remembered them, usually to their own advantage. Some people set themselves rules about lying, when it was all right and when not acceptable. There were those whose words were never false, but whose actions invariably were. The best liars, in Ward's experience, were those who knew how to embroider, to stitch together truth and fiction into a seamless fabric. What sort of a liar was Owen Cadogan? As he mused, Ward found himself looking not at Cadogan, but at the secretary working in the next office, separated from them only by a partition that was half glass. He wondered how much she could hear. It was only a single pane, and Brennan's voice was rather loud. The secretary seemed to be going about her work with a kind of forced concentration that led him to believe that she could hear it all. At this moment, she had her back turned and was typing furiously.

Ward rose and ventured out to her desk, closing the office door behind him. "I wonder if you could point me in the direction of a water tap?" The woman raised her head and pointed wordlessly to the galley kitchen across the hall. "I'm supposed to take this tablet an hour before my dinner," Ward offered, by way of explanation, "and I nearly always forget. Thanks, Miss . . ."

"Flood. Aileen Flood."

Ward ducked across the hall and downed his aspirin tablet with a sip of water, throwing back his head to make sure it went down properly. She regarded him curiously. Then he came back across the hall and observed that the sound from the inner office was indeed perfectly audible, as though there were no partition at all. "Thanks," he said again, and rejoined Cadogan and Brennan, who hadn't missed a beat.

"All right. All right. The lad's name is Charlie Brazil. He got himself into an awful twist about her last summer. If you ask him, he'll deny it. Some people say he's not the full shilling, but he's all right. A good lad— a bit odd, but a good worker. She'd no business messing with him."

"Does your wife know about your talks with Ursula Downes?" Ward asked.

"Leave my wife out of this," Cadogan said. His eyes narrowed as he looked across the desk at them.

"I'm afraid we can't leave your wife out of this, Mr. Cadogan, because you're on our list as a suspect, and we're going to have to talk to her about where you were last night."

Cadogan looked down with the dejected air of someone who was well and truly in it. "She took the children up to her mother's place in Mayo. They go every summer for a fortnight. She left two days ago."

"So no one can vouch for your whereabouts last night?"

Cadogan looked away, then back at Brennan. "No, I was home. Alone."

"And no one saw you at the house, no one phoned you there? I'll remind you, Mr. Cadogan, that we're investigating a murder, and that you're under very serious consideration as a suspect. Can anyone give evidence about where you were last night?"

"No." Even as his lips formed the word, Cadogan's eyes flicked over to the window, where his secretary was continuing the pretense of going about her work. But the woman's stony facial expression, her overprecise movements, betrayed her intense agitation.

"Look, if someone can tell us where you were between one and four o'clock this morning, we'd be delighted to cross you off our list."

Ward made a point of turning, ever so slightly, so that he was looking straight out at the anxious woman in the next office. But Cadogan wasn't going to bite.

"There's no one, I swear. I was alone all evening. All night."

Brennan regarded Cadogan evenly, giving him a last chance to come clean, then glanced over at Ward. He closed his eyes to tell her he had no additional questions, so she stood, and said, "That'll do for now. We'll be in touch when we have any more questions, and of course you can always ring us if you remember anything further."

Cadogan looked slightly surprised that they were finished with him so soon. He tried to mask it, placing his hands on the table and making a show of getting out of his chair. As they took their leave and headed down the corridor to the exit, Ward glanced back briefly, to see Owen Cadogan crouched by his secretary's desk. It wasn't his submissive posture, but the woman's worried face that piqued Ward's interest. He turned back to Maureen.

"We won't have time today, but do you fancy calling in on Ms. Flood at home tomorrow?" he asked.

"Already in my diary," Brennan said.

7

Charlie Brazil wasn't hard to find. They entered the workshop's open maw, where a man in a stained boilersuit was working on aligning the swamp treads on a huge tractor. They showed their IDs and asked for Brazil. "You'll have to wear these," the man said, tapping his own goggles, and ducking into the shop foreman's office to pull down two pairs from the board inside. He handed them each a pair, then pointed with his thumb to the next repair bay, where a young man in safety glasses worked on a machine part with a grinder. Ward put his goggles on, noting the row of illustrated calendars at the back of the shop, featuring posing, pouting women whose breasts looked like they'd been inflated with a bicycle pump. The workshop seemed to be organized into different areas, according to type of repair and equipment needed. It was impossible not to be overwhelmed by the scale of the machines and the sharpness everywhere: dull blades being honed with grinders, shiny new blades waiting to be fitted on these huge tools for scraping the skin of the earth. He wondered if these men understood that every day they came to work they were destroying their own livelihood. Bogs were finite, not like his line of work, which relied upon wellsprings of anger and greed and stupidity that seemed to have no end.

As they approached, the fair young man at the grinder pressed metal to metal, and a rain of sparks fell near their feet.

"Charlie Brazil?" Ward shouted above the noise, holding up his ID. The young man nodded and turned off the grinder, and Ward noted the fingers black with grime. They had it from two sources that their victim had been interested in the lad. But what was his interest in her? "We were just having a chat with your boss, Mr. Brazil. He tells us you knew Ursula Downes."

Brazil eyed them suspiciously through his safety goggles. "So did we all. She was here on the bog last year as well." Ward stood facing the open door to the next repair bay and watched as the police presence seemed to reverberate around the building. He marveled at how such knowledge was passed, like a scent, a feeling in the air. Some of the workers strode by purposefully; a few stood and gawked from a distance like curious cattle. Every once in a while, a figure would drift by the open door, pretending to check the yard for the next job. It was clear they all knew why the police were there. When the third boilersuited figure came into view, Ward turned to Charlie Brazil and said, "Look, we can go somewhere else if you'd like."

Charlie gave a kind of resigned grimace and shook his head. "I'm used to it." Ward noted that Charlie was the only youngish man at the workshop; all the rest seemed to be middle-aged or older. He could imagine the slagging, the thinly veiled envy, the superiority of knowledge. Charlie Brazil had the same look Ward remembered from boys who had been picked on at school, for being too intelligent, too introverted, too quiet. They might as well have had signs hanging around their necks. He watched Charlie Brazil's long fingers fiddle with the clamps that held the machine part. Did he know what Ursula Downes had called him behind his back?

"I didn't know her all that well. They sent me over to put up some steps for her, just knock together a wooden staircase so they could get in and out of their supply shed—it was up fairly high off the ground. When she needed some drawing frames there the other day, she asked if I'd make them."

"So you were often out at the excavation site."

"Fairly often, yeah."

"Did you look for opportunities to be out there, to help Ursula whenever you had the chance?"

"No. I only did what I was asked to do."

"Was there any change in how you got on, between last summer and this one? Any difference in her that you noticed?"

"Not really. She liked to get people to do things for her. She was always asking me to help her out, and I did."

"Why?"

Brazil didn't answer immediately; he looked away and pulled at his lip. His voice dropped a notch or two in volume. "I suppose I felt sorry for her."

"What?" Brennan's voice was incredulous, and Ward flashed his eyes to tell her to tread lightly here.

"It seemed like she needed attention," Brazil said. "I helped her when she asked me."

"I see." Brennan opened her mouth to ask another question, but this time Ward jumped in: "Did you ever see Ursula away from the job, Charlie?"

"No. Never."

"Did you ever have a sexual relationship with Ursula Downes?" Ward asked.

"No!" The lad's nostrils flared as he raised his head, and his chest heaved as if he couldn't take in enough oxygen. "I never. I swear."

Ward remembered the comment from one of the archaeologists. "What were you doing in the archaeologists' shed a few days back?"

Charlie Brazil stared at them with a new wariness in his eyes. "I was looking at a map they've got in there, trying to see where the next cuttings were going in."

"Ursula found you in there, didn't she? Why was she upset or angry to find you there?"

"No, she wasn't—"

"You left in quite a hurry," Ward said. Charlie couldn't understand how they knew all this. He was unsure of himself, and they kept the pressure on.

"When was the last time you saw Ursula?" Brennan asked.

"At the excavation site a couple of days ago, about five o'clock. They were finishing up for the day. I didn't speak to her."

"That's not what we heard," Ward said. "We have a statement from someone who overheard you talking with Ursula. She said she'd been watching you, didn't she? She threatened to expose what you'd been hiding unless you did something for her. There's a word for that sort of proposition; it's called blackmail. What are you hiding, Charlie? And what did Ursula want from you in return?"

Charlie's fingers gripped the metal cylinder more tightly, and his eyes hardened into steely blue stones. "Whoever told you all that was a liar. It never happened. Who was it told you that—Cadogan? He's the one you ought to be asking about his relationship with Ursula Downes."

"Are you saying you've seen them together?"

"If he denies it, ask him about the pipe shed on the back road to the old power station. I'll say no more about it."

"Where were you last night, Charlie?" Brennan asked.

He didn't respond immediately, and his feet shifted nervously. He couldn't look either one of them in the eye. "I had nothing to do with Ursula's murder. I swear it."

"Just tell us where you were. Start from the time you left work."

Charlie finally looked up at Maureen. "I finished my shift at four and went home to get my dinner. After that, I fed and watered the cattle and mended a fence across the road where my mother keeps her sheep. One of the posts was a bit wobbly, so I had to see it was mended straightaway."

"And what time did you finish all that?"

"About half-eight, I suppose. I don't really know. I don't wear a watch."

"Well, what time did you get home?"

There was a brief silence. Charlie's voice was low as he answered. "I didn't."

Ward saw Brennan glance over at him before she proceeded. "So where were you?"

"Up the hill behind the house. I had a big pile of dry scutch I'd been saving for a bonfire that night. It took a while to get the fire going well and I stayed beside it all night. I didn't want it to burn out. I got home around half-six to do the foddering."

"Where was this fire, exactly?"

"Top of the hill directly behind the house."

"Did anyone else see it?"

"I don't know. I didn't build it for anyone else. It was my own thing."

"What was the occasion?" Ward asked.

Charlie's eyes remained downcast. "Midsummer's eve. It's supposed to bring good luck, putting ashes from the fire over the cattle."

Brennan said, "So you're telling us you just sat and poked at a fire all night? All on your own?"

"That's all." Charlie colored deeply. Was it something that innocent and personal, Ward wondered, or was he concealing something darker? Whichever it was, the boy couldn't seem to raise his eyes from the floor. It wasn't just luck for the cattle he'd been after. There was something more, something he wasn't saying.

"I don't know if you remember, Charlie, but you and I have had dealings before," Ward said. "The business about some animals killed out on the bog. It's a good few years ago now. I talked to you a couple of times about that."

The young man's voice was low and adamant. "I remember. And what are they saying now? 'It must have been Charlie Brazil, he knew her, and remember what he did to those poor creatures.' They all think I'm half cracked, but I'm not, and you know it. I didn't do those things back then, and I did not kill Ursula Downes. I've done nothing wrong."

They had reached a stalemate. It would be useless to go on, at least for the moment.

"Can I get back to my work now?"

Ward nodded, and Charlie Brazil switched on the grinder, ignoring them as they made their way back out through the workshop.

8

When they reached the Garda station, Cormac hesitated for a moment before they went inside. He pulled his car keys out of his pocket and handed them to Nora.

"Just in case you need them," he said. He might as well have said what he was really thinking: *Just in case they arrest me.* "You can wait here for a while if you like, but I'm betting it'll take more than a few minutes. Maybe I should just ring you when they're finished with me."

She took the keys, letting her fingers rest lightly on his upturned palm; then he turned and walked through the door. "Cormac Maguire," he said to the officer at the front desk. "Here to see Detective Ward. He's expecting me."

Just a few moments after Ward had taken Cormac away to an interview room, Detective Brennan stuck her head through the inner door. "Dr. Gavin? If you'd come with me, we can have you sign your statement upstairs."

They passed through what appeared to be a squad room and turned into a stairwell at the building's rear. Their feet clattered on the concrete stairs, making a hollow, metallic echo in the stuffy stairwell. More desks, more phones upstairs, then a nondescript room with a table and several chairs—an interview room. Cormac was probably just next door. Nora knew they would not have brought her here just to sign a statement; they weren't finished with her yet, and it was this woman's job to get something more out of her.

Brennan set a sheaf of typed papers on the table, just out of reach. "We have your earlier statement here ready for you to sign, Dr. Gavin, but we wanted to give you the opportunity to add to it, if you wish to do so."

Nora studied Detective Brennan's face: broad, with a generous mouth; thick hair cut in a style that said she was a woman who tolerated a minimum of fuss.

"I'm not sure what you'd like me to add."

"You live in Dublin, but are staying out here for the moment at—"

She checked the typed sheet. "—the Crosses, a house owned by Evelyn McCrossan, is that correct?"

"Yes. You know all this; it's in my statement."

"Just want to make sure there's nothing you've inadvertently left out. Now, as I understand it, you're assisting with the excavation at Loughnabrone, and the archaeologist in charge of that excavation was Ursula Downes."

"It's a bit more complicated than that. Ursula was in charge of the bog road excavation, and in the course of that work, her team found the remains that the National Museum team was recovering over the past few days. I was consulting with the National Museum on that secondary excavation."

"I see. And Ursula's crew also found the body of Danny Brazil, who apparently was murdered at Loughnabrone Bog twenty-six years ago."

"Yes."

"All rather strange and coincidental, isn't it? It's also coincidental that your fellow houseguest up at the Crosses is an archaeologist and knew Ursula Downes—knew her quite well, according to our information. Working with her must have been a bit awkward."

Nora said nothing, but she felt her hands tightening into fists under the table. Brennan, despite her pleasant appearance, was quite good at this.

"Whose idea was it for you and Cormac Maguire to spend time here?"

"I don't remember, exactly. When the body turned up at Loughnabrone, the museum asked me to come down and consult on the recovery, and when I mentioned it to Cormac, he suggested that we stay at the Crosses."

"You came out here together from Dublin? When?"

"No. Cormac drove out here on his own last Sunday, and I came out on Monday morning. I wanted to have my own car while I was here."

"And why did you say he came along on the trip out here?"

"I didn't. But he told me he was working on some writing and thought a few quiet days in the country might help his concentration."

"I see. Or maybe he thought it would be interesting to put the two women he was seeing within reach of each other? Maybe the danger of that situation appealed to him. Surely he'd seen Ursula Downes being interviewed on television about the bog body. Surely he'd heard she was working on the site. Isn't that why he came out here?"

He'd never said anything to her about Ursula before they'd made their plans. "No. I had to be here for the excavation, and he came along to write."

"Did he mention anything to you about Ursula Downes visiting him at the Crosses on Sunday evening?" Brennan asked.

"Yes, he told me she stopped by just after he got in."

"This was something he volunteered on his own when you arrived?"

"No, he told me this morning—" Only this morning, after he'd found out Ursula was dead. But what Detective Brennan was suggesting could not be true.

"Can you tell us where Dr. Maguire was last night?"

"He was with me."

"All night?"

Nora hesitated slightly, trying to feel her way through this minefield, to tell the truth without damning Cormac. "We were together all evening. I fell asleep about eleven-thirty, and he was with me. When I woke up at seven this morning, he was there as well."

"And in the intervening hours, from half-eleven to seven a.m.?"

"I told you, I was asleep."

"You didn't wake in the middle of the night?"

"No, I was very tired." She felt the calm gray eyes survey every inch of her face. Brennan switched gears again.

"I suppose all archaeologists have their own gear that they bring to an excavation—do you know anything about that? I'd no idea they actually use bricklayers' trowels; I suppose I thought it would be something more sophisticated than that. And everyone all done up in waterproofs. I suppose the weather doesn't make all that much difference out on a bog. Wet above, wet below."

"Yes. It's very soggy work." A whirlwind of images swirled in Nora's brain: all the genderless figures out on the bog, Cormac's waterproof jacket hanging on the hook above his wellingtons last night, and the empty peg she'd seen this morning, the arterial blood spray on the wall at Ursula's house, and, though she tried to resist it, the image of an arm encased in a yellow rubber sleeve pulling a blade in a sharp motion across Ursula's slender throat. She knew Detective Brennan was watching these visions pass in front of her eyes.

"Cormac kept his waterproofs outside the back door of the house. Anyone could have taken them." She realized her misstep a second too late.

"*Kept* them outside the door? So you're saying they're not there now? When did you notice they were missing?"

"This morning as I left the house to go to the bog."

"So just before you discovered Ursula Downes's body?"

"Yes."

"And when did you last notice Dr. Maguire's waterproofs hanging in their usual place?"

"Yesterday evening, when we got home from a walk after dinner. He wore his wellingtons on the walk, and put them back under his waterproofs when we got home."

"What time was that?

"It was almost dark—about ten-thirty, I suppose."

"So between approximately ten-thirty last night and half-seven this morning, Dr. Maguire's waterproofs went missing."

Nora had the sinking feeling that she was digging Cormac in even deeper, but she couldn't lie without making things worse. She couldn't hear the rest of Brennan's words. The world had gone pear-shaped in front of her eyes. Was there anything Cormac had not told her about his visit to Ursula? *Stay calm,* urged the voice in her head. *They're doing this on purpose, to get at you. It's all part of the interrogation technique, to get you to question Cormac's word, tell them something you shouldn't tell. But you've told the truth.* Who had told them Cormac had been involved with Ursula? Had he told them himself, or was there some other evidence? Or maybe it was just speculation on their part. The police had to sort fact from fiction all the time, and they, like all humans, made mistakes, and jumped to conclusions, too eager to find connections where there were none.

"Put yourself in my position, Dr. Gavin," Brennan was saying. "We have to follow all possible leads, and when we see a past relationship with a victim, physical evidence at the scene, and an eyewitness account, we have to look into it."

Nora tried to focus, to slow her racing thoughts. "Of course you do," she said. "I understand perfectly. But I hope you're looking into all the other possible suspects as well."

"Oh, we are. But did I happen to mention that Ursula put up quite a struggle, and that we found blood and skin under her fingernails? We ought to be able to match that with the person who strangled her and cut her throat. I'm encouraged by that news, but I'm afraid Ursula Downes is beyond encouragement."

"You don't have to tell me, Detective Brennan. I found her body, remember? I couldn't be more aware of a victim's plight. But Cormac Maguire is not the one you're looking for. He's not, and I'd stake my life on it."

"Well, Dr. Gavin, let's hope it doesn't come to that." She pushed the statement in front of Nora and offered a pen. "Just sign and date the statement, if you would. Then I can see you out."

Emerging from the station, Nora felt as if the world had changed while she was inside. The faces of the people passing by looked harder, more sinister; the very light looked harsher and more unforgiving than it had less than an hour ago. She had two talismans, the car keys Cormac had handed her and her mobile phone. She checked the phone's battery—still good, for another while at least. He'd said he would ring as soon as they were finished with him. Surely they wouldn't—no, she couldn't let herself imagine that they would keep him in custody. But if they tried, he might not kick up enough fuss about it, thinking that everything would come right somehow.

Gazing across the busy street, Nora saw another little whirlwind like the one she'd seen out on the bog, only smaller, more compact, and remembered Owen Cadogan's words: *The fairy wind. They say nothing good comes after.* A strong gust suddenly pulled a spout of dust and leaves several feet up into the air, where it lost cohesion and fell apart, once more becoming just a harmless heap underfoot—*the stuff we tread through day after day,* she thought. *And it's the same with evil; it comes from nowhere, from the things and people around us every day, and recedes back into them.* How else to explain lynch mobs, death squads, mankind's cruel history of spontaneous, senseless slaughter? Ancient people everywhere had explanations for it: tricksters, evil spirits, ill winds; the eyes they saw everywhere, leering, grimacing, taking glee in the disruption of order. Nora found herself offering up a tiny, wordless prayer for Cormac's safekeeping, and for her own.

Another thought struck her as she walked toward the jeep. They might just take a cheek swab or blood sample for typing and DNA analysis, and be finished with him within a few minutes. It would be silly to go home if that were the case. Nora crossed the street and pushed open the door of Coughlan's Hotel, then the door under a sign with three carved wooden knots that read "Lounge Bar." Inside was a rather old-fashioned blend of burnished wood and brass, tapestry-upholstered stools and benches. Nora ordered a cappuccino and sat at a table near the bar, stirring a sugar lump into the coffee hiding beneath the white foam.

Three knots. There had been three knots in the cords that strangled both Danny Brazil and Ursula Downes. Maybe that wasn't the only connection. If only she could get her thoughts to order themselves. She needed a logical plan of action, not this chaotic jumble of half-drawn connections and questions.

She wondered whether the certainty she felt about Cormac's innocence was the same certainty felt by people whose loved ones maintained their innocence when they really were guilty. Cormac might be guilty of other things—guilty of gallantry laced with stupidity in venturing over to Ursula's house that night, without a single witness to support his story. Why hadn't he brought her with him, if he'd only gone to assuage Ursula's fears? Detective Brennan had done an excellent job of raising all the unanswered questions that had been lying dormant in her mind.

She looked across the bar and saw a half-familiar figure. The man from Ursula's house this morning—Quill. When people said a man looked distinguished, they meant he looked like Desmond Quill, who had the sort of face that weathered nicely over time. He was probably over sixty, but broad-shouldered and trim, with well-defined, even features, a square jaw, and a full head of silver hair. Something in his upright posture suggested an elegant wading bird, a gray heron. Nora didn't know the man, but as she approached, the set of his shoulders and the double whiskey in front of him filled her with a spreading ache.

"Mr. Quill?"

He didn't turn; his eyes only flickered upward briefly, and did not rest on her face.

"You were at Ursula's house this morning," he said, his speech noticeably slowed by alcohol. "I'm sorry, I don't know your name."

She slid onto the bench across from him, and he didn't object. "Nora Gavin. I'm so very sorry about Ursula. I heard you say that you were a friend—"

"They won't let me go, you know. Not until their investigation proves that I'm not a cold-blooded killer. As if I—" He rubbed his temple as if massaging a vein that throbbed there, closed his eyes and breathed in deeply through his nose. Nora stared at his crinkled-tissue eyelids, the deep lines in his face that actually enhanced rather than detracted from its attractiveness. "I told them everything I know," he said. "That she phoned me in Dublin last night, said someone had been bothering her. She didn't say who it was, only that she was a bit anxious. I asked if she was in any physical danger, and she said—" He couldn't go on for a moment. "She said she didn't think it would go that far. I told her I'd be down first thing, to help her get things sorted out. I wasn't going to let her stay in a place where she might be in danger. She promised to ring the police if anything else happened." He looked up, his eyes searing into Nora's face.

"I knew her only briefly. I wish—"

"What do you wish?"

"I wish there were something I could do."

"Do you know who killed her?"

"No. I mean—I don't know. You said someone was harassing her?"

"Yes, that's what she told me. Ringing her at all hours, spraying paint on the windows. I offered to come out here last night, but she said no, nothing would happen, I should wait until the morning. And so I played my usual game of chess, and I lost."

He lifted his eyes to meet hers, and she felt a sudden transfixion. Then he looked away, as if he'd felt it too. The amber whiskey before him looked thick and sweet, clinging to the clear glass as he lifted it and swallowed. Nora studied the way his Adam's apple rose and fell above the crisply pressed white shirt. Quill had one of those faces that seemed almost not to have any pores, so fine and fresh was the skin. She looked at his necktie, pulled loose at the collar, but still secured with a very unusual pin: a bronze disc, into which an ancient design had been engraved, a triskelion, a graceful trio of spiraling curves.

"I'll tell you the same thing I told the Guards," Quill said. "I have a suspicion about who might have been threatening Ursula. She told me that she had a brief—and, by her account, wholly unsatisfactory—liaison with Owen Cadogan last summer. It was long over, at least on her part, but Cadogan was evidently having trouble letting go." So the contempt she had seen in Ursula's face, and the anger in Cadogan's eyes, had been real, Nora thought. She had been witness to the unraveling of a relationship, with all the pain and bitterness that entailed.

Quill drew back slightly and studied her expression. "You think it strange that Ursula would tell me about her affairs."

"No, not necessarily."

"You do. That's all right, too. She wanted to make sure I knew what I was getting into with her. Thought that, if I knew the worst about her, I'd be warned off; but it didn't work that way. She fascinated me, absorbed me. Why am I telling you all this?" He stared down at the whiskey, then up at her. "She wanted to tell me about her lovers. And I wanted to hear because she felt the need to tell me. No doubt some people, maybe even most people, would think that strange. I can't say it's not. I don't defend or deny. It's just a fact. It is. And I daresay there are stranger things in the world than the need to confess, to take someone into your confidence. Lets you feel, perhaps, slightly less alone."

"Why you? Why did she choose you as her confessor?"

"I don't know. Maybe because I've refrained from passing judgment. Isn't that what love does?"

Nora thought it quite possible that she'd never had such a peculiar conversation with a complete stranger. Sometimes death had a way of cutting through polite social customs. And, in a way, she found Quill's lack of embarrassment quite exhilarating. His fingers circled the glass in front of him. They were long and slender, almost out of proportion to the rest of him, and Nora felt as if she could see clearly, through the skin, how each finger's knobby metacarpal fitted against its cuplike base.

"I didn't really know Ursula," she said. "I only met her a few times, out on the bog. But I found her this morning, and I suppose that makes me feel as if I should have made an effort to know her better."

"What do you want to know? I wonder what it says about the human race that we're so much more interested in the dead than in the living. While she lived, no one inquired after Ursula—what sort of a person she was, what moved her, excited her, allowed her to get out of bed each morning. Now that she's dead, you're just the latest in a series of people who've asked me that same question. I'm not trying to make you feel bad, Miss Gavin; it's just curious to me. Being with Ursula was like getting a strong electric jolt. Everything she did crackled; there was no sitting things out, no passivity. Who would want to see that extinguished?"

Nora thought of the Ursula Downes she'd seen, provoking Owen Cadogan, mocking Charlie Brazil, and wondered whether Desmond Quill's judgment had been clouded by his feelings. Then she remembered the ghastly sight that had greeted her only a few hours earlier and knew that, no matter what she'd done, Ursula Downes hadn't deserved the death she had met today.

"We met only a few months ago," Quill said. "An exhibition opening at the National Museum. We were strangers, passing at a reception. I know it seems ridiculous, but sometimes you experience a kind of sudden recognition, and that's what I felt from the start. No illusions. Ursula was the only person with whom I ever felt that sort of kinship. The world saw us both in the same light, I suppose: cold, a little hard, perhaps. I prefer to think of it as being unsentimental. But there was ample reason for Ursula's mistrust of the world. It's a common reaction to betrayal. Think of it; the one person you depend on for protection, turning around and using that very vulnerability against you." He stared into the nearly empty whiskey glass, his expression distant, remembering.

"I don't think Ursula ever told anyone except me what her stepfather made of her. He used her mother's illness as an excuse, started coming to her room when he'd closed up the dry-cleaning shop for the night. She was just a child, and there was no safe place to run. Eventually he stopped. She grew up, you see—became a young woman, not a child anymore, and so she no longer fit within the bounds of his twisted fixation. Ursula said that sometimes, after everything else, it still felt as though the worst cruelty was the way in which he finally rejected her. That she actually came to hate herself for growing up. Can you imagine such a monster? He left his mark on her. It wasn't just the physical scars that remained forever."

There was nothing Nora could do but listen. Of course all the tiny facets of Ursula she'd seen were not the whole picture. But what became of all the other undetectable, irreducible essences that made up any human being, when the person was no longer there? One of the most terrible things about murder was that it made for an unfair summing-up, a life abridged far too soon. She still wasn't sure why Desmond Quill was telling her all this. Perhaps he hadn't planned to do so; maybe the shock had been more than he realized. After all, it was only this morning that he had arrived at the house to find that Ursula Downes, his singular vision of the future, was dead.

"I suppose some people would look at Ursula and me and see an old man using a younger woman to regain the illusion of lasting life. I was laboring under no misconceptions, mind you. I'm not young—I'll be sixty-seven in October—and I understood completely that Ursula had certain needs, certain desires that I might not be able to fulfill. I wouldn't have stood in her way. She didn't belong to me; it isn't—wasn't—that kind of possessive relationship. But in many ways we were uncommonly well-suited. If only she'd let me look after her, she wouldn't have been out here again. But she could be terribly willful. Exasperating at times." He took another swallow of whiskey, and Nora wondered how many he'd had before she arrived. He began shifting the change that sat beside his glass on the table, arranging the coins into triangles, then rows of three, like some elaborate game of noughts and crosses. She watched the elegant fingers moving slowly, surely, deliberately.

"You said you wished there was something you could do," Quill said. "Maybe there is. You can tell me about her last few days here." He seized Nora's hand; she tried instinctively to pull it away, but he held her fast. "I need to find out what happened to her. I've got to know." The muscles in his jaw went taut; then his head drooped toward his chest, and he let her go. "I'm sorry. . . . Do you know what she asked me, just before she rang off last night? She asked whether I thought three was a lucky or an unlucky number. What do you think she meant by that?"

Nora looked down at the coins on the table, neatly arranged in three rows of three. Just then her mobile began to chirp and vibrate against her hip. She couldn't answer it, not now; she needed room to breathe and think. She had to get out of here, away from Desmond Quill with his deliberate hands and his disjointed grief and his sweet whiskey breath. She stood up suddenly and said, "I'm sorry, but I have to go now." Desmond Quill stood as well, at least a head taller than she was, but unsteady on his feet.

When she reached the jeep, she sat in the driver's seat, flipped open her phone, and retrieved the voice mail message. It was Cormac. "It looks like I'm going to be here another while. Why don't you go home for now? I'll ring you again when they're finished with me." A pause. "Talk to you later, Nora." How strange that the device she held in her hand could contain all that was in those final words: disappointment, puzzlement, a plaintive sliver of hope.

9

The conversation with Desmond Quill had unsettled Nora, and she arrived back at the Crosses unsure what to do next. Climbing out of the car, she saw the empty peg where Cormac's waterproofs had hung the previous night. Where were they now, and why had Detective Brennan been so full of questions about when she'd seen them last? The detectives must have thought they had something concrete; otherwise Brennan wouldn't have wasted precious time asking pointed questions. Surely they didn't think Cormac would be that thick—to wear his own protective gear while committing a murder, and then stash it near the crime scene? She thought of him in a windowless interview room, trying to explain what seemed inexplicable, even to himself—why he'd gone to Ursula's house, how her blood had gotten all over his clothing. Things looked bad for Cormac unless they could come up with evidence placing someone else at the scene as well. And with a prime suspect who had conveniently presented himself on their doorstep—at her insistence, she recalled—would they even try?

After hearing Desmond Quill's suspicions, Nora was more convinced than ever that Owen Cadogan had something to do with Ursula's murder. But what was she going to do—phone up Cadogan's wife and ask if he'd been home all night? Surely the police would do that much. Her statement on its own wouldn't be enough, of course; they would need hard evidence. Quill said that someone had sprayed paint on Ursula's windows; maybe there was some way Cadogan could be tied to the scene through that. . . . She knew she was grasping at straws, jumping to conclusions too fast. Maybe Quill's suspicions had made her too focused on Owen Cadogan.

If it wasn't Cadogan—well, Cormac wasn't the only person who might have traveled to Ursula's house on foot. Michael Scully had told them that the Brazils were his closest neighbors, that Danny Brazil's apiary was just over the hill behind the house. And Danny's apiary was now in Charlie Brazil's care. From the conversation she'd overheard between

Ursula and Charlie, it seemed that Ursula had been for some reason keenly interested in the recovery of Danny Brazil's body. Nora tried to remember exactly what Ursula had said—something about Danny's triple-knotted cord not being such a good luck charm. Was that what Ursula had meant, asking Quill if he thought three was a lucky or an unlucky number? *I've been watching you,* she'd said to Charlie. *I know what you're hiding.* But when Charlie had asked what she wanted from him, she'd said, *Maybe I have something to give you.* Her words had been a proposition, in more ways than one. *Come and see me,* she'd commanded. As if he'd have no choice but to obey.

Nora closed her eyes and went back to the previous night, trying to picture what they'd seen from the top of the small hill. From what she remembered, anyone up there could have seen down into Ursula's kitchen. Cormac said he'd seen Brona Scully at the fairy tree; maybe she'd been up there last night. But that hopeful idea was immediately tamped down by reality. Even if she had been, even if she'd seen something, how was that supposed to do Cormac any good? The girl didn't speak a word. One might as well try to coax testimony from a silent standing stone. If Brona had seen something . . . the more Nora thought about it, the more that possibility disturbed the edges of her consciousness. It wouldn't hurt to find out what the girl could have seen from the fairy tree.

The scrappy whitethorn bush made an arresting sight even in the bright light of day. The setting was just as Nora had remembered: from the pasture atop the hill, a person could indeed see straight down into Ursula's back garden. The empty kitchen window still yawned jaggedly, and crime-scene tape still marked out the perimeter of the house and garden. She tried to picture Ursula's figure in the house—and Cormac coming up over this hill and down into Ursula's yard. She didn't like to think about what had followed, but she had to, if she was going to help Cormac. She stood in the spot where a witness might have stood only a few hours ago and imagined how events must have unfolded.

Cormac was not guilty of murder—he couldn't be; but Brona Scully's silence might be his undoing. How much would Brona have been able to see at night—presuming she even came here after dark? There was no sign of the girl, but Nora still felt ill at ease, wondering if there were eyes upon her. She had a distinct, unsettling feeling that someone was watching her from the tangled bushes at the edge of the field. She turned slowly back toward the fairy tree, searching the hedgerows for signs of life, but nothing stirred.

She heard the sound of breathing behind her, and whirled around to find a red bullock with a creamy-white face regarding her curiously from a few yards away. From what Michael Scully had told them, Nora guessed the cattle grazing in the surrounding pastures belonged to the Brazils. Charlie's apiary was probably somewhere up here as well. She kept thinking of Ursula's words: *I've been up at your place, Charlie—the place where you have the bees. People have told me Danny used to keep bees there as well. . . .* Was it blackmail, or another kind of threat that had lingered in her words? *I've been watching you, Charlie. I know what you're hiding.* What if it was something in that forbidden knowledge that had gotten Ursula killed?

Nora had another vision of Cormac sitting in that dreary interview room, answering the same questions again and again, facing disbelieving expressions on the faces of the detectives across the table. Ursula's blood was on his clothing, and she had left scratches on his neck. It was possible that unless Nora found some other path for them to follow, Cormac's whole life might be forfeit for something he hadn't done.

She checked her watch. Charlie Brazil wouldn't be at the apiary just yet. At midsummer bees had to be tended quite closely and checked at least once a day, she knew, but Charlie probably worked until at least four o'clock on the bog. She wasn't sure what direction to choose, until she saw several bees, heavily laden with golden pollen, rise up out of a wild rose hedge beside her and fly off unsteadily away from the Crosses and the way she'd come. She followed the cattle path and saw the circle of trees first, then the hives, set like standing stones around the open ground in its center. Off to one side was a house, with door and window frames gaping open to all weather. No one was about except for bees, buzzing in the midsummer plenty amid the globes of clover. She had no protective gear, but she didn't feel nervous. The insects were consumed in their business, and not interested in her.

Walking into a house with no door didn't seem as intrusive as breaking and entering, but Nora still felt strange, venturing into Charlie Brazil's beekeeping shed. Two things drove her past the discomfort: the image of Cormac being interviewed as a suspect, and the lingering regret she always carried with her that she had not done more, had not pushed harder to find things out when her sister was still alive. She couldn't afford to risk timidity anymore.

The door frame had once been painted green, and the whitewash had long ago crumbled from the walls with damp. She stepped across the threshold and saw a ragged curtain tacked to the window frame with nails. You could imagine a father and mother in their traditional places by the fire, and thin-faced barefoot children in pinafores. Was there no place in Ireland that wasn't hip-deep in ghosts?

Charlie Brazil had stacked new frames along the walls. His bee suit, hat, and veil hung on a hook beside the doorway, and his smoker—a small can with a built-in bellows that keepers use to control their bees—sat ready on the window ledge with a box of matches beside it. Under one of the small windows sat a plain metal cot, blanket neatly tucked under the mattress. Someone stayed here—if not every night, then at least from time to time. A dozen or more small holes in the thick, crumbling quicklime of the wall at the bed's foot said something had been tacked up there, and fairly recently, too. Nora got down on her knees to look under the cot, and saw something like a postcard lying facedown on the dirt floor next to the wall. Reaching one hand in, half afraid of what she would find, she felt the thick, smooth paper.

The image on the other side was not a photograph, as she'd half imagined, but a detailed pen-and-ink drawing, like those she'd seen in Cormac's archaeology books, only this one was graying slightly with mildew. Its subject was a plate or shield, with decoration that was vaguely familiar; something about it said Iron Age. She let her fingers travel over the sinuous S-curves and scrolls, drawn on paper here as they had been engraved in the original metal. What was a drawing like this doing in Charlie Brazil's beekeeping shed? She noted the pinhole in the paper, with a thumbtack still through it, and counted the pinholes in the wall; seventeen, regularly placed, as if more drawings like this had once hung there. Was this what Ursula had found?

Nora slipped the drawing into her jacket pocket and looked around the tiny room once more. She wondered what had become of the people who had lived here. The house seemed to have been abandoned more or less intact; the worm-eaten shelves built against the dividing wall were still stacked with cracked cups and saucers. Someone kept the bare floor swept fairly regularly, presumably with the broom that stood in the corner, and the wooden steps up into the loft had been mended recently;

several nail heads shone against the weathered wood. She tested the first step, and, finding it sturdy enough, ventured up the short ladder into the attic. An open suitcase lay on the floor. She stooped to examine the contents scattered about: clothing that looked as if it had been torn to shreds, a jumbled pile of newspaper cuttings, and some old photos, faded with time and weather. The top photograph, sticky with honey, showed a young woman. From the clothing she wore, the picture seemed to have been taken some time ago. Nora closed the suitcase and looked for initials, a tag, anything that would tell her whose belongings these were; but the warped cardboard shell gave up no clue, just fell apart where the hinges were coming loose. She continued looking around the cramped attic room, strewn with old junk, rusted nails, and wire. Maybe Charlie was digging up artifacts like the disc in the drawing, and that was what Ursula had been on to. According to Niall Dawson, digging up antiquities without a license was a criminal offense—but would such a thing be worth killing for?

A noise came from below; someone was in the house. Nora felt a surge of adrenaline as she flattened herself along the floor. The smell of dust and damp filled her nostrils, and she prayed that she wouldn't sneeze or choke and give herself away. There were wide cracks between the floorboards, and she could see into the room downstairs.

It was Charlie Brazil. But he made no move toward his suit and gloves. He was here for something else. Nora held her breath and watched as he knelt by the fireplace. With the poker he prised up a gray flagstone at one corner. He removed a flat tin box from the place beneath and set it on the floor beside him, then moved the stone back into place and scattered a few ashes over it. Nora tried to pull herself along the floor without making a noise, to get a better vantage point.

Charlie opened the box, lifted out a handful of drawings like the one Nora had tucked in her pocket, then checked through the other objects the box contained. She heard the sound of metal on metal, and saw ring money, bracelets, an ax-head, coins. Charlie reached into his pocket and pulled out what looked like a primitive dagger, and drew the blade from its sheath. The dull bronze glowed in his hands, and it was clear to Nora, even at a distance, that the knife was not a modern implement. A thrill of cold fear traveled through her. This could be the knife that had been used on Ursula Downes. If Ursula had found out about Charlie's hoard of artifacts, what would she have done? Perhaps she'd wanted in on it.

Charlie had said people asked him where the gold was buried, the things Dominic and Danny Brazil had supposedly kept from the Loughnabrone hoard. Nora tried to remember exactly what Ursula had said to Charlie that afternoon. *I know what you're hiding.*

She felt something on her left ankle, down near the place where the roof met the floor. One of Charlie's bees had found the space between her trouser leg and sock, and was crawling slowly up toward her knee. She couldn't move for fear of making a noise, so she held her breath and willed the bloody insect to turn around and go back from whence it had come. She'd have to be very careful not to provoke it; she knew from experience that a stinging bee gives off a pheromone that encourages other bees to join in the attack. And she'd seen what kind of damage a swarm of angry honeybees could do. The alternative was giving herself away and getting out now—a prospect she did not relish, looking down on the knife that might have cut Ursula's throat.

Charlie slipped the dagger back into its sheath, then placed it carefully in his pocket and slid the tin into a cloth sack he'd pulled from another pocket. He was shifting these things; maybe Ursula had found them, and he feared another discovery. The bee inched its way toward her left knee, and Nora had to fight the urge to smash it and run. If only Charlie would get out, so she could move, get away from here . . . He stood, looking around the room. Nora twitched involuntarily as she felt the bee move again, then froze as Charlie started to mount the staircase. He stopped with his head just inside the upstairs room, listening intently, and Nora hoped that her breathing wasn't audible from where he stood, that he couldn't feel the vibration as her heart wrenched violently against her ribs. She felt the bee sting, like a nettle's hot-cold touch, until the pain blurred together into a single throbbing mass. She tried to still her mind, deaden her senses, breathe silently despite the awful fear that she would cry out.

After a few seconds, Charlie's head disappeared, and he climbed back down the ladder and left the shed. Nora waited as long as she could, then peeled off her jeans, batting at the bee, which retaliated by trying to sting her bare fingers. She scrambled to her feet, flailing her arms and legs to shake it off, and almost tripped down the ladder. She ran out of the house, up onto the pasture above the apiary, trying desperately to put distance between herself and the angry insect, waving her empty trousers behind her. Her left ankle already felt swollen and hot as her body's natural histamine rushed to fight off the poison. She began to limp, and stopped at the pasture gate to catch her breath and put her trousers back on. The ankle had started to swell. Stepping into her jeans, she heard a noise in the bushes behind her, and turned to see Charlie Brazil, red with embarrassment at her state of undress.

"What are you doing here?" he asked.

Nora's mind raced through possible responses. Charlie had nothing in his hands now; he must have hidden the artifacts somewhere nearby. "I was just out for some air," she said. "I wanted to thank you for the honey, if you were around. I'm afraid I strayed too close to the hives." She lifted her trouser leg and showed off the swollen ankle. "Stupid of me. I should have known better."

"Let me see that," he said, dropping to one knee and cradling her ankle in his hands. His touch felt cool against her skin. "You're not allergic to bee stings, are you? Do you need some help getting home?"

Nora remembered the dagger Charlie had removed from his pocket. "I'm sure I can make it on my own," she said. "There's no need—"

"You shouldn't put your full weight on that ankle. Come on, I'll walk you." He was close enough that she could smell the tang of sweat his body gave off after a day's work. It was possible that she'd completely misread Charlie Brazil from the start. He stood and was about to put one arm about her waist, but the thought suddenly struck her: What if he found the drawing in her pocket? She pulled away.

"No, really, I can make it on my own. I'm all right."

His eyes narrowed slightly. "Why are you afraid of me?"

"I'm not. You've rescued me once already, that first day out on the bog. I just don't think it's necessary. You've things to do, I'm sure, and I'll be fine on my own." Her eyes brushed involuntarily across the knotted cord around his neck, then slid away, but he'd seen her hesitation.

"What is it—this?" Charlie lifted the cord between his fingers and looked at her accusingly. "Ursula was very interested in this too."

He wasn't prepared when Nora bolted, ducking under his arm and fleeing headlong down the path toward the Scullys' house and the Crosses, as fast as she could run on her swelling ankle. Charlie probably could have caught her if he'd really wished to, but he let her go.

Nora's hands were trembling when she finally made it into the cottage and bolted the door behind her. Her ankle throbbed, and she limped to the fridge to see if there was any ice. One tray—it would have to do for now. She dumped the cubes into a plastic bag and twisted it shut, holding it to her still swelling ankle.

At first she had been almost certain that Owen Cadogan had something to do with Ursula's death. But after what she had seen just now, she couldn't be sure that Charlie Brazil wasn't involved as well. There were too many connections between Charlie and Ursula to rest on mere coincidence. She had nothing substantial enough to bring to the authorities, just a vague collection of hunches and suppositions. And yet she knew that all the things she'd seen had to add up somehow. Remembering why she had come here in the first place, to find out more about a man who had been either executed or sacrificed, Nora realized with a sinking feeling that she couldn't possibly stop now; there was too much at stake. Owen Cadogan had called the superstitions surrounding the fairy wind a load of old rubbish but, thinking back to that day, Nora knew that nothing good had come after it.

10

Ward left the superintendent's office and walked slowly back to his desk. They would have company on the Ursula Downes murder, as he had suspected. The unusual nature of the case, not to mention the whiff of ritual killing, had piqued the attention of the National Bureau of Criminal Investigation, and they were sending down a contingent to assist the local detective force. To the Bureau, "assist" meant something slightly more than the term generally implied. It meant he and Maureen Brennan had only a few more hours to come up with results before the Dublin boys in the expensive suits rolled in to take over the case.

He came up behind Brennan, who was pinning up crime-scene photos and other pertinent scraps of information on the board behind her desk, lining up a neat column for each of their lines of inquiry. "They'll be here Monday afternoon to set up their incident room." Her lips pressed together in a subtle expression of annoyance. "I know, but we'll have to just bear it."

"What did the superintendent say about the search for Rachel Briscoe?"

"I told him we've got several men and some local volunteers out looking for her already, handing out photos, asking if anyone's seen her, and that they're having no luck at all. We'll mount a coordinated search in the morning if there's no word."

"What are we calling her at this point—suspect or material witness?"

"She's only wanted for questioning, but that could change. Some of her coworkers seem convinced that she was obsessed with Ursula Downes, possibly stalking her. From the binoculars—and the way her colleagues describe her attachment to them—it seems likely that Rachel was at the house last night."

"What about that knife found at the scene?"

"It's being processed, but Dr. Friel didn't seem to think it was the murder weapon."

"Why not?"

"The blade is serrated; from what she's seen so far, Dr. Friel's of the opinion that the knife that cut the victim's throat had a straight edge. I still think Rachel Briscoe is probably the key to everything. If she didn't kill Ursula Downes, there's a chance she might have seen the person who did."

It was still early in the investigation, Ward realized, but they were very short of information on the victim. The house where Ursula Downes had been staying was only temporary quarters, and it had yielded very little useful information about her; the testimony they'd been able to gather so far from people who'd had contact with her here was sketchy and incomplete. They needed a fuller picture of the victim in order to imagine the crime.

He reached for the rucksack he'd brought back from the scene, and started to go through the contents. Brennan listed and described each object on an inventory form as he extracted it from the bag. "Appointment diary—not much in it; I'll have a look through that. Clipboard and paperwork—related to the excavation, looks like. Pens and pencils. Small purse with identification, driving license, business cards, fifty-seven euros and—" He counted out the change. "Forty-three cents. Mobile phone. Why don't you have a look at the phone—check all the calls made and received in the past few days. By the way, what's the word from Dublin— have they been in touch about the search of Ursula's flat?"

"They're sending a team over right now," Maureen said, looking at her watch. "Anything else you need from them? What about Desmond Quill—hadn't we better check his alibi as well? I mean, it's unlikely that he drove out here, cut her throat, and then hung around to see who might discover the body, but we've still got to check him out."

"Yes, see if they can send someone 'round to check Quill's story for Thursday evening. He says he was playing his usual chess game that night, and was occupied with that until quite late. Dr. Friel puts time of death between midnight and four a.m., so if we can eliminate Quill, we can concentrate on a few of the others."

"Ah, yes—the others."

"Let's go over the interview notes, see where we might have a few holes where we can start digging."

Maureen reached for her notebook and flipped back a few pages to the start of the interviews on the case. "Nora Gavin says she saw Owen Cadogan making threatening gestures toward Ursula Downes on Monday afternoon last. Dr. Gavin also says that the following day, Ursula turned the tables, giving Cadogan a slap in the face and a right old tongue-lashing. A couple of very public quarrels with the victim in the days running up to the murder, and no alibi for that night."

Ward remembered Cadogan's tight-lipped secretary. "Unless perhaps Aileen Flood has a slightly different story than the one he gave us. Let's wait and talk with her tomorrow. And don't forget we also have Desmond Quill's statement, saying Ursula was seeing Owen Cadogan last summer, and that he'd been harassing her since she arrived last week—ringing her mobile, leaving crude messages on her windows. There was something that looked like red spray paint on the broken window glass in the bin in Ursula's kitchen. I sent it along to the lab; if it was one of those messages Quill described, they might be able to reconstruct it, tell us what it said. Her mobile also ought to tell us if Cadogan was the person ringing her up day and night."

"His story about warning Ursula off Charlie Brazil sounds to me like a complete load of rubbish. But that doesn't necessarily mean Ursula wasn't somehow involved with Charlie Brazil."

Ward considered that possibility. "We've got Dr. Gavin's statement that she overheard Charlie speaking with Ursula Downes—she was blackmailing him, threatening to expose something he'd been hiding."

"What do people normally want to keep hidden?" Brennan said. "Bastard children, buried treasure, family skeletons . . . Whatever it is, though, we're going to have a job finding out, since he flatly denies that conversation ever took place. We should also check out that place he mentioned—the pipe shed on the road to the old power station."

"What do you think of Charlie's story about building a midsummer bonfire?"

"Ah, come on, Liam. Nobody does that anymore."

Ward thought back to Charlie Brazil's guarded expression when he'd talked to them about the bonfire. Brennan wasn't often wrong, but he thought she was mistaken in this case. The attraction of fire was deep and instinctive, inexplicable, and there were certain areas, especially in the West, where people still made huge bonfires on special nights. Ward felt suddenly pierced by the memory of an incident that had happened more than thirty years ago, one of his first official tasks as a young Garda officer. He'd been asked to put the boot down on a Saint John's Eve bonfire, at the request of a parish priest who had no time for such remnants of pagan foolishness. He had driven out to the spot thinking it was probably harmless enough, wondering what the hell he was doing there. Then he'd seen the huge fire. He had stood for a long time, watching as flames and embers reached skyward, through them seeing human faces, their reddened features exaggerated and transformed into surreal masks by the firelight.

The memory receded, and Ward said, "We'll have to go up there and check the place where Charlie Brazil said he built his bonfire. It won't tell us if he was there all night, but at least we'll know if he was telling the truth about the fire. Did anything turn up in the files about other ritual murder cases?"

As if reading his thoughts about conflagration, Brennan said, "There was a body found burnt to a cinder in Wicklow last winter. At first there was speculation that it might be some sort of ritual thing, but they eventually found out it was a disagreement over drugs. The victim had a bullet in him, and the fellas who put it there tried to make the killing look like a sacrifice to throw investigators off."

"That's it? Nothing else?"

"Nothing local, at least nothing with a human victim. Just that case you mentioned to Charlie Brazil." She took a file from a stack on her desk and tossed it over to him. Ward opened the file and perused the reports and photographs it contained, stopping at the pictures of the butchered kid goat suspended from a slender branch. He studied the detail shots of the narrow noose, the animal's protruding tongue, the deep gash in its distended throat, the blackening entrails. Poor harmless creature. The ground beneath the kid's hind legs was exactly as he remembered it from the scene: stained a deep rust red, with three circles drawn in blood. A hideous prank, or some demented notion of a sacred rite?

"Tell me more about that case," Maureen said. "You said you worked on it?"

"I'd only been here about three years. There were three separate incidents, two lambs and a kid goat killed in some apparent ritual sacrifice. It was bad—you've seen the file. I had a suspicion at the time that Charlie Brazil was probably just a convenient scapegoat. Now I'm not so sure."

"What about Maguire?" Brennan turned the pages of her notebook to their most recent interview. "He says Ursula Downes reported a prowler and asked him to come over and investigate, which he did. He says she'd cut herself on glass from the kitchen window, which was broken when he arrived, and he got blood on his clothing when he helped her bind up the wound."

"There was a fairly deep cut on Ursula's left hand. We should ask Dr. Friel to check for any fragments of glass in the wound."

"Right, but Maguire also admits that it's his skin under the victim's fingernails. He claims she attacked him when he questioned her story about the prowler and refused to stay any longer. He says he put his bloodstained clothing into the washing machine when he arrived home. Claims he doesn't know what happened to his waterproof gear. He did keep it outside the back door of the house where anyone might have taken it. And why would you wear your own kit if you're planning to kill someone? Wouldn't you get a nice disposable mac? But I suppose that sort of mistake makes sense if it was a crime of passion, spur-of-the-moment. You've done the deed; you're covered in blood, and for some reason you can't take the time to get rid of the evidence. So you plant the waterproofs somewhere and hope someone will buy the idea that you're being stitched up."

Ward remembered the plumes of blood on Ursula Downes's bathroom wall. She had probably been unconscious but still alive when her throat was cut, a fact that didn't square with Maureen's spur-of-the-moment theory. And the tableau, all that peat heaped around the bathtub, also smacked of ritualistic obsession, not crime of passion. "But why bring the waterproofs in the first place? It wasn't raining on Thursday evening. And what about motive? Maguire admits he was involved with Ursula Downes years ago, but it doesn't seem to have been a terrible secret. Not worth killing for."

"Maybe it's something else. They're both archaeologists; maybe it's professional. She knows something about him that he doesn't want other people to know—something to do with his academic work, his research; something that might compromise his career, his ambitions to be department chairman one day. We've got to at least check him out."

"Agreed. Let's add him to the list for the boys in Dublin, get some background on him."

"It would be so nice and simple if it was Maguire."

"Wouldn't it, though? Somehow I doubt this case is going to untangle that easily. I keep going back to this thing with the three knots," Ward said. "Both bodies found in the bog had knotted leather cords around their necks. One's a couple of thousand years old, one's more recent. But the cord was how the newer body was identified; Teresa Brazil said her brother-in-law Danny always wore a similar cord with three knots, some sort of good luck charm. And then, three days after Danny's body turns up, somebody strangles Ursula Downes with the same sort of triple-knotted cord. Both also had their throats cut. One was found in a bog, one in a bathtub that had been heaped around with peat."

"What's the peat supposed to mean, do you think?"

"Dr. Gavin mentioned at Danny Brazil's postmortem that his injuries were very like some she'd seen on ancient corpses from bogs—like the one that turned up here last Friday. She said it's not certain, but some archaeologists think they might have been human sacrifices. The idea was niggling at me, so I called around yesterday evening to ask her a few more questions about it, and she referred my questions to Maguire. He seemed well up on ancient sacrificial rites, especially the triple death Dr. Gavin mentioned—it's supposed to have included strangulation, throat-cutting, and drowning."

"Unfortunately, a lot of people could have had all the pertinent details on the manner of Danny Brazil's death." Maureen started ticking off the witnesses on her fingers. "There's Ursula Downes, for a start, all six people on her crew, and Nora Gavin. And Maguire obviously knew about it, if you talked to him. We know for a fact that Charlie Brazil told his mother about the triple knots, because that's how she came to think it might be Danny. And that's not even mentioning all the people that any one of those witnesses could have spoken to after that morning. You know how information travels here; I'm betting that half the county was well up on it by Tuesday afternoon."

She was right, of course. Still, they would have a look at the two cords. It was at least a possible connection, and there might be others as well. Ward reached for the preliminary autopsy report on Danny Brazil, and turned to Dr. Friel's description of the injuries: *The initial wound is present on the left side of the neck, over the sternocleidomastoid muscle, 6 cm below the left auditory canal.* There was something tentative about the injury, as if the assailant hadn't quite maintained control of the situation, and the victim had struggled. They didn't have the autopsy report yet, but it was clear from what he'd seen this morning that Ursula Downes's throat had been cut from side to side, deeply enough to sever the main arteries. Danny Brazil had drowned. Even though the modus operandi seemed similar, the two attacks had had very different results. Were they looking at the same killer, or at someone who for some reason only wanted Ursula's death to look like Danny Brazil's?

"What else do we know about Danny Brazil?" Ward asked. "He was twenty-four years old when he was last seen in June 1978. He was unmarried, employed at Bord na Móna as a fitter, and helping his brother, Dominic, work the family farm. Played for the Offaly senior hurling team until he suffered a career-ending injury in 1977. That was also the summer he and Dominic found a significant stash of Iron Age artifacts out on the bog. Just before Danny disappeared, they'd each received ten thousand pounds in reward money."

"Must have thought they'd won the Lotto," Maureen said. "Especially at that time. Nobody had two shillings to rub together."

She was right. The amount seemed almost paltry now, but ten thousand would have been a huge sum in those days. And there were the stories that the Brazils had held out, kept some of the best pieces from the Loughnabrone hoard. People took it for granted that the rumors were true. The brothers had mostly kept to themselves, and hadn't gone out of their way to refute the common assumption. Ward had thought at the time that the suspicions of the older generation might have been a factor in the whispered accusations against Charlie, but those were things that you could never quite describe or quantify in a file. Some people said that finding the hoard had actually brought bad luck on the Brazils. The question remained: Was there some connection between Danny Brazil's death and the murder of Ursula Downes, or did someone just want them to make a connection?

"I know it's tempting to make a link with the older murder," Maureen said, "but I think we're looking for something much more recent. At this point I'm still leaning toward a jilted lover, which would lead us straight to Owen Cadogan or Cormac Maguire. They both have motive. Cadogan's been rejected, and after his carry-on with Ursula the previous summer, that probably wouldn't sit well. He'd probably feel entitled. Maguire told us his relationship with Ursula Downes was long over, but suppose it wasn't. Suppose he goes over there hoping to cool things off, and she refuses—maybe threatens to tell his new girlfriend about them. He admits arguing with her; we've got traces of his skin under her fingernails, and her blood is all over his waterproofs, for God's sake. Sometimes it is just that simple, Liam."

No, it isn't, Ward thought. Things were never that simple. Not just every crime, but every second of existence was fraught with complications, misunderstandings, lies, and cock-ups. Ninety-nine percent of their work was sorting through the chaff to find one solid clue. They could follow dozens of leads in this case, waste precious time pursuing every twisting road to its ultimately fruitless end. Their job over the next few days or weeks would be to try to find the connections between people, connections those people were often trying very hard to hide.

It seemed to Ward that he spent half his life immersed in a shadowy, fictional world, conceiving scenarios that may or may not have happened. Most people imagined detectives as people who dealt in facts, in hard evidence—and that was a vital part of what he did. Still, much of his life remained in the subjective tense. He breathed speculative air, and so, he realized increasingly, did everyone else around him.

Once the ice pack had reduced the throbbing in her ankle, Nora reached into her jacket pocket for the drawing she'd robbed from Charlie Brazil. She wasn't even sure why she'd taken it, except that it seemed somehow significant. She tried to collect her thoughts, to impose some order on all the possibilities that tumbled about in her brain. What use could her feeble theories be against the powerful reality that two people were dead? Danny Brazil and Ursula Downes had been brutally murdered. There were similarities in the way they'd been killed, but she couldn't shake the thought that something else connected them as well, something that no one had yet grasped. The line back to Danny Brazil went even further into the past, to the time when he and his brother had discovered the Loughnabrone hoard—and, according to the rumors, gold. But if this place was anything like the other places in Ireland where she'd spent time, folklore and legend were on a fairly equal footing with fact.

Just because Charlie Brazil might be involved, that didn't mean Cadogan was innocent. They could both have been mixed up with Ursula, for similar or very different reasons. Maybe they had all three been in something together, and no one had yet figured it out. And the boyfriend, Desmond Quill . . . he seemed to have no illusions about Ursula's character, despite the fact that he was in love with her. What had Ursula thought of Quill?

Nora looked down at the drawing, its edges curled and speckled with black. Struck with a sudden idea, she carried the sketch to Cormac's work table and rummaged through the papers for his magnifying glass. The artist's pen strokes leapt out at her through the thick lens. The detail was exquisite; the shield's curved surface appeared as tiny dots that blended together to form a shadow. She turned the drawing over and saw a series of circles lightly sketched in pencil, and a scribbled inscription: *Below a city of sisters, beside a lake of sorrows.* That was the way it was here; double and even treble meanings hidden everywhere.

The door rattled against the jamb. Was Charlie Brazil coming after her? She slipped the drawing into the nearest book and kept very still, until she heard Cormac's voice calling through the stout door: "Nora? Are you there? I haven't got my key."

She crossed quickly to the door to let him in, throwing her arms around him, pressing herself into his chest. He seemed a little surprised at her greeting, but not unhappily so. "I wasn't gone all that long, was I?" he asked. "Everything's fine. They just asked me a lot of questions."

"And have they finished with you now?"

"For the moment, anyway." He tried to give her an encouraging smile, but she sensed his worry.

"How did you get home?"

"The Guards gave me a lift. I tried ringing your mobile, but I couldn't get through. Did you have it switched off?"

"No, I was waiting for you to call. I was out of the house for a bit; maybe the signal is weak out here in the middle of the bog."

"You shouldn't really be wandering around by yourself, Nora. It's not safe, not after what's happened. Where did you go?"

"First I tried to find Brona Scully. I thought if she'd been out at the tree, she might have seen you leaving Ursula's house the other night. Then I went over to Charlie Brazil's apiary. Something Ursula said to him the other day made me think about it." She limped back to the work table where she'd hidden the drawing.

Cormac's alarm was immediate. "Nora, what happened to your leg?" She could hear the anguish behind his words, the jangling fear that she might have gone somewhere she shouldn't have, on his behalf.

"It's just a bee sting. I'm fine. I've put ice on it, and the swelling's already starting to go down. I found out some things about Charlie Brazil that I don't think anyone knows. He's got a stash of what I'm fairly sure are illegal artifacts hidden somewhere up near his apiary. It makes me wonder if Ursula's death isn't somehow tied to all that." She decided not to mention that she'd actually met Charlie on the expedition, or Cormac might lose sight of what was most important here—finding some connections in this ever more vexing puzzle.

"How do you know all this?"

"I was just looking around in the shed where he stores his beekeeping supplies, and I saw where he'd hidden the other things under the floor. He doesn't know I was there. I found this, too." She flipped through the pages of the book where she'd hidden the stolen drawing. The pages opened to the place where the postcard-size drawing lay facedown, but when Nora turned the paper over, it was not the same picture as the one she'd slipped into the book. It showed some kind of intricately decorated circlet, though whether it was a bracelet or a necklace was difficult to tell from the scale. The thick paper had been pierced by a pin about a half-inch from the top, just like the drawing she had found in the shed.

A wave of nausea swept over her, and her fingers suddenly felt clammy and cold. Turning a few more pages, she found the shield sketch she'd put in the book and compared it to the new drawing. Both were clearly the work of the same artist.

Cormac was close behind her now, looking over her shoulder. "What are those, Nora? Where did you get them?"

Nora felt her breath catch in her throat as she wrestled with how to respond. The question seemed in earnest. How else could she answer him? She held up the shield drawing. "I found this one in Charlie Brazil's beekeeping shed this evening. And this one—" she held up the sketch of the circlet "—I just found here in your book."

He seemed to grasp the unspoken question even before she could think it. "It's not mine, Nora. I've never seen it before, I swear."

"How did it get here?"

"That's the book I lent Ursula. I hadn't even remembered it. When she stopped by the house the first night I was here, she wanted to know what I was working on. She started looking through the books I was unpacking, and asked if she could borrow that one for a day or two. There didn't seem to be any harm in lending it to her. Last night I saw it just beside the door at Ursula's, so I took it back. I put it on the kitchen table when I came in, never even thought to open it."

Nora thought back to the morning, which seemed so long ago now, and remembered moving the book from the kitchen to Cormac's work table. She examined the spine. *The Exquisite Art: Masterpieces of Irish Metalwork.* "Why would Ursula be so interested in this book?"

"I don't know, Nora. It's an academic treatise on artifacts and antiquities," Cormac said. "Pretty dry reading, even for an archaeologist. She didn't say why she needed it, and I didn't ask."

Ursula Downes hadn't struck Nora as the kind of person who devoted herself to scholarship. There had to be some reason she had been interested in this particular book. Nora opened the thick pages at random, finding photographs and drawings, charts full of numbers that looked like location coordinates, maps documenting where certain types of artifacts—gold gorgets and hoards of bent and broken weapons—had been found. Cadogan's words about the Brazils holding back some things from the hoard suddenly circled through her head. Had Ursula found out something she didn't want anyone else to know? *I know what you're hiding. . . .* The discovery of a previously unknown artifact would certainly put a new spin on the murder. And there were three knots in Ursula's cord, just like in Danny Brazil's.

"Can I have a look at it?" Cormac took the drawing and the book and started going through the illustrations, comparing the sketch in his hand against the book's drawings and photographs. "This has a catalog of all the known gold artifacts recovered on Irish soil."

"So what are you doing?" Nora asked over his shoulder.

He quickly flipped to a page showing a drawing, and held it open to show her. "The Broighter collar, a gold neck-ring from the first century B.C. The style of decoration—these intricate, curving designs—marks the piece as Irish-made. The drawing you found in here seems to be a collar similar to this one. The thing is, I don't think anything exactly like the piece in your sketch has ever been found in Ireland—or maybe I should say, nothing like it has ever been reported. The Broighter collar is one of the few examples of La Tène metalwork found in Ireland, and one of the few gold artifacts from the Iron Age. You must have seen it at the National Museum. Look at the decoration on your drawing, those raised whorls and trumpet curves—see how similar they are to the Broighter details? It's astonishing."

"So if the collar in the drawing is real, and not just a figment of some artist's imagination . . ."

"It would be an unbelievable find. Priceless. And whoever found it—presuming that they turned it over to the state, and that it was found legitimately and not through illegal means—would get a pretty whacking great reward. Once an artifact has been dug up, its provenance comes into question. It loses a lot of archaeological significance if we don't know where it came from—but of course the monetary value always remains. I'm wondering now about the other drawing—whether it's an actual object that exists, or as you said, just a figment of some artist's imagination."

Nora handed him the shield drawing, and they both began to search through the books of artifacts, comparing it to the objects pictured. The names of all the findspots started to blur in front of her eyes: Dowris, Ballinderry, Moylarg, Lagore, Loughan Island, Lisnacrogher . . . The organic forms snaked and twisted and curled across the pages, mirroring the natural world in abstract. Eyes and animal faces were everywhere. She imagined the metalworker hunched over his tools, making delicate herringbone patterns, birds whose beaks formed the heads of pins. She paged past a triskelion disc and felt a tug of familiarity; where had she seen that image before? The graceful spirals, everything counted in threes . . . She scoured her memory, but could not place the image. Never mind; it would come back sometime, probably when she wasn't even trying to remember.

"Here it is," Cormac said. "A shield boss, part of the Loughnabrone hoard." Nora looked over his shoulder and saw a photograph that matched the drawing exactly. She thought of all the other drawings, probably at least ten or twelve of them, that Charlie Brazil had in his tin box.

"I have an idea," she said. She ran to get her mobile, and scrolled through the memory until she found Niall Dawson's home number. She heard his familiar voice over the background noise of children chasing one another, breathless with laughter. She could imagine them in the back garden of the Dawsons' house in Sandymount, getting ready to take the food off the barbeque, and the sound of normal life suddenly made her feel like weeping.

"Niall, it's Nora Gavin. I know it's the weekend, and I'm calling to ask a favor. I'm wondering if there's any way I can get a complete list of all the items found in the Loughnabrone hoard." She waited for a moment, while the children's voices carried on in the background. "I wouldn't ask, Niall, except that I think it could be vitally important."

"No, I'm happy to oblige, Nora. It's just that I'm a little astonished, because you're the second person in two days to ask for an itemized inventory of the Loughnabrone objects. I faxed the same list off to Ursula Downes yesterday evening."

BOOK FOUR

DEVOTE TO DEATH

. . . in such cases they devote to death a human being and plunge a dagger into him in the region of the diaphragm, and when the stricken victim has fallen they read the future from the manner of his fall and from the twitching of his limbs as well as from the gushing of his blood . . .

—the Sicilian historian Diodorus Siculus, writing about the Druids in the first century B.C.

1

Ward drove out to Illaunafulla on Saturday morning in bad humor. Rachel Briscoe had not turned up at her lodgings in Offaly or in Dublin, so he'd arranged for a ground search of the area around Loughnabrone, starting in Ursula Downes's back garden where the girl's binoculars had been found. So far, however, the search arrangements had not been progressing satisfactorily. There was too little manpower available, and it was taking too much time to mobilize and organize the extra officers and volunteers. Nothing was going right. A contingent of men would have to be sent to Ferbane, where the Leinster Fleadh Cheoil was on this weekend. The once-a-year regional traditional music competition meant extra security would be needed, since the town would be overflowing with people in the pubs and on the streets, and unguarded handbags and musical instruments would be ripe for the picking. And to top everything off, after a near-record fortnight of fine weather, a slanting rain had begun to fall.

"They're all assembled, Liam." Maureen Brennan leaned in through the car window he'd cracked open. "Waiting for your instructions. I told them to wait in the shed, around the back, to keep out of the rain while they could." Low, shifting gray clouds moved silently across the sky, making the space between heaven and earth seem even narrower than usual.

Someone had set up a table in the hayshed, a sheet of plywood over a couple of sawhorses, and Ward set to rolling out the maps while Maureen gathered the collected force around. Several held steaming cups of tea, and one or two stubbed out their cigarettes at the entrance as they turned to follow Ward under the curved sheet-metal roof. They gathered around the makeshift table, their lean faces reminding him of his own first years as a Guard. There were a few more women here than when he'd started out—a good thing.

He said, "Some of you may know that yesterday morning, just beyond the wall in the back garden here, we found a pair of binoculars belonging to Rachel Briscoe. She's not been seen now for more than twenty-four hours, and her employer has officially reported her as missing. Rachel Briscoe is twenty-two years of age. She's five feet, six inches tall, and has long dark brown hair and brown eyes. She was last seen wearing a dark blue hooded anorak, jeans, and blue and gray trainers. Distinguishing marks may include some healed scars on the hands or wrists. Here's the photograph from her company-issued identity card." He passed a stack of computer-printed photos to Maureen to hand out to the search party.

Ward unrolled the Ordnance Survey map he'd brought along. The Grand Canal ran east-west along the top half of the paper; on the eastern edge of the map was the bridge at Carrigahaun. The map showed all the ancient monuments, ringforts and tower houses, monasteries and holy wells. He showed them where they were, the farmyard marked carefully on the map, and pointed out the bright yellow line he'd highlighted around the area they would search. He looked up at their concerned faces and saw that it didn't matter that most of them didn't know this girl. They'd search for her, seeing in her place their own sisters, their own daughters, and praying that she would be found, alive and well.

Once the searchers had set out, Ward stood in the shelter of the shed behind Ursula Downes's house and watched the line of uniformed Guards in their yellow rain gear inch up the hill. The line moved slowly, foraging in the long grass, using sticks to poke into the hedgerows and undergrowth. It was going to be a very long day. The heavy clouds seemed only feet off the ground and the rain had started to come down harder—a desperate, soaking rain, just as they were beginning the search in earnest.

He remembered taking part in just such a search as a young Garda— a profession his educated family had disdained, a job for plodders and born civil servants. He'd been part of a line just like this one, stretched across a forested hillside in the Wicklow mountains, searching for a woman who'd been missing for six days. The sun had been shining that day, and he remembered the sound his fellow officers' feet had made as they worked their way up the slope. And he remembered what they'd eventually found. He couldn't remember what he'd noticed first; perhaps the peculiar odor of death, then the still, silent form, and the way the dappled light strayed across the woman's mottled skin amid the verdant undergrowth. He hoped none of his officers would have a similar experience today.

2

Nora awakened on the sofa in the sitting room, and heard Cormac rustling around in the kitchen. Niall Dawson's fax had come in shortly after their call to him the evening before, and they'd worked into the wee hours looking through the records of the Loughnabrone hoard. To see the whole list of items recovered was astonishing; the hoard was an unparalleled cache of Iron Age swords and daggers and spearpoints. All that beautiful ancient scrollwork still snaked across her drowsy consciousness. They'd have to bring Charlie Brazil's drawings to the police, she knew, but it would be so much better if only they could bring some other useful information as well.

"It's nearly eleven o'clock," Cormac said from the kitchen. "Fancy a trip into town? We can have some lunch there."

Forty minutes later they walked into the bar at Coughlan's and took a table near the window. Desmond Quill sat only a few tables away, staring into his coffee, looking as if he'd spent the previous twenty-four hours gazing at the bottom of a whiskey glass. He probably had, Nora thought, considering the state she'd seen him in yesterday afternoon. Everything about him—the slumped posture, the deep lines in his face, the pain that flowed from his downcast eyes—whispered devastation and loss. The plate of food before him looked untouched. It was as if the other restaurant patrons knew what he'd been through and, fearing the contagion of death, were determined to keep a safe distance.

Cormac must have noticed her looks in Quill's direction. "Do you know him, Nora?"

"Not really. I met him for the first time yesterday. Desmond Quill; he was Ursula's—" She stopped, not knowing what to call him. Friend? Lover? Companion? None of those designations seemed adequate, given the visible depth of the man's grief.

Cormac seemed to understand. "Poor fella."

Nora felt tempted to tell Cormac more about her conversation with

Quill the previous afternoon, but she held off, feeling that to do so might violate Quill's confidence.

Their lunch had just arrived when Nora looked up to find Quill approaching the table.

"You asked if there was anything you could do," he said to her, picking up where their conversation had left off the day before. "You said you would help me if you could." He turned slightly to look at Cormac, his bluntly handsome features pulled downward in an expression of puzzlement. "You look familiar; I'm sorry if I don't know you. Desmond Quill."

"I don't think we've met," Cormac said, taking Quill's hand. "Cormac Maguire. Nora told me you were Ursula's friend. I'm very sorry for your trouble."

Quill nodded once, accepting the condolence. If Cormac had been one of the men Ursula had mentioned by name, it didn't seem to register. Quill put his hand on the back of the chair beside Nora. "May I?"

She gestured for him to sit, curious about what had brought him over to speak to them.

"I've just remembered something Ursula told me, about the place where she used to meet Owen Cadogan. I don't know where it was— somewhere out on the bog; a rough sort of a shed filled with bags of peat moss and dry concrete. Could be any one of a dozen places, I suppose."

"Have you told Detective Ward about it?"

"I left a message, but he's out on a search, they tell me, looking for a young woman gone missing—one of the girls on Ursula's crew. No one's seen her since late Thursday evening. A couple of Guards came 'round and asked me about her this morning." He raised hollow eyes to look at Nora. "It's like a nightmare, all this. A nightmare. I don't know anyone here. I don't know this place. But I wondered if you knew anyone who might recognize the building from that description. I don't know what else to do. I'm going mad sitting here, and if I could just find something, some little piece that would help the police find the person who killed her—" His right hand flew up to cover his eyes for a moment, and he stood to leave. "I'll go now; I won't stay and disrupt your meal. But if you know anyone who could help me, please . . . it's all I'd ask of you." His red-rimmed eyes held a desperate, silent plea. Without waiting for Nora's answer, he turned and walked away.

She waited until Quill was out of the bar before speaking. "Ursula told him that Owen Cadogan had been harassing her since she broke off the relationship. I think he believes Cadogan killed Ursula, but he can't prove anything. You know the area—do you have any idea about the place he was talking about?"

"There are dozens of Bord na Móna buildings at Loughnabrone. It could be any one of them. Nothing comes immediately to mind, but his description was pretty sketchy. What was he saying about the missing girl?"

"That's the first I've heard of it. Did they ask about her when you were in for questioning?"

"They did, actually, but the name didn't mean anything to me."

"What name?" She knew before he said it.

"Rachel Briscoe."

"I gave her a lift home the other night, Cormac, and she dropped something in the car. It turned out to be an overdue notice from the Pembroke Library in Ballsbridge—but it wasn't addressed to Rachel Briscoe; it was sent to someone named Rachel Power."

It was Cormac's turn for astonishment. "Rachel Power? You're absolutely sure?"

"Of course I'm sure. I can show you the letter—it's still in my car back at the house. I was going to give it back to Rachel yesterday morning, but I forgot all about it when I found Ursula. Why—does the name Rachel Power mean something to you?"

"It's a long, complicated story," Cormac said.

"Tell me."

"I have to say first that I never really knew how much of the story was true and how much was exaggerated, or even outright fabricated. I don't think anyone really knew but the people involved, and they weren't talking. I had a colleague at the university years ago, Tom Power. An outstanding archaeologist, one of the best scholars I've ever known. But he suffered terribly from depression. Used to go into these downward spirals that lasted for weeks. He got involved with Ursula in one of his really down periods. That much I know is true, because he told me himself. A moment of weakness, he said. He felt rotten about deceiving his wife, and he wanted to break off with Ursula; he knew it had been a terrible mistake. But by that point he couldn't figure out how to extricate himself. He tried several times, but she wouldn't let him go—threatened to tell his wife."

"What happened?"

"This is the part I only heard second- and third-hand. I don't know how much is true."

"Tell me anyway. It could be important."

"Tom's wife and daughter walked in on them one afternoon in his office. His daughter was only about ten or eleven at the time. And the way I heard it, the confrontation wasn't exactly an accident; it may have been deliberately set up."

"By whom?"

"By Ursula. It's awful, I know. I just don't know if that part is true; it was just what people said. But Tom's wife left him; that was a fact. And the scandal didn't end there. There were rumors that Ursula was trying to discredit Tom's academic work, saying she'd actually done his research and most of the writing he'd had published for the previous several years. I can't believe that part is true. Tom Power was, and is, a brilliant man; he had no need to hide behind a colleague's work. But he was consumed with guilt about what he'd done to Sarah and he wouldn't even defend himself. He had to leave his teaching position, and no other university would touch him. In the end he took a job cataloging a large private art collection somewhere in France, cut his ties to everyone he knew. I can't imagine that he's had an easy time of it the past ten years."

"And Rachel is his daughter?"

"Tom's daughter was named Rachel, and she'd be about the same age as the girl who disappeared," Cormac said. "Briscoe was Sarah's name before she married. There's got to be some connection."

Nora's thoughts went back to the scene at the excavation, when the young man had borrowed Rachel's binoculars. Rachel's temper had flared, but it was Ursula's seemingly benign gesture, handing the binoculars back, that had nearly put her over the edge. "Rachel might have had reason to despise Ursula, but to take a job out here just to get close to her? I can't see someone her age concocting such an elaborate scheme just for revenge."

"She may have seen Ursula as the person who destroyed her family. People have committed murder for much more trivial reasons. If no one has seen her since Ursula was killed—"

"But that doesn't mean she did it. She could have just been a witness." Either way, the Guards would be anxious to find Rachel and talk to her. Nora considered the way Ursula had been killed and tried to imagine Rachel Briscoe pulling tight the leather cord, drawing a knife. None of it seemed to connect with the defensive young woman who'd sat in the passenger seat of her car less than two days ago.

"We're probably getting ahead of ourselves," she said. "Maybe she just got fed up with the job and went home. We don't even know that she is your friend's daughter, not for certain. Maybe we should go back to the house and think this through at least once more before we call anyone."

3

At half-past five, Maureen Brennan set a steaming mug of milky tea on Ward's desk. The daylong search for Rachel Briscoe had turned up nothing, so they'd come back to the station to dry off and go over their notes, getting ready to brief the Bureau officers who would be coming in on Monday.

"Don't worry, Liam. She'll turn up. If she's anywhere to be found, we'll find her."

He didn't need reassurance on that score. They would find Rachel Briscoe eventually, he was sure of that; he just hoped it wouldn't be too late. They had found no footprints, no traces of hair or blood, no debris that could tell them any more about the girl's whereabouts. The only thing they had turned up was a small area of bent grass and leaves under one of the hedgerows, as if someone or something had been sleeping there recently; even the most experienced searchers couldn't tell whether the marks had been left by an animal or a human. Ward sighed. "What's the latest from Dublin—and how are we doing on Ursula Downes's personal effects?"

"She didn't keep much in her appointment diary, as you saw yourself, so it's been difficult to find anyone who claims to know her well. But here's what we've been able to get so far. She was born and raised on the north side of Dublin, an only child; her father left before she was born, and the mother either married or remarried—we're not quite clear on which it was—when Ursula was ten. The father's whereabouts are still unknown, but both the mother and stepfather are now dead. Ursula was single, lived alone in a flat in Rathmines. The Bureau say they'll let us know what turns up there, but they said it might take a while; her place is an absolute tip."

Ward felt annoyed. He knew it made sense to have the Bureau handle the search, but he couldn't help wondering if they'd miss something, even one tiny thing, that might help color the case. He also knew the Bureau lads wouldn't be in any particular hurry to get things done until

Monday, when their own officers would be safely in charge of the investigation.

A sideways glance from Brennan told him that she understood and shared his irritation, but she went on: "Ursula Downes's mobile had only a couple of numbers stored in it; her office in Dalkey, Desmond Quill's mobile."

"That's strange, isn't it—that she wouldn't keep more friends' numbers on her mobile?"

"Not if she didn't have any friends. Some people don't, you know. Or it could be that she was just too lazy to program them all in." Ward thought of the empty directory on his own mobile.

Brennan continued: "Several neighbors interviewed in Dublin yesterday said she kept to herself and was often out late, all night. I also spoke to her boss at the archaeology firm. Ursula had a decent job there, but the boss didn't seem completely satisfied with her performance. Nothing he was willing to spell out, but he hinted that she'd probably not have been going back to them after the excavation season this year. That seems to have been a pattern in her employment history. She worked at six different contract archaeology firms over the past ten years."

Ward turned to his own notepad. "All right, what about the timeline? Several witnesses place Ursula Downes leaving the excavation site at half past five. She drove into the village to pick up some take-away and a few other items, including four bottles of wine, according to the shopgirl who came forward yesterday. From there it looks as if she went home and started in on the wine; two of the four bottles were empty, and according to the toxicology, her blood alcohol level at the time of her death was almost double the driving limit."

Brennan said, "From her mobile, we know that she rang Desmond Quill on his mobile around eight, and they talked for about thirty minutes. He says they were making plans for the weekend, and that they agreed he would arrive on Friday morning."

"What do we know about Desmond Quill?"

"Owns a shop off Grafton Street—antiques, very posh. Lives in Ballsbridge. He says he was in Dublin the night Ursula was killed, playing his regular Thursday chess game at home with Laurence Fitzhugh, a banker. Fitzhugh confirms the story, says they were together at Quill's house until nearly half-two in the morning. If he's telling the truth, that wouldn't give Quill time to drive all the way out here and commit the

murder—Loughnabrone is a good three hours from the south side of
Dublin. Quill says he left the city at eight o'clock on Friday morning."

"And what time did Ursula ring Quill on Thursday evening?"

"Ten past eight—and again at twelve fifty-five."

"She rang him twice? If they'd made all the arrangements for the
weekend in the first conversation, why would she ring him back?"

"Quill says Ursula told him that someone was bothering her. She
could have been calling him for help. He says he didn't receive the second call, that his phone was switched off. And it lasted less than a
minute. Maybe she decided not to leave a message."

"And what time does the phone say she rang Maguire?"

"Twenty past twelve. That matches his story."

"So she rings up Maguire at twelve-twenty, and Quill again thirty
minutes later? Say Maguire was threatening her. If she was truly frightened, why would she call Desmond Quill, who was seventy miles away in
Dublin, instead of emergency services? This isn't lining up quite right."
With the new wireless technology, they could find out from the phone
company exactly where Quill had been when he'd received the second
call. It probably wasn't worth pursuing at this point, unless there was
something funny about his alibi, and so far, at least, it seemed pretty
solid. "What about calls to Ursula's mobile?"

"The phone's memory keeps a record of the last ten calls made and
received. The last ten received were all from Owen Cadogan's mobile.
They were spaced only a few minutes apart, all on the night of the murder, between a quarter past ten and three o'clock that following morning.
All very brief, as though she knew who it was and didn't answer."

That was an interesting detail, but there was no way of knowing
whether Cadogan had just given up trying to reach Ursula, or stopped
phoning because he knew she was already dead.

"Who else did she call?"

"The last ten calls she made included one to Niall Dawson—you
remember, that fella we met out at the bog—he's Keeper of Antiquities
at the National Museum. There were four calls to Desmond Quill, the
one to Maguire, and four other numbers I'm still checking out."

"What did you find on the laptop?"

"Let me show you." She switched on the computer, and Ward brought
his chair around so that he could look over her shoulder. "From the
browser history we can tell that someone—maybe it was Ursula, or

maybe it was someone else—was online the night she was killed. Here's a list of all the sites browsed that evening: the *Irish Times* archive, the *Examiner* archive, the Dúchas Sites and Monuments record—"

"Can we tell what was she looking for at any of those sites?"

"All of them. Which one do you want?"

"I don't know—one of the newspapers."

Maureen scrolled down the screen to show him: Ursula Downes had dug up a series of brief news articles on the animal mutilations about which Charlie Brazil had been questioned. None mentioned the boy by name, but Ursula may have picked up enough local gossip to make the connection. That could have been what she was holding over Charlie Brazil—though as horrible as the crimes had been, why would anyone care about three slaughtered animals all these years later?

Ward looked up at Brennan. "What were the other sites you mentioned?"

"She went into several excavation databases, searching for information on the Loughnabrone hoard. But she was an archaeologist, so it's possible that some of those searches might have been work-related. I'd have to spend a bit more time digging to tell exactly what she was looking for—if it was just general information about the hoard, or something more specific."

Ward looked down the list that glowed on the flat screen. The Loughnabrone hoard was another connection to Charlie Brazil—perhaps not directly, but it had been Charlie's father and uncle who had discovered the hoard. And Ursula's crew had just uncovered the uncle's body three days previously. Perhaps there was a pattern he wasn't seeing in the way these facts aligned themselves, a combination that would open it up. "Right. Keep at those searches a bit longer, if you would, Maureen. They might turn up something useful."

"I had another thought today while we were out in the fields. Both eyewitness statements we have on Ursula Downes and her confrontations with Owen Cadogan and Charlie Brazil came from Nora Gavin."

"What are you saying? You think Dr. Gavin is making things up to draw our attention away from Maguire?"

"It's possible, isn't it?" Maureen looked down at her notes again.

"Definitely possible. But we also have Desmond Quill's statement that Cadogan was harassing Ursula, and evidence that Cadogan placed repeated calls to her mobile. I don't think Dr. Gavin is making up stories, but maybe she's being somewhat selective in what she tells us. At this point maybe we should concentrate on Owen Cadogan and Charlie Brazil—and those flat denials that they ever had anything to do with Ursula Downes. Anything back from forensics on fingerprints or other evidence from the house?"

"Nothing yet—probably not until tomorrow at the earliest."

"Well, if we don't have physical evidence, we can start on witnesses. Were you able to find out where Cadogan's secretary lives?"

Brennan lifted her notebook. "Right here."

"Let's talk to her, see what we can find out. We've also got the phone calls from his mobile to Ursula's. We can use that to rattle his cage a bit."

Ward stood up and stared at the crime-scene photos on the board while Brennan collected what she would need for an off-site interview. For him, this process of painstakingly working through all the evidence—even at such an early stage in the investigation—was a necessary winnowing, a process that helped to separate kernels of relevant fact from the surrounding chaff. He was glad his partner had no objection to the method, because he wasn't sure he could work any other way. The station was even quieter than usual today; everyone had been sent home after the unsuccessful search for Rachel Briscoe. Maybe Brennan was right and the girl would turn up eventually, unharmed, wondering what all the fuss had been about. He hoped so. The trouble with this case was that nothing was shaking out. They were already buried in chaff, and it would only get worse the more they found out. All he could do was to keep shaking the frame.

4

"Sorry to be calling around so late," Ward said, noting the surprise on Aileen Flood's face at the sight of two detectives on her doorstep. "I'm sure you can appreciate how busy we've been."

"Of course. Won't you come in?" She led them into an immaculate sitting room, antimacassars set with grim purpose as though aligned and placed with a template. Everything was exactly as it should be—china lined up in the cabinet, dinner dishes all washed and put away, the faint whiff of lemon oil and disinfectant in the air. It was a space that seemed to Ward essentially and inordinately female, as though it had never been contaminated by a man's presence. Everything reeked of cleanliness and decorum.

"You live here alone, Ms. Flood?"

"For the last couple of years, yes, since my sister married and moved to Banagher. Her husband runs a boat there." Aileen Flood had a round, earnest face that flushed easily; her trim, tailored clothes spoke of rigid standards that must be maintained, whatever the cost.

"Would you like a cup of tea?" She looked at him expectantly, but he glanced at Maureen, with whom she'd hardly made eye contact.

"I don't think we'll trouble you that long. It's late—"

"I'm dying for a cup of tea, actually, if you wouldn't mind," Maureen said, leveling her eyes at Aileen Flood and smiling with her lips only. She wasn't fond of overly demure women. Didn't trust them. And Ward knew that she didn't want tea at all; she only wanted to get Aileen Flood out of the room so she could have a better look around.

When they were alone, Brennan sidled to the kitchen door and cracked it open to peer through. Ward heard the sound of a refrigerator opening and closing; then his partner shut the door and came back to sit beside him. She leaned over and said in a whisper: "Three pint bottles of Guinness in the fridge. Does Aileen strike you as a solitary pint drinker, by any chance?" Maureen's nose for scandal was unrivaled in his experience, and she often picked up cues their male colleagues were just too thick to see.

When Aileen Flood reentered the sitting room a few minutes later carrying a tray, Brennan asked to use the toilet, knowing that Aileen would be too busy with the tea to bother worrying about her.

"I'm sorry," Ward said, "we shouldn't be putting you to so much trouble. We're only here to ask a few questions as part of the inquiry into the death of Ursula Downes." He saw Aileen's tea-pouring hand begin to quake, despite her best efforts to keep it still. Her face looked pinched, and she flushed an unattractive blotchy scarlet. This physiological reaction wasn't of much use to him; some people started to sweat the moment they saw a policeman, whether they were guilty of anything or not, and Ward suspected Aileen Flood might be one of them.

By the time the tea had been poured around, Brennan had returned from the toilet, and when Aileen Flood's attention was turned elsewhere she took the opportunity to tell Ward with a subtle shake of the head what she'd found there: nothing.

"Thank you for the tea," he said. "Now, we have a few questions to ask you about the night of the murder, the twentieth of June. Can you tell us where you were on that night, say from the end of your work day onward?"

"I left the office at five o'clock on Thursday, the usual time, then drove to the shop in Birr for a few things. My sister and her husband were coming over from Banagher for dinner that night. I stopped at the off-license to get some Guinness; that's what Phil likes to drink. They arrived about seven; we ate our dinner and watched a bit of an old film on television, and they went home about half-ten. Phil does have to be up early in the mornings on the boat."

She paused, her fingers twisting the fringe of a plump, perfect pillow that lay beside her on the chair, and suddenly her soft face looked as if it were about to crumple in on itself. "I know what Owen said when you came to him in the office, that he was on his own on Thursday night, but it isn't true. He was here with me. He said he didn't want to involve me in this mess, but I told him it's no use; I'm already involved."

"You're telling us that you've been sleeping with your boss?" Maureen asked, her voice as flat as she could make it. "How long has that been going on?"

Tears streaked down Aileen Flood's face as she answered. "Since last March. He had a bit too much to drink at a farewell party for one of the other regional managers. His wife never comes along to any official functions anymore, and he really was in no state to be driving himself, so I gave him a lift, and it just happened."

Brennan said, "I suppose he comes here to see you, here to the house?"

"Yes, of course. He doesn't generally stay over, but he did on Thursday—the night you're talking about, the twentieth. He arrived after my sister left—about half-eleven it was—and left again about seven in the morning. He was with me all night, I'll swear it. His marriage was a sham, and everyone knew it, including his wife, so it didn't seem wrong. A person deserves a little happiness." Ward couldn't decide if she was speaking about Owen Cadogan or herself.

"So everything had been going fine since March. Your neighbors must have seen Cadogan's car here a few times, then?" Brennan asked.

"I'm sure they must have."

"Does he keep any of his things here—spare clothes, a razor, a toothbrush?"

"I said he doesn't usually stay the night." Ward thought he heard Aileen's voice catch in her throat. He knew where Brennan was going, and knew it was his turn to take up the questioning.

"You must have been quite surprised when Ursula Downes came back to Loughnabrone this summer."

Aileen Flood's voice and expression hardened in a single heartbeat. "Why should that be of any concern to me?"

"Because you know what happened last summer, when all Ursula Downes had to do was crook her little finger . . ."

The fierce battle Aileen was waging with herself was visible on her face. "Owen was through with her. He'd no interest in Ursula; he said he hated her."

"Hated her enough to kill her?"

"No, I didn't mean that." Aileen was evidently having trouble keeping a lid on her own pent-up emotions about Ursula Downes. Ward realized they'd never considered the possibility that the crime had been committed by another woman—or by two people working as a team.

"Did you help Owen murder Ursula?"

"No! I told you—"

"You both hated her, did you not?"

"Yes," she said. "Yes, I hated her too, and I'm not sorry she's dead." Ward had been around canals and locks enough to know how to stick in a wedge and keep the floodgate open once it was cracked. His job right now was to lever it further open, keep the flow going.

"We have it on good authority that Cadogan's affair with Ursula Downes was not over."

"Who told you that?"

"We have an eyewitness who saw them engaged in—what would you call it?—a rather intimate conversation." Ward watched as this information did its corrosive work on Aileen Flood's pride.

"She was a right scheming bitch, that Ursula—thought she could just come back and start ordering Owen about. She never cared about him. You should have seen her, coming into his office and asking had he worked up the courage to ask me for a ride, in that horrible, mocking tone. She laughed at him, then expected him to fall down on his two knees and adore her—"

Ward said as gently as he could, "But he did adore her, didn't he? He was still obsessed with her. Couldn't stop thinking about her. And there was nothing you could do." He watched as Aileen Flood's eyes filled with tears once more. "You've never actually slept with Owen Cadogan, have you, Aileen?"

Her voice came out in a choked whisper. "No."

There it was, Ward thought, the strange and shameful truth—and it was not that Aileen Flood was carrying on with someone else's husband, but that she was in love with a man who had so little regard for her.

"It hardly seems fair that if Owen Cadogan killed Ursula and only came to you afterward, you can still be charged as an accessory to murder, just as if you had helped him."

Her eyes grew large. "It's not true. You're just saying that."

"It is true, Aileen. But you didn't stop to think about it, did you, when he came to you for help that night? You've gotten much better at lying since all this began, haven't you? But one thing I can promise you is that Owen Cadogan has gotten much better than you. It's become so easy for him that he does it all the time now. No bother on him at all. He lies to his wife, he lies to his friends. He lied to you about Ursula once, Aileen, when he said he was finished with her. Why wouldn't he do it again?"

Brennan said, "Do you know what he did to her, Aileen? Shall I tell you—"

"No, please, please, I don't want to know. And I'm telling you, whatever was done, Owen didn't do it. He arrived at my house at a quarter past two and said he'd been at Ursula's and that she was dead, someone had murdered her, and he needed my help. I couldn't say no. He said she was dead when he arrived, and I believed him. I had to believe him, didn't I?"

"Do you want to go and talk to Cadogan now?" Brennan asked, once they were in the car and headed back toward the station. "We might not have any reason to hold him, but we can let him know what we've got—his own admission that he was at Ursula's house on the night of the murder. We can at least make him sweat. I'd like that."

"Let's go, then. You know where he lives?"

Brennan nodded. "It always amazes me," she said, "how men can go on behaving like such absolute shite hawks, and women still manage to be astonished. Stupid cows."

Aileen Flood's performance seemed to have touched a nerve, but Ward wasn't sure it would be entirely appropriate for him to go probing into his partner's personal life. It wasn't only women, he reflected, stealing a glance at Maureen's strong profile beside him. All of us insist upon our illusions, upon substituting dreams and distorted memories for the real thing. He'd certainly done it himself, and did it still, as the beautiful, quiet girl he'd fallen in love with became brightly polished over time, and the real Eithne—the thin limbs, haggard face, and compulsive gestures—had almost faded away in the reflected light of the favored image. It seemed to him that delusion was the most natural of human states; it was honesty that was the aberration.

5

"We're going in circles," Nora said. She looked at all the papers she and Cormac had laid out on the table before them: Charlie Brazil's two drawings, the book about Iron Age metalwork, the list of Loughnabrone artifacts from the National Museum. They'd spent the entire afternoon and evening going through all the facts, an exercise that had proved almost entirely fruitless. Cormac had tried placing a few phone calls to establish whether Rachel Briscoe was the daughter of his former colleague, but no one he'd spoken to so far had been able to make that connection.

"Maybe we should quit trying to work it out," Nora said, "and just bring Ward all these scraps of things we've found. He's got different pieces of the puzzle as well. Maybe some of this will make more sense to him than it does to us." She began searching under the papers for the policeman's card.

"Hang on one second," Cormac said. "Before you call anyone, I was thinking that I may know the place Desmond Quill mentioned at lunch. There's an abandoned shed on the road out to Loughnabrone, from the time when they used to manufacture concrete drainpipes out here. The place I'm thinking of hasn't been used in years, but it would probably still be full of dry concrete. Might be worth a quick visit before dark, to see if anyone appears to have been using it."

The midsummer twilight lasted for hours, but darkness was just beginning to settle in the east as they left the Crosses and turned out onto the main road to Birr.

"How do you happen to know about this place?" Nora asked.

"Well, I'm not absolutely sure it's the place Quill was talking about. But I used to know this whole area pretty well. There's no guarantee that the place I remember is still there, but abandoned places tend not to change too much."

The shed was exactly where Cormac remembered it, down a lane in a thick tangle of brushy trees. "Let's leave the car out of sight if we can,"

Nora said. "If someone's there, it would be better to approach on foot."

Cormac steered the jeep behind a huge bale of black polythene on the overgrown verge, took a torch from his glove box, and handed Nora another from his site kit. The twilight was fading fast. They approached the shed, a single-story rusting metal structure with a few dusty windows about ten feet off the ground and a huge padlock on the door. Nora checked the lock, careful not to touch the metal for fear of marring any fingerprints that might remain. It didn't look brand-new, but it probably hadn't been there more than a couple of years at the most. "I'd love to look in the windows," she said. "There's nothing around we could climb on, is there?"

"I hear a car," Cormac said, and they both scrambled for cover, just managing to duck around the corner of the shed before Owen Cadogan's silver Nissan pulled up beside it. Cadogan popped open the boot of his car and jumped out, fishing in his trouser pocket for the key. He let himself into the shed. Nora made a move to look inside the open door, but Cormac held her back. They heard rustling inside, and small groans of exertion; soon Cadogan emerged again, carrying a bulky bundle wrapped in black plastic over one shoulder. He dumped it without ceremony into the open boot, then locked up the shed again and drove away. As soon as he was out of sight, Nora sprinted toward the jeep, and felt Cormac close behind her.

They kept their distance out on the main road, and followed Cadogan when he turned down a narrow byway that led to the canal. There was no sign of his car ahead of them on the one-lane road. The jeep's headlights fell on a ruined cottage, its windows blocked with weathered boards, once someone's home, now an outbuilding of some kind. Nettles and blackberry brambles, signs of neglect, grew thick along the verge. Not many people would pass this way anymore, especially since the canal was so little used. The lane began to narrow suddenly, and the overgrown hedges at the roadside slapped against the car. But movement in the branches ahead told them that Cadogan had passed this way only a short time earlier. Eventually, after about a quarter-mile of winding road, they came to an abrupt stop at the canal. The hedge outside Nora's window was chopped and twisted, as if it had been trimmed recently with a large, dull blade, and the pulpy bone-white wood inside lay exposed. A gravel towpath stretched in both directions, with no sign of a car either way. There was no other road Cadogan could have turned onto, but there was a small humpback bridge about fifty yards to the left. He might have gone over it; there was no way to tell, and going over the bridge might give them away. Nora was about to give up hope when a pair of red taillights suddenly appeared off to their right.

"Stay here," she said, opening her door and climbing out of the jeep. By the time she'd made it around to the driver's side, Cormac was out of the car as well.

"Wherever you think you're going, Nora, I'm going with you."

"Just down the towpath to see what he's doing there."

He nodded and followed behind her, crouching close to the hedgerow for cover. The rutted path was little used and filled with potholes. Nora saw the swordlike leaves of yellow flag growing along the canal bank, heard the birch trees on the far side rustle in the night wind. Ahead, Cadogan's car bumped slowly down the path, sometimes swerving to avoid the deepest holes. They might be able to get impressions of his tire tracks, Nora thought, if that became necessary. Suddenly the car ahead stopped, and she and Cormac stopped as well, crouching just beside a stand of tall reeds that grew at the water's edge.

Cadogan had just climbed out of the Nissan when his mobile began to ring, and he answered with an exasperated sigh: "What now?" He listened for a moment, then said, "Hang on a minute, Aileen. They've got nothing. No, they don't know anything; they're just—"

Again he listened; then he took the phone away from his ear and kicked the car tire savagely. "Fuck!" He kicked a few more times, letting out a stream of curses with each blow, until his anger was spent; then he put the phone back to his ear. "Do you realize what you've done, you stupid—Ah, Aileen, don't cry. Jesus . . . No, I'll think of something. Listen, I've got to go now—right." He pulled the phone abruptly from his ear, switched it off, and landed one last savage kick. Then Cadogan rounded the car's boot and opened it with a key. He leaned into the dark space and pulled out his heavy bundle, which they could see clearly now was the precise shape and heft of a body. He lifted the bundle to his chest, cradling it in his arms, but it sagged and slid down to his knees; he struggled, trying to maintain his grasp. Nora felt Cormac's grip on her shoulder tighten, and felt his breathing stop as the heavy bundle slipped into the water without a splash. Cadogan stood on the bank for a few seconds as it sank, until the only sound was the swishing sigh of the wind in the tall reeds. Then he turned on his heel, climbed into the car, and drove away, his tires spitting gravel in their wake.

As soon as he was out of sight, Nora went to the water's edge, overgrown with grass and weeds that were bent and broken where Cadogan had dropped his bundle. Without hesitation, she jumped over the bank into the opaque green water, not even bothering to remove her shoes. Cormac was left to watch from the bank as she gulped a deep breath of air and dived beneath the surface.

She emerged a few feet away, gasping, her hair and face streaming with water and algae. "He's got it weighted down—you'll have to help me." She tried lifting one end of the bundle by the ropes that tied it, but couldn't manage to shift it. "It's too deep," she said. "I can't get a foothold." She was too far out from the bank, as well; there was no way he could reach her. "Hang on," Cormac called. "I've got a rope in the car. Don't let go."

He scrambled up and ran headlong for the jeep. Nora tried to hold on to the heavy bundle, but she couldn't help coughing and spluttering as it kept pulling her under. Cormac backed the jeep into position and rummaged through the supplies he kept in the back until he found a coil of rope. He tossed one end to Nora and quickly looped the other end to the car's frame. "Tie this to it, and hang on to the rope if you can," he shouted down at her. "Let me know when you're ready. Make sure you have a good grip; try and walk up the wall if you can."

She dived under again, tied the rope through the chain that circled Cadogan's bundle, and came up spluttering. "Okay, ready. Go ahead."

Cormac climbed into the driver's seat and inched the jeep forward until the bundle came up over the canal bank, with Nora trailing behind it. When she was safely over the bank, she let go of the rope and fell upon the large bundle, tearing at one end of the black plastic. Her body was filled with pounding dread as she anticipated finding what Cadogan had secreted inside.

When the plastic finally broke open, what came spilling forth was not what she had expected, but a mass of loose brown peat. Nora pulled at the twisted chains and tore at the plastic until she'd completely opened the length of the bundle: peat, only peat. Dizzy with confusion and relief, she started digging through it with her hands, just to be sure, and felt something solid beneath the surface. She brushed away the covering peat and extracted a rolled-up sheepskin. Inside it she found a handful of silk scarves, a velvet hood, several feathers, and a bright pair of nickel-plated handcuffs. Nora sat back and stared at the strange array of items laid out before her.

"Well, thanks be to God," Cormac said, coming around the side of the jeep. "I thought it was—"

"A body," she said. "So did I."

Cormac crouched down beside her and picked up one of the scarves, apparently just as mystified as she was. The scarf was still dry; the canal water hadn't had time to soak through the peaty bundle. "I can't see anything here that's even remotely incriminating," he said. "So why would Owen Cadogan go to such lengths to hide this stuff?"

Nora felt discouraged, exhausted in the wake of fear and exertion, and chilled by the wet clothing against her skin. The dusk had completely settled now, and she looked out over the black and blue landscape, imagining Garda officers out here with flashlights, sifting through wet peat and Cadogan's harmless bondage gear. There was no point in calling Ward; they had nothing that would help him find Rachel Briscoe, or identify Ursula's killer. She had been so sure that Cadogan was capable of murder. She'd seen it in his eyes when he had Ursula by the throat.

On the other hand, these things didn't mean he was off the hook. They'd just have to find some better proof.

"Let's go home," she said. "I can't see anything here to make it worth calling the police."

6

Nora was in the bathroom at the Crosses, rubbing her damp hair with a towel, when she heard Cormac's mobile ring. Who would be calling at this hour? It was after midnight. She could hear his voice from the sitting room say: "Michael, what's the matter? Are you all right?"

Nora went downstairs to find Cormac putting his shoes on. "That was Michael Scully. He can't find Brona. She hasn't been home all evening, and he's worried. I told him we'd come over."

Scully answered the door looking haggard. His thin skin seemed to hang loose on him, and he moved even more slowly than he had on their previous visit. He led them into the kitchen, where he'd evidently been trying to fill a medication dispenser. The box containing all the tablets and capsules had overturned, leaving a colorful mélange of pills on the tabletop.

Scully smoothed his disheveled hair back into place. "I heard on the radio this evening that one of the young women from the excavation has gone missing, and I—" His voice caught in his throat.

Cormac said, "I know, Michael, I know. We'll find her for you. You mustn't worry." When he'd gotten Scully settled in a chair, he turned to Nora and spoke under his breath. "I don't think we should leave him alone. Will you stay here while I see if I can find Brona? I think I know where to look." At the door, he said, "Lock this after me. Don't let anyone in. Promise me." She nodded, and for the first time Cormac's eyes betrayed his own worry.

Nora helped Michael Scully get all his medications back in the proper boxes. As she counted out the pain pills, he said, "Who knows where I shall be this time next year?"

Nora looked into his eyes and saw fear, not for himself, but for the daughter already so isolated from the world. "Who knows where any of us will be? We can't know that. Don't worry, Cormac will find her. He said he would."

Scully smiled faintly and said, "I wish Gabriel could see the two of you.

He often talked about how uncommonly well suited he thought you were."

"I'm sure he does see us, somehow, aren't you?"

"I'm not sure I believe in spirits, exactly, but I do believe that what happens in the world never really goes away. Everything that has been remains somehow, makes an impression. Some things make stronger impressions than others, but it all leaves something behind, some change, some ripple in time, don't you think? It's probably the best we can hope for."

Nora changed the subject. "I was wondering if you have anything in your files about the Loughnabrone hoard—any newspaper cuttings or official reports."

"I've quite a large file on it, yes." He faltered trying to stand, and Nora took his elbow.

"Are you all right?"

"It doesn't take long for the painkillers to take hold. I'll be fine in a few minutes. Not a bother on me. But maybe you'd look up the file? It should be on the far left, second drawer from the top."

Scully kept talking as she opened the drawer and began scanning the file headings. "My daughter has been helping me with this work since she was a child. She's read nearly everything in those files. I'm not sure whether she'll want to keep them. . . . I've often thought about this place, and everything that has passed here over the last nine thousand years, and how little we'd know if someone had not seen fit to set things down, incomplete and imperfect as those things certainly were."

Nora looked at the files, all neatly arranged and labeled in the same precise hand. She couldn't help marveling at the time and effort it must take to maintain all this, and at the astonishing capacity of the human memory, to be so steeped in all this that you carried it around inside you. What she beheld was nothing less than a life's work, and it was a humbling sight. Eventually paper records like these would probably be replaced by digital databases, just as the monks' written annals had replaced the twenty years' learning that the Druids had to undertake in order to qualify as high priests and judges. Faced with the whole wall of heavy files, representing as it did every fragmentary repository of human knowledge, she couldn't help wondering at how transitory it all was, in the long run, and how necessary to existence to engage in this kind of gathering and hoarding of knowledge. She wanted to tell Michael Scully that she understood his fear, his need to see it all carry on, even without him. Instead she said, "There's no need to talk if you don't feel like it. You should rest."

"I'd like to talk, if you don't mind. There's something I need to ask you."

Nora pulled the Loughnabrone file out of the drawer and set it on the table in front of the sofa and sat, so that she could give her full attention to Michael Scully and his request. What could he possibly need from her?

Scully leaned forward slightly as he spoke, his grip on the chair arms occasionally betraying either social discomfort or physical pain, or both. "I hope you can understand a father's apprehension. Brona is all I've got now. My wife died shortly after she was born and my elder daughter, Eithne—" He couldn't go on for a moment. "Eithne wasn't well for a long time, and disturbances of the mind are the most difficult to comprehend or confront. She suffered terribly, and nothing we did could help her in the end. Eithne drowned herself when Brona was just a child. I'm sure Cormac told you that Brona hasn't spoken since that time. What I wanted to ask you was this: I have one sister who lives down in Waterford, and I don't want her to interfere with Brona's future. Now, it's not that my daughter isn't well able to take care of herself. Even though she doesn't speak, she's not in the least simple. But my sister cannot understand that, and treats her as if she's somehow impaired. I've made all the necessary provisions in my will for Brona to have this house, as well as all my other assets, but I need to make sure that she has at least a few allies, just in case there's any dispute about the provisions of the will after I'm gone. Evelyn McCrossan already knows everything that I'm telling you, as does Brona herself, but I wanted to explain the situation to you and Cormac as well, since you'll have the cottage. I don't know that anything would be required of you, and since Brona is more than competent there would be no legal arrangement, but it's a possibility that she would from time to time need some . . . assistance, perhaps, in communicating with my lawyers or some other authorities. I don't know who else to ask, besides yourselves and Evelyn. I realize it's a rather strange and heavy responsibility, since it's an unknown quantity, and particularly since you won't be here most of the time. But as time passes I feel a greater urgency—"

"Of course we'll do whatever we can to help," Nora said. "I know Cormac would be more than willing as well. I'll tell him. He may have some questions for you. We both may, as we think about it more."

"Of course. Of course. It may be that nothing is required. I hope that will be the case." Michael Scully looked as if a heavy weight had been shifted from him; the deep crease in his forehead seemed to soften, either because the painkillers were kicking in or because he'd been able, finally, to unburden himself. "Thank you," he said, closing his eyes and letting himself sink back into the chair's upholstered softness. He looked very frail and ill, and Nora felt the urge to take his hand and offer some gesture of reassurance or comfort. But as she reached forward she realized that Michael Scully was fast asleep, and she withdrew her hand, not wishing to disturb his rest.

7

Rachel Briscoe was awakened by the beating wings of a large bird flying only a few feet over her head. She opened her eyes and for a moment felt as if the earth were falling away beneath her, but it was only the clouds moving across the deepening blue of the night sky. She had fought sleep so long, resisted closing her eyes, to keep away the terrible vision that kept rearing up in her head. And was this slumber from which she had just awakened a real sleep, or one of those mysterious absences, a blank, a hole in time? She had no idea how many minutes or hours had passed since she came to rest in this thicket, or even how she came to be here. She had seen policemen out searching for something, and had run as far as she could in the other direction.

She didn't dare come in contact with anyone, not yet, in case they heard the change in her voice and saw it in her eyes, that she was a person capable of shedding blood, of taking a life.

In her fitful sleep she had dreamt of a giant insect, its flattened eyes only reflecting what they saw, its sharp mandibles working. The thing had reached out to her, and she had opened her mouth to speak or cry out, but what had emerged was not words nor any other sound, but a warm torrent of blood. The memory of the dream made her feel ill. She could taste the blood in her mouth. Or had it been a dream? The line between what was real and what was dreaming had grown increasingly blurred over the past two days, since she'd found herself beside Ursula's body, her hands covered in gore.

She was in a hedgerow, thick grass beneath her back and arching brambles in haphazard latticework above her head. She was burrowed in like an animal, and yet she had no recollection of how she came to be here, just a hazy memory of panic, of searching the perimeter of the field—was it this same field?—for a way out. And of weariness, of being worn down by noise, like metal on metal, in her head. Clanking noises, one, two, three. Always three. How long had she been here? How many days? Time seemed elastic here, seemed to expand and contract at will.

The long drains glowed silver in the moonlight against the black peat. Her mouth was dry, but she dared not venture from the shelter to drink. The water here wasn't safe anyway. At times she had been certain that she was being followed. Several times she had doubled back, but found no one where she was sure someone had been. She had no idea how far she'd traveled, but the short nights were a hindrance; she couldn't get very far before it was light again. She pressed her face into the wet grass and tasted the dew, feeling no hunger, just insatiable thirst.

The field was on a little rise, and from it she could see all the bog she'd have to cross to get to the canal. A person could walk to Dublin on the canal. She'd plucked the idea from nowhere, it seemed. It was something that held together, when everything else seemed to be breaking apart. The night noises of animals, the sounds that had been her only comfort for days, seemed suddenly sinister. She heard rustling in the grass only a few inches from her head, and turned to find a badger baring his teeth at her, his black eyes reflecting the crescent moon. She scrambled backward, her clothes and hair catching in the brambles, imagining the sharp razor teeth biting into her flesh. There was no refuge from the blood. It would follow her, find her, punish her. She could see the stonelike forms of sleeping cattle in the field, the few stars emerging into the darkening night sky. If she stayed in this place, vines and brambles would grow over her, tying her down to the earth overnight. She'd never escape. Images and sounds traveled through her consciousness, her father's eyes, brimming with remorse. Too late. And the clanging, metal on metal, never silent, and the searing pain behind her eyes. She gathered her strength for putting one foot in front of the other, counting each step, louder and louder, the pressure building, the blinding pain, louder when she closed her eyes, even louder.

All at once before her was a pasture gate. Again she wondered how long she had been trapped here; and now the gate had appeared. As she stood still for a moment, she felt darkness gathering in her, pushing her forward. She felt its presence like the wind, knew that it was getting into her head, seeping in there. Soon there would be no daylight left at all, only darkness and noise. She climbed over the gate and began running toward the blank darkness that was Loughnabrone Bog.

She tried to stop thinking about the tattoo beating in her head, but it was always there, waking or sleeping, sometimes just a soft thrum, sometimes a deafening din. Always the same pattern. One, two, three. One, two, three. She felt as though her thoughts were in danger of being drummed right out of her head. The one imperative that remained was to get home, back to Dublin, whatever way she could. She dared not close her eyes at all anymore; she had to keep moving, keep hiding so they wouldn't find her. She could walk back to Dublin if she had to; she could find a way. Keeping out of sight was the main thing.

Whenever she closed her eyes, it came back—the blood, the spattered walls. Even with her eyes open sometimes she could see it, and hear the noise in her head again. She had not wanted it to happen that way. But when she had opened her eyes and seen the horror there, she'd dropped the knife and run. She looked down at her wet hands, expecting them to be covered in blood once more. She felt as though the knowledge of death would seep out of her; she imagined blood oozing from her pores like sweat.

From her hiding place on top of the hill, she had seen the canal cutting through the bog, straight as a road, a line into the heart of Dublin. That would be her path, if she could only get there. A huge expanse of bog lay between her and the canal bank, and a shivering body of water. Loughnabrone, lake of sorrows. She would have to cross that way. Every time she closed her eyes she saw it: the blood, and then the looming mask, the insect face, its raspy breathing sending a panicky chill into her veins.

The drains were deep and blacker than night, and she half expected something to rise up out of them after her. A hare, frightened by her sudden movement, zigzagged out from under a clump of rushes and brushed so near her that she lost her balance and tumbled down into the inky, water-filled ditch. She went down hard on one knee; she could feel the joint pop as she landed, and a sharp pain shot through her thigh. She sucked in her breath and bit her lip to keep from crying out. She lay still for a few moments, immobilized by the tearing pain in her leg, then scrambled upward, trying to stay focused on climbing out of the murky water, on trying to outrun the cacophonous clanking noise that grew louder and more clamorous until all other sound was shut out: One, two, three. One, two, three . . . It grew to such a pitch that she barely felt the blow that fractured her skull.

8

Nora settled the woolen blanket over Michael Scully's sleeping form in the chair beside her, then took up his file on the Loughnabrone hoard and rearranged herself on the sofa. She was contemplating what Scully had said about humankind's incomplete and imperfect attempts to set down what they had seen and heard and learned—and how much more imperfect they must be if the times you tried to document had no written language. It must be nearly impossible not to misinterpret or exaggerate the significance of everything that had been passed down, since the fragments were so rare.

She found John O'Donovan's letter to the Ordnance Survey office, with notes about the townland called Loughnabrone. The older residents he had interviewed described it as a very gentle place, by which they meant that it had more than its fair share of fairy rings and raths. The water from the holy well on the northeast side of the hill supposedly cured all ailments of the throat.

She dug a bit deeper into the file and came across a photograph of Owen Cadogan, taken when he was appointed manager at Loughnabrone. Nora remembered her first impression of the man: restless, dissatisfied, a little dangerous. Maybe that had been the initial attraction for Ursula Downes, but maybe it was the sort of attraction that didn't last forever.

A rap sounded on the Scullys' front door, and Nora went to answer it. Cormac had been gone about an hour and a quarter. Remembering his warning, she checked through the window and saw him leaning on the doorjamb. The person who'd knocked was evidently Brona Scully, who stood beside him. When the door was opened, the girl darted past Nora without a glance, went straight into the sitting room to her father, and shook him gently awake. Scully clasped his daughter tightly to his chest without a word.

Nora said quietly to Cormac, "Where did you find her?"

"I didn't. She found me. I was looking up into that tree, thinking she might be hiding there, and she was. She pulled back one of the branches and let me have it." He rubbed the raised lump on his forehead where the tree limb had evidently made contact. "She would have done more, but I started shouting about how her father had sent me looking for her, and she came along peacefully enough then."

"Who did she think you were?"

"I don't know. But I think someone must have frightened the life out of her before I got there. If she hadn't known me, hadn't known Michael had sent me to look for her, she would have fought like a demon."

"I've been wondering if Brona might have seen you leave Ursula's house. That tree has a direct view into the back garden there. I know she might not be able to tell us anything, but do you think it's at least worth asking?"

Cormac looked into the sitting room, where Brona was helping Michael to his feet.

"It's nearly three o'clock. Let's let them be for tonight," he said. "We can talk to Brona in the morning."

BOOK FIVE

A SACRED CHARACTER

The dark color and unfathomable depth of their water has conferred a sacred character upon some pools.

—the Roman writer Lucius Annaeus Seneca (4 B.C.–A.D. 65),
describing the Celtic peoples of Europe

1

Benny Smollett felt the wind raise goose pimples on his exposed, pale flesh, and knew he'd better get into the water quick. He finished stripping off down to his swimming togs, folded his shell suit neatly and placed it beneath his towel, ready for when he emerged from the lake. The sun had already been up for more than an hour, but for some reason going for a swim in midsummer always made him colder than it did in chillier times of the year. The wife thought he was off his nut coming here at all, but the lake was handy to the house, and cost nothing. Sometimes in the depths of winter he used the pool in town, but he disliked the chlorine smell that seeped from his skin all day. No, the lake was far superior. It was clean, as well, with the bog all around acting as a natural filtration system.

Benny cast a glance skyward as he walked down the dock and dived into the water with a splash. He knew he was taking a chance, being out here on his own; the place was deserted, and if he took a cramp he would sink like a stone. But the solitariness of the place was one of its attractions. He knew people around the town thought him daft, but what did that matter? Out here he imagined himself as young and strong. In his own mind, he was fit, and getting fitter. He imagined that he could stave off decrepitude and even death itself.

He pulled the water back with strong strokes. He was almost used to the chilly temperature now. The lake wasn't large, and he would swim once across and back. That was his daily routine. He plunged forward into the small waves, sliding into the easy rhythm of a crawl, conscious of his progress when he turned his head for air. He dared not miss a day, or his rhythm would get clogged up and it would take him days to find it again. He felt his muscles glide over his bones, felt the tendons tighten and loosen as they should, propelling him forward. He was a machine, kept in good repair by constant use, leaving the dock behind and seeing his goal, the opposite shore, nearly within reach. His legs felt strong and useful. He was glad he'd started doing his rounds on the bike in good weather. Driving the postal van everywhere was death on a man. He shuddered at the prospect and kept swimming, feeling the air flowing in and out of his lungs. He reached the far shore, felt the lake bottom with his fingertips on the forward stroke and turned, starting in on the back-stroke for the trip back. High overhead a tall wading bird flew by, its long legs trailing awkwardly in its wake. He would have to start learning about all the birds he saw here. There were hundreds of them, nesting ducks and other waterfowl among the reeds near the shore, tall waders and small, wrenlike birds that he'd seen catching damselflies with one quick sideways twist. The streak of fine weather had been uncanny, and it lifted his spirits. He was blessed with work he enjoyed, fresh air and freedom. In the evenings, he had the refereeing at the local football pitch, and then home to bed by ten. He never touched a drop of liquor. All in all, a good life—not without its disappointments, but whose life had none of those?

When he reached the shallow water again, he headed toward the ramp that was built down in the lake for boats. The shoreline could be boggy in places, and difficult to get over without sinking into it, so the ramp was the best place to get in and out. He stood, dripping, exhilarated from the long swim, his brain firing on all cylinders. Great for clearing the head, it was. Losing his waterborne weightlessness, he trudged up the ramp, now knee-deep, until he stumbled over a submerged branch. Not a tree in sight, but he knew that these bog lakes often held huge trunks, whorls of roots that had been preserved below in peat. If he could manage it, he'd better move the thing so it wouldn't trip him up again tomorrow.

He grasped the branch end with both hands and heaved upward. Once it was loose he could shift it out of the way. What he didn't antici-pate was that the branch would be easily six feet long, with smaller branches and leaves still attached. As he dislodged the thing from the lake bottom, it sent bits of dirt and peat flying, flecking his face and bare chest with slimy black mud. He reached into the water again, expecting to touch rough bark, but instead he felt something smooth and slippery bob to the surface. He moved to retrieve it. That was when he saw the marks where the branches had pressed into it, and knew that what floated in the water before him was pale flesh. A body.

2

Liam Ward turned away from the lakeshore feeling light-headed. He hadn't been prepared for the sight of Rachel Briscoe's body floating in the lake, her long hair a dark aureole spread out around her head. The unwelcome vision dredged up memories that he did not want to face again this morning. He was rescued from his thoughts by Catherine Friel's arrival. Ward felt his heart tighten when she glanced over at him, and was suddenly conscious of the gold band he'd replaced on his left hand.

Twenty minutes later he was consulting with the crime-scene officers on their search of the area when Dr. Friel emerged from the white police tent and signaled for him to join her. As he entered the surreal diffuse light inside the tent, the sight of the girl's waxen face and blue lips made his stomach lurch unsteadily once more, but he fought off the nausea and stood beside her.

"I'm afraid it's all too familiar, Liam," Dr. Friel said. "The garrote is a narrow leather cord with three knots tied in it. And her throat was cut—looks like left to right again, just like Ursula Downes. She also seems to have been hit on the back of the head, but I'll know more about that after the postmortem. From the temperature and the condition of her skin, she'd probably been in the water about six to eight hours when she was found, which puts time of death maybe between one and three in the morning. No obvious signs of struggle or sexual assault. She does have some unusual scarring on her wrists." She unzipped the body bag a few inches to gently lift one of Rachel Briscoe's arms and show him. "They look like deliberate cuts. Completely scarred over, and at least several years old. If I had to venture a theory, I'd say probably self-inflicted."

"You're not saying this may have been a suicide?"

"Oh, no, I don't think it's possible that the fatal injuries were self-inflicted. Just that she may have had a history of self-injury. It's not as uncommon as people might think. I don't know if that detail might be relevant to your investigation, but I thought you should know." She reached over and pressed his forearm. Her hand felt warm against his wrist, and surprisingly strong. "I am sorry, Liam. I know you were trying to find her."

Ward nodded and looked out over the lake. The strong wind stirred up tiny wavelets that rippled its surface, driving a pair of mute swans on the far side of the water hard against the rushy lakeshore. How had this place come to be called Loughnabrone, and what other deeds were hidden beneath its waters? These three triple deaths—three lives sacrificed, and for what? Perhaps it was for something beyond rational understanding, something deeper than the motives he could grasp. He'd been fighting the notion. But with this third victim, perhaps he ought to admit there might be some dark connection to the past.

3

The pounding on the door downstairs gradually made its way into Nora's consciousness. Cormac still slept soundly beside her. They'd been up half the night, over at the Scullys' house, and had looked forward to a lie-in this morning. She climbed out of bed and went to the window, to find Liam Ward looking up at her, one hand shielding his eyes from the light. Behind him stood Detective Brennan. She hurried into her clothes and down the stairs.

"Dr. Gavin? Sorry to disturb you so early, but we need to have a word with you and Dr. Maguire."

"About what?"

Ward pursed his lips and frowned. "I'm afraid there's been another murder. Rachel Briscoe's body was found this morning at Loughnabrone."

Nora backed up into the entry, feeling jittery, as if she'd had too much coffee instead of too little sleep. Could something she had said or done in the last few days have placed the girl in even greater danger? "Another triple death," she said. Ward's face remained impassive. "It was, wasn't it?"

"I'm afraid I can't discuss the details—"

But what else would have driven them straight here, to check on their prime suspect in Ursula's murder?

Cormac came downstairs, struggling into a shirt, with his hair still standing on end. Nora could see that he wasn't quite awake, and she also saw each of the detectives noticing the reddish marks on his forehead.

Ward addressed Cormac: "I was just telling Dr. Gavin the reason that we've disturbed you so early this morning. A young woman named Rachel Briscoe has been found dead at Loughnabrone. We'd like to ask you a few questions."

A look of helpless disbelief crossed Cormac's features. "Of course. Anything I can do to help." He waved them into the sitting room.

Brennan took a seat on the sofa and brought out a small notebook and pen; Ward remained standing. He said, "I have to ask you both where you were last night between the hours of midnight and four o'clock."

Cormac ran one hand through his uncombed hair and looked over at Nora. Her stomach leapt, knowing what he'd have to say, but Cormac didn't seem tense at all. "After midnight, maybe about twenty past, Michael Scully rang. His daughter hadn't come home all evening, and he was worried."

"We went over to the house right away," Nora said. "Michael was quite agitated, so I stayed with him while Cormac tried to find Brona." Was it her imagination, she wondered, or did Ward's reaction to this news seem a bit odd? She said, "I don't know if you know the Scullys, Detective."

Ward cut her off, saying in a low voice, "Yes, I know them. Michael Scully is my father-in-law." Nora had a sudden vision of a slender form slipping silently beneath clear water, and grasped that Michael Scully's elder daughter must have been Ward's wife. He would know all about Brona's silence. Her face burned and she felt ashamed for being so obtuse. Ward looked away for a moment, then calmly resumed his questioning of Cormac. "Where did you go looking for Brona?"

"I started behind the house, just cutting through the pastures. I'd seen her once before near a whitethorn tree at the top of the hill, so I thought I'd try there first. I didn't go down to the lake."

"Did you have a torch? Did you call out? What I mean to ask is whether anyone might have seen or heard you."

"I don't know. I did have a torch, and I did call for her, but I doubt whether anyone heard me."

"How long did you carry on the search?"

"I suppose about an hour or so, maybe an hour and a quarter. I didn't really pay attention to the time."

"So from about one o'clock to approximately two-fifteen. And you eventually found her?"

"Yes. She was hiding in the top branches of the whitethorn tree I mentioned. It's in the clearing on top of the hill behind Ursula's house. I shone my light up into the tree, and she let go a branch that hit me square in the forehead. That's how I got this." He indicated the raised reddish bump near his hairline. Brennan noted all this in her book.

"Why would the girl attack you like that?" Ward asked.

"I don't know. She seemed terribly frightened, as though someone had been after her and she thought it might have been me. I tried explaining that her father had sent me to look for her, that I couldn't leave there without her. I just kept talking, and eventually she calmed down and came along with me. We got back to the house between two-thirty and three."

"And then what happened?"

"After we'd got Michael and Brona settled, and all their doors and windows locked, we came home again and went to sleep. It had been a very long night. I think I fell asleep just after dawn, maybe around five."

"Did you see anyone besides Brona Scully when you were searching?"

"No. I didn't see anyone. Look, I didn't have anything to do with any murder—last night or any other night."

"Nevertheless," Ward said, "I'm afraid we'll have to ask you to answer a few more questions down at the station."

Cormac stood up, resignation visible in his face and posture. "I suppose the sooner I go in, the sooner you'll be finished with me."

"We would appreciate your cooperation."

Despite the strong sunshine, the wind was brisk when they went outside. "Can I just get my jacket from the car?" Cormac asked, and Detective Ward gave a quick nod.

Cormac opened the jeep's rear compartment to retrieve his anorak, and Brennan stepped up behind him.

"That yours?" she asked.

"Is what mine?" Cormac's voice was muffled as he slid the anorak over his head.

"That," Brennan said.

Cormac's eyes went cold, and Nora and Ward stepped forward as Brennan pointed to a rucksack, nearly hidden by the site tools in the back of the jeep. A shiny pink fabric heart hung from its zipper.

Brennan's eyebrows arched as she looked at Ward and lifted the rucksack out of the boot. She unzipped the main compartment and opened it. Inside the flap was an address label, filled in with Rachel Briscoe's name and address.

"Wait a minute. I've never seen that rucksack before," Cormac protested. "And I don't know how it got there. I don't believe this—"

Brennan opened the car door for him. "We can talk about all of this down at the station," she said.

4

After the detectives had taken Cormac away, Nora stood in the kitchen and tried to think. There had to be some way through all this, but her head felt as though it was made of felt. Somebody was trying to make it look as though Cormac was mixed up in these murders. Someone must have been watching them last night; how else could anyone have known that Cormac was out searching for Brona at the time Rachel Briscoe was killed? Unless they'd been drawn out of the house on purpose. For a split second she wondered if someone had tried to set them up. But who— Michael and Brona Scully? She didn't like to think it, but she and Cormac would have been at home all night if it hadn't been for Michael's urgent call. A wave of paranoia, and then a backwash of disbelief, rolled through her. No, not possible, not possible. Michael had been Gabriel McCrossan's good friend. It had to be coincidence that Michael had phoned when he had.

She suddenly remembered what Cormac had said about finding Brona Scully—that it seemed the girl had attacked because she thought someone was after her. She had to talk to Brona, try to find out whether that had been the case, whether she knew anything—and whether she'd be willing to go to the police. But how would that help, having as their only material witness someone who could not speak?

Or maybe it would be best to go all the way back to the beginning— start with Danny Brazil, the first victim found with a knotted cord around his neck. Ward had refused to tell her how they'd found Rachel Briscoe, but Nora had a terrible, sinking feeling that there had been a triple-knotted cord around her neck as well.

This whole mess was beginning to resemble a tangled knot, with strands looped back and twisted around themselves. But getting frustrated wouldn't help. Unraveling any knot needed a careful attack, following one filament at a time, working at it until it slid free; that was the way to undo this puzzle too. That was the way she could best help Cormac.

What could Ursula have found out or surmised about Danny Brazil's death? Ursula had asked Quill if he thought three was an unlucky number. And the next morning she was dead. It was impossible to shake the impression that her murder had something to do with the Loughnabrone hoard. After all, Ursula had stolen one of Charlie Brazil's drawings, one that seemed to document the existence of a priceless gold collar never registered in any museum. This was just the sort of discovery that would add fuel to all those myths about hidden treasure, gold buried underfoot. If Ursula had known of the collar's existence, she might also have had some theories about who had killed Danny Brazil to get it. And maybe she was prepared to use that information—perhaps for blackmail, trying to squeeze money out of Danny's killer. Or maybe it was even more complicated than that. Maybe, like Danny Brazil, the collar had never gone away. Maybe it was still here, still a motive for murder.

Nora crossed to Cormac's desk and opened the book where Ursula had stashed the stolen drawing, turning on the table lamp to examine it more closely. The paper was black in places from mildew, but the draftsmanship was exquisite, incredibly clear and detailed. She reached for Cormac's magnifying glass and sat down to get closer to the image. Maybe there was something she was missing, some double meaning hidden in it somewhere. The magnifier made the image bulge before her eyes, shading and hatch marks blurred into three-dimensional illusion. She traveled up and down the lines, looking for something, anything that might leap out.

She turned the paper over and saw a series of nine smaller circles inside the arc of a larger ring. The way they were drawn, she saw eyes peering out of the paper, a face that seemed somehow familiar, but not quite right. She turned the paper upside down, but that didn't help. Did the numbers mean something—three and three and three?

Nora jumped as she heard a heavy fist beating on the cottage door. She closed the drawing into the book and slipped it under a pile of papers as quickly as she could. The pounding had stopped; with her heart still thudding in her chest, she moved to the door and peered out the diamond-shaped window.

No one was visible, but someone had left a small white envelope wedged into the window frame. The handwriting on it, plainly visible through the window, read "Nora Gavin." Nora wondered why anyone would leave a note instead of talking to her. Could it be some communication from Brona Scully?

Remembering Cormac's warning, she crossed quickly to the fireplace, grabbed the heaviest poker, and returned to the door. Still no sign of anyone outside. If only the window were a little larger, a little lower, so she could see if someone was there. . . . She unlocked the door as silently as she could, reached for the envelope, then closed and locked the door once more.

Safe inside, she turned her attention to the envelope. It was only lightly sealed, and Nora opened it carefully, conscious of the value it might have as evidence. Inside was a black leather cord with three figure-eight knots. Was it intended as a warning, or an accusation? She felt the thin roundness of the cord between her fingers, and knew with sudden clarity that the person who'd killed two people had just been outside the house.

She raised her head to peer through the window once again. Only then did she perceive the shadowy presence behind her and hear the soft whistle that split the air. Her head snapped forward, and the solid world beneath her dissolved, swallowed up in black and blinding pain.

5

"Look, I've told you already, I have no idea how that rucksack got into my jeep," Cormac said. His eyes burned and his head ached from lack of sleep. Detective Brennan had been going at him for nearly an hour. He glanced up at Detective Ward, sitting silently by Brennan's side, arms crossed over his chest.

"Why would I have opened the car if I'd known the girl's rucksack was in there? It doesn't make sense. We're wasting time here, going around in circles."

"So tell me something new," Brennan said.

Cormac said, "All right. I think Ursula Downes was murdered over buried treasure." Silence greeted his pronouncement; not a good sign.

"And why would you think that?" Brennan finally asked.

"I think she suspected—as a lot of people did—that not all the items in the Loughnabrone hoard had been turned over to the National Museum." Cormac detected a subtle movement in the chair beside her, perhaps no more than a blink, but he knew that the idea had piqued Ward's interest.

"Go on," Ward said.

"But I think Ursula found some proof that there were items in the hoard never accounted for. I don't know that much," Cormac said, "but I'll tell you what I do know." And so he told them everything, about the drawing Ursula had apparently left in one of his books, about the similar one Nora had found in Charlie Brazil's shed, about the letter Rachel Briscoe had left in Nora's car, and his theory about her true identity. He carried on, despite the skeptical turn of their lips, the doubt in their eyes.

"You think Ursula Downes thought she'd found proof of a gold collar found at Loughnabrone?" Brennan asked.

"Yes. I don't know who she thought was in possession of it. And I don't know who she might have been working with—Charlie Brazil clearly has some connection, since he has a number of similar drawings. I think Ursula may have been carrying on an affair with Owen Cadogan. There's nothing to say he was involved in the sale of illegal antiquities, but he'd have better connections in the right places than most of the men who work for him."

Ward said, "Let me ask you, Dr. Maguire—if you believed these drawings to be so significant, why did you not bring them forward earlier?"

"It was a question of provenance," Cormac said. "People would want to know where I'd got my hands on them. Plus, there was no way of knowing whether the collar really existed or whether someone just made it up. All the same, if it is real, then it would be incentive enough for murder."

"How much incentive?" Brennan asked.

"You mean how much would something like that be worth?" Cormac shrugged. "Hard to say—whatever the market will bear. And when you're talking about one-of-a-kind ancient gold objects on the black market, it'll bear a lot."

"So why should we believe your version of this story?" Brennan asked. "Why shouldn't we just flip the whole thing back to front? You found proof of the collar, and Ursula tried to get a share of the selling price, so you killed her. And then killed Rachel Briscoe because she'd seen you that night at Ursula's house."

"Even assuming that were the case, why would I tell you about the collar? Why would I not just keep mum? Take me home right now, and I'll show you the drawings if you don't believe me."

Ward and Brennan exchanged a glance; then they both stood up to leave the interview room.

"What's happening?" Cormac asked. "Where are you going?"

"We'll be back in a moment, Dr. Maguire," Ward said. "I just want a quick word with Detective Brennan. Can we get you anything?"

"No, thanks." When the detectives had left the room, he let his eyes wander around the stark space. If only he and Nora had been able to make more progress on the details surrounding Ursula's death: her interest in Danny Brazil's murder, the collar. He hoped Nora wasn't up to anything rash, trying to get him out of this jam. They wouldn't be able to hold him forever; they'd eventually have to either charge him or let him go. Surely she would see that. But somehow he didn't feel overwhelming confidence on that point.

He might not even be here if someone hadn't deliberately planted that rucksack in the back of the jeep; if he could only work out why . . . Perhaps so that he would have to be questioned again; but to what end?

He couldn't believe the police would actually charge him for Rachel Briscoe's murder. It didn't make sense, thinking that he'd killed the girl while out looking for Brona. So why lead them down the wrong track—unless it was just to get him away from the house?

And with a sudden, awful horror, he knew. Whoever had planted the rucksack wanted the drawings. He couldn't believe he'd been so thick. He'd said it himself: Ursula's drawing was the only evidence that any Loughnabrone collar existed—and to some warped mind, probably well worth killing for.

He leaped from his chair and started pounding on the door of the interview room. "Detective Ward! Somebody—open up!"

As they made their way to the galley kitchen across from their office, Brennan spoke first. "I can't believe he wants us to swallow all that—a gold collar, for God's sake."

"Does sound a bit outlandish, all right, but you have to admit it's not impossible. Look at that fella stumbled across those Bronze Age gold necklaces at the beach on his holidays up in Mayo." She must remember it; the case had made national headlines.

Brennan gave a grudging nod, and Ward continued: "Dr. Gavin's statement says she overheard Ursula Downes telling Charlie Brazil that she knew what he was hiding. What if he and the father still have a whole pile of stuff from the hoard? Ursula finds out, and they have to get rid of her." As he spoke, a gauzy notion dragged across Ward's consciousness. The way Ursula Downes and Rachel Briscoe had been killed—just like Danny Brazil, one of the brothers who'd found the Loughnabrone hoard in the first place. It was Maguire who'd known so much about triple death, but Charlie Brazil who'd been suspected of carrying out bloodletting rituals. "Even if he is blowing smoke, Maureen, it wouldn't hurt to see these drawings he's talking about. And we should probably pull Charlie Brazil and Owen Cadogan this morning, see if they can give us details about what they were up to last night. Maybe we'd better split up, when we're done with Maguire. I'll take Brazil; you take Cadogan."

They both turned to the uniformed officer who'd just stuck his head in through the doorway; he appeared slightly winded from legging it up the stairs.

"Ah, Detective Ward, there you are. Thought you were in the interview room. I've got a phone call for you."

"I am in the middle of an interview," Ward said. "We're just on a short break. Take a message, will you?"

"I would, but she says it's urgent, sir, and she won't speak to anyone but you."

Ward crossed the hall to his office and picked up the phone.

"I'd like to speak to the officer in charge of the murder." The woman's voice was smooth and educated, with a recognizable Dublin 4 drawl, but tentative. Ward guessed that she didn't often ring the police about murder—or anything else, for that matter.

"This is Detective Liam Ward. I'm heading up the murder inquiries."

"Inquiries?" Shock registered in the silence on the other end of the line. With one hand, Ward signaled to Maureen to pick up her extension. "Does that mean there's more than one? I only heard about one on the television."

"As of this morning there's been a second murder. Are you calling with information?"

The woman's tone was matter-of-fact. "I'm ringing to tell you that Desmond Quill's alibi for Thursday evening is a lie." Ward pictured her slender and fair, with expensive rings on her manicured fingers, but he could not see her face.

"And how do you happen to know this?"

"Because that Thursday chess game was something he and Laurence Fitzhugh cooked up years ago, the two of them, as a convenient cover for when they wanted to misbehave. Every week they work out who wins and who loses—plot every move, in fact, so that they can back each other up if that should be required. The game actually does take place, you see—not on a chessboard, but in their heads. I don't know where Desmond Quill was that night. But I do know he wasn't with Laurence Fitzhugh, because I was—as I have been every Thursday night for the past six and a half years."

Ward wanted to believe the cool, anonymous voice. It could be a vital lead, but his inner skeptic made him pull back. "We appreciate your coming forward, but of course we'll need to verify—"

She cut him off. "I haven't come forward. I won't give a formal statement, and I'll certainly never testify in court. I have far too much to lose. I'm sure you understand, Detective Ward. And you needn't bother tracing this call; I'm ringing from a telephone box. I just had a notion that you ought to know the truth."

She rang off abruptly, leaving a loud, flat buzzing in his right ear. He looked up at Maureen, who was setting her receiver in its cradle. She made a face. "Worthless. Could be anyone, a crank, someone trying to take the pressure off Maguire."

"But it is something new. We can ask the Bureau to follow up with Fitzhugh. Maguire can wait another few minutes downstairs; let's head over to Coughlan's, will we, and see if anyone can tell us exactly where Desmond Quill was at the time Rachel Briscoe was murdered."

6

Coughlan's Hotel was a small but very formal inn—directly across the square from the Garda station, but not the sort of place that would be happy to welcome police officers on duty, even if they were neighbors. Ward showed his identification at the front desk, careful to keep his voice low as he asked to speak to the manager on duty. A neat, middle-aged man in an expensive suit came out of a side office almost before the receptionist had set down the phone. He introduced himself as Noel Lavin, the general manager, and ushered them discreetly into his office. "Now, then, if you could tell me what the problem is, exactly . . . ? And if there's any way my staff can assist you, they certainly will."

"We're inquiring after one of your guests, Mr. Desmond Quill. We'd like to speak to the staff members who may have had some dealings with him."

Lavin seemed to waver for a moment between his civic and moral duty to assist the Guards and his professional duty to maintain a screen of privacy and discretion for his paying guests. He smiled insincerely. "Is Mr. Quill in some sort of trouble? I assure you he's done nothing here—"

"We're just making some routine inquiries," Ward said. "Which members of your staff would have had the most to do with him during his stay here?"

"The restaurant and bar staff, certainly. He took quite a few meals in his room, obviously. We were all shocked to hear about the murder. A dreadful thing, just dreadful and terribly, terribly sad."

Ward proposed that Lavin should fetch the people they needed to see, and Lavin liked the idea. "Much more discreet that way, yes. Saves you from chasing all over the hotel . . ." Ward finished the thought in his own mind: . . . *and letting the guests see you question the staff.*

From the barman, Ward learned that Quill had gotten desperately drunk on Friday, the first day he was there, and that it had taken the barman and the night manager and two others to get him into his bed. The following day, Saturday, he'd spent more quietly. He'd stirred out for lunch in the hotel restaurant, but otherwise stayed in his room, ordering in drink—plenty of it.

The night manager backed up the barman's story, saying Quill had spent most of the time in his room, drowning his sorrows. "At least I assume that's what he was doing, from the amount of whiskey he ordered up. I check all the rooms before I turn in, and you could hear him in there, drunk as a lord and snoring his head off. You'd feel sorry for him, the poor sod."

"What about the cleaners?" Ward asked Lavin. "I'm particularly interested in talking to the person who cleaned the room today."

"You'll be wanting Cara Daly, then. Only works at weekends, but she should still be here. I'll see if I can find her for you."

While he was gone, Ward sat and pondered the anonymous phone call. What did the woman on the other end of the phone have to lose if she came forward? It might have been just an elaborate decoy maneuver, an attempt to deflect attention from Maguire—and if that was the case, he was wasting time here. He was on the brink of packing it in when the door opened and Lavin returned with a slight, frightened-looking young woman with a puffy face and circles dark as bruises under her eyes. As she sat down in the leather armchair beside him, she crossed her thin legs and twisted them together, as if half afraid they would start moving of their own volition. Ward felt a twinge of guilt, knowing he didn't have time to find out her story. Lavin, clearly nervous about leaving the girl in Ward's care, started straightening the items on his desk and wouldn't leave the room until Ward asked him to. What was he afraid the girl might say?

"I asked to speak to you, Cara, because according to Mr. Lavin, you cleaned Room Thirty-eight yesterday and this morning—the room where a guest named Desmond Quill is staying. Is that right?"

"I always clean Number Thirty-eight. It's on my list. I meant to tell him, Mr. Lavin, about the room right away, but I forgot."

"Tell him what, Cara?"

"There's nobody in it today. Mr. Quill's stuff is gone, all his clothes and shaving things."

Ward felt a prick of apprehension, but he needed to know more, much more.

"Was Mr. Quill in the room when you were cleaning yesterday?"

"No, he was out." The girl's muscles went rigid and her hands clenched into fists. Her anxiety was contagious; Ward felt a tightening at the base of his throat.

"When you were cleaning the room, Cara, did you notice anything unusual, anything out of the ordinary?"

Her eyes flicked toward him suspiciously, and she licked her lips. "I don't want to get in trouble."

"You're not in trouble. Just tell me what was unusual about Mr. Quill's room."

"I shouldn't have touched anything. They could fire me for that."

"No one is going to fire you, Cara. What did you see in Number Thirty-eight?"

"Didn't see. Heard. I was tidying up the bedside table, and there was a tape recorder on it. I was just curious. I wanted to hear what kind of music he liked, the man in that room. He was nice; he left me a whole tenner the day before."

"And what kind of music was it?"

"It wasn't music at all." She hesitated again, her hands and fingers twisting into elaborate knots in her lap. "It was just a whole lot of noise. Sounded like me dad, snoring." Ward had been prepared for almost any answer but that. Snoring? Suddenly he heard the voice of the night manager, sitting in the same chair only a few minutes earlier: *You could hear him in there, drunk as a lord and snoring his head off.*

A few minutes later, Lavin was letting him into Number 38, which as Cara Daly had reported, had been completely vacated. "I'm sure it's just a misunderstanding," Lavin said, unable to imagine his venerable establishment tarnished by scandal. "He left a credit card number with us. I'm sure he's going to come by the desk later to settle things up."

Ward stood at the door and let his eyes sweep up and down the hallway, noting the glowing red EXIT sign at one end. He turned back to the hotel manager. "Supposing someone wanted to leave the hotel without going by the reception desk, without being seen. Is that the only other way out?"

"Well, yes," Lavin said. "Although the door at ground level does lock so no one can get in from the street."

"May I have a look?"

Lavin led the way to the fire exit at the end of the hall, and down the concrete stairwell that must have been added to the old hotel in the past few years. He pushed open the door at ground level, showing how the exit led into a narrow alleyway. There were no windows above, which meant there would be no one to witness comings and goings.

Ward crouched on his heels to examine the door more closely, and found that someone had taped the latch open. Desmond Quill could have come and gone at will without anyone seeing him.

7

Nora gradually regained her senses in darkness. Her eyes slid open, but there was nothing but impenetrable blackness before her; solid black, a total absence of light. The ringing in her ears and the throbbing pain radiating from the base of her skull told her she was still alive. Why? Was the killer just toying with her, saving her for later?

That grim prospect was enough to get her moving, despite the stiffness from lying in one position too long. It had been a couple of hours, anyway, judging by the way she felt. Propping herself up on one arm, she reached the other in front of her, feeling for surfaces, edges, shapes of recognizable objects. Her fingers closed around a long, round broom handle, a mop and bucket, two walls within reach. A closet, then. She was still in the cottage, in the broom closet under the stairs. She felt washed in relief, and drank in the mingled scents of cleaning liquid, dust, and lemon oil. She had been spared for some reason. That showed the killer wasn't panicking, but proceeding according to plan. But what was that plan? Maybe it hadn't been necessary to kill her, just to get her out of the way for a while.

But she had to get out of here. Climbing to her feet, she felt the door's beaded lath; no handle on the inside. It wasn't completely dark now; she could see a thin thread of light around the door. She tried to remember what the latch was like. A simple bar, if she recalled correctly. Depending on how the door frame was constructed, she might be able to lift it from inside, if she could find something to use as a tool. Even if he was here waiting for her when she escaped from the closet armed only with a mop, it was still better than just sitting there waiting for him to return.

Something thin, and strong enough to lift a latch. She set to work, down on her knees, methodically running her fingers over every object, leaving everything where it was, in case she needed it later. A strong wire might work, if only such a thing could be found. On the floor she found a box of rags; nothing in the bottom of the box. After a few minutes, she had examined and rejected every item. There must be something, something she hadn't found, or something she could take apart to find the sort of flat tool she needed—

A noise came from the other side of the wall, and Nora froze in panic. She felt her skin flush with adrenaline, preparing for a fight. Maybe she should let him think she was still out—no, better to be ready as soon as anyone opened the door. . . . The scrabbling noises from outside continued, until she finally realized that it was just a pair of birds who'd built a nest under the eaves, arriving home and fluttering against the outside wall.

She relaxed a little, and her hand slid down the wall behind her, touching something she hadn't felt before—a slight raised edge, a cold surface. She knelt and followed the edge, and prised up the flat piece of sheet metal from against the wall with her fingernails. Too big, probably, but worth a try. She'd have to be careful of the sharp edges. She felt around for a couple of rags and used them to lift the metal sheet. It seemed to be about eighteen inches long and eight inches wide; it might slip through the crack between the door and the jamb. She turned around in the cramped space and felt for the tiny crack, trying to remember how high off the ground the latch was, and hoping against hope that Gabriel and Evelyn had hired a carpenter who didn't see any absolute need for square corners.

The thin sheet slid about a half-inch into the crack. She shoved it in another quarter inch, until she heard the distinctive sound of metal touching metal. Trying to keep a grip on her two makeshift handles, she wrestled the wobbling sheet downward, trying to find the bottom of the latch so that she could slip the metal under it and lift the bar. Her head still pounded dully, and beads of sweat were forming on her forehead and down the middle of her back. *Let it work*, she prayed fervently to whatever deity might be listening. All at once the metal sheet slid forward, and her shoulder bumped against the door. Now just to jimmy the sheet upward, and—

Nothing. The door didn't budge, though the latch had lifted; she'd distinctly heard it click. Maybe something was blocking the door. She threw her shoulder against the stout wood and heaved with all her strength, but it wouldn't move. She lifted the sheet metal higher— maybe the bar hadn't quite cleared the latch. She joggled the flimsy metal up and down a few times, still pressing on the door, and all at once it burst open and sent her flying out onto the flag floor, sheet metal warbling and vibrating as it skidded across the stone.

After the deafening crash reverberated several times, the house was quiet. Nora lay still and listened, but heard nothing. Raising her head to look around, she saw that the house had been ransacked. The sitting area was in shambles, cushions tossed around, lamps broken, all of Cormac's wine bottles and Evelyn's beautiful crockery smashed. The floor was knee-deep in books that had been pulled from the shelves, as if someone had been searching the place in a frenzy.

Still jangling with fear, she went into the front hall to get the mobile from her jacket and tried ringing 999 with shaking fingers. The emergency operator's voice kept cutting out, only half audible over the poor radio signal, and Nora knew her own voice was just as unintelligible. She hung up and tried again with no better luck; after the third failure she jammed the phone into her jeans pocket in frustration.

How had the attacker managed to get into the house? Both doors had been locked; she'd checked just after Cormac went off with the detectives. If someone could gain access to the house so easily, there was no protection in staying here. She could drive into town for the police. But what would she say? She hadn't even seen the person who attacked her. She did have a nasty lump on her head, but even so, they might even think she was making it up, trying to draw suspicion away from Cormac. *Think, Nora. Just clear your head and try to think,* she told herself. *There's got to be something here, some clue to hold on to.*

She checked the floor of the entryway. There was no sign of the envelope with her name; the attacker must have taken it. But the message it had contained was a triple-knotted cord. Was there something symbolic about those three knots, something she was missing? She remembered what Cormac had told Ward about a triple sacrifice making an offering more powerful. Danny Brazil had suffered a triple death. So had Ursula, and maybe Rachel, too. She put one hand to her own throat, and thought how simple it would have been for the assailant to slip the slender cord around her neck when she was unconscious, to cut her with the blade. For some reason she'd been spared. Maybe her death would have made one too many, disrupted the mysterious power of three. No, it was absurd even to think that way.

She looked into the sitting room, and amid all the jumble she saw the book into which she'd tucked the drawing of the collar. The book lay sprawled open, its pages torn and crumpled. She stumbled through the debris and riffled through the pages; nothing inside. Whoever attacked her had been after the drawing—had probably watched her hide it. She might just as well have opened the door and let him in.

But the killer had shown his hand by going after the drawing. It was the one thing that definitely linked Danny Brazil's death with Ursula Downes. Rachel Briscoe might just have become an unfortunate liability, if she'd seen someone at Ursula's house the night of the murder—or perhaps there was some other reason she'd been singled out. Loughnabrone . . . It suddenly struck Nora that last night the lake's poetic name had become literally true. She didn't even have to close her eyes to imagine Rachel Briscoe's pale form pitching forward in the moonlight, helpless and alone as her blood mingled with the water. What desperate need had required so terrible a sacrifice? She felt a clench of regret and felt hot tears come to her eyes, reliving those fleeting moments in the car the other day, remembering the defensive pitch of Rachel's dark eyebrows, her self-protective posture, and most of all the naked confusion and anger in the girl's face. She should have made an effort, done something more. What good did it do now, wiping away useless tears when they were too late? *Stop it, stop it,* said the voice in her head. *Stop beating yourself up and think about the drawing.*

It had come from Charlie Brazil's shed. He must have known that Ursula had taken it. Nora thought of Charlie's hands around her ankle, his own triple-knotted necklace, how terrified she had felt when he mentioned Ursula's interest in the significance of the three knots.

If Charlie was involved, it was possible that he wasn't acting alone. What if dealing in stolen antiquities had been a family endeavor, the thing that had gotten Danny Brazil killed? It could be that Charlie was acting on his father's behalf. Ursula might have found out what they were up to, and threatened to expose them.

Owen Cadogan wasn't completely off the hook either. She'd spent some time thinking about him after they'd gotten home last night. Those things he'd dumped in the canal may have been evidence of his connection with Ursula, or Rachel Briscoe, or both of them. It looked as if he enjoyed tying people up. Maybe things got out of hand, and the whole staged ritual was just a cover-up for an accidental killing. But it was possible that Cadogan was involved in smuggling artifacts as well. His relationship with Ursula could somehow have been connected.

All these elaborate conspiracies were just possibilities—and pure conjecture, really. She knew from bitter experience that what the Guards would need was concrete proof.

Nora suddenly remembered that she and Cormac had been planning to talk to Brona Scully, to find out whether someone had frightened her last night. If Cormac was right about somebody being after Brona, maybe she could identify the person. Charlie Brazil she'd know, certainly; but she might not know Owen Cadogan, except by sight. Nora remembered the picture of Cadogan she'd seen last night in Michael Scully's file on Loughnabrone. She dived into the jumble of books and papers on the floor, found the file, and flipped quickly past the raft of yellowed newspaper cuttings.

She came to a stack of black-and-white news photos. Most of them featured only the Brazils, with Danny in front holding up a corroded metal blade. One of the pictures was the same shot she'd seen in Cadogan's office, of Dominic and Danny Brazil accompanied by a third man. This picture had not been cropped, and the lower part of the third man's face was visible. There was something vaguely familiar about him, she thought—perhaps the posture, the body language; she couldn't pinpoint it exactly. Was it just that she'd seen him in the other photograph?

Then her eyes fell on the perfectly knotted tie and the unusual pin. The image was minuscule but unmistakable, a testimony to pleasing and deceptively simple Iron Age design: a triskelion.

All this time, they had been so focused on the objects in the hoard that they hadn't paid enough attention to the people involved. She looked more closely at the hands in the photograph, remembering the elegant fingers arranging coins on a table into triangles and rows of three. The missing link between Ursula Downes and Danny Brazil had been staring her in the face since the day she'd arrived, but now she knew his name: Desmond Quill.

8

Teresa Brazil set her small brown suitcase by the kitchen door. She had packed the case only twice in her life before, once the day before she was to be married, and once—

It was all right to think about it now. The past had been blocked off, dammed up; but the sight of that triple-knotted cord on the policeman's desk a few days ago had started a slow drip that had grown into a steady flow, and finally into a deluge that she was powerless to stop. The long-dry lakebed of her soul was flooded with images, words, feelings, and sensations long denied. Staying here would be fatal; it would mean drowning in memory.

She had awakened this morning dreaming once more of hard yellow earth, sunlight, and dust, the reverse of this place with its soaking ground and dark drains slowly bleeding life away. Here, lives were confined by narrow roads, closed in by hedges and ditches and ivy-choked oak trees, hemmed in by a place that was perpetually dark, secret, and damp. She would leave this dying bog in midsummer, and arrive at midwinter in a place where the seasons stood on their heads. People said even the water spiraling down the drain went contrariwise. Nothing would ever be the same, and that somehow felt right and necessary.

She had let the sheep out, and sent Charlie to gather them up. She needed to make sure he'd not come back to the house for at least a few hours. She didn't bother to look into the sitting room. It was where Dominic always was, these days, tied to his oxygen tank and his television. She could hear the noise of the television—bright, false laughter.

The hackney driver would be here any minute, and there was one more thing she must do before she left. She dug through the pile of discarded clothes at the bottom of her wardrobe until she found the square tin box, rusted shut and covered in dust from many years of neglect. She prised off the lid and stood holding the tin in her hands; she stared at its contents, feeling herself at once rooted to the earth and hurtling backward into the past.

Dominic Brazil had not been her own choice. He'd been twenty years older than she was, for a start, with roughly handsome dark features and a manner that was by turns brutal and taciturn. She had been only twenty-five years old, but her own family would keep her at home no longer; they'd made that clear. Dominic was dead keen on having her, her father had said. And she hadn't had the will, nor the resources, to oppose any of them. It was only years later that she grasped what had really happened; that she had in effect been sold, in a ritual that shared more with animal husbandry than with true marriage. She had crossed this threshold an ignorant girl, led here from her father's household like a prize heifer. She still felt shame, remembering the way old Mrs. Brazil had turned her around, poked and prodded, practically checked the teeth in her mouth. She had been judged too weak, too thin, too contrary to be of any use.

At first she'd wanted to prove them wrong, to show what she could do, until she realized that it would do no good. Nothing she did would ever be good enough. She was the outsider, resented all the more because she was necessary. The Brazils were a dark family. The darkness didn't just reside in their coal black hair and sloe eyes, but seemed to emanate from their very souls, from the secretive habits and closed doors, the walls constantly built up between them. Danny had some of that darkness as well, but he was a bit different from the rest. He was the only real ally she'd ever had.

At first what passed between them had been very innocent. About eighteen months after she'd come here, she began finding small gifts in the henhouse when she went out to collect eggs—shiny stones, snail shells, and cocoons—compact treasures that fit in the palm of her hand. She started keeping them in a small box hidden at the bottom of the wardrobe. She knew who'd left them, but nothing was ever spoken or even acknowledged between them. No communication at all but these small, secret offerings and their silent acceptance. On the surface, everything carried on as it had before, but she could feel the current quickening below, threatening to pull her under.

The day that everything changed, she found a strangely formed lump of beeswax in one of the usual hiding spots. She held it to the light, admiring the pale, translucent form—like a tiny cathedral, she had thought; like a photograph seen in a book, something delicate and fine. Suddenly her husband's dark form had filled the doorway, and she had instinctively folded the wax into her palm. Dominic had asked her something about the eggs, which she'd answered without even hearing the question. When he left, she opened her hand and saw the imprint of her palm and fingers in the ruined, misshapen wax, and knew at that moment that some part of her soul had suddenly been transformed. She could not go back, only forward. Why that single, accidental act of destruction had set off everything that followed, she would probably never fully understand, but she had held the wax tightly in her palm until she reached the apiary.

Danny was sitting on the cot against the wall when she arrived, hands clasped around his drawn-up knees, staring off into the distance. She distinctly remembered simply standing before him, uncurling her fist to show the melted lump of wax. And somehow she had known that he already understood everything she had come to say, and that there was no need to speak. When he finally pulled her down on the cot beside him, the sensation was not one of submission or capitulation, but of long-awaited freedom.

She and Danny had planned to meet early on that Midsummer's morning. She walked the two miles to the crossroads at dawn. He would come from the apiary; they would meet at the cross and thumb a lift from a lorry driver heading toward Shannon. From Shannon they would make their way somehow to Australia. A dense fog had spread low over the bog that morning, and a frisson of anticipation had bubbled through her, dissipating all fear and fatigue. When the sun broke across the horizon, she sat on her suitcase under the shelter of an overgrown hedge, listening to a lark's celebratory chorus. She remembered how the minutes had slid by, but it was difficult to recall exactly when her hopeful anticipation had begun slipping toward disappointment, then apprehension, and finally bitter despair.

She had never seen any tickets. He'd said they ought to wait until they arrived at Shannon. At six o'clock, nearly two hours after the appointed time, she concealed her small suitcase in the hedgerow and began walking home, feeling with every step a heavy inward strike, burying disgrace and humiliation far down in the depths of her soul, never to be acknowledged, ever again.

She had arrived home just in time to put the kettle on. After starting the rashers and sausages for Dominic's breakfast, she had begun preparing his lunch for the day. He would have to be up in a few minutes for the eight o'clock shift on the bog. The cuckoo clock in the kitchen sang its mechanical song at seven. Everything was as it had been yesterday, and as it would be again tomorrow. There had never been anything else; it had only been temporary madness, an illusion.

And she had remained steadfast in her denial. When the monthly blood stopped and she began to feel the quickening flutters in her abdomen, she had simply accepted the child, never once looking at him in search of some feature that would tell her which of the two brothers was his father. Never once, that is, until Charlie had brought home news of a blackened corpse with a triple-knotted cord about its throat. It had felt like a car crash, that moment, filled with sounds of tearing metal and shattering glass. It felt as if a yawning void had opened in the ground beneath her feet, and everything that existed these last twenty-five years had slipped away, suddenly devoid of meaning.

She carried the tin box outside into the haggard behind the house, where she had made a pile of straw. She lit a match and touched it to the golden stalks, watching the fire falter at first and then take hold. One by one, she dropped the treasures from the tin into the fire, watching as it consumed each one with bright, chemical confidence. When the last object was gone, she turned away from the fire.

As she opened the kitchen door, the hackney driver was just pulling into the yard. She waved to signal that she was ready, and went into the house for the last time. One by one, she unscrewed the valves on the three oxygen tanks that stood in the corner of the kitchen. Then she crossed to the cooker. She had already extinguished the pilots; now she turned the gas on at each of the four hobs, and in the oven as well. Teresa let her gaze sweep the room one final time before she grasped the handle of her brown suitcase and stepped outside, closing the kitchen door carefully behind her.

It was strange how calm she felt, riding in the back seat of the cab—how well she could envision the journey ahead, if not its destination. When it was finally time, she would make her way down the long corridor that led to the departure gate. A few hours from now she would emerge naked and new on the other side of the world. She had tried to keep from feeling each minute seeping into the next, bleeding away, until there was nothing left. But now she felt as if her veins had run dry. She was a husk, light and free. If by chance she should cut herself, nothing would flow from the wound but a meager trickle of dry yellow dust.

9

Nora tucked the photograph of the Brazils and Desmond Quill into her jacket pocket, and set out to find Brona Scully. If Quill had been out here at Illaunafulla last night, and she could get Brona to identify him from the photo, it would be something to take to the police. It still wouldn't be absolute proof that he was involved in the murders, but it would be one step closer.

Michael Scully seemed surprised to see her when he answered the door. His hair and clothes were rumpled as though he'd just awakened from a nap.

"I'm very sorry to disturb you, Michael, but I need to speak to Brona."

Scully let her in and called for Brona from the foot of the stairs, but received no response. "I don't think she's here at the minute," he said. "She must have gone out while I was resting."

Nora saw last night's dreadful worry creep back into Michael Scully's face. He might not know about Rachel Briscoe's murder, and there was no point in making him worry needlessly. "I'll go and have a look at the place where Cormac found her. But if she does happen to come home in the meantime, would you give me a ring?" She fished a card out of her pocket and scribbled her mobile number on it. "Just ring me on that number." Scully nodded gravely.

All these paths, Nora thought as she picked her way up the small boreen at the back of the Scully property; all these trails twisting around and leading nowhere. The grass was deep, and there were blind corners everywhere.

If Quill had been part of the Loughnabrone excavation team all those years ago, he could have been involved in Danny Brazil's murder. And maybe Ursula had found out about his connection, and had been using that knowledge as leverage to get something she wanted—the gold collar? The drawing was documentary evidence that it existed. If it had already been sold, maybe it was a share of the money Ursula had been after.

Nora's head still ached, and her joints were stiff from the time she'd spent in the broom closet. If she couldn't find Brona, or if the girl couldn't identify Quill, then she could try to track his movements last night—find out if he'd left the hotel, who might have seen him in the town. It was impossible to know whom to trust, but she couldn't stop now. The facts were starting to fall together, piecemeal though they might be, and it would all come out eventually. She had to believe that.

She quickened her pace, scanning the hedges at the pasture's edge for Brona Scully's dark head. It was probably crazy to think she could find the girl, but Cormac had done it last night. She climbed through a hole in the hedge and emerged amid a crowd of cattle, heads down at their grazing. A young bullock raised his head to inspect her, his innocent brown gaze raising a host of specters of fatted calves and sacrificial lambs. She had to find Brona, before it was too late.

No figure appeared near the fairy tree. Nora peered up into its swaddled branches, feeling once more the strange intensity in the hundreds of ragged and colorful supplications. She called out Brona's name, not daring to speak above a whisper, as if the tree might catch and hold her plea in its gnarled limbs.

She crisscrossed the patchwork of fields a half-dozen times, poking at the base of any ditches where a hiding place might lie, skirting any low-lying spots. There was no sign of the girl anywhere. She suddenly realized that she was at a distinct disadvantage. Brona Scully knew this place, every hedge and bush and pile of stones; she could even be watching from some protected place. Nora turned, taking in the vista, the brown bog stretching into the distance, the lake below the hill. She hadn't yet looked in Charlie Brazil's apiary. The thought of running into Charlie again after their last meeting was not a prospect she relished, but she had to find Brona. She would advance on the place slowly, circling around it first, in case anyone was there. Brona might run if she was surprised, and Nora didn't want to meet anyone else.

She traced the edge of the pasture above the apiary, sticking close to the framing hedge and crouching as low as she could. There was the bee-keeping shed that she could use for cover. She circled cautiously around the outside of the whitethorn ring that surrounded the hives, and came up behind the abandoned house. No one seemed to be about, but the breeze carried a lazy, intermittent buzzing, depending on which way the wind shifted. Brona could be hiding; she'd have to check inside.

As she turned, she felt a strong hand clamped over her mouth and another person's wiry strength against her own. Her captor pushed her back against the wall, and it was a moment before she realized that the wide, frightened eyes only inches from her own belonged to Brona Scully. With her free hand, the girl lifted a finger to her lips; then she pulled Nora down into the weeds.

The reason for her urgency became immediately apparent; the grass began to rustle no more than a few yards away and two figures came into view through the overgrown grass and clover. Nora recognized one of them as Dominic Brazil; the other was Desmond Quill. Brona Scully's whole body tensed, and she pulled at Nora's arm as if to beg her to come away. They might be able to get away without being seen, but it was risky. If they stayed put, Nora reasoned, she might be able to find out what was going on. She shook her head. Brona stopped pulling, but remained where she was.

Dominic Brazil was speaking. "I don't know what you think you're going to find. I told you a long time ago, there never was any gold. It was something Danny made up to try and get some extra money off you. If there was any gold, why would I have just carried on all these years?"

Desmond Quill followed about five paces behind Brazil, carrying a spade in his left hand, and keeping the right jammed in his coat pocket. "It took me a long time to figure that out. You know, I almost believed you, back when that story was new—about how there was no gold, how Danny had made off with both shares of the reward money. But you ought to know it won't wash anymore. Give it up. And keep walking." He prodded Brazil's back with the spade handle, making him stumble. "I admit that I underestimated your fortitude—sticking to that story all these years, never wavering."

Brazil marched stoically through the deep grass, but his pace was slowing. "I've got to rest for a minute," he said. "It's me breathin'. I can't cover ground like I used to."

"We're nearly there," Quill said. "Keep going."

"Nearly where? What are you on about? If you know where the fuckin' thing is, why didn't you just take it? Why did you have to drag me here?"

"Because I'm a curious man, Mr. Brazil, and you're the only person who can satisfy my curiosity—let's put it that way." Quill's mouth turned upward into a grim smile; he drew his right hand from his pocket and looked down at the dagger it held. "I understand that you're a bit worried about this. But consider my position. How was I to know you wouldn't try the same thing with me as you did with Danny? You seem to be on a downward spiral, my friend. I might have been next."

"You're fuckin' crazy."

"Wouldn't it have been simpler just to tell me you'd murdered your brother? Why the need for such elaborate dissembling? I'm disturbed at your total lack of trust in me. I suppose you thought I'd go to the authorities. But let me ask: In all these years, have I ever done so? Have I ever raised one single objection to your acts of thievery or fratricide? You could have eliminated your whole sorry family as far as I was concerned. Stop there."

Dominic Brazil was wheezing now, and pale, but Quill seemed not to notice. They had passed the beekeeping shed and stood within the circle of the hives. Quill looked at the three hives that marked the top of the circle, then turned and faced the other two sets of three. He stuck the spade into the soil at the base of the ninth hive. "Here's where we're going to dig. Where you're going to dig, to be more precise." Brazil looked as if he wanted to cut and run, but didn't dare. Instead he reached for the spade. Quill said, "Despite everything, I'm going to be reasonable. We're both going to be reasonable men, aren't we?" Brazil glumly set the spade at the spot Quill had pointed out. Placing one heavy foot on the spade's neck, he dug in.

Quill stood close by and watched Dominic Brazil dig. "Clever, wasn't he, your brother? Much cleverer than you. And always just that much ahead of you in everything, even though he was younger by—what, six years? At first I thought the reason you killed him was something to do with the farm. It must have been difficult, having to share with your brother—like you'd had to share everything with him your whole life. Nothing was your own. And even though you were the eldest, you were always the less favored son; everyone knew it, even you. Especially you. They didn't even pretend. He got everything, eventually. Everything."

Brazil's face and shoulders twitched. "You don't know what you're talking about." He kept digging, but each spadeful was smaller than the last.

"Faster," said Quill. "And then I thought, no, of course you wouldn't kill your own brother, not just for the sake of a miserable few acres in the middle of a bog. Besides, you told me you had it worked out, all that. He was going away to Australia, and you were buying him out with the reward money. He could have the money and you could have the farm. But why should you be satisfied with that arrangement when you could have everything?"

Dominic Brazil scratched at the earth, and his breathing was becoming more labored. "I didn't need everything. The way we were working it, the place would be mine. I'd not have to worry about him coming back and taking anything away. He signed the papers. He was going away for good, he said. What need had I to kill him? He said he was never coming back."

Nora's thoughts were racing, zigzagging through what she'd just heard. They had conspired together, all those years ago, to keep something back from the Loughnabrone hoard. Quill must have made a deal with Dominic and Danny Brazil to sell whatever it was and split the proceeds. But if Dominic was telling the truth, and there was no gold left, what was Quill making him dig for? Nora heard the spade's rhythmic scraping against the soil. She couldn't see the ground for all the weeds, but she had a clear view of each man's face; the sweat gleaming on Dominic Brazil's forehead; Quill's cool, detached expression as he watched the digging. She thought about creating a distraction, something that would draw Quill away, but she had no idea what he might do. Maybe it was better to keep still and wait until they left.

The two men stopped speaking, but she could hear the spade. It struck something that reverberated with a hollow, metallic sound. The next sound she heard was a struggle, a cry, the sound of flesh slapping against the wooden spade handle. The two men were rolling on the ground, and Dominic Brazil was holding the spade handle to Quill's throat.

With a fierce shove, Quill threw Brazil off balance and scrambled to his feet, wielding the spade like a weapon. "I thought we were going to be reasonable about this," he said. "There's no reason for either of us to get hurt. We're partners, after all."

She could hear Brazil's labored breathing, each exhalation coming in a slow wheeze.

"Dig with your hands," Quill commanded, and Brazil complied, reaching down into the shallow trench and scooping out earth until he had freed the object that was buried there, a large round black-and-gold biscuit tin. "Open it," Quill said.

Still kneeling, Brazil pressed the tin to his chest and prised off the lid.

Bundles of old hundred-pound notes fell onto the ground, and Quill's face went rigid when he saw what else was inside. "Give it to me," he said. Brazil lifted out a cloth-wrapped bundle and handed it over to Quill, who dropped the spade, putting one foot on it before he began pulling at the corners of the cloth.

It was probably the color—a luminous, deep yellow-gold—that made the most immediate and indelible impression. It must have been easy to believe that the wearer of this object possessed some supernatural power, such was its exquisite and incorruptible beauty. The rich golden metal seemed to give off its own light.

Quill stood frozen, mute, and Nora began to believe that this was the very first time he'd laid eyes on the collar, after dreaming about its existence for twenty-five years. He had been waiting almost half a lifetime to gaze upon this object with his own eyes, and now he couldn't tear them away.

"I have a confession to make," Quill said, finally. "I've been toying with you. I know the real reason you killed your brother." Brazil's head came up, his haggard features displaying honest curiosity.

"As I said, at first I almost believed that Danny had gone away. There was no other explanation for the fact that the collar was gone. I've been watching you all these years, and I have excellent contacts; I would have known if either of you had tried to take it to someone else. But you never did.

"The idea only occurred to me after Danny turned up dead. He might have been planning to swindle both of us. It's easily done: he moves the collar, plans to take it with him when he leaves the country. But if that had been your reason for killing him, you'd still have the collar and the money. So how did it happen that Danny is dead, but you don't know where the collar is? There's only one explanation: you killed him before you found out that he'd taken it and hidden it somewhere else. But, I asked myself, why would Dominic Brazil do something so extraordinarily stupid?

"And suddenly I grasped the whole picture. It was nothing whatever to do with the gold, the money, or the farm. The collar wasn't all that Danny was taking with him, was it? If you let him get away, you were going to lose a treasure worth more than any gold. This was where you found them, wasn't it?"

Dominic Brazil didn't speak for a moment. "They were going to go away, the very next morning. I was just outside, under the window, and I heard them talking, and—" Brazil's voice and face transformed as he relived those dreadful, decisive moments. "After she'd gone home, he was still lying there in his pelt, smoking a fag. He didn't even hear me come in. I caught him by that stupid fuckin' leather cord; all I had was my penknife, but I was going to cut his thieving throat. I got one good cut in, but he started fighting like the devil and knocked the knife away. That's when he ran out onto the bog—it was all wild bog around here that time. I couldn't find the knife, so I picked up a hurley and followed him. I caught up to him and hit him a clout, and down he went. I thought he was dead, so I dragged him to the bog hole. I was just looking for someplace to hide the body until I could come back. I saw his eyes open down there at the bottom of the hole. But I couldn't stop; I just kept piling in everything I could find, down into that hole, until he was gone. He was just gone, and everything was peaceful and quiet."

Dominic Brazil looked as if he hadn't much more life in him. His complexion was ashy, and his face telegraphed pain with every shallow exhalation.

"You didn't know he'd taken the collar?" Quill asked.

"Not until afterward—when I went to the spot where we'd hidden it. It was all Danny's idea to keep the fucking thing. I never gave a curse about the gold. I knew it was bad luck having anything to do with it, with the likes of you. He could have taken every one of those bloody yokes we found, and good riddance, if he'd only let me have my Teresa, my own wife. When Danny was gone, I thought she'd belong to me. Fuckin' daft, I was then. It took me another twenty-five years to suss it out, that she never belonged to anyone but herself." He looked up at Quill, and Nora felt an icy finger down her backbone as she wondered why Dominic Brazil used the past tense in speaking about his wife.

Neither man moved or spoke for a long moment; then Quill broke the silence. "What about the whole ritual, then—the triple death?"

Dominic Brazil's shoulders sagged. "I don't know what you're talking about. There was no triple anything."

Quill shook his head in disbelief. "You're telling me it was accidental? What about Ursula Downes and the other girl, Rachel Briscoe? Don't tell me those deaths were mere accidents as well?"

"Look, I don't know what you're on about. I didn't kill those girls—"

Dominic Brazil started to protest, but Quill twisted behind him, wrenched his forehead back with one hand and with the other drew the dagger sharply across his throat. A fountain of blood gushed forth. Nora felt Brona Scully go rigid with terror beside her, and quickly clamped a hand over the girl's mouth to keep her from crying out. There had been no warning. A man was dead, and they hadn't even had time to react.

Dominic Brazil's suddenly lifeless body sagged sharply sideways, his mouth still open in protest. Quill leaned forward to close Brazil's staring eyes and murmured, "No, you didn't. You might as well have. They never would have died except for you."

Nora watched in frozen horror as Quill felt for a pulse. Satisfied that there was none, he reached into his pocket for several lengths of knotted black cord and laid them beside the body, pressed Brazil's right hand firmly around the dagger handle, and then let it fall. No doubt he had taken the same exquisite care in arranging the bodies of Ursula Downes and Rachel Briscoe. Nora pressed herself to the wall and felt the air closing in around her.

10

At last Desmond Quill moved away, stopping to cast one last glance back at his ghastly tableau, as if considering the effect the scene might have on the person who eventually discovered it. Nora felt Brona begin to tremble beside her. Quill was still lingering, considering his handiwork, when she felt her mobile phone begin to vibrate against her hip. She reached for it instinctively, but by then it was too late: the quick double ring had given her away.

Quill's voice was chilling. "Come out where I can see you."

If he came any closer, he might see them both. Nora climbed to her feet, pressing Brona Scully's head to the ground and willing the girl not to move.

"Closer," Quill said. She moved toward him, stepping to the side to draw his vision away from where Brona was hidden in the weeds beside the shed. The phone had stopped ringing by the time she stood face-to-face with Desmond Quill. He'd taken the dagger from Dominic Brazil's hand, and he used it to direct her movements. "Give me that mobile."

She tried to press the call button as she passed it to him, but he must have seen the slight movement; he deliberately switched the phone off before putting it in his pocket. Then he picked up one of the knotted leather thongs and marched her ahead of him to the lakeshore, where he hurled the mobile as far as he could out over the water. "Thousands of years from now, they'll dig up that curious artifact and display it as a votive offering. So now you know the whole story, Dr. Gavin."

Nora knew she had to keep him talking as long as she could. One way was to appeal to his vanity. "Not quite. I still don't know how you knew where the collar was."

"I have Ursula and young Charlie to thank for that. And you." He reached into his coat and pulled out the drawing he'd taken from the cottage. "When the Brazils came to me with their proposition, I was naturally skeptical about the gold collar. But Danny Brazil was clever. He knew it probably wasn't wise to go around showing off the real artifacts, so he made drawings of every object they'd found—even the ones they hadn't shared with the museum. Quite an expert draftsman, wasn't he?

"After Danny disappeared, Dominic tried to tell me that there had never been any gold collar, that it was just a ruse. But Danny had made this wonderful drawing, you see. I had a hard time believing he'd made the piece up. I used various methods of persuasion to get Dominic to tell me what really happened. I'd almost given up hope—almost. Isn't it strange? This summer I was going to make one last stab at Dominic Brazil. That's why I arranged to meet Ursula. She was a good cover, a plausible excuse to be here. And then Ursula's crew very conveniently stumbled over Danny Brazil's body. Wonderful timing.

"I have to say that one of the qualities I actually admired most about Ursula was her tenacity. Once she'd found Danny Brazil's body, she just kept worrying those old rumors of illicit gold, hoping something would shake out. And eventually something did. She found several of Danny's drawings here. Charlie had them tacked up on the wall in that shed. Didn't even know what they were, poor sod—but Ursula did. She couldn't wait to tell me about the collar drawing with a strange bunch of circles on the back. I was coming out to take a look at it. But Ursula was sloppy. She let your friend Maguire walk off with the drawing that night. I watched him take it, not knowing it was in the bloody book. I was there, outside the house, the whole time he was with Ursula." His features took on a slightly sardonic sneer. "What did he tell you—that she attacked him and he fought her off? Not that it matters very much at this point, since you won't be seeing him again, but that wasn't exactly what it looked like to me."

Nora said nothing. She knew he was just testing her, trying to see what would provoke a reaction.

"So what were all the circles on the back of the drawing?" she asked. She tried to keep Quill's back to the shed, in case Brona might be able to make a move, but there was no sign of the girl. Maybe she was too frightened, or maybe she didn't understand that she ought to run for help.

"It was a map of this very spot, the nine hives, although a person might not recognize it if he wasn't a bit familiar with the area already."

"Why did you take Cormac's waterproofs?"

"Why not? He'd already done himself in by going over to Ursula's that night. And they provided another handy diversion, a way to get the Guards sniffing around him and leaving me alone."

"How did you get into the cottage? The doors and windows were all locked. I checked them myself."

"Doors are only locked against people who don't have keys. Ursula told me where the key was hidden, outside the back door. She'd been there dozens of times; she sometimes used it as a trysting place when the owners were away. Very careless of them, leaving the key there—and not like Mrs. McCrossan at all. Ah, no, Mrs. McCrossan likes to do the smart thing, the prudent thing." His tone was contemptuous.

"How do you know Evelyn?" Nora asked.

Quill's eyes flashed. "Just couldn't stay out of it, could you? Couldn't let things run their course. Everything would have been settled, Dominic Brazil would have taken the blame for the murders, your friend would eventually have been let off for lack of evidence, and everything would have gone back to the way it was before. One brother pays for the death of the other. Everything comes back into balance."

"And what about Ursula and Rachel? How do you balance their deaths?"

"They were necessary sacrifices. I'm afraid you're looking for saints, hearts of gold where there were none. Beneath her damaged exterior, Ursula Downes was nothing but a vicious, drunken slag. I was actually quite fond of her, but that is the truth. And did you even know Rachel Briscoe? She came into Ursula's house that night with a knife drawn. I'm sure she would have slit Ursula's throat in a heartbeat—if I hadn't done it already. She saw me and tried to get away. It took me until last night to find her, the daft little bitch. I gave each of them something more: a triple death. A perfect death."

Nora stood still, hoping for a chance to reach for the dagger, as he drew closer. Quill reached up and put his fingers around her throat. His face was only inches from hers, and she knew he could feel the pulse beneath her skin.

"I'll be sorry about you, Dr. Gavin. I've actually enjoyed talking with you. And not everything I told you about Ursula was a lie." Quill's plummy voice resonated in his chest; she could feel its vibrations traveling through his flesh and bones into her own. His eyes regarded her without feeling.

If she could create a distraction, maybe Brona could escape. She reached up and felt Quill's fingers around her throat. Her voice came in a hoarse whisper: "Don't you want to know what gave you away?" She let her eyes slide down to the triskelion design on the pin that held his tie in place. "You were wearing that same tie pin in the newspaper pictures taken after the discovery of the Loughnabrone hoard. Is it real, or a replica? You must be very attached to it, to have worn the same piece for twenty-five years. That's how Ursula knew you were involved, and that's how I figured it out as well."

Quill's lips curved in a mirthless smile. "Aren't you clever? Ursula thought she was clever, too, thought she'd outwitted me." He shook his head in disbelief. "Do you know what her grand plan was? First of all, she assumed that I had murdered Danny Brazil. Her plan, if you could even call it that, was to use the paltry evidence she'd scraped together to blackmail me—as though fear of exposure would be enough to make me do whatever she wanted. All she wanted was enough money to buy a one-way ticket to someplace warm. She thought all this was about money."

"So if it's not about money, what is it about?"

"I doubt you would understand."

"Let me try. If you're going to kill me, you owe me some sort of explanation. I want to understand."

He moved behind her, tipping her head back and looking down into her eyes. His upside-down face looked distorted and strange. "You know, somehow I believe you do. But how do you explain something that isn't based in reason? Look out there—" He tipped her chin down again and gestured toward the lake and bog that stretched before them. "You might as well ask for reasons from the earth, the water, the wind.

"It grieves me when people talk about an artifact only in terms of its monetary worth. As if its significance can be quantified, reduced, vulgarized in that way. I used to work in museums, and now they depress me unutterably—the contents of votive hoards, fallen from powerful talismans to mere trinkets and curiosities, and all those throngs of bored schoolchildren and gaping tourists trooping past, sullying sacred objects with undeserving, jaded eyes." He held up the collar with his free hand. "Can anyone be blamed for wanting to keep this from them? Apart from its exquisite form, an object like this is nothing less than a window through which we can gain access to a mind that grasped the most astonishing and sophisticated concepts. The person who created it worked in a miraculous material that never decays, never corrodes. He shaped it truly believing that his inspired creation would confer superhuman

power on the person who wore it. Who are we to disparage his beliefs?
We carry them within us still. What is Christianity but blood sacrifice
masquerading as modern religion? We've lost our faith in the world
around us, in our own deeper selves—in the sacred connection between
blood and death, the places on earth that can lead us deeper within ourselves. The destruction of this bog is a case in point. I detest that superior
attitude we hold today toward ancient people; it releases a kind of fury in
me. You probably can't understand that, can you?"

"To a point. But is any object—even something so exceptional and
exquisite and powerful—really worth the lives of three people?"

"What a small circle you live in, Dr. Gavin; your tiny moral universe.
It's four people, in point of fact, or soon will be—you've forgotten yourself. And yes, something like this collar is worth four lives, four hundred
lives, and many more. No matter what's been done to thin the popula-
tion, I think it's impossible to deny that human beings still remain in
constant, practically endless supply. You think me callous, unfeeling.
That may be true, but I'm not unique. Governments and corporations
routinely treat human beings like cattle—because the people allow
themselves to be treated that way, to be led to the slaughter like dull-
witted beasts. But I have the utmost reverence for the sacredness of
human life and death. Those who've never shed blood with their own
hands should never presume to judge me for what I've done. And you'd
be surprised at the number of people who actually wish to die, though
sometimes they don't really know it. People like Ursula, who can hardly
contain their curiosity about death, who enjoy pushing at the threshold,
though they're too frightened to make the final, fatal leap."

He was moving closer, and Nora didn't dare try to slip away. She tried
in vain to see whether Brona Scully had made a break. There was no sign
of the girl. Quill's hand moved, and Nora felt the cold dagger blade flat
against her cheek.

"Shall I tell you what surprised me most about killing someone?" Quill
asked. "How the act itself has such breathtaking beauty. I didn't expect
to find the color of blood so astonishing—that glorious crimson. Have
you ever been present at a death, Dr. Gavin? Even with those who aren't
the most—acquiescent—there is undeniable gratitude; you can see it in
their eyes, just before the light passes. Do you know what this place, this
patch of land is called?" His voice was low, almost hypnotic.

"Illaunafulla," she said.

"Very good; someone's been giving you lessons, haven't they? You must also know what it means, then."

"Island of Blood."

"And how do you suppose it got that name? An island of blood in a lake of sorrows. We've given up thinking of the spilling of blood as a necessary part of existence. I can't understand why. We go to such lengths to deny the intense joy to be found in death—the ultimate joy, really. And in your line of work, Dr. Gavin, I'm sure some part of you has felt it quite keenly, too. What's the difference if you choose the time and manner for yourself, or someone else chooses for you? Death by sacrifice is a sacred privilege. Now kneel."

Nora looked at the heavy dagger only inches from her face. She was not going to get down on her knees. She started to twist away, but the dagger handle made contact just below her left ear, and she went down on her side in the soft grass.

When she opened her eyes, her vision blurred, then came into focus. She was lying facedown in the grass, with her hands tied behind her. As he tested the knot that bound her hands, Quill whispered in her ear, "Haven't you ever wanted something so much, Dr. Gavin, that you were willing to do anything to get it? I suspect there's something you want above anything else in the world, right this minute. I'm so sorry I'm going to have to cut your opportunity short."

As he dragged her upright, she saw the dagger in his right hand, a shiny blade with an ancient-looking handle. Her feet were free; maybe she could manage a well-placed kick. She lunged sideways, trying to catch him off balance, but he deflected the tackle and reached for something at the back of her neck. She realized what it was only as the ligature cut into her flesh and she felt three knots pressing into her skin. He pushed her ahead of him, onto the dock that led out into the lake.

Once they'd reached the end, he forced her to kneel and jerked the cord tighter, cutting off her air supply. She was starting to get light-headed. She thought of her parents, wondering how they would survive another murdered daughter, and she knew they would not. The ancients had it right; their gods were corrupt and demanding, childish and wrathful by turns. The idea of a benevolent deity was off the mark. She fought the darkness that welled up in her blood and tried again to wrestle free from Quill's grip, but he was strong. She felt the cold blade against her throat.

At the same moment she heard a cry, like an animal's throaty howl. Desmond Quill whirled around, pitching Nora forward and letting go of the ligature. She felt a rush of blood to her brain, and turned to see Brona Scully at the end of the dock, triumphantly holding the golden collar above her head.

Nora bent her knees and launched her feet at Quill's ankles, aware of the dagger only inches above her head. He staggered sideways and fell to one knee, making a desperate swipe with the knife, but Nora kept her feet in motion, striking out at any part of him that moved. She heard Brona's quick footfalls on the dock, and looked up to see her bring the heavy collar down on Quill's head, stunning him.

Brona dropped the collar and went for the knife, but by that time he'd recovered. He lunged, pinned her to his chest with one hand, and with the other lifted the gleaming knife to her throat. Nora struggled to her feet, panting, with her hands still bound behind her. Quill's clothing and hair were disheveled. Brona's blow had opened a gash on his forehead, and blood was now trickling into his eyes. The golden collar lay on the rough wood planks between them.

"Right back where we started, Dr. Gavin," Quill said. "What was the point of all that? It just means that another person has to die."

Brona's eyes were still defiant. She drilled Nora with her gaze, then let her eyes sweep down toward the collar, and Nora knew she had to do something.

All at once the sound of an enormous explosion split the air, and a huge ball of smoke and fire erupted from the other side of the hill. Nora had no time to wonder what was going on; realizing that this was her only chance, she tipped the collar with the toe of her shoe and, with one fluid kick, hurled it into the air. She saw the whole thing as if in slow motion: the collar gracefully turning end over end, flashing gold, and Quill's eyes following it. He flung out his right hand, the one holding the dagger, but he couldn't reach the collar; he lost his balance and toppled over the edge of the dock into the water below. There was a cry and a splash.

Nora's eyes traveled back to Brona. She'd been cut. The girl looked down at the scarlet tide advancing down her chest; then her head dropped forward and she sank into a small heap on the weathered planks. Nora ran to Brona's side, but her hands were still bound, and she watched helplessly as the stain grew larger. There was nothing she could do to stop the bleeding. She felt tearing pain in her chest as she lifted her head and shouted to anyone who might hear, "Help! Help! Please, someone, help us!"

She thought she was dreaming when she heard heavy footsteps pounding down the dock, and Charlie Brazil's terrified face appeared beside her. "Have you got a knife?" she gasped. He just looked at her. "To cut me loose! We've got to stop the bleeding if we can." Without a word, Charlie took a penknife from his pocket and sliced through the leather cords that bound her. Nora went to work, oblivious of the blood on her hands, keeping pressure on Brona's wound while Charlie removed his shirt to use as a bandage. He looked dazed, slightly singed and sooty, and Nora remembered the explosion. A growing wail of sirens was audible in the distance.

"The house is gone," Charlie said. "The house is gone and my father—" His gaze turned toward Dominic's body in the apiary.

"I know," said Nora. "I'm sorry; there was nothing I could do."

When help arrived, Nora heard voices as if through a fog. It wasn't until the Guards lifted her away from Brona's side to let the ambulance attendants take over that she felt her knees falter, and noticed the sharp bite of the wind. "Can someone get a blanket over here?" the Garda beside her shouted.

As they draped the blanket around her, she saw Cormac moving toward her through the blue-and-yellow crowd, his face haggard and drawn. His mouth dropped open at the sight of all the blood on her. "Not mine," she said. "It's not my blood." She looked down at her hands and fell against him, suddenly so tired she could barely stand. She felt his chest contract as he let out a long, ragged sigh of relief and pulled her close. "Ah, Cormac, I never meant for any of this to happen."

"Shhh. Be still now. Be still." They stood in the middle of the dock as the Guards and emergency medical personnel moved in a constant mill around them, hurrying with stretchers, blankets, and rescue equipment.

"Don't let go of me," she whispered. "Please don't let go."

A few minutes later, the ambulance men took Brona away on a stretcher, but her face was uncovered. Detective Ward, following, stopped to speak to them. "She's lost quite a lot of blood, but she's alive," he said. "I believe you saved her life, Dr. Gavin."

Nora wanted to tell him that wasn't the way it had happened at all—

that it was Brona who had done the saving, who had nearly made the ultimate sacrifice to save her. She would tell him later. Ward turned to leave, and Nora caught his sleeve. "Wait—what was that explosion? Does anyone know? Charlie said the house was gone."

"It was the Brazils' house. Looks like a gas explosion. I don't know any more, Dr. Gavin."

"And what happened to Quill? He admitted killing Ursula and Rachel, and I saw him murder Dominic Brazil with my own eyes."

"Yes, we know all that, Dr. Gavin. We know."

"Then what happened to him? We were struggling, and he fell into the water. He didn't get away?"

Ward's eyes narrowed. "You really don't know?" She shook her head. He put one arm around her shoulder and led her to the end of the dock. A hard breeze blew over the lake, raising a shiver on the water. "This lakeshore is treacherous, like quicksand. Struggling only makes it worse."

In the marshy area below their feet, all that remained visible of Desmond Quill's body was a pale hand sticking up out of the water. Gripped tightly in his fist was the bright gold collar, cast once more into its role as a votive offering, a dreadful sacrifice to appease the capricious gods.

BOOK SIX

TO HEAL SORROW BY WEEPING

If it were possible to heal sorrow by weeping and to raise the dead with tears, gold were less prized than grief.

—*Sophocles, Scyrii. Frag. 510.*

1

Eleven days after Desmond Quill's murderous spree had ended at Loughnabrone, the cottage at the Crosses was nearly restored to its former order. In the aftermath, Nora had focused on cleaning the house. It was something to do, something concrete. On hands and knees, scrubbing the wine stains from the floor and walls, she reflected that it might easily have been her blood spilled here. What had stopped Quill from slitting her throat—and why was she obsessed with the thought, unable to let it go? She knew enough about survivor guilt by now to recognize the signs, but that didn't prevent her from seeing it again and again: Dominic Brazil's inert body slumping sideways, the red flood creeping down Brona Scully's chest, Quill's dead hand grasping the bright gold collar.

Having something useful to do had helped to break up those visions over the past few days; they came less frequently now. And every minute she spent clearing away the damage down here was another minute she could avoid going upstairs and packing her suitcase, avoid thinking about how her time with Cormac was nearly at an end. The future loomed before her, unknown.

She considered the nameless, faceless creature her brother-in-law was supposed to be marrying in only four weeks' time. It was easy to imagine the woman as reckless or desperate, perhaps not terribly bright. But Tríona, beautiful and brilliant and usually very cautious, had fallen for him as well. Intelligence had little to do with it. Every relationship meant taking a chance, leaping headlong into the void, suspended by hope. And only some were lucky. She remembered the jumble of silk and the handcuffs from Owen Cadogan's hidden stash, and the thin leather cord she'd seen around Ursula Downes's throat. Maybe Ursula had been taking ever-greater chances, flirting with death, trusting that Owen Cadogan, or Desmond Quill, or whoever, for whatever reason, would loosen the cord in time to pull her back from the brink. For the first time Nora saw Ursula's actions for what they had been, a cry for understanding and connection, born of a need as deep as that for food or water, or shelter, or warmth. Even Desmond Quill's attraction to blood could be seen that way. A deep need for connection to something beyond themselves had been the very reason that ancient lake dwellers made sacrifices, sank weapons, gold—sometimes even fellow creatures—into dark and seemingly bottomless pools. Quill had been right about one thing, Nora thought; that we shouldn't look back with contempt before taking a closer look at our own currently acceptable behavior.

She looked around at the books stacked back on the desk, the pictures repaired and rehung, the crockery—what was left of it—back on the sideboard shelves. She opened the box of new stoneware she'd found to replace the set Desmond Quill had smashed. Everything else that had been shattered in the past few days would be much harder to repair or put right, but this much was easy. Each piece was wrapped in crumpled tissue paper, cushioned against its fellows for transport. As she took out each new plate, unwrapped it and set it on the sideboard shelf, the same thoughts kept tumbling through her consciousness: Quill had known enough pertinent details about sacrificial victims found in bogs, and he had used that information to mislead the police into thinking that the recent murders might be some sort of ritual killings, stringing them together with Danny Brazil's death. They had been rituals of a kind—Desmond Quill's own blood homage to the talisman, the sacred object he sought.

Nora stood back to observe her work. The last plate was in place, and the dresser looked almost as it had before Quill had torn up the cottage looking for the drawing of the Loughnabrone collar. That was what they were calling it, now that it was safely in the hands of Niall Dawson and his fellow curators at the National Museum. The newspapers were calling it the find of the century, the television reporters breathlessly describing this spectacular new addition to the material heritage of Ireland. Once it had been examined, analyzed, and authenticated, it would no doubt go on display at the National Museum. She couldn't help thinking of all the schoolchildren Quill had so scornfully envisioned, trooping past it, bored and jostling one another, oblivious to the collar's ancient power and its recent bloody history.

It suddenly struck her that Quill had destroyed more than was necessary in searching for the drawing. He knew the drawing was in the book;

all he'd had to do was find the book and take it. But he'd done much more: smashed all the crockery and the wine bottles, knocked over furniture; pulled random books out of the bookcases that lined the walls. This room was filled with evidence of a virulent anger and hatred, something she hadn't witnessed in the admittedly brief time she'd spent with him. Contempt, yes, annoyance, condescension; but nothing like this. It was too late to find out what had triggered this fury. No one would ever know for certain.

Nora attacked the loose photos that had been dumped on the floor. She had previously just scooped them up and put them back in the box, but now she sat down to reorder them. She had a box like this herself, photographs that wouldn't fit in any album, odd sizes, or single shots of events no one remembered. Most of these pictures were ruined, curled and with mottled, berrylike wine stains. She'd have to take them back to Evelyn and let her decide what to do with them. She started sorting through old black-and-white photographs of Gabriel and Evelyn in their younger days; snapshots taken at parties where everyone was drinking and smoking; pictures of Gabriel at work on an excavation; a copy of an image she'd seen at Cormac's house, of himself and Gabriel in a trench, proudly displaying their discovery. About halfway into the pile was a faded color photo, crumpled into a ball. She opened up the wrinkled print and saw the image, faded now; Gabriel and Evelyn McCrossan, and Desmond Quill. Their hair had been darker in those days, their faces unlined. From the clothing, the men's haircuts and long sideburns, Nora guessed the picture had been taken sometime in the early seventies.

Quill's words came back to her like an echo. *Haven't you ever wanted anything so much, Dr. Gavin, that you were willing to do anything to get it?* She'd assumed he was talking about the collar, but perhaps he had meant something else as well. It suddenly came to her what Quill had meant out on the bog about Evelyn McCrossan being careless, leaving a key where anyone could find it. A shiver slid down her spine.

The front doorbell sounded, and Nora instinctively shoved the picture back in the box and put the lid on. She checked the small diamond-shaped window and saw Liam Ward standing outside the cottage door, head bent, his expression thoughtful.

"Good evening, Dr. Gavin. Sorry to be disturbing you again—"

"Not at all. Please come in, Detective." Cormac was just coming down the stairs.

"Good, I'm glad you're both here," Ward said. "I have a bit of official business, one last question, if you have a minute."

Nora was about to show Ward into the sitting room when Cormac's mobile sounded. He looked at the number and said, "Sorry, I should take this." He headed back upstairs, and they could hear him answer. "Hello, Mrs. Foyle. Is everything all right?" Geraldine Foyle was the neighbor Cormac had asked to check on his father from time to time, at the house up in Donegal—something that had proved a source of tension with his father several times before. Nora hoped it wasn't something more serious this time.

She led Ward into the sitting room, where they settled in a couple of chairs near the fire, but the policeman seemed somewhat ill at ease. Nora studied his ever-present olive raincoat, the slender wrists and hands that emerged from the sleeves, the long nose and soft brown eyes, the wiry salt-and-pepper hair. This was a man who projected an air of gentleness, and Nora wondered again what had pulled him into police work. No doubt the same thing that drove her and countless others: intense curiosity, a need to know, to learn, to connect the dots—though now it seemed to her that the more you actually learned, the less it was possible to understand.

"I've just come from Michael Scully's," Ward said. "He said you'd be taking him to the hospital to see Brona in a while. I wanted to thank you for that, and for everything you've done."

"It's nothing. We're happy to do it. You said you have one last question, but I hope you don't mind if I have a few as well. I've been trying to work out how everything fits. Nothing is straightforward, is it? It all seems tangled up. How do you begin to unravel it?"

"Like untying a knot, I suppose; one thread at a time."

"How do you know when to stop?"

"In my case, it's usually not a matter of choice. Other cases begin pressing, and eventually the old ones have to be abandoned. It's got to be that way; otherwise there would be no end. Not what you wanted to hear, is it?"

"No, but I understand. That's the way it happens."

Cormac rejoined them wearing a worried expression.

"Is everything all right?" Nora asked.

"It's nothing urgent. I can tell you later," he said. "Carry on."

"I was just going to tell you that we found a lot of interesting material in Desmond Quill's house in Dublin, including keys to a lockup that was filled with artifacts—mainly Iron Age, from what the experts are telling us. There were also detailed records showing that he'd been doing a great business in stolen antiquities, items nicked from museums. No one even knew they were missing. In addition to the items he'd sold, there were hundreds more he'd apparently kept for himself, all cataloged and documented. Quill was working for the National Museum at the time of the Loughnabrone hoard, overseeing conservation of items from the hoard. He would have had contact with the Brazils, working out here."

"And they showed him drawings of the things they'd found," Nora said. "Things they hadn't handed over to the museum. Can you imagine someone like Quill, only able to see a drawing of that collar, one of the most magnificent archaeological finds in the last fifty years? It must have driven him nearly mad. You said his obsession was Iron Age artifacts?"

"There are a few items from other periods, but that seems to have been his particular fancy. All the items he'd kept were Iron Age, give or take a century."

"That may be one reason he was so interested in the whole idea of triple death," Nora said. "He tried to explain to me how he saw bloodletting and sacrifice as spiritual, as though he was giving Ursula and Rachel and Dominic Brazil something greater by killing them. He talked about the astonishing beauty of blood."

Ward said, "We found at least a half-dozen ceremonial bronze daggers in the lockup, like the one he used on Dominic Brazil, and probably on the other victims as well."

"One thing I don't understand," Nora said, "is why the Brazils would try to sell the collar in the first place. Why wouldn't they be satisfied with a reward? Even if it was only a fraction of what the collar was worth, it would have been more money than they were ever likely to see in their lifetimes."

"But to qualify for it," Cormac said, "they'd have had to prove that they had acquired the collar legally, legitimately. The minute they moved it from the findspot, the provenance became suspect, and their claim would most likely be rendered invalid. Under the treasure-trove laws, the state could have seized the collar, and the Brazils wouldn't have seen a penny of any reward. Quill was probably smart enough to make it seem as though their best choice was to turn it over to him."

"And it's easy for us to sit here and analyze after the fact. Situations like that only seem simple from the outside," Ward said. "Mistrust is a very corrosive force, especially among three people. If Quill set the Brazils against each other, he knew exactly what he was doing. He probably hoped for a betrayal of some kind; he just didn't anticipate that he would end up without the collar."

"Here's something I don't understand," Cormac said. "Why did Quill wait so long to try to find the collar? Danny Brazil disappeared twenty-six years ago. If Quill didn't believe Danny went off on his own, why would he not try to find him, prove that he never went anywhere?"

Ward said, "I imagine he did try to trace Danny, and came up empty. He probably even suspected that Dominic had done away with his brother, but without a body or some evidence of foul play, there was no way he could prove anything."

Nora said, "But from what Quill said out on the bog, it sounded as if he'd kept pressure on Dominic Brazil all these years. Dominic never broke, because he didn't know where the collar was. But Quill didn't know that for certain. He couldn't risk killing the person who was his only possible lead. But when Danny Brazil turned up, Quill knew exactly who was responsible. He must have heard enough about Danny's body to assume it was a triple death, and he made sure that his victims' wounds matched Danny's—maybe to throw you off, or maybe because he felt some attraction to the method, some connection to the idea of sacrifice. I think in some strange way, it pleased him to see the ritual angle being pursued."

"All of this was buried for so long. What opened it up again?" Cormac asked.

"I suppose you could think of Ursula as the catalyst," Nora said. "When Danny Brazil's body turned up, she started investigating rumors about gold in the Loughnabrone hoard, and eventually she found the drawing. She knew it was a key to finding the collar, but she needed Quill's help to decipher it."

"The map wouldn't make sense to anyone who didn't know the area," Ward said, "but to someone who'd been here dozens of times, as Quill had, it made perfect sense. He could see the lakeshore and the nine hives, and the inscription provided another clue. The bees made a nice protective shield. Who would think to look underneath a hive?"

Cormac pulled at his ear, puzzled. "I understand the whole connection between Quill and the Brazils, but what I can't understand is how Ursula managed to figure it out."

"Sometimes it's just a tiny thing," said Nora. "Ursula must have seen the same photograph that I saw hanging in Owen Cadogan's office, showing the Brazils with their discovery. Desmond Quill was in the picture too; you couldn't see his face, but he was wearing a tiepin that he still wore all these years later—a pretty distinctive triskelion. It took me a while to put my finger on where I'd seen it before. Once you start thinking about it, Quill is quite recognizable in the picture—something in the way he holds himself, that upright bearing. I can't explain it beyond that, really." It remained a small twist of fate, she thought, a mystery that would probably never be solved. She turned her attention to Ward. "No word on Teresa Brazil?"

"No, not a word," Ward said. "No body turned up in the Brazil house, as you've probably heard by now. It's as if she vanished into the air. The fire investigators tell me all the oxygen tanks and the gas taps on the cooker had been left open. All it took was one spark from the oil burner to set it off. Have you ever seen the aftermath of a gas explosion? The house was completely leveled. Nothing left."

Nora had not mentioned to anyone how the explosion had transformed the sequence of events—how Quill's attention turning to the Brazils' house as it was blown to bits had given her one last chance to fight back. Or how the resulting conflagration had brought the fire brigade so quickly, and ultimately saved Brona's life. All that, and more besides, they owed to Teresa Brazil. She had saved them both by destroying the lie she had lived for so long. Nora imagined her leaving the house, pulling the door shut to the hiss of gas escaping.

"Will you be staying the rest of the summer, then?" Ward asked.

Nora looked over at Cormac before answering. "That's another thing we wanted to mention. I'm headed back to Dublin tomorrow, for the postmortem on the Loughnabrone bog man."

"What is it you hope to find out from him?" Ward asked. He sounded genuinely curious.

"We look for a rough date and cause of death, any pathologies, and explanations for anything that does turn up. For my own research, I'm looking for a better understanding of what happens to preserve a body in a bog. We may be able to analyze his stomach contents, and that can tell us a lot about his diet and about social conditions at the time. I'm sure he'll stir up a whole chorus of new debate about sacrifice. We look for all the same things you look for in investigating a crime, I suppose—who and how, but most of all why. It all comes down to human motivation in the end."

"And what about you, Dr. Maguire? Is that your sort of thing as well?"

Cormac's face darkened, and he glanced at Nora. "Normally it would be, but I won't be able to go. I've just had a call from the woman who looks in on my father. She says he's not doing very well at the moment, so I'm heading up there tomorrow. I'm sorry, Nora."

Ward put his hands on his knees and stood up, his curly head nearly touching the low ceiling. "I'd better be off."

He lifted his raincoat from the chair and turned toward the door, but Nora stopped him.

"Did we answer your question, Detective Ward? When you arrived you said you had a question for us."

"Oh, yes—I almost forgot. It's this," he said, reaching into his breast pocket and pulling out a small black-and-white photograph, which he showed to each of them in turn. The picture showed a dark-eyed young woman in a peasant blouse. She was looking back at the camera over her left shoulder, and her eyes held the photographer in a frank and playful gaze. The immediate impression was one of luminous youth and startling intimacy. "Do either of you recognize this woman?" Ward asked.

"Yes, of course," Cormac said. "I'm surprised you don't know her yourself. It's Evelyn McCrossan, the woman who owns this house. It's an old photograph, though. She's over sixty now."

"The name on the back here is Evelyn Fitzgerald."

"That was her family name, before she married," Cormac said. "Where did you get this picture?"

"From a locked drawer in a desk at Desmond Quill's house in Dublin. There were nearly a hundred photographs of the same woman—some taken a long time ago, like this one, and dozens taken more recently. Some were dated in the past few months." The chill that had fingered Nora's spine returned. Ward asked, "Any idea why Quill was so interested in Evelyn McCrossan?"

"Not a clue," Cormac said, and Nora could only shake her head. One photograph in a jumble didn't mean anything. Her heart fluttered as she spoke. "I suppose it wouldn't be too startling if Quill knew Gabriel and Evelyn. He was an archaeologist years ago, and worked at the National Museum; I'm sure he and Gabriel were probably acquainted from way back. And if that was the case, he couldn't help knowing Evelyn as well."

"You can always ring me if you think of anything further," Ward said. "When a suspect dies before the whole case is resolved, there are always these questions without answers. I do appreciate your time."

As soon as Ward had gone, Nora went to the sideboard, to the box where she'd hidden the photograph of Quill with the McCrossans. She turned it over and read the inscription: *Desmond, Evelyn, and Gabriel, Loughnabrone, 1967.* She held it out to Cormac. "I found this photograph of the three of them this morning," she said. "What year were Gabriel and Evelyn married?"

"I think about 1969 or '70. I'm not exactly sure."

"But they weren't married when this picture was taken?"

"No, definitely not." The question hung between them, unasked, unanswered.

"If they knew each other, I wonder why Gabriel never mentioned Quill. Maybe they parted ways, had a falling out."

"Over Evelyn?"

"I suppose it's possible."

Nora studied the grainy faces in the photo. Did the atmosphere seem strained somehow, as if the two men were vying for the affections of the beautiful girl who sat between them? Quill's arm snaked up behind Evelyn's back on the snug cushion—a proprietary gesture. But how could you see the nuances of relationships in a snapshot, a fleeting moment frozen in time? They knew who had ultimately won Evelyn's affections, and it was not Desmond Quill.

Nora said, "If Quill was interested in Evelyn, then some of the things he said to Dominic Brazil down at the lake—things about losing a treasure worth more than gold—make a lot more sense. Maybe he felt he deserved the collar, as compensation or reparation for some slight he'd suffered. Rejection by Evelyn would be one explanation."

"Jesus, poor Evelyn. I'm sure she'd no notion about any of this."

"Now that Quill is dead, surely it's all over." Nora slipped the photograph from Cormac's hand; before he could object she had lit a match under it and cast it into the ashes in the fireplace. She watched the edges curl and blacken. The last fragment of the image to disappear was Desmond Quill's smiling face. With any luck, Evelyn might be spared the anguish of being Quill's final, posthumous victim.

2

Cormac dropped Michael Scully and Nora at the hospital's front entrance, and Nora stood by anxiously as Michael climbed out of the passenger seat. He moved slowly, but she wasn't sure how much assistance to give, and didn't know whether he might be offended by the offer of a wheelchair. When they'd made it through the sliding doors into the hospital foyer, Scully turned to her and tipped his head toward several wheelchairs that stood waiting just inside the entrance. "I think it may be a good idea to take a lift in one of those," he said, "if you wouldn't mind."

She went to fetch one of the wheelchairs, and Michael sank into it, exhausted, though he'd walked only about thirty yards from the car. Taking her place behind the chair, Nora looked down at his thin shoulders moving up and down from the effort of breathing, his face showing the weariness of constant pain. His hands gripped the wheelchair's arms, and she saw the veins standing out between the tendons. They would probably not meet again, after she left this place.

As they approached Brona's room, Michael Scully raised a hand for Nora to stop the wheelchair outside the door. He looked in at his daughter, asleep in the bed, her injured throat still swathed in bandages. Brona had lost quite a lot of blood by the time they got her to the hospital, so her condition had been critical for the first couple of days, but she seemed to have suffered no brain damage from oxygen deprivation. In the past several days she was much improved, and yesterday they'd found her sitting up in bed. She would probably have a scar, but by some miracle Quill's blade had missed the major vessels in her throat.

"Let her be," Scully said. "I can wait a few minutes to see her." Nora turned the chair around, and they went back down the hospital corridor in silence.

Scully finally spoke. "I've been thinking. There's not much more I could do for Brona, even if I were going to be here. She'll have to make her own decisions. But I want to be sure that she can make up her own mind, and not have others trying to do it for her."

"I'm sorry that we have to go away tomorrow," Nora said. "How will you manage your doctor visits?"

"I'll drive myself as long as I can, and when she's recovered, Brona can drive me, if I'm not able." He looked at Nora's startled expression. "Oh, yes, she has a driving license, and a Leaving Cert. She's a very capable, independent young woman. But you can see the kinds of preconceived notions she faces, even from people like yourself."

"I shouldn't have assumed—"

"Nearly everyone does," Scully said. "No harm done."

"I'm curious about how you communicate—or I suppose a better question would be how Brona communicates with you. How does she tell you what she feels, what she needs?"

"You'd be amazed what can pass between two people without a word being spoken," Scully said. "I'm not saying it isn't difficult, but we've always managed. Even people who speak have trouble making themselves understood."

Nora felt the words acutely, knowing how difficult it had been for her to tell Cormac she was leaving. "But she doesn't write, she doesn't use any kind of sign language?"

"Not really," Scully said. "It's difficult to describe. She does make herself understood in our daily life. It must be a terribly lonely life for her, out here on the bog with me, but she doesn't complain. She cooks and keeps the house, she helps me with my work, she reads. We used to look forward to Gabriel and Evelyn coming down every summer; it took away some of the loneliness for a while. I sometimes thought of leaving here, but I didn't have a notion where else to go. Where on this earth can a person be spared from loneliness? And I understand it's sometimes far worse when you're surrounded by people. Here it may rain enough to drown fish; it may not be the most picturesque part of Ireland nor the most desirable—but it's my place, this."

As he was speaking, Nora felt the stab of longing for her other home, where snow buried broken cornstalks in the prairie winter, where the river bluffs glowed golden in the autumn light, and the glorious, towering sky dwarfed all that lay beneath it. There was a great flatness and openness that she missed dreadfully, even out here on the black bog, and she envied Michael Scully that feeling of belonging somewhere.

"I've decided that I'd prefer not to be in here, when the time comes," Scully said. "I'd rather be in my own home, on my own patch. I know I've asked a lot of you already, but is there some way you could help me arrange that?"

"If you're talking about hospice care, yes, I could give you the names of some people who would be able to help."

They continued down the corridor, both carried in the constant flow of their own thoughts. Nora wondered what would happen to the hoard of knowledge Michael Scully had built up over a lifetime—more than a lifetime, if you considered all the people from whom he'd gleaned bits of history over the years. He had all those incredible files, of course; but reading them wasn't the same thing as walking out with someone who could take you to the very spot where three ravens had sung over the grave of a king.

Down the long corridor a white-coated figure was approaching, a brisk, clean-shaven young man, probably a resident. Nora stopped the wheelchair when he reached them, and saw the nervous way the man gripped the chair's arm and ducked his head to speak to Michael. "Mr. Scully, before you go in to your daughter, I wonder if we might have a word—in private."

Scully said to Nora, "Dr. Conran has been minding Brona." He turned back to the physician. "This is Dr. Gavin, who has been looking after me. If she doesn't mind, I'd like to have her with me, whatever the news."

"As you wish," said Conran. "We can go into the office here." He led them a few yards down the hallway into a small room where three cluttered desks were pushed into the corners. The young doctor began cautiously: "Yesterday, as you know, Brona seemed to be having quite a bit of pain in her lower back and legs, and this morning we decided we should check to see whether she might be suffering from a compression fracture. It's routine, when scheduling a pelvic X ray, to perform several blood tests before exposing a woman of child-bearing age to even such a small amount of radiation. One of those routine blood tests is a pregnancy test." He shifted uncomfortably in his chair. "I have to inform you that your daughter's result on that test came back positive."

"Are you saying Brona is pregnant?"

The doctor ran one hand over his chin. "Yes. I had the laboratory run the test a second time, to be sure it wasn't a false positive. The thing is, Mr. Scully, when your daughter was brought into casualty, we didn't do any sort of examination for sexual assault. No one asked for it—"

Nora's mind raced over the details of that awful day. Was it possible that Brona had been hiding in the weeds at the apiary because she'd been attacked?

"Do you have some reason to believe my daughter was sexually assaulted?" Scully asked. "Something I didn't know about? Was she injured in some way—"

The young resident was alarmed "No, no, nothing like that. But, as I said, we didn't examine her . . ."

Michael Scully was silent for a long moment. When he did speak, his voice sounded rough and tired, but not unkind.

"Thank you, Dr. Conran, for being forthright about all this. I do appreciate it. But I have two questions for you. First, I wonder why you would assume that Brona was the victim of an assault?"

"Well, she—I thought—" Nora watched the resident's face and knew he was terrified that Michael Scully would be angry about an oversight that might get him, his colleagues, and the hospital into trouble. It was also clear that he thought Brona suffered from somewhat diminished mental capacity. Nora pitied the young doctor, but couldn't fault him; hadn't she assumed the very same thing?

Scully went on: "Second, if you have some news about her medical condition, I wonder why you'd convey that news to me and not to the patient herself. My daughter is twenty-two years of age, Dr. Conran. She's not deaf, and her mental faculties are perfectly intact."

"I'm sorry. I didn't know—that is, I wasn't sure. She's been sedated, and—"

"I'll go and speak to her. You can consider yourself absolved of that duty."

The relief that broke across the resident's face was almost unseemly. He had a bit of work to do on his bedside manner, Nora thought; but when he spoke, her irritation lifted somewhat. "I appreciate your honesty as well. I'm very sorry if I jumped to any wrong conclusions, Mr. Scully, and I apologize sincerely if I've offended you. I'll remember our conversation before making any assumptions." He offered his hand, and Michael Scully took it. "I'll leave you now," Conran said. "You can stay here in the office for a while if you like."

When he had gone, Nora took her place behind the wheelchair and maneuvered Scully down the hall to Brona's room again. When they were perhaps ten feet from the door, Michael put up his hand to stop the chair once more. Nora looked into the room to see what had made him pull up short; Brona was still asleep, but tossing in the bed, her hands clasping the bedclothes.

"I have a confession to make," Scully said. "The night Brona was out until late—the night I rang you—it wasn't the first time. She wasn't at home at all the night Ursula Downes was killed. Something awakened me that night. It was a quarter past two, and I went to make sure she was all right. But she wasn't in her room; she wasn't anywhere in the house. She didn't come home all night, and the next day her clothes smelled of wood smoke. When I heard about the murder, I should have said something, told Liam that Brona had been out that night, but I kept quiet. I was worried for her safety, and I thought the fewer people who knew she'd been out that night, the better off we would all be."

Nora looked down at Scully and saw his shoulders lift in an involuntary sigh, saw the furrowed face, the bright tear trembling at the margin of his eye. "I thought I could protect her. But if I find that someone hurt her, and I kept quiet . . ."

At that moment, Brona's eyes opened. She saw them outside the door, and gathered her father in with such a look of affectionate devotion that, standing beside him, Nora felt herself gathered in as well.

Then Brona looked straight into her, past all the fear and trepidation, and Nora felt her breath flowing in and out, felt herself transfixed by the girl's eyes. Her look was a benediction, a blessing, a knowing acknowledgment of all they had shared. Then Brona's eyes drifted shut again, and Nora felt as though she'd been released from some sort of thrall.

3

Liam Ward stood in front of his open cupboard, feeling uninspired by the tins of beans, the bottled curry sauce that met his gaze. He was standing there out of habit, talking to Lugh, who was doing his usual pointing routine at the sight of the dog food tins in the cupboard. This was a ritual they followed every night, and one that still delighted both of them, after all these years together.

"What will it be this evening—mutton stew, or steak and kidney pie?" Lugh raised his tail like a flag. "Steak and kidney pie it is. A wise choice."

As he opened the tin and filled the dog's dish, watching him lunge hungrily at the meat and gravy, Ward's thoughts turned to the case again. He had difficulty letting go until he'd worked out the major knots, though there were always some that refused to disentangle, no matter how much time and patience were applied.

Charlie Brazil's story about building the bonfire had checked out, but they had no indication of how long he'd stayed there. He'd also omitted one major detail; he had not been alone. Ward had conducted his own search of the scene, and had trod on something in the ashes. Beneath his foot was the bracelet he and Eithne had given Brona for her tenth birthday. It was made of several slender strands of gold metal, twisted into a kind of torc. As far as he knew, Brona always wore the thing, never took it off.

He had picked the bracelet up and slipped it into his pocket, guilt clawing at his conscience. He'd told himself he would not keep its existence hidden if it proved to be significant. But he had already tampered with possible evidence. He pulled the bracelet out of his pocket and stared at it for a few minutes, turning it in his fingers. Time to return it to Brona.

He thought of all the things, like this bracelet, that had something to do with the case but would never find their way into his report. There were too many connections, too many stories that the case did not require, though they were part and parcel of it. Things such as the box full of trophies in Ursula Downes's flat, things she had evidently nicked from dozens of men. Each object was tagged and documented with a first name and a date, and sometimes there were as many as three or four dates within the space of a single week. What pathological need, what lack had Ursula Downes been trying to fill?

Rachel Briscoe had indeed been the daughter of Thomas Power, as Maguire had surmised. After her parents divorced, the girl had moved to England with her mother, and they'd taken the mother's maiden name. All of this had been confirmed for them by Sarah Briscoe, who had arrived more than a week ago to claim her daughter's body. She'd not been interested in what they'd found in Rachel's flat in Dublin: notebooks filled with tiny, crabbed writing, meticulously documenting her surveillance of Ursula Downes in the weeks and months before the excavation.

They were almost impossible to read, the scribblings of an increasingly disordered mind, but the one thing Ward had taken away from it was that Rachel Briscoe was not a killer, despite what Desmond Quill had said—unless you counted suicide as self-murder. Because that had been the girl's plan: to find Ursula Downes, to get close to her somehow, and finally to cut her own wrists before the woman who had poisoned her existence.

His own blood had gone cold as he read those words, perhaps written at the very moment the idea had taken shape in Rachel Briscoe's mind. It had been a long and difficult night, but he had forced himself to continue reading, living through her writings the tormented existence of a young woman who truly wished to die, thinking of another suffering he had been unable to ease.

He looked down at Lugh, who was just finishing the last bit of gravy in his bowl, nudging it across the floor.

"Nice work, old son. Hunger is great sauce, isn't it? I suppose you'll be ready for your walk soon." Lugh's head lifted at the word "walk," another of their evening rituals, so Ward fetched the lead and fastened it to the dog's collar. Their customary path was out the road by the hurling pitch, to the crossroads, up the hill past the castle ruin, and back home again on the small road that ran along the Silver River. They both looked forward to it on an evening like this, when the long light stretched over the hills. But when Ward opened his front door, he found Catherine Friel standing on his doorstep.

"Hello, Liam," she said, recovering quickly. "I hope you don't mind my dropping in on you like this. Maureen Brennan told me where to find you." She handed him an envelope. "I wanted to make sure you got my report as soon as possible, and—"

Lugh poked his nose out the door and nuzzled her free hand, looking for a scratch, and she stooped to stroke his soft ears and look down into his face. Ward had to admit he felt slightly unsettled. Why would Dr. Friel drive all the way out here just to deliver a report he'd have had in the morning anyway?

The dog moved in closer, appreciating the unexpected attention, and tried to lick their visitor, but she held him off. "He's terribly affectionate. What's his name?"

"Lugh."

"Lovely name. God of light, victorious over darkness." Her glance upward was quick, as if to gauge by Ward's expression whether Lugh had managed to live up to his name. "My son has been lobbying hard for a dog for the past eighteen months. I've been telling him I don't know. I'm away from home so much with this new job. But I suppose to him that's as much an argument for having the dog as against it. I keep hoping he'll give up and let it go, but he's been very persistent."

"What's your son's name?"

"Johnny—John, after his father. I keep forgetting that he wants to be called John nowadays."

"What age is he?"

"Ten in October. Both his sisters are away at school, so he's on his own a lot. I suppose it would be good for him to have a companion."

"And what does his father say?"

A look of pure astonishment crossed her face, and she turned away slightly before answering. "I lost my husband, three years ago."

"I'm sorry, Catherine—I didn't know. I didn't want to presume—" He looked down. "Not much of a detective, am I?"

She met his gaze with a wry smile that made his chest tighten alarmingly. "Nonsense. You're a fine detective. You've had a lot to deal with these past few days." She suddenly leaned down to give Lugh one last scratch behind the ears, evidently a gesture of farewell. "I really should go."

Ward felt his chance slipping away. In a few seconds it might be gone forever, and he couldn't let that happen. He heard himself say, "I had a wonderful time at dinner the other night."

"I did too, Liam."

Ward was remembering how much he had held back during dinner, how many times he'd struggled to keep his emotions reined in so that hope wouldn't get the best of him. Now, faced with his first real opportunity, he was nearly paralyzed.

They both stood motionless in the open doorway, until she finally spoke again. "For a time after my husband died, I tried living my life backward. But I found that it doesn't work. The only direction I can live is forward. It's terrifying, but it's the only option I can see." She reached up and brushed her lips against his in a brief farewell, but let her face remain close to his, so that he felt the warmth radiating from her skin. He felt momentarily unable to breathe, to think. But when she began to pull away, he caught her arm with his left hand.

"Catherine—I don't suppose I could prevail upon you to stay one more night, to have dinner with me again?" Something in her eyes lit the dry tinder of his soul, and he felt a slow flame, damped down and presumed dead for so long, suddenly flicker to life in his chest.

"You could, Liam," she said. "You could indeed prevail."

4

Charlie Brazil picked his way through the charred remains of the house in which he'd been reared, searching for familiar remnants, any bits of his former life that might be worth salvaging. But the destruction was complete; all he saw was singed upholstery, charred bits of chairs and wardrobes, broken glass and shattered concrete. The fire brigade said it had been a gas explosion. His mother had known exactly what she was doing. She'd turned the sheep loose herself to keep him away from the house and out of harm's way. He'd been confused, but he now saw it as the proof that she had wanted him to live. He didn't want to think about his father.

Where was his mother now? He tried to imagine her, contained within herself, casting a shadow that moved somewhere across the earth, and knew he'd never see her again. He wasn't quite sure what he felt. Maybe the anger, the worry would come later. For now, he was just relieved that she had not been in the house. He wanted her to live, too. He dug a toe into the debris, turned over the blackened radio that had rested on the kitchen shelf since his earliest memory.

Now he had a reason for the feeling he'd always had about this house—that there was something wrong here. His father had always talked about the house being unlucky, but Charlie was convinced, more than ever, that it wasn't the house, nor the ground it was built upon. And yet there was something to the claim. Some negative force resided here. Never once did he remember his father turning in at night without checking the doors and windows, without shaking holy water over the doorjambs and the fireplace, warding off whatever might come in. It was as if he had expected an invasion. No doubt he had known of all sorts of dangers, of which Charlie and his mother had lived unaware.

After the rescue workers had taken his father's body from the apiary, they had removed the body of the man they said had killed him, a man called Desmond Quill. The corpse was wearing a collar and tie, but the object that caught Charlie's attention was the tie pin, a simple bronze disc with three whorls. He looked back at the dead man's pale face and saw it younger, nearly twenty years younger, smiling out of the window of a car that had pulled up beside him on the road. The man had said he was a friend, that Charlie's parents had been called away on a family emergency and had sent him to collect their son, to take him out for supper while they were away, and then bring him home. Charlie had been afraid to go against his father's wishes, so he had agreed. He remembered being mistrustful at first, but the man had done exactly what he said he would. They'd gone to a posh restaurant somewhere in the Slieve Bloom mountains. He remembered the drive into the mountains with the sun still high. It had been early summer, and the bushes on either side of the road had blushed pink with blossoms. He remembered the greed that had overtaken him at the sight of the food brought to their table; he had eaten extravagantly: roast beef and gravy, and two desserts, and all the while the man across from him had watched, smiling and smoking and saying very little. After dinner, with the man's warm hand resting uncomfortably on his neck, they had phoned his father from the restaurant lobby, and he'd had to speak on the phone. But before he'd had a chance to tell about his magnificent meal, the man had pulled the phone away and spoken into it: *You know what I want. I think it's a fair exchange,* he'd said. *I just wanted you to know how easy it was.*

Charlie remembered the sound of his father's voice, no words, but the notes desperate and pleading. After that he'd been afraid on the ride home, but the man had dropped him at the gate and driven off without a word, the taillights of his car growing smaller and smaller and then disappearing into the night. His father had come out of the house then, shaken him by the neck and cuffed him, and told him never to get into a car with a stranger, no matter what, and never to tell his mother what had happened that evening, because it would surely kill her. He never had told his mother; and since no great harm had come of it, eventually the memory had simply faded away. It was after that extraordinary evening that his father had begun checking the doors and windows each night. Now he realized what grave danger he'd been in, and why his father's reaction had been so extreme. But the question still remained: Why had Desmond Quill decided to spare his life?

He had never seen Quill in the intervening years, but he had seen that same desperate look come into his father's eyes. It was when the Guards had come to the house, asking questions about some animals that had been mutilated and killed out along the bog road, two lambs and a kid goat taken from his mother's small flock. Everyone had thought he was responsible, Charlie knew well, but they had all been wrong; he could never have done those things to any animal. The memory of blood in the pictures they'd shown made him feel ill, even now.

Charlie whirled as something brushed against him from behind. Turning in place, he found that he was alone. He had felt a distinct touch— unless he was imagining things—in the very same place where Desmond Quill's hand had once rested on the back of his neck. Trying to shake off the feeling of disquiet, he moved through the ruin, surveying the splintered mass of debris where a few days ago there had been a house. If there had been no explosion, the structure would eventually have collapsed from the weight of knowledge, the roof beams finally unable to withstand the burden of shame and guilt they had supported for so long. All the things he had wondered about—his mother's secret absences, the photograph of her he'd found in his beekeeping shed, the artifacts hidden under the flagstones—were fragments of the picture beginning to take shape in his mind.

If it was true, what Ward had told him, then Danny Brazil might have been something more than his uncle. He remembered the first jarring sight of the body in the bog, the cord around its neck, and his fingers moved unconsciously to his own leather charm. He'd tied it there nearly ten years ago and had never taken it off since, believing those three knots somehow held the power to protect him from harm. No one had explained to him exactly how Danny had died out on the bog. They didn't have to; he'd seen enough for himself to imagine how it had happened. He couldn't avoid thinking about it. Over the past several days, going about his work out on the bog, he would suddenly picture the scene, and the earth would feel as though it were dropping away beneath his feet. He would stumble or tip backward, feeling unbalanced, disoriented, and dizzy.

It didn't help that he'd hardly been able to eat or sleep for worry about Brona. He had to see her again soon—he couldn't keep away. He understood that if he showed his face at the hospital everyone would know, but none of that seemed to matter anymore.

Three times over the past eleven nights he had sneaked into the hospital to see her. The first two times he'd just watched her as she slept. But last night she'd been awake, and when he'd reached out to touch her face she had taken his hand, placed it over her own beating heart and then down over the curved softness of her belly. He had closed his eyes and traveled back to the night of their third miraculous meeting.

He had lit the bonfire and was watching the flames, thinking of Brona, aching inside to see her again, to feel her fluttering pulse beneath his hand, when suddenly across the fire he saw her face, illuminated in the flickering blaze. She started circling slowly around the fire, and for some reason he moved in the opposite direction, away from her. Three times they circled the bonfire. He knew almost instinctively what had to be done, and felt the hair prickle at the back of his neck. For the first time in his life, he felt no hesitation. He seized Brona's hand and together they took a few steps back, then threw themselves forward and hurdled the fire. He felt its scorching heat and the flames licking at the soles of his shoes. If they fell they would surely be done for—but he knew they wouldn't fall. They landed safely on the far side, heels first, and toppled forward. Before he could recover himself, Brona Scully was lifting him up, taking his face in her hands. Her fingertips felt lovely and cool.

Standing beside her hospital bed, he had opened his eyes again and looked down at the place where his hand rested, and had felt filled up, vibrating and brimming over with life. The vision of Brona cloaked in living insects still haunted him and filled him with wonder. In a flash he had understood what she must have felt.

Charlie moved through the debris and stood in the place that had once been his room. He saw how few steps it actually was from the door, the sitting room, the kitchen. He finally saw the very small universe in which his family had traced the separate orbits of their daily lives, avoiding one another more often than not. He lifted a piece of roofing to find that the shelf where he'd kept all his beekeeping books was flattened sideways, the books charred at the edges and warped from the water used to douse the fire. He felt their loss acutely, although he knew that everything he needed from them had already been absorbed, and was locked up safe inside his head, worn into his consciousness. He needed no more lessons; he knew what was to be done simply by gauging the temperature and rainfall, feeling the dampness in the air, anticipating the seasons for trees and meadow flowers, reading the moods of the bees themselves.

He began climbing the hill and looked back at the empty space his parents' house had once occupied, and knew at that moment that he didn't want or need to know which of the Brazil brothers had actually been responsible for his existence. When the time came, he would bury two fathers. There was no need to think about it right now. At this moment he had Brona to think about. Besides, it was midsummer, and the bees needed looking after.

5

On their return from the hospital, Nora tried once again to persuade Michael Scully to come and stay at the cottage, or at least to let her or Cormac stay the night with him, but he scoffed at the notion.

"Haven't I survived here on my own this last week and a half? I'm not so bad that I can't endure one more night. Go," he said, "and enjoy the time you have together. You'll not budge me on that, so you may as well give up and be gone, the pair of you."

"All right," Nora said, "but we'll be back to say good-bye before we have to leave tomorrow."

"Just one more thing before you go," Scully said. "Do you happen to know what's become of Charlie Brazil? Has he any place to stay? I should have inquired before now, I realize, but—"

"You've had plenty of other worries, Michael. And Charlie's all right. I saw him in Kilcormac the other day and he told me he'd found a bedsit above one of the shops there. Probably not ideal, but he's got a roof over his head, at least."

Scully nodded. "Good. That's very good."

Nora returned to the Crosses thinking about Michael Scully's question. Had it just been neighborly concern, or was there some other reason he might be interested in Charlie Brazil's welfare?

"Fancy a walk up the hill before the sun is gone?" she asked Cormac.

"Lead on," he said.

They walked up the hill, close but not touching, as they had when Nora first arrived. With each step they took toward the setting sun, she felt time diminishing, slipping away. Night's cloak would cover the landscape for a few short hours before the daylight came again, and with it, as the song said, a dreary parting.

At the topmost point of the hill they came upon a huge pile of ashes, the remains of a bonfire. They walked around it, either side. Nora saw two sets of deep footprints, the heel marks deeper than the rest. "Look at this," she said to Cormac. "What do you suppose happened here?"

"Did you ever hear of midsummer bonfires?" Nora shook her head, and Cormac continued, "It's one of those leftover pagan traditions that's probably fallen off in most areas. Sometimes it was just a family, but sometimes a whole community would come together and build a fire big enough to burn all night. It was supposed to be a time for blessing the house, the crops, the animals. People walked three times sunwise around the fire to ward off sickness, and sometimes young people would leap the flames."

"You think somebody jumped over this fire?"

"Looks that way to me. After the fire died down, you were supposed to drive the animals through the ashes or singe their backs with a hazel wand. Everyone carried a burning stick home from the bonfire, and the first one to bring it into the house was supposed to bring good luck with him. They'd also take home a glowing ember from the fire and carry it around the house three times, and save some of the ashes as well, to mix with the seed for the following spring. I didn't know anyone here still built a midsummer fire. I'd love to know who it was."

You could ask Brona Scully, Nora thought, but she said nothing. Perhaps Brona and Michael Scully would like to keep their family matters private, and she wasn't about to talk about things that had been told to her in confidence, even with Cormac. "I meant to ask what Mrs. Foyle said about your father. Is it something serious? You've never had to go up there to sort them out before."

"No, it's not that. My father's had a small stroke," Cormac said, trying to downplay it, no doubt for her benefit. "Not life-threatening, but Mrs. Foyle doesn't want to be overstepping her bounds, she says. I've got to go and see what's going on. I'll probably be back in Dublin before you have to leave; I just won't know what's happening until I get there."

"I could come with you for a couple of days—"

"Ah, no, I couldn't ask you to do that, to miss the exam on the bog man. It's important."

"You're important to me too."

He took her hand. "Thanks. I appreciate the offer. But I know how much that examination means to your work. You'll never have another chance at him, not like this one."

"Why does Donegal have to be so far away? Why couldn't your father be from Kildare?"

"I suppose he could be, but then he wouldn't be my father, would he?"

Nora thought of Joseph Maguire, whom she'd never seen except in pictures, a fierce-looking, white-haired oak tree of a man. "No, you're right."

They came over the top of the hill and the sudden sight of Brona Scully's fairy tree, bedecked in all its ragged finery, once more took Nora's breath away. She leaned her back against its trunk and looked up into the twisting branches. "What is it about this place that I love so much? I just wanted to come here once more, because it might look very different when I come back, and I want to soak up every detail."

Cormac leaned on a low branch beside her. "Are you saying you will come back?"

His doubt was a quick knife. "I know I've not been very forthcoming. I hope you can understand why I have to go home. It's not that I want to be away from you—"

"I understand loyalty. I understand keeping a promise. So even if you have to go away for a while, it can't be for too long. Too long doesn't exist."

"I want to believe that. . . . I just don't know that we should make any promises." The searching look in his eyes unsettled her.

"Maybe you're right," he said. "Maybe it's best if we just leave things as they are. But wait here for a minute, will you?"

She stretched out beneath the tree while he crossed to a stand of hazel wands growing from a nearby stump. Taking a penknife from his pocket, he sliced through several narrow green shoots, cutting pieces about twelve inches in length. Then he came back and stretched out on the grass beside her. "It's well known that hazel is a powerful charm against mischief," he said. She watched intently as he bent the supple greenwood in his hands, then quickly fashioned a simple plait, like those she had seen in museums— a love knot. "Here," he said, "keep this with you."

She took it, knowing that, whatever happened, she would never let it go. She would carry it with her always, that hopeful pledge, unspoken. She pulled him down beside her and they lay in the tall grass, limbs tangled together, gazing up into the fairy tree's wild profusion. She thought of what faced each of them in the days to come—an opportunity to look death in the face, to find out more about themselves and the people they loved than they ever wished to know. She would be far from this sanctuary. She knew it was just an illusion, that there was no real protection here, no place of safety, and yet she felt it more strongly than in any other place she'd ever been.

As if he'd been reading her thoughts, Cormac turned to her and said, "There's just one thing . . . I don't want you to go around thinking you're invincible, now that you have that." He reached out and fingered the hazel knot. "It may be powerful, but it doesn't mean you can throw caution to the wind. Please be careful, Nora."

She hadn't told him the real reason she was going home. How would she have explained it—that she hoped to prevent her sister's killer from claiming any new victims? But at that moment she realized that Cormac knew why she had to go and that, even if he feared for her, he understood.

The sun hung just above the western horizon, a bright orange disc in the dark haze of churned-up peat dust. She thought once again of Mide, the middle province, and felt Cormac close beside her. If she left now, it was possible that they would never find their way back to this place. Would she remember this spot as a sanctuary, or as a place of sacrifice? Perhaps the ancients had been right in their belief that those things were one and the same.

Keeping Cormac's hand tightly clasped in her own, Nora sat up and faced out toward Loughnabrone, Lake of Sorrows, thinking of the ancient people who had named this place. What sacrifices, what sorrows, what infinite griefs had they borne here? What riddles had they tried to answer about the beginning of life and its end? She held very still and watched a solitary heron wading slowly, elegantly through the shallows until a passing flash of silver caught its downcast eye.

ACKNOWLEDGMENTS

Many thanks to the people who helped with research for this book: Barry Raftery, for help with all things archaeological, and for his wonderful book *Pagan Celtic Ireland*; archaeologists Jane Whitaker and Ellen O'Carroll, who answered hundreds of questions, and allowed me access to their bog excavations; Conor McDermott, Cathy Moore, and Cara Murray, of the Irish Archaeological Wetland Unit, whose knowledge of bog archaeology could fill volumes; Dr. John Harbison, Ireland's state pathologist, for sharing his vast experience of crime scenes; Heather Gill-Robinson, for sharing her expertise on bog preservation; Kevin Barry, for showing me where he found the body in the bog, and his wife, Betty, for her hospitality; Eamon Dooley, for his fascinating history of Bord na Móna at Boora; Paul Riordan, Boora Bog general manager; Boora workshop foreman Cormac Carroll, and all the men at the workshop; Eddie O'Sullivan, of the Federation of Irish Beekeeping Associations, and John Donoghue, who let me tag along around his apiary one soggy afternoon; retired Garda Síochána officer Patrick J. Cleary, for continuing advice and information on police procedure; Dáithí Sproule, for helping once again with Irish translations; and finally all the wonderful musicians who have inspired the music in this book. Thanks also to my remarkable editors, Susanne Kirk at Scribner and Carolyn Caughey at Hodder & Stoughton; to Sarah Knight at Scribner, for her invaluable support; and to my incomparable agent, Sally Wofford-Girand. To all who offered encouragement, most especially my writers' group, my family, and my wonderful husband, *go raibh míle maith agaibh*.

A SCRIBNER
READING GROUP GUIDE

Book Club Questions for *Lake of Sorrows* by Erin Hart

1. *Lake of Sorrows* opens with a graphic scene: a young man sinking and eventually drowning in a bog. After reading the whole story, can you be certain of the young man's identity, or is it still ambiguous? What does the opening chapter foreshadow about the rest of the book?

2. The industrial bogs of the Irish midlands provide a most unusual atmosphere in this novel. The bog has played many roles in Irish history, as a place of spirituality, mystery, and commerce. What does this unique environment contribute to the story? What elements of the bog landscape can you see reflected in the psychological development of the characters?

3. The bog has often functioned as a hiding place for secret treasure. Many of the characters in *Lake of Sorrows* have hidden or buried physical objects, or intangible things such as their personal history or emotions. Can you think of examples? Which are revealed in this novel, and which still remain buried at its conclusion? What do the things people hide reveal about them as characters?

4. Sacrifice is one of the major themes in *Lake of Sorrows*. The bog that was once a mysterious place of sacrifice in ancient times is being sacrificed in modern times to generate electricity. In what other ways do ideas about sacred offerings and sacrifice still resonate in the characters' daily lives?

5. Nora wishes she could see Ireland the way Cormac does, "under the skin of the landscape down to the bones." Later, Theresa Brazil compares the water that runs in local bog drains to the lifeblood of the place. Are there other references to the earth as a body, a living, corporeal entity? How does this relate to the theme of sacrifice?

6. Several characters in the book draw modern parallels to the ancient practice of human sacrifice: war and famine, industrialization, politics, the cult of celebrity. Do you think any of these parallels are justified?

7. Early on in the story, an ancient corpse is discovered bearing evidence of a grisly practice known as "triple death." The number three or the concept of trinity appears throughout *Lake of Sorrows*. Can you think of other examples? What is the significance of the number three?

8. Gold is another recurring image in the story, both literally and figuratively. Can you think of examples? What are the qualities that have given gold such power and significance within the human imagination?

9. Bees and honey figure prominently in this novel. Discuss their many roles, from the mystical to the practical.

10. Nora comes to realize early in this story that she does love Cormac, but she is still haunted by her sister's death. Is unfinished business at home in the United States reason enough for her to leave their relationship up in the air, or do you think that given the events of this story Nora has some deeper fears about Cormac's honesty and faithfulness?

11. Several of the characters in this story are eccentrics or outcasts: Charlie Brazil, Rachel Briscoe, Brona Scully, and even Ursula Downes. What sets these characters apart from others, and do you identify with them, even though they are misunderstood?

12. One of the characters, Brona Scully, is mute. How is Brona, despite her lack of speech, able to make herself understood, and why do you think some of the other characters—even those capable of speech—still struggle to communicate?

13. Michael Scully is described at one point as carrying on the tradition of the hereditary historian. People give him old photographs, letters, and journals, pieces of the past they haven't the heart to dispose of but don't want to keep either. Do you know anyone who fulfills this kind of a role in your family or in your community?

14. Does Ursula Downes's background, including the damaging, abusive relationship with her stepfather, make her adult relationships—especially those with men—more understandable?

15. Charlie Brazil has always believed that Dominic, the man he knew as his father, never felt anything for him. Late in the novel, Charlie is remembering his narrow escape from a potentially dangerous situation as a child and his father's reaction. Do you think Charlie is mistaken about Dominic's regard for him?

16. Teresa Brazil's life story is told in a single chapter late in the book (the only part of the story told from her point of view). Does the drastic action she takes in the end make sense given her history?

17. Does the book's final chapter leave you with a sense of hope for Nora and Cormac and their future together, or do you have any lingering doubts about whether things will work out for them?

18. Which were the most memorable scenes in this story? What ideas or images stayed in your mind after reading the book? What was the most interesting bit of insight or information you gained from reading this story?

19. How does Erin Hart's work fit into the tradition of mystery/crime writing, and which authors—past or present—would you consider similar in style or tone?

Fishing for Invitations on *Lake of Sorrows*

An Open Call to Book Clubs from Author Erin Hart

Reading and talking about books has always been one of my favorite pursuits. And as I was thinking of ways to give something back and really engage with readers, it occurred to me that one of the best ways might be to become an even more active participant in book clubs.

Since my first novel (*Haunted Ground* came out in 2003), I've visited dozens of local book clubs—and made contact with even more book club readers across the country with the help of a speaker phone!

It's always a great experience, so with the publication of this trade paperback edition of *Lake of Sorrows*, I wanted to extend a hand to book clubs everywhere. Invite me to your book club and I'll be delighted to join in your discussion. Really.

Monday through Friday, from 7 to 11 P.M. CST, I'll be available to join your book club by phone anywhere in the United States or Canada. (Book clubs should have at least ten members and a speaker phone.)

Just contact me directly at: mail@erinhart.com.

Looking for some suggested discussion questions? Check the back of this book, or look in the Book Clubs section of my website (www.erin hart.com/clubs.htm), or under the Book Club Resources tab at the Simon & Schuster website (www.simonsays.com).

Of course, the published discussion questions are only suggestions—you may have your own. We can also talk about how the novels came about, the landscape and culture of Ireland (especially the bogs and all the riches found there), the road to publication, and lots more.

Looking forward to our chat!

Sláinte,

Erin Hart

ABOUT THE AUTHOR

Erin Hart is a Minnesota theater critic and former administrator at the Minnesota State Arts Board. A lifelong interest in Irish traditional music led her to cofound Minnesota's Irish Music and Dance Association. A theater major from St. Olaf College, she has an M.A. in English and Creative Writing from the University of Minnesota, Minneapolis. She and her husband, musician Paddy O'Brien, live in Minneapolis and frequently visit Ireland. Erin Hart was nominated for an Agatha Award for her debut novel, *Haunted Ground,* and won the Friends of American Writers Award in 2004. Visit her website at www.erinhart.com.